MAD
IF Y' DO...

I0737808

David Kolff

Published 2022
by David Kolff

ISBN 978-0-473-62966-3 (Softcover)
ISBN 978-0-473-66041-3 (Softcover – print on demand)
ISBN 978-0-473-62967-0 (Epub)
ISBN 978-0-473-62968-7 (Kindle)

© Copyright David Kolff 2022
All rights reserved.

This novel is a work of fiction. Unless otherwise indicated, all the names, characters, businesses, places, events, and incidents in this book are either the product of the author's imagination or used in a fictitious manner. Any resemblance to actual persons, living or dead, or actual events is purely coincidental.

Except for the purpose of fair reviewing, no part of this publication may be reproduced or transmitted in any form or by any means, electronic or mechanical, including photocopying, recording or any information storage and retrieval system, without prior written permission from the publisher.

Book cover design – Link Choi

Designed and distributed in New Zealand by The Copy Press,
Nelson, New Zealand. www.copypress.co.nz

For Mariana and Lucien, with love.
You finally get to read this book.

1

Leaving

When I broke the news, I could see consternation play out on Mum's face as my words sank in. I don't recall the details of our discussion exactly, but I can still see the expression on her face. Her forehead wrinkled into deep lines and her eyebrows tensed and screwed up slightly.

"You need to be careful," she said. "Things are different overseas."

"Mum, Australia isn't exactly overseas, more like across the ditch."

"Sam, if you want to call it a ditch that's fine! But remember, it's not a ditch or even a river you can swim across!"

The old man's reaction was quite different.

"How long are you going for?"

My parents didn't want me to go to Australia. I could tell there was something in the way they reacted when I told them of my intention. I sensed they expected me to go off the rails somehow. After all, in their eyes I'd already shown a tendency not to stay on the tracks.

"We don't really know," Tania butted in. "I just want to go home and see my folks. I thought we might go to the mountains and get work on the ski fields."

Mum was obviously concerned about me going to another country with a woman I barely knew, and she tried to get the old man to talk me out of it. There was no way anyone was going to persuade me otherwise, least of all him. Hey, I was bulletproof and full of life, everything excited me.

* * *

Tania was my girlfriend. She was twenty-five and I was younger. I thought I was pretty cool to be going out with her, probably as much because of her age than for any other reason. It was 1980, and we'd met earlier that year, in February, picking apples together on an orchard in the Tasman district. At the end of the season, she decided she was going back to Australia to see her parents and had asked me whether I'd accompany her.

"Yeah," I had said. "I've never been to Oz. Let's fly from Christchurch so I can see m' parents 'n you can meet them, they'd like that." Though I knew they wouldn't like anything about it — not me going to Australia, nor that I was going out with a woman seven years my senior — but I really did want to see them before I left the country.

* * *

Picking apples was hard work but paid good money for a young person needing to make a buck or two quickly. One night out at the local pub, and a few drinks too many, saw Tania and me in bed together. In the morning I couldn't even remember the night before, all I knew was that she was lying naked beside me. Pairing up was a common occurrence during the apple harvesting season. Inevitable really, given a group of young men and women working together and sharing a bach with not a lot to do in the evenings except sit around, drink and talk shit, or watch television. Tania became my bedtime companion and we fucked like rabbits the whole season long with the assistance of alcohol and mind-altering drugs.

2

Our intimacy was a continuous experiment of various sexual positions, just to keep it interesting. After all, for how long can you enjoy sex with the same person? Let's be honest, the novelty wears off fairly quickly! That would've been the case this time too, except that we found inspiration in the common ground we shared — an adventurous curiosity about sex. We were the best bunny rabbits in the house.

* * *

"Why do you want to go and work on an Australian ski field?" the old man asked.

"Why not?"

"The real ski fields are over here. It's common knowledge that Australians come here to ski because the snow's better, the runs are better and …" he said, grinning like the cat that got the cream, "they're real mountains here! Over there, Sam, they're just hills on tablelands. The country's so old there is no ruggedness to the mountains, it's all been eroded down. Half the time they don't even get any snow!"

"That's not true!" Tania protested, placing her hands firmly on her hips. "We do get snow. Not always as much as would be desirable, but most years up at Mount Kosciuszko — at Thredbo and Perisher ski resorts — the snow is awesome."

"Really?" said the old man. He was on a roll, about to launch into another assault, when he caught a sideways glance from Mum: Butt Out! He changed tack. "Then if that's true, I apologise. I'd heard differently."

"Whatever the case might be, it doesn't really matter cos we're goin' anyway!" I announced with conviction. *End of story!*

"Fair enough," mumbled the old man, eyes diverting to the worn rug on the floor.

Mum was giving him the glare, shaking her head, and he was shrugging his shoulders, looking sheepishly at her. What's the problem? Dad conveyed with a glance. My mother wasn't an easy woman to please in any respect, so I didn't blame the old man for switching off like he was doing now, but I was concerned that he allowed himself to switch off far too often. I feared that one day he might not be able to find the 'On' switch again. The old man gave way to Mum far too much, allowing her to be the one making most of the decisions. She wore the pants in the house and watching this little enactment of their relationship dynamic reminded me of how happy I was not to be living at home anymore.

* * *

We spent a couple of nights at Mum and Dad's before flying out to Sydney. The night before we left, I went to see a movie, *Midnight Express*, selected simply because I liked the title. The opening scene was set at an airport, with a young guy in a toilet cubicle strapping blocks of hashish to his waist, then the scene cuts to him at Customs Control, appearing rather anxious. The movie was well-paced and intense as the young man sweated his way through Customs. On the point of boarding the plane from the apron, he was stopped by Security and held at gunpoint. A guard patted him down. They obviously thought he had a bomb strapped to his waist. The guards laughed when they realised it was hashish he was attempting to smuggle out of Istanbul. Billy was the character's name, Billy Hayes, and he was in a power of shit.

Imprisoned, Billy went to trial and was sentenced to four years in a Turkish jail. Just as he was close to finishing his prison sentence, the Turkish authorities swept the carpet from under his feet. The prosecutor had petitioned for a life sentence in a higher court and had succeeded. There were a few more foreigners in the same prison as Billy, and in a

4

similar situation, and as the story unfolded, so too did the hopelessness of their predicament. When one of his friends was taken away to be beaten at the hands of the prison guards, and subsequently dumped in the sanatorium, Billy decided he had to take matters into his own hands or he would end up stuck in the asylum himself. Daringly, he managed to escape, and with help he somehow made it back to the United States. The credits that rolled revealed the movie was based on a true story.

When I arrived home from the cinema, Mum asked me what I thought of the movie. She was always keen on going to a screening herself and liked to hear the recommendations of others. I told her that I thought it was great, well worth going to see, without elaborating further.

"I'll add it to my to-see list," she said. I'd never seen her to-see list or witnessed her write anything down.

* * *

My parents wanted to drive us to the airport, and I wasn't about to persuade them otherwise. I wanted to keep Mum happy. At the airport we checked our bags in, which took a bit of time as there was already a fair queue banking up. For some reason, all the flights departed to Australia at approximately the same time: one to Melbourne, one to Brisbane, and ours to Sydney. In some cases, there were two flights to the same destination but with a different airline. We were travelling with Air New Zealand; they had a good reputation for their service and food, so I was happy. Until the Mount Erebus disaster in 1979, the year before, they also had a good record for safety in the air. *They never saw what was comin' till it was too late. The poor souls.*

Once our bags were checked in and we'd paid our departure tax, there was still enough time to have a look around Duty Free and buy a bottle of Glenfiddich for myself and Bombay gin for Tania. They were good deals at half the normal selling price, so one couldn't complain. I could've stayed browsing in Duty Free for hours, looking at sound equipment and watches, but it was time to say farewell. Our departure time was approaching, and we still had to go through Customs.

Mum had tears in her eyes as she hugged me goodbye. "Don't worry, Mum, it's only Australia," I said, giving her a big squeeze as she held me tight.

"You be careful," she said, holding onto me, her tears saturating my right shoulder.

"I will, Mum."

She finally released me and briefly hugged Tania goodbye, whispering something in her ear that I was never meant to hear. I embraced the old man. He even looked like he might shed a tear.

"Stay in touch, Sam," he said.

"I will, Dad. I'll send y' the odd postcard." I'd maybe give them a call once in a blue moon.

"And have a good time." Dad looked like he meant it.

There'll be no doubt about that!

Tania kissed my dad lightly on the cheek and thanked him for having us, then we were gone, dancing excitedly through the doors into the departure area to have our passports stamped by Customs. Before the doors completely swallowed us up, I turned and waved to my parents. They enthusiastically waved back, standing arm in arm, Mum with tears streaming down her cheeks, Dad remaining stoic by her side. Tania took my arm, and my parents were gone as the doors swung shut.

2

Sydney

We arrived in Sydney and passed unchecked through Customs. For a fleeting moment, Billy Hayes came hurtling to mind, and I couldn't resist observing the overbearing customs officers in their blue uniforms, glaring at everyone passing through to collect their luggage from the carousels spitting out suitcases, packs and parcels. People rushed and shoved to grab items they recognised. One of the officers had a well-trained beagle sniffing at the luggage as it went trundling past.

Poor fuckin' Billy! He really got himself in a pickle, but I guess they would expect that kind 'f shit in a country like Turkey. He was always goin' to be up against it at an airport like Istanbul's, carryin' that shit!

We stumbled wearily through the exit doors into the arrival concourse to hordes of expectant relatives and friends, people of every creed and colour, waiting for their family, their spouse, or their lover to appear. Tania hadn't arranged for anyone to pick us up. We walked outside to the taxi rank, engaged the closest taxi, and piled our bags into the boot. The driver looked as though he'd just arrived from darkest Africa, his accent was strong, his English stilted. As we drove, I became increasingly overwhelmed by Sydney's size. Nothing could have prepared me for this. The city was densely populated and so busy, there were people, cars and buildings every way I looked. My eyes boggled with excitement as we neared the city centre with all its high-rise buildings reaching forever into the sky. Towering above them all was an unusual building called Centrepoint which resembled a giant hypodermic needle pointing skyward. I'd never seen anything like it before. I wound down the taxi's window and immediately felt intoxicated by the smells and sights of this strange world, the heady scent of frangipani and pollution, the exquisite light that fell on the subtropical foliage, the buildings and the people's faces as we zoomed along.

We pulled up at traffic lights and I saw huge white cockatoos perched squawking in the eucalyptus trees. I'd only seen cockatoos on television before, and I felt an amazing sense of euphoria at being somewhere so exotic.

We stayed in Sydney for one night, in Bondi at the home of Tania's old friend, Sue. They seemed moderately pleased to see each other, but it was obvious they weren't the closest of friends. I had a sense that it was more of an obligation than a pleasure on her part. In fact, it was probably an inconvenience having us stay. I wondered if they had been schoolmates, once the best of friends, but as time passed so too had the closeness of their friendship.

Sue showed us to our room, neatly made up with folded towels on the end of the bed just like in a hotel. She told us to help ourselves to anything we wanted and smiled at me, but it wasn't a warm smile. Sue would've been pretty if she smiled more often. Her face had a harshness to it, and her eyes wore a flinty look of disappointment, as though she had been let down once too often. Life appeared to sit heavily on her young shoulders, and I felt an unexpected rush of compassion for her. I smiled back and watched her face soften a little before she looked away, and then directed her gaze at Tania.

"I'll show you around," she said.

After our tour, she abruptly announced, "I'm afraid I'm going to have to leave you two to your own devices. You see, I've got an essay due tomorrow. It's very important." Sue forced another smile as if that would excuse her. She was doing Tania a favour. It didn't really suit her to have us there.

"She's a cheerful thing, isn't she?" I whispered under my breath to Tania.

"Just be grateful," Tania rasped back at me.

* * *

I had no real idea about the layout of Sydney, or where we were in relation to the city, except that Bondi Beach was where all the Kiwis lived when they moved to Australia. I wanted to explore, and I was excited to be there. Tania showed no interest in going out, she claimed she was too tired. That was fine with me, but I needed fresh air and a walk after spending three plus hours on a plane and another hour in a taxi. Now that I didn't need to play at polite conversation with our host, it was the perfect opportunity. Besides, we would be leaving the next day and my only claim to being in Sydney would be to say, *I stayed a night in Bondi at a stranger's apartment with m' girlfriend. She was so uptight cos she was gettin' her rags. She wouldn't take me out t' show me the sights, 'n her girlfriend was such a goody two shoes she wouldn't do anythin' with us cos she had an essay due.* Bloody hell! Where was the fun?

Sue's apartment was a couple of blocks back from the beach. I had a sense of where the beach was in relation to her apartment because Tania had waved her arm in the general direction. It felt good to be out in the fresh air. The temperature was mild compared to Christchurch, and there was the distinct smell of sea air mixed with frangipani. It was late afternoon, the sun low in the sky, causing an orange haze to rest over Bondi. As I reached the main street, I saw the beach with the sun glistening on large, perfect waves breaking along the shore. The waves were splattered with black dots. Surfers were out, competing for the ultimate wave. I was amazed that such a beautiful beach existed amidst a large city. I'd never seen a beach that had shops and restaurants all the way from one end to the other. At the southern end, where most of the surfers were, a saltwater lap pool, Bondi Baths, was built into the rock, the ocean waves surging over the concrete edges.

The jagged, rocky cliffs of the coastline looked spectacular in the late afternoon sun, a kaleidoscope of terracotta, yellow and bright orange hues. I walked onto the beach and noticed how fine the sand was, so fine it squeaked beneath my feet with every step I took. It was late May and women were sunbathing topless, a sumptuous feast for my wayward eyes, and I showed no discretion in where I looked. I was indeed in a place called heaven on Earth. *Why are we only in Sydney f' one fuckin' day? I could happily stay here for a week.*

The next morning, we caught a bus to Bondi Junction where we went underground to access the rail network. I was mesmerised and intrigued to be catching a train that travelled beneath a city. We arrived back in daylight at Central Station. There were numerous stations along the route, and platform after platform of trains constantly coming and going. *How the fuck did people know where t' get the right train from? I s'pose the trains always depart from the same platform, 'n in time y' know which platform y' need t' be on t' get y' where y' want t' go.* Our next train would depart from a platform inside the main part of Central Station. The station was a grand old building with a spectacular ceiling high above a beautiful, slightly faded terrazzo mosaic and marble floor.

We caught a train to the small town of Nowra, about an hour and a half south of Sydney, situated on a river and not far from the coast. Tania had decided that to save money, we should hitch from Nowra to

Wodyn, where she would get her parents to pick us up. She said it was just over three hours as a straight drive, easily doable in a day, especially with the early start she insisted on. It was ten o'clock as we walked with our bags from the station out onto the road. There we stood with our thumbs out, hoping some kind soul would give us a ride. The day was beautiful and sunny with a vast, clear blue sky and white cockatoos squawking in the eucalyptus trees overhead.

3

On the Road

An hour passed and we'd had no luck, no one seemed interested in picking us up. I was becoming extremely bored and hungry. The nearest shop was a hundred metres or more down the road.

"Shall I risk it?" I asked Tania.

"Please yourself," she said, shrugging her shoulders as though she didn't approve of the idea.

"The perfect ride could come along while you're in the shop, and I'd have to decide if I wanted to wait for you."

"Would y' really think about takin' a ride without me?"

She grinned at me, going all soft in the face. "It would be a hard decision," she said, putting her arms around my waist and kissing me. She put her thumb out for a car that was hurtling towards us, still embracing me with her free hand.

A beige VW Beetle with a surfboard strapped to a roof rack pulled up on the loose gravel in front of us. Tania released me, rushed over to the car and opened the passenger door.

"Where are you off to?" I heard her asking, then saw her nod her head enthusiastically. She lifted her head out of the car and waved her arm, signalling for me to come over. "We've got a ride!" she yelled.

A man emerged from the vehicle as I gathered up our bags and struggled to the car. He was tall with a dark complexion and shoulder-length, black curly hair contained by a white-and-blue paisley headband. He was casually dressed in a long-sleeved white cotton shirt, jeans and thongs — what we called jandals back home.

He opened the front boot of the Beetle. "Those bags should both fit in here," he said, jovially.

I placed our bags in the boot and the man closed the lid on them, pushing it down firmly. We clambered into the car. I scored the back seat but didn't mind, being happy we weren't still on the roadside.

"So … you're off t' Wodyn, eh?" he stated more than asked as he turned the key over in the ignition. I felt the engine start up behind me. He pulled back onto the road, craning his neck to check it was all clear.

"Yeah," I said. "Thanks for stopping."

"Not much happenin' in Wodyn. What do y' want t' go there for?" He changed through the gears; the engine made that classic VW throaty hum.

"We're going to Yaringa, actually," replied Tania.

"Oh, that's a diff'rent story. Nice little place, Yaringa," he mused.

"So I believe. I've never been there before," I replied.

"It's great f' surfin' all up 'n down that coastline."

"I wouldn't know, don't surf."

"What, y' don't surf? Get the fuck out 'f here!" he jibed, checking me out in his rear-view mirror.

"I'm not from 'round here."

"Where y' from?" he asked in his Ozzie twang.

"NZ."

"Yeah, thought so, but you're not, are you?" He nodded his head at Tania.

"You guessed it, I'm a true-blue Ozzie girl, born and bred in Yaringa," she said, and casually flicked her hair back in a flirtatious manner.

"Y' were blessed, then. Y' could do a whole lot worse than Yaringa."

They both laughed too loudly. The ice was well broken, this guy could probably talk the hind leg off a donkey with three legs.

"Hey, look, I was about t' roll a spliff when I saw you folks. How about it?"

"Sure," I replied, thinking of the three or so hours we were going to be stuck in his car. A smoke was a fantastic idea.

"Yeah, that'd be great," Tania said, nodding her head keenly.

"Right then. We just need t' turn off somewhere so we aren't drawin' attention t' ourselves. The cops can be complete cunts when y' in a car like this if y' get m' drift."

We continued a few more kilometres down the road until our quirky driver found a side road leading toward the coast. He drove down the dirt road to the quiet end of a beach and pulled up in an empty picnic area.

"M' name's Josh," he said, turning to Tania, offering his hand.

"Tania. Thanks for the lift, Josh." She took his hand and loosely shook it.

He turned to me. "And you are?"

"Sam," I replied, reaching out my hand to shake his.

"Alright, Sam! Pleased t' meet y'. Best I roll this spliff."

Josh reached under his seat, pulled out a cereal-size wooden bowl and set it on his lap. In the bowl was a small ornate wooden box. He opened it and took Zig-Zag cigarette papers and a couple of tailor-made cigarettes from it. Underneath the papers and cigarettes were several good-looking marijuana heads.

"This is the stuff I grew last summer. It's very smooth and delivers a great stone, a nice balance 'f mental 'n physical." He removed one of the heads and began breaking it up into the bowl. "Can y' pass me the lighter in the glovebox please, Tania?"

Obliging, she plucked out the lighter sitting at the front of a very messy glovebox and passed it to Josh.

"Thanks," he said, reaching for it. In his other hand he held one of the cigarettes from the wooden box and ran the flame of the lighter up and down the length of it while rolling the cigarette over and over to avoid burning it. Once the paper was completely browned, he peeled it away from the first half of the cigarette and let the tobacco drop into the bowl with the dope. He put the other half of the cigarette back in the wooden box, then began mixing the dope and tobacco together, rubbing it gently as he went until it was all nice and fine.

"That just about does it," he said, picking up the Zig-Zag papers and plucking three from the packet. He licked one and stuck it to a second paper, then licked the third paper and stuck it running the other way across the two papers he'd already joined together.

Christ almighty! All this effort seems barely worth the final result! It was all going to go up in smoke anyway as we sat listening to Bob Dylan's *Masterpieces* compilation album that Josh had just put in the car's cassette player.

"Alright," was Tania's response, bobbing her head to Bob's 'Lay, Lady, Lay'.

She'd prob'bly love t' lay across the car seat and suck Josh's knob. I sat in the back seat waiting impatiently for Josh to finish his own masterpiece. He'd managed to roll a fine-looking joint and was twisting one end of it. *We're almost there, thank Christ.* But things came to a halt again. He put the spliff in the bowl and picked up the packet of Zig-Zag papers. From nowhere a pair of tiny scissors materialised, and he cut a piece of cardboard off the flap of the Zig-Zag packet. *What the fuck are y' doin' now?* He rolled the cardboard up tightly and placed it in the end of the spliff. *Ahh, I see!* He'd just made a filter for his creation. He popped the twisted end in his mouth, running it in and out quickly.

"Makes it burn more evenly," he said as if he'd read my mind. Finally, he placed the filtered end between his lips and put a flame to it, sucking timidly as if he expected it to blow up in his face. Satisfied, he passed it to Tania who took it from him, smiling. His cheeks were ballooning from the smoke he was holding in. Tania gave it a fair rip, no mucking around, then she turned and passed it to me. It must've been almost half an hour since the ritual had commenced.

M' first toke on an Ozzie spliff. It went down smoothly, but I failed to see the overall benefits of Josh's long-winded ritual. We each got two very good hits, and my world became all warm and fuzzy as a feeling of euphoria washed over me. Josh put the remnants back in his little wooden treasure box, and the box into the mull bowl, then shoved it all back under his seat.

"That was a pleasant interlude, don't y' think?" He looked to me for approval.

"Yeah," I said, nodding and smiling simultaneously. The dope had definitely kicked in.

* * *

The drive south was relaxing with light conversation and great coastal moments mixed in with long stretches of cruising through forests of elegant eucalyptus trees. At one stage we had a pit stop in a small coastal town with few redeeming features. Other than that, the trip was uneventful. Tania fell into a deep, stoned sleep soon after we left the beach, while Josh and I talked about nothing in particular until the conversation diverted to skiing in Oz versus NZ. We could only go on what we'd heard about one another's country since I'd not skied in Oz and Josh had not skied in NZ. We rambled on for a while, neither of us particularly focused, still feeling some effects of the smoke. Our final consensus was that people who'd skied in both countries thought the snow better in New Zealand, more reliable with steeper runs. Although in Australia, apparently, the runs are scattered with snow eucalyptus that you can ski amongst, and the snow is often of better quality amidst the trees. The idea of tree skiing appealed to me.

Josh offered to drop us off in Yaringa, which, he said, wasn't too far out of his way. We approached Yaringa along the coastal road, passing beautiful waterways and gently sloping, eucalyptus-clad hills that fell away to the sea. Yaringa was a small fishing and resort village, picturesque and sleepy, but full of life during the summer months, according to Tania. The beach looked spectacular, the bay glistened turquoise and emerald in the late afternoon sun, and the light was exquisite.

Tania provided directions, and Josh pulled up outside her parents' house, located on a street near the bowling green. Their home was a large, 1950's-style brick building with a sprawling garden and a concrete driveway that led to an open double garage with two cars parked inside.

"Here we are," said Tania. "Thank you so much for the ride, Josh. Would you fancy a cup of tea before you go?"

"Thanks, but no thanks. I'm just goin' t' carry on. I'm in a groove with the drivin', no point in breakin' it up now."

"Hey, no problem. It's been fun." Tania opened the door and clambered out.

I pushed her seat forward and pulled myself out awkwardly. "Cheers, Josh. Great ride, and safe travels."

We took our bags from the front boot, thanked Josh again, and watched him drive away before we headed inside.

4

Winter

Yaringa in winter was beautiful but boring, and to top it off, I wasn't particularly enjoying living with Tania's parents. They both smoked like chimneys, drank like fishes, and argued incessantly. So we left to find work up in the Snowy Mountains. We'd bought an old classic Holden Special station wagon that had been on the side of the road for a while with a 'For Sale' sign placed in the front window. It was cheap enough and served a dual purpose: with a mattress in the back, we could also sleep in it if we needed to, wherever we ended up. We drove up to the mountains with Tania's parents' caravan in tow, which they'd kindly offered us, and found a place just out of Jindabyne to park up at a reasonable rate. Within a few days, I had a job on the ski lifts and Tania had a job in a pizzeria making coffees and waitressing.

Tania lasted a week before she decided she didn't like being in the mountains. She didn't want to work in the snow any more, it was too cold, and she wanted to be closer to her parents. She said she would visit me from time to time. I had to admit that with her gone, I had a lot more fun. Our relationship had gone stale; it had drifted into a state of staid and boring. Once she left, I could be more spontaneous, meet interesting people, have greater exposure to the mountain party-scene, and indulge in my fair share of mind-altering substances that were on offer.

At the end of the season I went back to Yaringa, with more than a little trepidation. I'd hardly seen Tania all winter and I didn't know what to expect. I really should have called things off and gone my own way, gone to Sydney or Melbourne. I'm sure I would've landed on my feet. Instead, I went back to Yaringa.

Hindsight's a marvellous thing, apparently. I'm not sure where the sayin' comes from, but how can hindsight be a marvellous thing when it's retrospective, when it's too late t' change what's already happen'd, when the events that've taken place are irreversible?

Tania and I found a house to rent with her ex-boyfriend, Bruce, and his girlfriend, Sally. We all became closely acquainted, mainly because they were the only people we really hung out with. I did meet a few other interesting people up at the local pub on the hill, including reacquainting myself with the charismatic Cosmo whom I'd spent time with up the mountain. He happened to show up in Yaringa and nobody wanted to know about him. I didn't really understand this as he seemed like a good enough bloke to me, but everybody got fidgety when he arrived in town. People said he needed to leave.

One day not long after his arrival, Bruce asked me if I'd give Cosmo a ride to Canberra as a favour. I'd never been there, and I fancied a drive up-country. There wasn't a lot happening in Yaringa; anything for a change of scenery. I drove him there in the Holden Special. It had become my pride and joy and was such a pleasure to drive. Upon arrival in Canberra, Cosmo suddenly became extremely demanding, wanting me to act as a chauffeur. I reluctantly drove him around here and there and by the end of it, I was quite happy to be rid of him. By the time we parted company, my opinion of Cosmo had changed. I was glad to see his backside as I drove out of Canberra.

5

New South Wales Cops

It was past midnight, and I was only a few kilometres from Yaringa when I noticed flashing blue lights in my rear-view mirror. I pulled over, hoping the vehicle would pass, but the lights remained behind me. Josh, who'd picked us up hitchhiking, had informed me about the cops in Oz and their attraction to old cars driven by young people. *He couldn't've seen me in the dark! Maybe he hasn't even noticed the age of m' car. Fuck!*

He seemed to come from nowhere, but cops often did, tucked away on a side road or out of view behind a tree or a bush. Under this blanket of darkness, I would never have been able to see a car half hidden in foliage. Besides, I wasn't speeding, and I had nothing to hide. In my rear-view mirror I saw the solid silhouette of a man emerge slowly from the vehicle and shut the door. I watched him walk the distance to my car, heavy steps crunching in the gravel. As he approached, I lowered my window.

"What's the problem, officer?" I asked, looking up into the face of a man who must've been in his early thirties, stern looking and unhappy to be on duty at this time of night. He immediately got all shitty, as if it was obvious what I'd done.

"Y' put y' lights on full beam while I was chasin' another car," he snarled aggressively.

We were off to a great start. I'd not seen another car since coming off the mountain highway. I didn't believe him but apologised nonetheless, insisting I was unaware of the situation. He wasn't interested in my apology and demanded I step out of the car. I did as he said and clambered out onto the tar-seal where I got to have a good look at him. Definitely early thirties, sporting a thick brown moustache. *Seems t' be standard issue in the law 'n order game. Seems that in the mind 'f the owner, it portrays a sense 'f power. Funny that it's viewed that way. It looks bloody terrible!*

He wasn't a tall cop, being quite stocky, perhaps a little overweight. His eyes were soft and pleasant, a contradiction of his official persona.

"I'm goin' t' have t' search the car. Please step away from your vehicle."

"On what basis?"

"No basis. Standard procedure. Now step away from the car," he stated firmly, simultaneously opening my driver's door.

Yeah right. Violation 'f an individual's rights more like it, y' fat pig! I stepped away.

"Now please stand off t' the other side 'f the car."

"What? Here?" I asked, moving to the passenger door.

"Yes, 'n place y' hands on the roof."

I did as he said. He was in my car instantly, flashlight beaming, going straight for the glovebox.

Fuck! I forgot about the chillum. The fuckin' chillum's in the glovebox 'n guaranteed t' excite him. P'haps he won't know what it is. Maybe it's all shrivelled up by now 'n won't resemble any kind 'f pipe.

He grunted his way around the front seat like a pig foraging for food. It didn't take him long to let out a few extra grunts, excited and curious at his discovery.

"What's this?" he exclaimed as he exited the car and waved the carrot in my face.

"A carrot," I replied.

"Yeah, I know that, y' funny cunt! But what's it hollowed out for?"

"F' fun."

His nostrils were flaring like a horse after a race and his eyes screwed up as he glared at me. "Y' think this is funny, don't y'?"

"Not really, I'm actually tired 'n just want t' get home," I said, shrugging my shoulders.

"Where's home?"

"Ahh … Yaringa."

"Yaringa, eh?"

From the darkness of the night, blue flashing lights appeared on the horizon, travelling at speed towards us.

"Yeah, Yaringa."

Within seconds the blue flashing lights pulled up on the verge across the road from where my Holden was parked. Gravel flew everywhere as the car came to a dramatic standstill. The driver's door opened, and shiny black boots trod on the gravel, crunching loudly in the stillness of the night. The officer stood beside the vehicle and placed his cap on his head. He was a tall, wiry man who obviously enjoyed the authority he got from wearing his uniform. He slammed the door closed and strutted with exaggerated casualness across the road like a cowboy, his right hand poised to remove his gun from its holster.

"Go 'n stand at the end 'f the car!" he demanded, pointing with his left hand, seeming quite happy to steal the porky's thunder. His face was ugly and snarled, and there was definite menace in his voice.

I took an instant dislike to him. Reluctantly I obliged and walked to the end of the car. The two cops talked briefly in hushed tones, then the cowboy entered the car and began frisking under the front seat before climbing into the back. After a few moments he clambered back out through the rear passenger door on the driver's side. He mumbled something to his colleague, then turned and walked towards me.

"Get y' hands on the roof where I can see them, 'n spread y' legs … nice 'n wide." He'd pulled his gun from its holster and pointed it at me.

Thinks he's in some kind 'f Clint Eastwood western. He was agitated and trying to intimidate me, though I still felt unafraid. It was as if the whole thing was an act. The cold steel of the gun barrel was on my temple.

"Come on! Spread those legs a little wider." Porky patted me down and I began to worry, but he was obviously homophobic and didn't get close to my crotch. I sighed with relief as he stood and shook his head to his mate.

Maybe the cowboy with the gun to my head detected my sigh, or maybe they'd just been playing with me up until then.

"Turn 'round t' face me," he demanded. I turned around, and he gestured aggressively, his gun aimed at my crotch as he stepped back from me. "What's that y' got down y' pants? A cunt, or what?"

"What are y' talkin' about?" I said defiantly.

"Y' can't fool me, mate. Get y' fuckin' pants down."

"Fuck off."

The gun was in my face and he was yelling at me. "Get y' fuckin' pants down before this fuckin' gun goes off!"

Suddenly I felt like everything was crumbling around me, I felt sick in the stomach, my knees went weak. I wasn't so optimistic about my situation anymore. I was dealing with a psycho and it was a whole new ball game as he continued to press the gun against my head. To undo my pants was to reveal what I thought I had safely concealed. *Well, did I get that wrong! It was all too late now.* I was between a rock and a hard place and there was no option but to expose myself and my well-packed underpants to Cowboy and Porky. *The good cop, bad cop scenario. Like in the movies where y' get one nice guy who gives y' a break, 'n then there's the fuckwit … the psycho I'm dealin' with now. Things sure are different here.*

I lost all confidence. My hands shook uncontrollably as they struggled to reveal the contents of my underpants. I knew the cop wasn't bluffing as he continued to hold the gun to my head. All I could think of was what my parents would say, and in those few seconds as my life passed before me, I sincerely hoped Mum hadn't seen *Midnight Express*. I gingerly handed the cops the Bakelite box from my underpants. Arsehole snatched it from my hand and opened it as though he was about to view something rare. His eyes lit up like a Christmas tree as he shared his discovery with Porky.

"What's this?" Cowboy demanded.

"Dunno," I shrugged.

He glared at me. "Yes y' do, y' smart cunt!"

"Look, if you've got a problem, take me in 'n I'll get a lawyer." As the words fell out of my mouth I knew, too late, that my tactics weren't the best. In an instant Cowboy had my arm behind my back, forcing it to the extreme, the pain was excruciating. If he pushed any further, I knew it would break.

As if on cue, Porky stepped in to pacify the situation. "Listen up. Y' can do this the easy way or the hard way. Either way we'll get what we want from you."

Classic fuckin' cop speech from the good guy. I hated them both for my predicament, but I hated Cosmo even more. My mind was racing, thinking of how I could resolve my futile situation. *I'm in the proverbial shit!* I took a deep breath. "Okay, Okay. They're capsules 'f hash oil," I blurted out in one breath, feeling the deflation of defeat.

"Right. We're takin' y' in, mate," said Porky. "You're under arrest. Anythin' y' say will be taken down 'n used as evidence."

I feel like I'm in a movie that I'm also watching. I feel like it's not me standin' there at midnight, but someone who looks like me. The real me is far away in the vast sky, watching ... hovering ... waiting.

The cowboy lowered the gun from my head and placed it back in its holster. I thought about running, jumping the fence and disappearing into the darkness. I fancied I could outrun them. The thought only lasted a few seconds as I imagined the psycho removing his gun and picking me off like some wild animal. I didn't fancy becoming his trophy. I wasn't going to give him that satisfaction. Porky attempted to handcuff my wrists, but one of the jaws had jammed on him.

"Fuckin' piece 'f shit! You'd think they could design somethin' as simple as this t' work more smoothly." No sooner had he uttered the words than it closed. "That's got the fuck'r." He closed it with such force that the cold steel bit into my wrists. There was no point in complaining, it would only escalate an already volatile situation.

"Right, y' little prick. Get y' arse in the back 'f the paddy wagon," said Cowboy as he dragged me in the direction of the vehicle that Porky had pulled up in. The blue lights of both vehicles still flashed unrelentingly in the darkness, like an empty disco hall. Porky opened the rear doors and Cowboy shoved me in aggressively. "In y' get, scum."

The door slammed shut behind me and I could hear their voices as they collaborated, the sound drifting in the still air. I was beyond caring what they were talking about.

The next minute the vehicle sparked to life, and I felt the husky throb of a large diesel engine. Porky pulled out onto the road, accelerating heavily. I could feel the back wheels spinning as they spat gravel. Through the grille of the rear door window, I watched my own car, headlights still casting a dull yellow beam, disappear into the night, only to be replaced by the blue flashing lights of Cowboy's vehicle taking up the rear.

* * *

Before long the vehicle's doors were being unlocked and opened.

"Out y' come," said Porky. I stood and walked to the edge of the police van, bent my knees and jumped. I kept my knees bent as I hit the road to avoid jarring my legs. I was quickly seized by my elbow and led up the path to the police station, identifiable by the well-lit 'Police' sign, presented in large blue letters with checkered blue-and-white squares below. The building was standard issue, Australian red brick with no distinctive features other than the external metal security grilles over each window.

The cops led me up the steps and into the reception area where Porky lifted up a portion of the bench set on hinges. Cowboy forced me through the gap and into the next room where an older man, dressed in uniform with sergeant stripes on his shirt sleeves, sat at a desk reading a *Playboy* magazine. He placed it on the desktop to reveal the centrefold.

"Check that out, Frank," he said, spinning the magazine around to reveal a busty brunette lying on a couch, naked except for stiletto shoes and panties around her ankles, her fingers parting her pussy's lips.

I looked at the sergeant who noticed me for the first time. *No wonder the cops've got the rep they've got here. Tho' she does look tasty.*

"What've you boys got here?" the sergeant hissed, glaring at me as though I was filth.

Cowboy, aka Frank, moved in close, salivating over the image as he spoke. "Some idiot who keeps 'is drugs down 'is pants, like he thinks he's got a cunt."

It didn't make sense to me, but he obviously thought it was funny as he laughed at his own joke. The other two laughed on cue.

"Right, son. Let's have y' details," announced Porky, leading me over to a different desk. He stood behind me and fiddled with my handcuffs until they were open. *Thank Christ.* Any longer and my hands would fall off from lack of blood circulation. He sat down behind the desk, I remained standing.

"Name first." He had a pad with a preprinted page to record details. There were boxes to put the answers in.

"Samuel."

"Y' full name."

"Samuel John Gorzman."

"Spell it."

"I, T." He started writing it down on the pad.

"Listen, y' smart fuckin' cunt!" he said, giving me the eyeball. "Y' can do y'self a favour or y' can make it really difficult f' y'self. Got it?"

"He givin' y' shit, Harry?" Frank was over and behind me, and suddenly grabbed my right wrist and shoved it high up my back with such force I had to bite my lip to stop myself from crying out, mainly because I didn't want to give him the pleasure.

"S-A ..."

"Y' surname!" Frank still had my wrist behind my back. He cranked it up, making me jolt. "Y' think y' funny, don't y'?" Frank said.

Funnier than you, arsehole. "No," I replied.

The sergeant sauntered over to join the circus. "Got a wise crack on y' hands, Frank?" He continued without waiting for an answer. "These two ..." he said, nodding his head like a chook from one to the other, "can make life very difficult for y'. *So play the game, shithead!*"

Spit flew in my face from his verbal assault. I wanted to wipe it off but couldn't move. I wanted to laugh hysterically, everything felt so fucked up, so unreal.

"Right, spell that surname f' me," snapped Porky, aka Harry, eyeballing me with anticipation.

"G-O-R-Z-M-A-N," I said, prolonging and exaggerating each letter.

"That's it?" he asked, looking at me as if I might've tricked him again.

"Yep," I said nodding. "Ahh!" My arm was rammed up my back again and I cried out as the pain shot up my arm.

"The word's 'yes'!"

"Yes," I promptly said, not wanting any more retribution.

"Where y' from, not from 'round here, are y'?" Harry asked, continuing to eyeball me, still armed with pen and notebook.

"I live in Yaringa."

"So y' said before. Whereabouts in Yaringa might that be?"

The air could have been cut with a knife as their curiosity increased.

"I live on the road by the lake entrance."

"There're only two houses on that road," the sergeant said, interrupting and looking all animated. "Fred Young lives in one, 'n George Peterson's away fishin', 'n he usually rents his out. He must be rentin' off George." The sergeant looked at Harry like he'd just split the atom or won the Nobel Peace Prize.

"That's right," said Harry, responding to the realisation, equally enthused.

My arm was forced up my back again as Frank's torture session continued.

"Is that right?" Frank asked, adding to the chorus in his monosyllabic dribble.

"Yes," I said, gasping to catch my breath.

Harry was waving the Bakelite box that housed the oil capsules, looking at me as if I was supposed to understand his latest form of communication.

"I bought it from someone up the mountains."

"What fuckin' mountains?" asked Frank as another shooting pain went up my arm and across my shoulder. It seemed he needed something to do to feel he was involved in the whole process. Harry looked at Frank as if he didn't approve of his behaviour. The look was fleeting, probably noticed by no one but me.

Frank's a fuckin' psychopath! The sort 'f guy who would've joined the New

South Wales Police Force f' the opportunity t' avenge his wounded childhood, the bullyin' he experienced at school as a boy. Each time he pulls someone in, it's his chance t' return the abuse he was subjected to ... or perhaps he was just born an arsehole. The cocksuckin' bully who enjoys taking advantage of those weaker than himself. Yeah ... that's the most likely scenario. Born t' bully!

"Kosciuszko," I replied, hoping for a reprieve on my arm, which didn't come.

"Would that be Thredbo or Perisher?" Frank asked, maintaining his grip. The pain still unbearable, but I couldn't afford to let him know that.

"Thredbo." He relaxed his grip. I sighed internally.

"So ... let me get this right," said Harry, staring me down. "Y' went all the way up the mountains t' get these capsules in this box?"

"No. I worked at Thredbo, 'n while I was there, I bought the capsules."

Harry looked at me sceptically and I sensed he didn't believe me. I still found it strange the way I had been pulled up in the middle of the night with some lame excuse that I'd had my headlights on full beam and directed at him while he was in pursuit of another vehicle. If I had, it certainly wasn't intentional, one car looked like another in the dead of night. *Why would he bother t' turn 'round t' chase me?* I smelt a rat and the stench was becoming stronger.

"So where were y' comin' from when I pulled y' up t'night?" Harry continued.

I didn't see any point in lying. "Canberra," I said, testing the waters, looking for any telltale signs from Harry. He showed far too much expression on his face to ever be any good at poker, let alone the interrogation game. Sure enough, Harry's eyes lit up too brightly and a small smile became visible in the corners of his mouth.

Fuckin' Cosmo! He must've been lookin' f' credits! What the fuck did he hope t' achieve dobbin' in a small fish like me? As I stood there, vulnerable, surrounded by these men in blue, I realised they were after a bigger fish than me. They planned on getting that bigger fish even if it wasn't by the book. *The Do's and Don'ts of Big Game Fishing* came to mind. In this circumspect moment, I saw an image of the book cover in my head — me hanging from a gaff hook, like a marlin, held up in mid-air by Frank and Harry, both grinning, the quintessential big game fishermen.

"Can I use the toilet?" I was desperate for a dump. I'd been holding out for some time hoping the need would dissipate.

"Let 'im cack 'imself," said Frank, unsympathetically.

"Y' want t' clean up? Cos I don't."

Harry grabbed me by my free arm and led me through a wooden door, then through a steel-bar door which led to the prison cells, where he pushed me into the first cell. In the corner was a dirty stainless-steel bowl with no seat. Harry stood in the doorway while I made my way over to the toilet.

"Y' gonna watch?" I asked, unbuttoning my jeans.

"Police regulations: *Keep an eye on the suspect at all times.*"

I was beyond caring. I dropped my pants and squatted over the bowl. There was no way I was putting my arse on that septic-looking thing. As I commenced my assault on the bowl, two more faces showed behind Harry's. I couldn't help myself. "You guys got nothin' better t' do than perv on some poor soul doin' Beethoven's Ninth? Y're all sick, I reckon!"

"Y' want t' watch y'self, sunshine, or there won't be no sun shinin' out 'f that arse no more." Frank had managed to string a bit of a sentence together and was looking menacingly at me.

I could see I was in for a long night, as I'd just given Frank the extra impetus he needed to do the job he thought he was made for doing. I finished my business with all three still watching, although they did turn away while I wiped my arse. *Must be squeamish after all.* I flushed the toilet and pulled my trousers back up. There was no basin to wash my hands, and I didn't see any point in asking. Harry led me back to the interrogation room.

"Okay," resumed Harry. "Where did y' get the goods?" He was playing lead interrogator, the good cop with the fundamental questions.

"I dunno the guy's name. He didn't offer it, 'n I didn't ask. Never met the guy b'fore … it was a one-off purchase."

"So have y' just come from Thredbo or from Canberra?" Harry asked.

"Both, kind 'f," I replied calmly. Harry was trying to angle things so I would fall into his trap, and I was convinced he knew more.

"I suggest y' do know who y' got it off and it would be in y' favour t' reveal this!"

"Look, I told y' I dunno."

My head was suddenly snapped back. Frank had me by my hair and was pulling on it, dragging me across the room. It felt as though my hair was going to come out at the roots.

"What the fuck are y' doin', man?" I gasped. As abruptly as he had started, he stopped, leaving me kneeling on the floor.

"Y'll talk, son, y'll talk … They all do in the end," Sergeant Playboy muttered randomly.

Frank left the room and Harry knelt down beside me. "Listen. Y' can do this my way 'n save y'self some trouble, or y' can do it Frank's way." He looked at me sincerely, like he really cared, but I believed it was all part of the performance, *the Frank and Harry Show — the crack team from Hicksville.*

I gave him my most sincere face as I pleaded, my eyes staring directly into his. "I seriously only met this guy once … alright, maybe twice, but I swear we were never formally introduced. I only ever knew 'im as Joe."

"How come I don't believe y'?"

"Come on, Harry." Frank re-entered the room through a side door for his turn on the stage.

"He's all yours, mate," replied Harry.

"Right, y' little prick!" Frank snarled, grabbing my hair in his hand and pulling me up. I tried to get to my feet to ease the pressure, but as I did so he hurled me across the room, smashing me into the brick wall. He came up close to my face so that I could feel the warmth of his breath on my skin and smell the stale garlic on his breath. He had his knee firmly up against my balls and the whiskers of his moustache brushed my lips.

"*Who the fuck did y' get that shit off?*" he demanded.

"I've got rights. I'm entitled t' a phone call. M' lawyer's gonna hear ab—" Wham! His knee rammed into my crown jewels. I shrieked with pain as it took my breath away and I collapsed heavily on the floor, pulling myself into a fetal position. "Y' cunt, y' fuckin' cunt!" I rasped. His hand was on my head and I was again being pulled up by my hair and slammed against the wall.

"Y' had enough?" Frank asked, a twisted smile spreading across his ugly face.

I spat in his face, right between his eyes, and watched it dribble down the bridge of his nose. He was in a state of disbelief, just standing there, not bothering to wipe it away but holding my gaze and looking increasingly psychotic.

"*Harry!*" he yelled, "get the goddamn phone book, will y'." Harry hesitated. I could see him over Frank's shoulder. He froze, and in that moment the sergeant whipped a phone book off one of the desks.

"Here, Frank," he said, all excited as he held it out to him.

"Y' know what t' do with it, just hold it nice 'n steady," said Frank as he stepped away from me. The sergeant put the book up against my stomach. Before I had time to realise what was happening, Frank charged at me and swung his fist into the phone book, hitting it repeatedly until I slumped to the floor gasping for breath. Frank was hysterical, completely out of control, repeatedly kicking me. Harry had to step in and pull Frank away, giving me the opportunity to catch my breath. He didn't say a word, just looked at me with his soft-cock eyes and let Frank take over again. I was still doubled up on the floor.

Frank was on his knees beside me. "No one knows y' here." Then louder, "*No one knows y' fuckin' here, cunt!*" Then softer, "I could take y' down some country road 'n beat y' unconscious. Y' could be lyin' in some ditch slowly dyin'. It might be several days b'fore someone finds y'. By then it could be too late, y' might be dead. That'd be too bad … *too fuckin' bad!*"

"Y're insane."

"It's been said before," he said, looking pleased about it.

Frank's hand was on my head and my hair was being pulled once more. I wished my hair wasn't long, he could get a fistful so easily. I was sure my hair was all going to tear away from my scalp as he dragged me to my feet. In his other hand he held the Bakelite box, which he put right up to my face and tapped my nose with it.

"What do y' s'pose would happen if someone were to take all 'f these at the same time?" he asked me with the look of the devil. An evil smile spread across his face. I saw horns growing out his forehead, and as he laughed his garlic breath burned in my nostrils like the smell of evil.

The capsules would blow someone's mind pretty big. I looked to Harry and the sarge, neither of them giving much away with their blank faces. They'd seen it all before. *The Midnight Frank Show — weeknights, Wodyn only.*

"I'm not sure," I replied as casually as I could manage, my voice sounding too high. Suddenly he was shaking my head like I was a rag doll. My head was hurting badly, my scalp felt swollen, and I was convinced that all my hair would fall out.

Opa's voice sounded in my head: *You've got beautiful hair, boy. Make sure you look after it.* I began to wonder what I'd look like with big hanks of hair missing, like someone's badly neglected pet, perhaps.

"What if I suggested t' y' that I'll force all this shit int' y' gob, 'n made y' swallow it. Y'd be pretty fuck'd up, wouldn't y'?"

"Guess I might be," I conceded, getting his drift.

"So…" he said, releasing my hair and placing his hand on the lid of the box. "I think we might have t' find out." He grinned and his dark eyes sparkled as he removed a capsule from the box.

"Y' won't get those in m' mouth."

"Three against one. Don't see too many problems with that."

The sarge was instantly in there, gripping my right arm and forcing it up my back to let his intentions be known and shown. Harry seemed less willing to play as he slowly sidled up to me. "Just fuckin' tell us where y' got this shit from and …"

"And what?" I started.

Harry suddenly had my face in both his hands, trying to force my mouth open.

"Y' cunts, y'all a pack 'f cunts!"

Frank had a capsule in his hand he was about to put in my mouth. Harry had forced me to open my mouth by pushing his hands on my jawbones on both sides. I'd tried half a capsule before, in a cup of coffee. It had been strong, almost too strong. Now I was about to get a whole one, then another and another. *They'll release me on t' the street 'n I'll be found in some gutter … unconscious … comatose … fuck'd forever. I might end up in a hospital bed, plugged in, a vegetable. Mum 'n Dad, m' brothers 'n sisters, all sittin' 'round tryin' t' decide whether t' switch off the machine. I'd hear them discussing it. I'd be powerless t' tell them I'll be okay. I just need time f' the oil t' wear off, but maybe it never would.*

"Okay … Okay. I'll tell y'!" I called out as the capsule fell onto my tongue. They hadn't heard me. My voice had been merely a squeak. Harry tried to close my mouth, so I'd have to swallow. The capsule was dissolving rapidly on my tongue and Frank had another one ready to go. I lifted my right foot and kicked out at Harry as hard as I could. I must've gotten him fair on the shin because he let go and started hopping around the room, clutching his right leg.

Frank was about to launch a punch at my solar plexus when my words sounded in his ears. "I'll tell … I'll tell y'." He stopped in mid-flight.

"We've got a winner here, boys!" he cried out, excitedly.

I'd never wanted to hit someone as much as I wanted to hit Frank at that moment. I looked at him with contempt and spat the capsule on the floor. It was all but dissolved and stuck to the floor like a big brown glistening blob.

"Where then did y' get this shit from?"

"A guy called Bruce."

"Listen y' little fucker, y' better not be takin' the piss, see. If y' are, I'll just pop another one 'f these in y' mouth." Frank was waving a capsule in his hand between finger and thumb, looking psychotic. "So … Bruce, y' say."

"Bruce Langer."

"And where might we find him?"

"In the mountains, I guess."

"Y' can call Fellini now, Harry," announced Frank. "I'll put this prick in a cell t' cool down f' a bit." Harry was still nursing his shin, staring daggers at me.

* * *

Frank took me by the arm and pushed me towards the door that led to the cells, then into the cell where they had been entertained at my expense a short time earlier. The cell door clanged shut behind me, the harsh sound of steel on steel. Frank turned the key and removed it from the lock. "That should sort y' out. We always get what we want out 'f arseholes like you." He smirked, turned and walked out, whistling as he went.

I lamented the fact that I had just dropped Bruce right in it, but felt I had no choice. I didn't know the full extent of what these cops were capable of, but Frank had demonstrated clearly how far he was prepared to go. He'd spooked me. *Fuck … Fuck … Fuck. What a fuckin' mess this is!* I sat on the side of the bed, waiting for the capsule to kick in. *Who the fuck's Fellini?*

I looked around at my cell. There was the stainless-steel toilet in the corner and a handbasin hidden in the shadows at the back wall — no windows, no frills. My bed was a rusted steel-frame with a lumpy kapok mattress, a pillow at the head, and one grey blanket. I lay down, stretched out my sore body, and placed my head on the pillow with my hands behind my head.

I was in a state of disbelief at my predicament. I looked at the back wall, noticing all the initials roughly engraved in the shit-brown paint. Someone had written "Cops take it up the Arse". *I bet Arsehole takes it up the arse. Hope he doesn't pay me a visit.* I began to shiver, and it wasn't even cold. I sat up and unfolded the thick, army-type blanket from the end of the bed and pulled it over myself as I lay back down. My scalp was throbbing and sore to the touch, and my entire body ached. The capsule didn't seem to be affecting me much. I just felt tired and strangely dreamy. I began to dream of home.

How far away it seems. It's not as though I can ring the old man at the end of the night, explain what's happened, and ask him t' pick me up. Hi, Dad. It's me … I just got out 'f the cop shop. I've been beaten up badly by the cops. I couldn't take it any more, so I confessed. I told them where I got large amounts 'f hash oil from. They should've arrested the guy by now, so I'm in big trouble … there'll be a price out on m' head. You'll prob'ly be able t' find me at the bottom 'f the Wodyn River. I'll be the body with the bricks tied t' it. If there's anythin' left 'f me, I've decided that I'd like t' be buried at the cemetery Oma 'n Opa plan t' be buried in. Dad, please come get me … it's not far … I'll be waiting.

I must've fallen asleep because I awoke, startled, to the sound of creaking hinges and the familiar clanging of steel. I jerked upright to see Harry walking into the cell.

"Wakey, wakey … hands off snakey."

I rubbed my eyes and sat up properly, instantly wary of Harry's upbeat mood. My scalp had definitely swelled. Reaching up to rub my head lightly, I found it was painful. *Who the fuck does he think he is, makin' light 'f my situation!*

"Chop, chop! Mr Detective awaits. Y' can't be keepin' him."

I peeled the blanket back and lowered my feet slowly to the floor, pushing up on the mattress, barely managing to hold my own weight. My whole body was in agony now, my brain too. I feared the interrogation was about to begin all over again. The cowboy had broken me and now the detective was here to finish me off.

6

Inspector Fellini

Harry led me out to the main room where Frank was talking with a man who looked like the main character in the *Godfather* movie. The godfather eyed me up as I was led across the floor. He was a tall, lean man of olive complexion, with jet-black hair combed back and held in place with Brylcreem. He had large dark-brown eyes that smiled at me even though his mouth showed no hint of warmth.

"This is Detective Inspector Fellini," said Harry. "And this is Samuel Gorzman." He waved his hand towards me.

Fellini? Wasn't there some famous Italian film director by that name? Huh! How appropriate to the situation. I boldly reached my hand out to shake his and to my surprise he reciprocated without hesitation.

"You can call me Fellini."

I smiled inwardly as I noticed Harry and Frank were servile in the presence of the detective. *I bet they lick his arse big time. They're scared 'f him! Their true nature reflected by a power mightier than themselves.* I allowed myself a slight snigger. The sarge was back at his desk, seemingly oblivious to us all, engrossed once again in his *Playboy* magazine. *Probably the closest he'll ever come t' a naked woman since his wife left him after she discovered what kind 'f animal she was married t'. I bet the only time he gets t' shoot his load is int' a hanky or up some whore's arse.*

"Come with me, Sam," said Detective Fellini as he ushered me towards an office with faded venetian blinds hanging in the windows. An old, tired freestanding fan rotated noisily in the far corner, creating a gentle breeze that ruffled the sad-looking pot plant beside it. A low-hanging ceiling lamp, coupled with an old-style banker's lamp on the desk, gave the room a sickly yellow hue.

"Harry, why don't you come and take notes," called Detective Fellini. Frank was obviously put out by this. He wore it blatantly on his face. I walked into the office grateful that I didn't have to deal with Frank anymore. Harry shut the door behind us. *Suck eggs, Frank, y' cunt!*

"Have a seat," Fellini said, pulling out a chair before making his way around to his own. His desk was a mess with files piled one on top of the other, without care or order. A large white notepad lay in the middle of the desk, and two ornate steel-framed photos sat side by side amidst the chaos. One was of an attractive young woman. It was all faded and yellow around the edges. *Must be his wife b'fore she got int' home cookin' 'n grew fat like most Italian housewives seem t', or maybe she still looks as good as in the photo. If so, he's a fortunate man.* The other photo was of two children standing together, smiling happily, obviously pre-teenagers — a girl about to blossom into a beautiful young woman and a boy with many of his father's features.

"Yes, they are my children," Fellini said as if reading my thoughts. "They're tucked up in bed where all good children should be." His eyes still danced warmly in his head as he looked at me gravely. *Don't let those eyes fool y'.*

Harry seated himself on a hard wooden chair in the corner, armed with a notepad and pen.

"Shall we begin?" asked Fellini, looking at me, then nodding to Harry. "Where do you live?"

"Yaringa." No reaction.

"Where in Yaringa?"

"Down by the …" Harry interrupted.

"Harry, for Chrissake let him answer the questions or we'll be here all night!"

"Sorry, sir," Harry apologised, looking sheepish, bowing his head like a boy who had been scolded.

"You were saying, Sam?" *I wasn't, he was.*

"Yeah, down by the lake on the road next t' the lake entrance, at George Peterson's."

"That place still standing?"

"Yeah, it's not so bad. I know it doesn't look like much from the outside, but the inside is good, it does us alright." Fellini's eyes lit up at the word 'us' and I realised my mistake. I wasn't any good at this game, but the cops already knew about Bruce anyway. I prayed that he had hidden his stash somewhere discreet.

"You say 'us'?"

"Me 'n m' girlfriend, another guy — m' girlfriend's ex — 'n his girlfriend," I reluctantly confessed. He sat bolt upright in his chair and I knew he was getting excited as to where this was leading. I loathed having to tell the truth, but I wasn't going back out there with Frank for a second round.

"That's a small place for four people. How do you get on with your girlfriend's ex?"

What? "I don't see how that's relevant t' the situation," I replied.

Fellini's eyes hardened as he leaned forward slightly and spoke softly but firmly, "Yes, but I do, and if the information helps me piece things together then I'll be expecting an answer!" He glanced towards the door suggestively.

I gulped and cleared my throat. "We get on alright. He's got his new girlfriend 'n they're very close, so it's not a problem."

I noticed Harry writing in shorthand. My mind diverted to thinking that he and Frank must've had to do shorthand classes, must've had to join a class of girls, studiously learning the different symbols. It was difficult to visualise them incongruously sitting there, trying to master the delicate symbols that make up teeline shorthand. Nearly all the girls in my class back at school learnt shorthand, but no guys took it up. *Sure would be handy, though, if I still want t' pursue a career as a journalist.* Harry caught me smiling and glared at me. Fellini's voice brought me hurtling back to the present.

"So you get on with him alright? What did you say his name was?"

"I don't believe I did," I replied. Fellini shifted in his seat, looking agitated. I maintained eye contact with him as I awaited his next question.

"So let's get this straight. You went up the mountains, Thredbo … right?" I nodded defeatedly. "You met a guy up there who sold you the capsules so you could sell them in Canberra."

"I never said anythin' about sellin' capsules!"

"Listen, young man. Anyone found with the number of capsules you were carrying is deemed to be in Possession with the Intention to Supply. So without even doing anything, you're viewed as having that intention. Are you getting the picture?"

"If y' say so then I believe y'."

Fellini was struggling to stay calm now, his eyes darkened, he leaned forward violently and spoke in slow, precisely accentuated words. "*You are in the proverbial shitter!* If you don't help us, we'll bring you down like a ton of bricks."

I was starting to get the picture, but I couldn't see how helping them was ever going to help me, even though I found myself nodding my head emphatically, hoping he would calm down. He continued to speak. "We don't believe you bought those capsules up the mountain. Do you get my drift?"

Images flooded my mind, images of Cosmo arriving in Yaringa, everyone so jumpy with him there, and Bruce asking me if I'd drive him out of town. I'd never had a problem with Cosmo until our arrival in Canberra. Up the mountain he'd treated me well. He was generous with his gear, getting everyone high before hitting the slopes, and was great to ski with. With his long red hair and full, flowing beard, he was like a character in a fantasy novel — a cross between a mad Scotsman and a wise old wizard. *Of course. Sure I'll take Cosmo t' Canberra.*

"Bruce … Bruce is my girlfriend's ex." I heard the words coming from my mouth, sounding as if from far away. *What the fuck am I sayin'? That's the nail in the coffin.* My heart was racing. I felt light-headed and overwhelmed. My head sank into my hands and I realised I was crying. Fellini was on his feet. I'd confessed. I'd broken the fundamental rule: Never grass on your mates or colleagues except …

I saw my life flash before my eyes as Fellini told Harry, "Jump to it man. Time is of the essence."

* * *

They were on their way to raid the house at the lake. My life was no longer worth living. *No wonder people take their lives in the wee hours 'f the mornin' in rural jail cells. Found hangin' by the threads 'f their clothes as the sun's comin' up, castin' light through the steel bars 'f the windows, silhouetting the poor fucker hangin' lifeless.* The more surreal my life became, the more reality hit me.

"Pete, get in here and put him in a cell until we check this whole thing out!" Fellini demanded, standing in the doorway of his office. Then he turned back to his desk and rifled through his drawer, pulling out a revolver. He opened the chamber to load it and rapidly inserted bullets before snapping it closed.

The sarge entered the room. "Get y'self up off that seat, boy. Y' can relax in the slammer for a bit, y' won't be goin' anywhere in a hurry t'night. Tho' it's mornin' actually, ain't it?" He laughed as if it were funny.

As the sarge herded me through to the cells, Fellini headed out the main entrance with his posse of Harry and Frank, all full of self-importance. I almost laughed out loud at how ridiculous they appeared, all hyped up, as if they were about to make one of the most crucial busts in the history of drug crime in Australia. *My world's gone mad.* The sound of steel slamming against steel made me instantly aware of my environment.

"That'll sort y' out f' a while, y' fuckin' little cunt." The sarge seemed to grow in stature and confidence in the absence of his superiors.

Get fucked y' pervert, y' weasel-headed jerk ... y' sick excuse 'f a human being. "Whatever y' say, mate," I responded flatly. I grabbed the familiar grey blanket and pulled it over my body as I lay down.

7

Cosmo & Others

I had met Cosmo up the mountain shortly after Tania and I arrived. He was a friend of hers, or so it seemed from the way they enthusiastically embraced when we stumbled across him. He was an interesting man, confident, an extrovert, and full of stories. By the way he dressed, he seemed to be a hippy — his clothes appeared self-made or second-hand. His stories were fantastical and full of creative licence. Cosmo was captivating and larger than life.

* * *

When Tania went back to Yaringa, she left me with the Holden Special and the caravan.

"Y' may as well take the caravan back if y' aren't stayin'," I had said to her. The caravan parks on the shores of Lake Jindabyne at the base of the mountains were pricey and unaffordable long term. We'd managed to find a more reasonably priced caravan park further out of town on a farmer's property.

"No, you'll need it and the car," she had replied.

"But I can stay up here in Thredbo village if y're goin'. I'll be able t' get a room in the staff quarters."

"You still might want the caravan," she had persisted. "It's here now, so you may as well make use of it. Anyway, how can I take the caravan without a car?"

I shrugged my shoulders. I couldn't be bothered arguing, and she had a point. "Hey, whatever y' think, baby."

The following morning, on the way to work, I had dropped Tania at the bus stop in Jindabyne.

* * *

Cosmo seemed to have a bottomless supply of drugs and for some reason he latched onto me. We hung out together a lot, and he never appeared to work or pay for a lift pass, and he was always up for skiing. He was much older than me and far more worldly. Initially I had imagined myself to be as experienced in life as he was, but soon I was constantly comparing myself to him. *Never compare yourself to others or you will always come up short,* Oma had told me once. At the time I wondered what she meant, but now it made sense. Cosmo was the kind of person I would've been happy to be. I admired his self-assured nature, his ease with everyone around him, his charm with the ladies, and his shrewdness in negotiating something for nothing.

On my free days I skied with Cosmo and a bunch of other people whom I'd befriended in my short time up the mountain. I was continually amazed at how quickly I made friends with people and how close we became within a short time. We all did cones together in the room of a couple of very spunky chicks. *T' die for ... I'd give m' right arm t' have one or both 'f 'em. Fuck what Tania'd think.*

* * *

I'd always dreamt of being able to ski every day for an entire winter, not that it had worked out that way this time. Being a lift operator meant that you stood all day in the freezing cold ensuring the 'turkeys' got on the T-bar, chairlift, or whatever other type of lift it was you were rostered on that day. Boredom would usually set in after five minutes on the job, but some lifts were more challenging than others and you could stay focused for longer. If you were working the chairs, you stayed in the warm cosiness of the control room, speeding up and slowing down the lift depending on the difficulties people were having getting on. Lunchtime never gave me enough time to go skiing. It was a total con-job — there was not one tiny bit of glamour in the industry. Being stuck in the ski hire section adjusting halfwits' bindings and telling them what size boots or skis they needed, didn't appeal to me any more than being a lift operator. The only good thing about being a 'liftee' was all the sexy chicks who slid around on skis in tight, fashionable ski outfits. Occasionally, I'd get a hot one who would slide and fall over right in front of me, unable to get back up. I was always happy to oblige in helping them slip and slide to their feet with my hands firmly planted around their waist.

One day up on the intermediate T-bar, a young, well-rounded babe with a pretty face and big tits slammed into me as she was approaching the lift. She pushed too hard with her poles to move herself forward and her skis shot out from under her. She landed on her well-cushioned arse with a mighty thud, like a small earthquake, but without the snow cracking and the earth parting to swallow her up. I did my usual male rescue thing, and she clung to me like crazy as I pulled her up, but I wasn't prepared for her weight. I staggered, and she pulled me down on top of her. There we were, in a compromising position at the front of a long lift queue. The crowd roared with laughter. I rose to my feet, composed myself, and took a bow before attempting to pull her up again. This time I was ready for the weight of her, and she came up rather easily, falling into my arms, totally intentional. As she pulled away, I saw her face more clearly, and was momentarily lost in her beautiful green eyes.

"Thank you for helping me. I'm really not that good on skis," she said and flashed a melting smile at me.

That night I was in the bistro bar getting my free evening meal, a prearranged deal struck at the beginning of the season with the girls who worked there. In return, we gave them free lift access. I'd just piled my plate up with three bean salad mix at the salad bar, a dish that looked like it had been poured straight out of a can, when there was a chirpy female voice in my ear.

"Hello," she said.

I turned to look behind me and almost dropped my plate. There were those big green eyes. She smiled her beaming smile again, as though she'd just discovered a long-lost friend. The young woman was all dressed up and looked surprisingly good for a fat chick.

"Hi," I said, far too animated. *Wonder what she'd be like from behind. Yeah, that'd give immediate access t' the best part 'f her body without havin' t' deal with the weight 'f her on top 'f me, 'n a nice plump arse t' pound away at.* I was surprised that I had imagined her in a sexual position so quickly, almost automatically, like a sonar fish-finder on a boat when schools of fish are near. The image stuck in my mind like a small crumb in the back of the throat that's not easily dislodged.

"Are you eating on your own?"

"No, I replied. "I'm eatin' with you, aren't I?" She seemed pleased at my response.

"That would be great," she said, lumping a large spoonful of mayonnaise-soaked potato salad onto her plate.

Fuck, all I want is m' dick up her fat arse 'n t' hear her moanin', beggin' f' me t' do it harder.

We sat down at a table near a window that in the daytime had a view of the mountain, but in the darkness of the night all we could see were the illuminated chair lifts and the flashing cabin lights of the snow groomers that smoothed the snow out, making it all pristine for skiing the next day. Most people didn't like all the ruts and bumps created naturally by the skiers.

"Pretty isn't it," I said, noticing her admiring the lights up the mountain.

"Yes, it is," she said, smiling at me as she probed her fork into a large piece of potato and raised it to her mouth.

I was getting a bulge in my pants just imagining doing it with her. The problem was I only had the Holden. The caravan was still down the mountain, not that I was worried, but she might be bothered by the idea. Some girls might dream of getting laid in the back of a Holden, but I wasn't holding my breath that this chick was up for that kind of adventure. For all I knew, she could be accommodated in a five-star hotel. Besides, there was no way I'd be able to take her from behind in the Holden without crippling myself.

"Where y' from?" I asked, and in the same breath, "I'm Sam, by the way."

"I'm Beth, from Melbourne originally. I moved to Sydney last year … the climate suits me better."

I would've thought that her surplus lard would've insulated her against the nippy Melbourne winters. "It's s'posed t' be the same latitude as Christchurch in New Zealand, which is where I'm from," I responded, trying to cut my way through my overcooked steak. I didn't like well-done meat. Opa always said, *Unless the juice still has some blood in it, it's not worth touching.*

"Are you really from New Zealand?" she asked. Behind those lips she had a wonderful set of pearly white teeth, and I began imagining her with those full-bodied, red lips going down on me, and I wondered if she was as turned on by me as I was by her. I often assumed that because I was turned on by a woman, the power of my energy would spill over and make her equally excited.

Immediately I wanted to ask Beth if she was feeling as horny as I was, but I'd been told that most of the time women don't respond positively to such blatant propositioning, so I didn't risk being upfront. Instead, I continued with the conversation. "Yes, I'm really from New Zealand."

"New Zealand's supposed to be a really beautiful place. I'd like to go there someday. Maybe next winter … and do some skiing."

It pissed me off that the only thing people seemed to know about New Zealand was that we have lots of sheep and the countryside is really beautiful. It was as though besides sheep and scenic beauty, New Zealand was void of any redeeming features, a modest country with modest people, not a place to stand up and be noticed.

"It's a pretty cool place. I grew up there, so I'm biased, but I like it. Oz is different; it's so much bigger, such a vast land in comparison, 'n y' cities are how I imagined large cities should be. But our population is so small that it makes our cities smaller too, they really aren't that big or flash at all compared with the likes 'f Sydney." She nodded thoughtfully.

"Listen," I said, wanting to change the subject, "do y' fancy a drink?" *Do y' fancy a fuck, I'm dead horny. Reckon I could have y' cryin' out f' more in a matter 'f minutes. What's y' favourite position?*

"Why sure, that'd be great." Her eyes really were something quite special. She was very pretty, and her breasts looked fantastic in the low-cut top she was wearing.

If I fantasised too much, I'd be coming in my pants before I even got her near the Holden. "What would y' like t' drink? I'm havin' a beer."

"Oh, a white wine would be great," she said, beaming that smile at me.

"Dry or medium?" I asked, trying to appear knowledgeable.

"Oh, just how it comes," she said, putting her hands together in her lap, shifting self-consciously from side to side, as you do when you're excited and you've got nowhere to direct your energy.

I'll cum inside y' like a volcano.

My mate Holly was working behind the bar. She was one of the two girls I smoked a lot of hash with, very cute, but older than me, and she seemed to fancy older men. Sure, she liked me, but I was too young for her, even though I knew I could please her in bed if she'd just give me the chance.

Out of the corner of my eye I saw Beth straightening her top and checking her lipstick in a small mirror. The situation was looking good. I just needed to relax a little and get her into the swing of it as well. Holly waived the charge on the drinks. "Cheers love, y' a real doll," I said.

I returned with the drinks, placing Beth's glass in front of her.

"Thank you, I don't usually drink," she said. "I'm trying to watch my weight."

I wanted to point out to her that the salad she'd eaten rated zero on the health front, that it had more calories than a few glasses of wine.

"Treat this as a special occasion," I said and raised my glass in a toast. She responded by raising her glass of wine and clinking mine. It was a cheap sound, epitomising the quality of the establishment we were in. We sipped our drinks, peering at each other over the tops of our glasses. The silence became uncomfortable.

Finally, her voice cut through the air like a sweet song. "Thank you for your help today."

"All part 'f the job."

"Do you fancy me?" she asked.

I almost choked on my drink, withdrawing it quickly from my mouth, trying to find some composure. "Y're, well … ah, very … pretty," I stammered.

"Do you think so, even though I'm not the slimmest of girls?" She maintained eye contact for what felt like forever. Defeated, I looked away, then into my drink as I attempted to find words in response.

"No … yes … y're voluptuous 'n beautiful," I replied, smiling genuinely. "Would y' like another drink?"

"I haven't finished this one yet," she said, raising her glass. "Are you trying to get me drunk?"

"No. Shit no, not at all," I replied far too quickly. "Look, shall we go somewhere else? How about your place?" She was shaking her head. I'd read her all wrong, she wasn't interested in me.

"We can't go back to my place, my roommate is there. She'd be peeved if we woke her. What about your place?"

Yes! "I don't have a place. I mean, I don't have a room. I do have m' Holden though. I use the staff facilities in the lodge. There was no accommodation left when I applied f' the job, so I told them I already had accommodation. I wouldn't've got the work otherwise."

"We could buy something to drink and have it in your car, couldn't we?"

Her candour surprised and excited me. I shrugged my shoulders. "Sure, why not." I could hardly contain my enthusiasm. Beth was up for a bit of adventure. I just hoped the height of the car's roof wouldn't be a problem.

We bought a bottle of cheap tawny port on the pretence that it would warm us up, then walked the short distance to the car park. It was a cold, clear night. The car would be like a fridge. I unlocked and opened the door on the passenger side. "Madame." I gestured for her to climb aboard.

"Aren't you the gentleman," she said.

I closed the door on her and let myself in on the driver's side. "There are glasses in the glovebox," I said, leaning across her, all too aware that

I couldn't avoid touching her. I felt the warmth of her body as I found the glasses. "Don't worry, they're clean, maybe just a little dust on them. This is the first time I've had any use f' them. Do y' mind holdin' the glasses while I open the bottle?" I handed the glasses to her, put the key in the ignition and gunned the engine.

"Are we going somewhere?"

"No, but if I leave the engine runnin', we can have the heater on."

"Yes, it's freezing, isn't it?"

"A few minutes 'n y'll be toasty," I said as I undid the seal on the port. I pulled the cork out, held the bottle up to the glasses in Beth's hands and poured a good drop into each.

She handed me a glass and made a toast. "To port and drinking with strangers in unexpected places."

"I'll drink t' that," I said and raised my glass, sensing we were one step closer. She threw her port back, taking it in one large drawn-out mouthful. I followed suit.

"That warmed m' cockles. Another?" I asked, looking at her.

She was looking at me strangely. She placed her glass carelessly on the dashboard and lunged at me. My glass fell to the floor. She was at my face, her hands wrapped around the back of my head as my lips found hers and she responded by pushing back violently. I grabbed her and pulled her towards me, and we were kissing as if our lives depended on it, kissing all over each other's faces, roving down and over each other's necks. I navigated my way through her maze of clothing and with extensive help from her, I managed to find flesh in the form of her left breast. I went to work sucking on it like a baby might in the hope of extracting milk. *What is it about m' obsession with breasts? Was I weaned too young, therefore always thirstin' f' it?*

Beth's hand was roving around my beltline, then my zip was going down. She'd manipulated my dick out and was down there in a flash.

Fantasy had become reality. Those juicy lips were as sensational as I'd imagined they might be. She took me in her mouth all the way. I felt like I might explode any moment and that wasn't how I wanted it to be, but I couldn't stop her, it was too good, and in a short time I was crying out with euphoria as she gobbled me up greedily. She came up for air. I could taste that sharp, salty taste of me in her mouth.

"Mmm, you taste so good," she whispered in my ear. "You're so fuckin' good. And we haven't even fucked yet!"

I wanted her badly. "Let's get in the back."

She didn't need any encouragement and clambered over the front seat to my bedroom, a double mattress with sheets and duvet. We tore our clothes off frantically and dived under the duvet even though it wasn't cold anymore, the heater had warmed the interior sufficiently. I decided it was my turn to go down on her, something I hadn't done a lot of before but had found it to be quite a turn-on. I made my way down her body, stopping at her breasts for a nuzzle, then moving down to her stomach, kissing it lightly all over. This action seemed to drive Beth wild as she arched her back and groaned. She was naked now except for her dainty, white lace French knickers. I spent some time around the inside of her thighs getting her aroused, then with her knickers still on, slipped a couple of fingers into her lovely moisture, experiencing great pleasure in watching her writhe and moan.

I could no longer resist, and I removed her knickers to reveal her sweet, small mound of perfect bush, one of the tidiest pieces I'd ever seen. I was so excited I had her legs parted in no time with me lying between them, my head well placed to taste her delights. She gasped at the first touch of my hot tongue on her very moist pussy, and soon she was writhing in ecstasy. I was glad she was so responsive and hoped she'd cum without delay. My neck was starting to hurt from the unnatural position my head was in. She let out her first real cry and I quickly pulled my head away and encouraged her to roll over. I wanted her doggy style and now seemed like the opportune moment as she begged me not to stop. I found her lovely wet entrance, slipping in nicely as she continued with her operatic solo. As I pumped her, I couldn't help smiling. *Only an hour or so ago this was a fantasy, a dream in m' head. Proves that what y' dream does come true if y' want it bad enough, 'n oh ... I do.* Her aria became louder and louder until soon we were a perfect duet, riding the pitch to a magnificent crescendo together, voices faltering only slightly at the climax as we went off on different notes. Sweaty and spent, I lay beside her.

"That was fuckin' fantastic," she said, turning to me, still panting and breathless. "I've never cum like that before. In fact, I haven't cum with a guy before."

What's that s'pose t' mean? I had to concede it was one of the better sexual moments in my brief history of sexual activity. I never expected a bigger girl to be such a good fuck.

We were woken in the morning to the sound of someone banging on the window.

"Rise 'n shine!" Even though the windows were steamed up, I knew it to be Cosmo's voice.

"What's happenin'?" I called out.

"Big day out, that's what. Everybody's meeting at the Ridgeback lift at nine o'clock sharp, so be there or be square. It's a great morning, so rise and shine, sunshine!"

"I'll be there!" I heard his departing footsteps crunching on the old snow, hardened by nightly frosts.

"Don't get too distracted!" Came his loud voice, further in the distance now.

I pulled myself in close to Beth and she rolled into me, her sleepy face soft and beautiful, her deep-green eyes looking at me, and for a moment I felt a warmth that I hadn't felt with Tania for some time. I leaned in and kissed her. She responded by pushing her lips hard against mine and I could feel myself growing hard against her stomach, then her hand was there. Suddenly we were at each other again with the same passion as the night before, only this time she'd managed to get on top of me. She looked like she needed a Stetson and cowboy boots with spurs as she rode me home with great gusto. I feared it would all be over too soon but as fortune would have it, we came through the ranch gates together with euphoric grins on our faces.

* * *

I made it to Ridgeback as the others were stepping into their ski bindings.

"I see you decided to join us," said Cosmo. "Something distracting you this morning?" He was grinning, trying to wind me up. "I saw you leave the bistro last night."

"Say no more then." I grinned right back at him.

"Sounds like Sam had company in his palatial dwellings last night," chimed in Al. Al was going out with Holly and for that I envied him. I don't know what Holly saw in him, though he was nice enough and knew how to have a good time, but there was something sleazy about him. I couldn't quite put my finger on it. I stepped into my bindings and pushed myself up to the chair alongside Al, Cosmo and Holly. The chair swung around the bull wheel, scooping us up and raising us quickly off the ground as our skis swung briefly back and forth from the momentum of the chair absorbing our weight. Cosmo wasn't kidding, it was a great morning. The sun was shining, and there wasn't a cloud in the sky. It was going to be a perfect day.

On the chair behind us was the rest of our party. There was Maxine, Holly's best friend and roommate, an extremely tidy piece of skirt. There

55

was Scott, I don't know how we knew him or where he came from. He was fairly quiet, ruggedly good looking, and a brilliant skier — self-taught like me — always committed to refining and improving his technique. He was never content to just slide down the mountain, being compelled to make each run the perfect run, to find a bit of air here or there, to take on the bumps. Any kind of challenge made it more interesting for him, and I felt the same way. And there was Billie. He was the pick of the bunch in my opinion. He didn't ski, couldn't ski. He was a humble guy who contracted polio while in prison doing time for some drug offence. Billie was an interesting character with great yarns about being inside and about his other crazy adventures. He was working in the café up the top of the mountain and on his day off, he'd go up there and hang out, read a book, chat up women, and generally talk to anyone who might want to listen.

Holly nudged me as she passed me the compulsory tonic: a pipe packed with tobacco and nuggets of hash on top. I took the pipe and sucked on it in one easy go, holding the smoke down as long as my lungs could comfortably bear it. We dismounted the chair at the top.

"I'm goin' f' coffee straight up. I need it."

"Bit 'f a hard night, Sam?" asked Billie, grinning mischievously.

"Y' might say that." I couldn't suppress the grin that was spreading across my face.

"That good, eh?"

It was the days off we hung out for. They were one big blast courtesy of Cosmo. I suppose it would've been someone else if it wasn't him. Billie was dealing hash at the café. It was the perfect place to offload, there were so many young people up the mountain desiring mind-altering substances. It was a winter of consuming copious amounts of drugs, a bit like *Animal House* and *The Blues Brothers* combined. Under the influence, it felt like my skiing transformed to another dimension — the skis, the snow and I became one, everything just seemed to click.

My night with Beth became a week. She was hooked on me after our first night in the Holden. Each night after meeting and eating, chased down with a few drinks, we'd head back to the car to steam the windows up and wreak havoc on the Holden's tired suspension. We went at it every night like rodeo riders, into the wee hours of the morning. At the end of the week, Beth had to return to Sydney. She gave me her address and told me to look her up, but within a few days it was as though the whole thing had never happened. I resorted to the reliable Mrs Palmer once again, imagining me and Beth in every position we'd experimented with, but it wasn't the same climaxing without her. The only physical proof that our torrid affair had happened was a pair of her sexy knickers I found at the base of my bed, and I hung them off the rear-view mirror like a petrolhead would his fluffy dice. At nights, after a feed in the bistro and a few pipes with the crew, I'd trudge alone through the ice and snow back to my Holden.

* * *

The season ended late September. The ski field could no longer justify being open, as there was no snow to speak of except for the main trails. With the warmer weather, the snow was melting off the mountain like an ice cream in a kid's hand on a hot summer's day, melting into the river that ran down the valley into Lake Jindabyne. On the Saturday night of the weekend the ski resort officially closed, the company put on a big staff bash. The theme was fancy dress — come as your Fantasy or Fancy. There was the usual bunch of us in Maxine and Holly's room, getting dressed up, helping each other in and out of costumes while smoking bongs and doing pipes. Cosmo had even managed to get his hands on some cocaine and people were lining up in the bathroom, taking up the hundred-dollar note he handed them to snort the generous lines he so meticulously cut up and laid out on an old-fashioned round mirror. The room was a constant cloud of smoke as we oscillated between smoking and adding to our attire for the evening. We were limited in our ability to dress up due to a shortage of wardrobe choices. Most staff came up the mountain with the bare essentials, so the boys were getting dressed up in girl's clothing, looking like tarts and transvestites.

By the time we left the room, it was approaching eleven o'clock and we were all completely shit-faced from our indulgences. We staggered down to the bar, cackling and carrying on, and our voices echoed back at us in the quiet of the mountains that rested close by, hidden in the shadows of the dark and faintly silhouetted by a crescent moon. Maxine was hanging off Cosmo, barely able to hold herself up, her body exposed, revealing her brilliant physique. Fortunately for her, winter had lost its bite. The spring temperatures that were melting the snow on the mountains continued to prevail. Cosmo was his usual charming self as he escorted Maxine down the path towards the bar. She giggled loudly as they walked, and he spoke nonsensical words. Al was well wasted, staggering along with Scott who was as aloof and quiet as ever. Holly appeared to have designs on the enigmatic Scott, even though she was going with Al. Billie and I followed at the rear, like the odd couple.

Billie refused to dress up and hobbled down the path dressed in his usual brown corduroy pants and black puffer jacket, with his best cotton shirt slightly exposed beneath it, and the habitual fag in one corner of his mouth while he spoke out of the other.

"We must look like a right couple," he said, as though reading my thoughts. I was dressed as a woman in fishnet stockings and a sequined dress I had borrowed from Holly. Billie and I broke into synchronised laughter as we stumbled down the final steps into the entrance of the bar and past the two doormen attired in tuxedos.

Inside, the full light show was on, with disco balls refracting light every which way and multicoloured strobe lights flashing on and off. The floor was heaving with people dancing to the cover band playing on stage, doing a fair rendition of 'I See Red' by Split Enz. Maxine and Holly were on the dance floor straight away, flaying their arms and limbs wildly to the music while us boys propped ourselves against the bar to watch the spectacle. Cosmo attracted the barmaid's attention and ordered the first round.

"What do y' think 'f Cosmo?" Billie asked me, leaning in close and raising his voice so I'd have half a chance to hear him above the music.

"I like him," I said. "He's a bit keen on himself but that's no reason t' dislike him."

"Yeah ... well, I beg t' differ."

I wasn't in the mood for discussing Cosmo, but I didn't say so. I liked Billie, so I half listened to what he had to say.

"In fact, I don't trust him one iota."

"Each t' his own. Looks like he's got Maxine 'round his finger t'night," I said with more than a hint of envy. Cosmo seemed to be able to have whoever and do whatever he wanted. With his confidence and ease with words, he was a man of the world, something I hoped to be one day too.

"Fancy her, don't y'?" Billie said, punching my arm jovially.

"That obvious, huh?"

"Y' problem is y' wear y' heart on y' sleeve too much."

He was right but I felt annoyed. I didn't want to know that, not tonight. "Actually, it's Holly I'm really hung up about. She does it f' me in all sorts 'f ways."

Cans of Victoria Bitter arrived, and we toasted Cosmo, throwing them back, guzzling greedily. Suddenly I was being pulled from behind. I spun round to see it was Holly.

"Come 'n have a dance with me, Sammy boy."

I put my hands up in protest. "I'm not the dancin' type."

"I've seen y' down at Edwina's on a Friday night shakin' y' booty. Don't think y' can get out 'f this that easily."

Holly wasn't going to take no for an answer. She took my hand and led me to the dance floor, and I was all too aware the boys would be watching and laughing. It was true, I did like dancing, and once I was up there, I managed to lose myself in the beat of the music. The band was belting out a Midnight Oil song, one I'd not heard before. Holly kept on pushing up against me, causing me to feel uncomfortable, knowing Al would be standing at the bar watching.

"Do y' want t' make it with me?" she asked as she pulled me in way too close.

"Y' what?" I asked, pulling away slightly, thinking I must've misheard her.

"Do y' want t' make it with me?" she said, louder. I was sure everyone around us must've heard. "I'm feelin' all turned on by y'."

I couldn't believe I was hearing this, all season long I'd watched and admired her but had not really given it any more consideration knowing Al was shacked up with her. *Of course I want t' make it with y'!* I was lost for a response, and I turned and looked towards the bar. Billie was standing there jiving to the music, grinning at me as if he knew what was going on, and I became even more self-conscious. Cosmo was kissing Maxine and Scott was talking with Al, they both had their backs to us. I turned to Holly. "Yes," I said.

"What y' waitin' for?" She took my hand and pulled me towards the door. It felt like madness, yet a strong urge within compelled me, probably my dick, but it was enough. I didn't resist. I eagerly followed her out the door and down the paved path where she turned and lunged at my face with her own. I was surprised by her ferocity as her lips smacked into mine and her tongue lashed at my tonsils, then she pulled away all breathless and excited. I thought she was going to have her way with me there and then.

"Can we do it in y' car? I can't really take y' back t' my place, but y' know that."

"Sure." I nodded and took her hand, finding some self-control amidst my excitement.

"Y've got a cute arse, Sammy. Y' know I've wanted a piece 'f it since the first time I set eyes on y'."

"Y' kiddin' me, aren't y'?"

"Not at all, Sammy. I really do fancy y'."

We reached the car, and I pulled the keys from my pocket, trembling with adrenalin. I didn't want to disappoint her. I struggled with the key in the lock since Holly was trying to chew my neck and get her hands up my fish net stockings at the same time. I finally got the door unlocked and open. We couldn't get into the car quickly enough, grabbing at each other in a frenzied burst, tearing at each other's clothing. Half-clothed, Holly found her way to my dick and was gobbling it greedily, all I could do was lie back in disbelief as she went to work on me. I'd had my dick sucked more in the last few weeks than in my entire sexual existence and these Ozzie chicks were good at it. This was the dream ending to a great winter. Holly was skilled. Most girls I'd had head from didn't really know what they were doing and just went through the motion. More often than not, it was like having your dick grated, all teeth and stilted motion. Holly had the action down pat: smooth, rhythmic and without a hint of teeth grating. It was unbearably good, so good I was going to cum and didn't know if I had the willpower to stop her. At the last possible moment, I reluctantly did so, pulling Holly up and close to me, and I could taste me in her mouth, in the same way I had with Beth, which seemed like an eternity ago. I worked my way down her and found the most magnificent soft, pink, sweet-smelling lips a guy could ever want. I pushed a couple of fingers in her wet hole, and she recoiled, groaning with delight. I fingered her until she was well worked up, then I planted my head between her legs and let my tongue do its own talking. She was wet and sweet beyond imagining and tasted better than grandma's apple pie.

She was moaning and groaning, begging me to stop. "Christ, Sam, it's too good. I'm goin' t' cum. I can't help it." I took no notice even though my tongue was starting to tire. When she did cum, it was with a huge jolting shudder and a mighty outcry that made me think she was in pain. Simultaneously, a great gush of juice burst forth from her, almost like a guy letting his load go. I pulled my face away while she was still crying out, moved up her body and stuck my dick where she needed it most, causing her even greater excitement. I began pounding my flesh against hers in swift motions, knowing she would orgasm for a while yet as she continued to cry out: "Oh yes, Sam! Oh no, Sam. Oh! It's too fuckin' good, Sam. Oh Sammy, I can't believe how good it is."

Not feeling like I was getting enough penetration, I pulled out and got her to roll over, entering her from behind and pulling her up on her knees. She twitched and convulsed as the dirty cries continued, only encouraging me to go harder. Before long, I was having my own convulsions as I came in great spasms deep inside her. Spent, we collapsed, holding each other in drug-enhanced bliss. I lay there in the back of the Holden with Holly's body draped around me and her gentle breathing blowing warmth on my chest.

8

Cold Reality

"Come on, sunshine, it's time t' get up 'n get y' arse outa here." It was Harry and he was rattling keys in the lock. I lifted myself onto my elbows and watched him open the door. "Come on, boy, I haven't got all day," he said, standing in the doorway. He seemed happy about something.

"Did y' find what y' were lookin' for?" I asked. He simply raised his eyebrows and tapped the side of his nose.

Out the front, Frank was at a desk typing. "This is a document sayin' y' must report t' the police station every day between the hours 'f eight in the morning 'n midday till y' appear in the Magistrates' Court in Wodyn next Thursday," uttered Frank as he wound the piece of paper out of the typewriter. "So we'll see y' daily. Doesn't pay t' be late," he smirked at me.

I'll punch y' fuckin' lights out before this is over. "Can y' please give me a lift back t' my car?" I asked cautiously.

"Don't think so, boy. It's not part 'f the service," he replied, maintaining his smirk.

"Thanks," I said, grabbing the document. I turned and walked out the door without so much as a backward glance.

The sun was up and just peering over the hills to the east. It was quiet on the streets of Wodyn, the town was still waking up — no cars, no people about. I trudged down the road that led to the main street. It

63

took me almost an hour to walk to my car, but the walk gave me time to think about the situation I was in. I'd read the document: Samuel Gorzman is charged with 'Possession of a Class B Drug with Intent to Supply'. It didn't sound good. Possession of a drug was viewed seriously enough, and Supply far more so. I was staring down a double-barrelled shotgun. On top of that, I didn't know what had happened to Bruce. *Have they found him? Have they found his stash?* Bruce wouldn't be impressed with me. Essentially, regardless of me being beaten up and threatened with a drug overdose, I'd snitched on him.

Just to add insult to injury, I arrived at my car to find it dead, not even a hint of life as I turned the key in the ignition. The bastards had left the lights on and the battery had no charge at all. Fortunately, I'd been pulled over on a hill, a nice gradual slope with a sweeping bend heading down into the river valley just north of Wodyn. I placed the car in gear and released the handbrake. With my foot on the clutch, the car began to roll forward. As it built up speed, I released the clutch to engage the gearbox. The engine struggled initially, jerking and shaking, before firing into life. *Come on, baby, y' can do it!* I put the accelerator flat to the floor and she surged forward. I was in business.

Tainted with dread, I drove towards Yaringa. As I drove, I tried to imagine what I was going to say. Not a lot came to mind. I thought about turning around and driving over the New South Wales border to Melbourne, but I barely had enough money to feed myself let alone put a full tank of petrol in the car. Reluctantly, I drove back to Yaringa to face the music.

* * *

No one was at the house at the lake when I pulled up. The van was gone, Bruce and Sally weren't there, and neither was Tania. I drove the short stretch to the village, wondering where they could all be, thinking that maybe they'd not been at the house when Fellini and his posse called. Town was dead. I drove around the block a few times, my mind still racing, my chest tight, wondering how I was going to resolve this enormous problem. Passing Kim and Ben's house, friends of Tania's, I stopped the car outside and sat with my head in my hands. Tears arrived, unwelcomed and unbeckoned, and I cried in great sobs.

After what felt like an eternity, Kim appeared at the car window, tapping on it gently.

"Sam! What are you doing out here?" I quickly tried to wipe the tears away. "What's wrong, honey? Do you want to come inside?"

I slowly emerged from the car with my head down, shoulders hunched. I must've looked bad, my face ashen, eyes overflowing with despairing tears, and my head all puffed up and swollen, a reminder of what had been done to me.

"My God, Sam. What happened to you?"

"Don't ask," I replied drably.

"You'd better come inside and let me take a look at you. Have you been in a fight?"

"Sort of," I replied.

She put her arm around my shoulder, ushering me inside. I allowed her to lead me into the kitchen. Ben, her husband, was at the kitchen table eating a cooked breakfast. The smell of food made my mouth water as it had been quite some time since I'd eaten.

"Jesus mate! Y've been in a fight or somethin', haven't y?" exclaimed Ben, his fork stopping in mid-air as he stared at my face. "Y' don't look too good." He shoved the forkful of food into his mouth and looked to me expectantly.

"It's a long story."

"Like that, eh?"

"Sit down, Sam, and I'll get you some breakfast," Kim ordered gently.

I gingerly pulled a chair out from the table and sat down gratefully. Within moments I was pouring the entire story out to an attentive audience of two. Kim occasionally interrupted me to ask a question, and at other times shook her head in disbelief. Ben was silent until I spoke the final words of my nightmare.

"Jesus mate, y're in the shit no matter how y' look at it!"

"Ben! That's the last thing he needs to hear," snapped Kim.

"It's alright. It's true, I'm in the shit 'n I dunno what the fuck t' do. I thought about fuckin' off t' Melbourne, but I don't even have enough money f' a tank 'f petrol. Besides, I dunno if that'll help me in the long run."

"Probably wise, Sam," responded Kim.

"Y' know …" I continued, "the other thing is … they might trace me back t' New Zealand, and if I do a runner …"

"Yeah, Interpol might have y' on their Most Wanted list," Ben said teasingly. Kim clipped him around the back of the head with her open hand. "Steady babe. I'm only tryin' t' make light 'f the situation."

"Hey, it ain't no situation to be making fun of!"

Kim was a real sweetie. I liked her a lot. She was easy to get on with and made me feel at ease in a small town wary of strangers. She seemed to understand completely what it felt like to be a stranger in town, and exuded warmth and compassion.

"Yeah, but if y' can't joke or have a laugh about it, what can y' do?" Ben added.

"It is kind 'f amusin'," I interrupted. "Y' know, the whole situation just seemed so bloody surreal as it unfolded. I never thought they'd find the stuff on me. I guess I was too fuckin' cocky about the whole thing. I never thought it would come down t' me being arrested. Bruce'll kill me, won't he?" I said, looking for some indication.

"Yep, you're right about that," said Ben, nodding.

"You don't even know if they found what they were looking for," Kim said soothingly as she placed a plate of bacon and eggs, which she'd miraculously knocked up, in front of me. "Eat that, Sam. It'll make you feel better."

Ben stood, picked up his plate, kissed Kim on the cheek and thanked her for breakfast. "Sorry … got things that need t' be done. See y' soon, Sam. It'll sort itself out."

"Yeah, cheers, Ben."

"See y' a bit later, babe."

"Okay, honey."

Ben put his plate on the kitchen bench and walked out the front door. I sat there staring at my untouched breakfast, my appetite had suddenly vanished.

"What are you going to do, Sam?" Kim pushed her cornflakes around inside the bowl with her spoon.

I shrugged my shoulders. "I dunno." I stood and paced the floor, anxiety overwhelming me. I didn't know whether the cops had gotten to Bruce, but I suspected they had or they wouldn't have let me go. And there was the good mood they appeared to be in.

"Look, Sam, you've had a totally gruelling night. Why don't you lie down on the sofa for a few hours, or even in the spare bedroom if you want? Get some sleep and think about things again when you wake up." I sat down on the sofa and looked at Kim sitting at the table.

She got up, came over and sat beside me on the couch. "Come here," she said, reaching out her arms. She pulled me in towards her, embracing me. I couldn't resist. I let her hold me and stroke my hair. I became aware of tears streaming down my face again. Although I felt embarrassed to be crying, the tears kept coming and I began to sob uncontrollably, my body convulsing as the events of the previous night caught up with me.

9

Mad If Y' Do,
Stupid If Y' Don't

I had been happy to drive Cosmo to Canberra. I hadn't understood what the fuss was all about, but it was pretty obvious he wasn't welcome in town, even though he knew a lot of people. No one, except Tania, was pleased to see him. Bruce in particular kicked up a real fuss at his arrival.

"What the fuck's that lunatic doin' back here?" he had asked Tania.

"It's a free country, isn't it? People can come and go as they please. It's not East fuckin' Germany!"

"Yeah, well. I don't want a parasite like that hangin' 'round in my backyard. Comprende?"

"Then you tell him he's not welcome here."

Bruce did tell him, in a roundabout way. He told him it might be in his best interest to leave because some people were agitated by his presence, that it was opening up old wounds. I was oblivious to Cosmo's past. Beyond life on the ski field, I had no idea who the real Cosmo was. I knew nothing of his history in Yaringa, only that he'd once lived and worked here. I did manage to ascertain that a business in the town of Wodyn, owned and run in partnership with someone, was the main source of animosity directed at him, but no one was prepared to divulge further details.

Cosmo didn't own a vehicle. He didn't see the point of it when there were so many cars on the road already. "I've got a good thumb," he said, waving it at me as if it were something special.

I said I'd drive him to Canberra in the Holden Special if he paid for petrol. He agreed and we shook on it.

Before we left, Bruce presented Cosmo with a large quantity of hash oil capsules. "See if y' can get rid of these for me."

Seems odd that Bruce trusts Cosmo t' sell hash oil f' him. It doesn't quite add up in my books. How will the money be paid back to Bruce? Or am I expected t' hang 'round till sales have been made? But hey, it wasn't my oil to be concerned about, I was simply driving Cosmo to Canberra.

* * *

We turned off the Main Coastal Highway and onto the Snowy Mountain Highway, heading toward Canberra.

"Ever had a chillum?" Cosmo asked out of the blue as I drove up Brown Mountain.

The route led towards the tablelands where it was relatively flat with craggy outcrops of rocks breaking up the tussock land. The area reminded me of the Mackenzie Basin in the South Island of New Zealand on the way to Mount Cook National Park. The road we were on went through a small country town called Nimmitabel then to Cooma, where it came to a junction with the option of continuing to the Snowy Mountains or turning off and heading north-west to Canberra. Brown Mountain was the route the logging trucks took and was always littered with dead wombats. I wouldn't have wanted to hit one with the Holden. A wombat could do some serious damage to a vehicle.

"What's a chillum?" I asked, feeling ignorant.

"Ahh … You haven't lived until you've tried my carrot chillum!" He laughed heartily from deep inside his chest. "A chillum is a pipe specially made for smoking hashish, and a carrot chillum is a carrot carved into such a pipe." He pulled a largish carrot from his bag and waved it around, laughing some more before he continued. "It's the most economical and brilliant way to smoke hashish and oil. You'll agree once you try it." He produced a small pocketknife and unfolded the blade, then set to work carving the carrot into a pipe as I continued driving.

"Okay, it's ready," Cosmo announced as we crossed the magnificent tablelands. "We should pull over and test drive this baby."

I obediently pulled up in a secluded picnic area dotted with eucalyptus trees. Cosmo packed the chillum with hashish, using tobacco as its plug, and took the first puff, demonstrating how it had to be held to get the most out of it. Instead of inhaling directly from the pipe, there was a particular way of clasping it, using both hands to create a small hole between your two thumbs, through which you then inhaled. The clasp was similar to the one I used to imitate a morepork call, only the pipe sits in the top of the clasp. It seemed to work as effectively as Cosmo had promised. His cheeks bulged as he endeavoured to hold the smoke in for as long as his lungs would allow. He repacked the pipe for me and I tried to emulate his clasp. Cosmo was eager for me to get it right.

"You've got to get all your fingers tightly woven around the pipe, and you only want the smallest of holes," he explained. He fiddled with my fingers until I had the right clasp. "Now you're talking turkey, brother!" He held the flame over the pipe, and I began to inhale. At first it felt as though nothing was happening, then the bowl at the top of the carrot began to glow. "Keep it going … keep it going. Oh yeah, now you've got it. Alright man!" Cosmo exclaimed.

My lungs were burning, and my cheeks must've looked like those of a pufferfish, but I held the smoke in as long as I could bear and released it slowly in a long stream of neat white smoke. I felt all light-headed from the tobacco rush.

"Whoa man, you sure did a nice job on that pipe," stated Cosmo, impressed by my effort.

"That's a nice way t' smoke it," I responded, beaming like a Cheshire cat.

"Want another?" He was already packing the chillum.

I shook my head. "Nah man, I couldn't. I've got t' drive. If I have another m' drivin' won't be up t' much." I liked the intensity of driving stoned but there was only so much I could smoke before it became a challenging task. I turned the key in the ignition and the engine fired into life.

"Suit yourself," said Cosmo as he lit the chillum again. He was the Chillum Master for sure. "Ever tried smack?" he asked casually as he put the flame of the lighter to the chillum.

"Smack? Is that heroin?" I asked.

"It would be known by that name as well," he replied.

"No, I've never tried it. I take it by y' askin' that y' have?" Meanwhile, he'd just hoovered up the most enormous lung full of smoke. "What's it like?" A few seconds passed, and he released a plume of smoke from his mouth.

"Mad if y' do, stupid if y' don't!"

I checked behind me and pulled out onto the road, gliding off nicely as we set out across the tablelands. As I drove, I realised how very stoned I was. Whenever I smoked too much, I tended to get deeply involved in my driving — every corner, every metre of the road became an obstacle course, challenging my senses. Usually, driving was second nature to me, like a woman who could knit and hold a conversation at the same time without missing a stitch, but as the effect became more intense, I felt as though I was driving too fast, the engine sounded louder, the corners became more difficult to negotiate. I glanced at the speedometer to discover I was doing only eighty kilometres per hour.

"You happy driving?" Cosmo asked.

"For now, I am," I replied, feeling self-conscious.

"You know you drive like an old lady."

"Come on! It's nice t' have a cruisy drive, 'specially after a smoke. What's the rush anyway?"

"No rush. Just wouldn't mind getting there today," he said, laughing.

"We will. We're almost at the turn off t' Canberra." We weren't far from Cooma, and from there it was a little over an hour to Canberra.

"So, what happens in Canberra? I heard it's a pretty dull place, full 'f politicians 'n students 'n not much else goin' on."

"It's all true. I'm stuck there trying to get off an LSD charge. I need to get out of the country or I'm looking at ten years in prison."

I glanced across at him to see if he was serious. His poker face revealed nothing. "Y're pullin' m' left tit, aren't y'?"

"Wish I was," he sighed, staring back at me grimly.

"Get the fuck out 'f here. What happened?"

"I got busted in a car park with a briefcase full of acid trips."

I looked at him in disbelief. "How come y're out 'n free? I thought they'd hold y' in remand f' somethin' that serious."

He shrugged his shoulders. "Guess I got lucky … had a good lawyer … got me bail."

"Y're lucky t' be out."

"Guess so," he said, not seeming to care.

"So when y' due t' go t' court?"

"Next month." There was silence for a few minutes. "Don't think I'm going to show up," he finally said, breaking the uncomfortable silence. "Think I'm going to leave the country."

"How do y' propose doin' that?"

"I've got someone doing me up a fake passport."

"Christ! Ain't that a bit risky?" I asked, switching my gaze between him and the road.

"I suppose so … don't feel like I've got much choice. I'm damn sure I'm not rotting in no prison."

I felt stunned by the information and caught between a rock and a hard place. *Fuck! That's why he wasn't welcome on the coast! Fuck! Why am I takin' him t' Canberra?*

*　　　　* * *

We arrived in Canberra in the early afternoon. Cosmo's personality changed. He was no longer the guy I thought he was, and I felt paranoid and trapped. He insisted on me driving him here, there and everywhere. I began to feel manipulated and taken advantage of. It was late afternoon when I said I really wanted to get back to Yaringa.

We'd driven all over the city. He'd visited his contact who was providing him with a false passport, and we'd smoked his chillum with a feral bunch of characters whom I wouldn't trust with my aunt's bone china or a five-dollar loan. At times I waited in the Holden while he went into various residences. Cosmo accused me of being a party-pooper when I said I wanted to go, but he didn't protest as strongly as I thought he might.

"Hey, alright, mate, you go," he said, throwing his hands up in surrender. "Oh, and you'd best take this stuff back. Tell Bruce I couldn't get rid of it," he said, handing me the Bakelite case. I was surprised he gave it to me. I thought Bruce had given it to him to help get rid of him. Cosmo wasn't usually one to look a gift horse in the mouth. But I didn't really have a problem with taking it back, so I took the case and placed it in my denim jacket's pocket. It wasn't until I filled the car up with petrol at a garage on the outskirts of Canberra that I transferred the small slim case to the inside of my underwear. I went to the toilet to piss and suddenly wished I hadn't agreed to take the hash oil with me. It felt uncomfortable at first as I sat back in the car, so I wriggled it around inside my pants for a better spot, and after driving for a few minutes, barely noticed it was there.

It was getting late. I was in two minds about whether to drive back to Canberra in the dark or to crash in the car for the night. I didn't like Canberra at all, so I decided to continue with the drive. As if guided by fate, the moment I decided to embark on the trip back to Yaringa, the engine died, and I was forced to pull over to the side of the road. Fortunately, I pulled up just short of a garage. I'd had problems with the car dying on me before and figured it was just a loose connection with the battery. Several attempts to solve the problem proved fruitless, so I made my way to the forecourt of the garage, not holding out much hope that the pimply young kid behind the counter would have much of a clue. He shrugged unconfidently at my request for assistance, suggesting that his colleague, who was outside pumping petrol into someone's car, might be a better bet.

"Do y' know anythin' about cars?" I asked as I approached the colleague.

"Depends what y' want t' know," he replied.

"It's electrical ... I think."

"Y' think or y' know? Cos if it's electrical, I can't help you. It's not my bent if y' know what I mean."

"Can't say f' sure."

He put the nozzle gun back on the bowser. "Are y' a member 'f the

NRMA?" he asked as he headed back inside with the money from the customer, me in tow.

"Yeah, I am. Well, I mean m' girlfriend is."

"Why don't y' just give them a call," he said nonchalantly.

I looked around for a phone. He read my mind and placed the one from behind the counter on the bench in front of me. I picked up the phone as he recited the number for me. Within moments there was someone on the other end greeting me and asking for my NRMA number. I fumbled with my wallet, pulling it out of my jacket and searching anxiously through my bits of paper for the appropriate card, eventually finding it.

"We should have someone out to you within the half hour, sir," the client service assistant said.

Feeling obliged to buy something after the help the garage guy had given me, I bought a cold drink.

"It's that simple when y' belong to NRMA," said the guy as he took my money. I thanked him and headed back to my car where I sat on the bonnet waiting for someone to show up. It wasn't long before a ute pulled up in front of my Holden, its flashing orange lights on the roof of the cab illuminating the dark night. A figure stepped from the vehicle into the shadows.

"What seems to be the problem?" the figure asked as it approached me with a kit bag in hand.

"Don't know … just died on me."

"Might be petrol."

"Don't think so," I said.

"Can you raise the bonnet, please?"

I had left it unlatched and reached for the release button at the front of the grille, pushing the bonnet up until the spring released. He removed something from his kit bag to test the battery, running wires to the terminals then looking at a meter to read its output. Satisfied that the battery was holding its charge, he began fiddling with the terminal leads.

"Not in the best condition, are they? This looks like your problem here," he said, pointing at the positive lead. "Too much crap around the terminal's not helping an already bad connection." He went to the back of his ute and returned with a terminal lead and a small toolbox. "You're in luck … just happen to have a spare one floating around on the back of the truck."

"Great," I said. "I'm tryin' t' get back t' the coast t'night."

"Bit late in the day to be heading there now, isn't it? Specially in a car like this. You never know what'll give out next."

"Yeah … guess y're right. But y' know how it is when y' just want t' get somewhere."

"Uh huh," he mumbled as he disconnected the old lead. "Get it all the time in this game. People just want to get somewhere or other and it's got to be five minutes ago. Anyway, once we sort out this problem you should be able to keep going." He cleaned up the deposits around the terminal and gave it a bit of a rub with fine sandpaper before he connected the lead. "I believe we have contact, Houston!" he announced. "Try that. I'd be surprised if she doesn't go now."

I jumped into the front seat and turned the key in the ignition. She turned over easily and fired into life within seconds.

He casually slammed the bonnet down, giving it an extra push to ensure it shut. "That should see you home," he shouted.

"Thanks very much," I said.

"Take it easy, eh. She's beautiful but she's an old girl," he said, nodding his head emphatically. "Nice car in its day."

I turned my lights on, pulled out into the night, and began to follow the white line. It was all that could be seen in the intense darkness. The further I drove, the darker the night became, and I had a sense that nothing existed other than myself and the white line I was following.

10

Bruce

I awoke on the couch to the sound of voices. Kim was at the door letting Tania in. I'd fallen asleep in Kim's arms and she must've managed to get up, leaving me to sleep. I felt self-conscious and disorientated as Tania walked through the door and our eyes met.

Tania looked concerned as she spoke. "Jesus, Sam. Are you alright?" I'd forgotten that my face was probably still puffy and swollen.

"Yeah, I guess so," I replied, trying to sit up and gently rub the sleep from my eyes.

"What happened?"

Kim made herself scarce in the kitchen, putting on the kettle to give us the space she probably thought we needed, but I didn't feel any closeness with Tania. Her sitting next to me now, with the events that had unfolded in the past twenty-four hours, only highlighted how much we'd grown apart. I explained my situation to her. She sat and listened without interrupting except for the occasional expletive.

"I gave them our address," I stated, choosing not to elaborate.

"I know! We had a visit early this morning. They took Bruce away. Sally's waiting for him to be released. Why did you tell them where we live, Sam?"

"Because I wanted them t' come 'round f' a barbeque!" I snapped.

"Why d' y' think I told them? Look, Tania, I just told y' what happened, 'n quite frankly, y' don't seem t' give a blind fuck!"

"Yeah, but ..."

"No 'buts', Tania. Do y' think I wanted t' tell? In the end I felt like there was no other option ... unless I sacrificed m' own life."

"They wouldn't have forced all that oil down your mouth, they would've just been bluffing."

"But they did, didn't they?"

"One!"

"That was just the start 'f things t' come. Y' weren't there, Tania. Would y've been prepared t' call their bluff, take that sort 'f risk in the same situation?" She looked away. "I didn't think so, y' weren't there t' experience what I did. I've had a gruelling fuckin' night 'n all y' worried about is Bruce. I'm the one in the shit!"

"Bruce is too," she mumbled, but with less conviction now.

"I'm the one they banged up." I aggressively pointed a finger at my head. "Y' really don't seem t' give a fuck!" I stood up exasperated and stormed out the back door into Kim's garden.

At the bottom of the garden, I found a seat that looked out over the coast and sat down, trembling, feeling alone and totally miserable. I began questioning the events of the previous night and wondered what would've happened if I'd refused to talk. I thought about Bruce and worried about seeing him again, afraid of what his reaction to me would be. He was in the police station now after no doubt being rudely awoken in the early hours and dragged out of bed to watch the cops grunt and sniff all over the property. He had probably been handcuffed and shoved in the paddy wagon and driven down to the station.

Strange how we choose t' survive. What becomes important when our existence 'n our safety's threatened. Suddenly an individual's will t' survive comes t' the fore 'n that's prob'bly quite different f' each 'f us, yet all 'f us must innately have survival instincts.

"Mind if I sit with you?" Tania had sneaked up on me and was standing beside the bench seat, looking reticent.

"If y' must," I grumbled, feeling unwelcoming but not wanting to continue the hurt.

"I must," she said, sitting down next to me and putting her arms around me while trying to pull me in closer to her. I was stiff and unobliging. I didn't want her mollycoddling me when I didn't feel as though I could trust her.

"Don't be so resistant, I only want to cuddle you."

"What if I don't want t' be cuddled?"

"Of course you do. You're upset. Who wouldn't be with what you've just been through?"

I hate the way some people feel they know what I need more than I do. Tania's one 'f them. The more she gets t' know me, the more she thinks she understands me better than I understand m'self. It's stifling. It's true, the sayin' that 'love is blind', or is it 'lust doesn't see beyond the dust'? Yes, I'm guilty 'f the latter. Love has never played a part in this relationship.

Tania had been a revelation in bed. For the first time, I'd found someone with the same libido as myself. The downside was that five minutes hadn't passed before all the psychoanalysing came into play, sending us on a downward spiral. One minute we'd be floating merrily down the stream, the next minute caught in a whirlpool sucking us under so unexpectedly it was difficult to fight against. By the time I realised the necessity to fight, any attempt was negated by the fact that I was in so deep I couldn't pull myself out.

I let her cuddle me because I couldn't be bothered with the grief it might cause if I resisted any longer. "Relax," she said, attempting a soothing tone.

"I can't. What's Bruce goin' t' do? Christ, he'll have it in f' me now."

"He'll be pissed but he'll handle it, just like you've got to handle it."

"Yeah, well … if he hadn't given Cosmo that shit t' sell in the first place, we wouldn't be in this mess. I was just tryin' t' help out by takin' Cosmo t' Canberra."

She looked at me with a beautiful smile and in that moment it was easy to think there was something special between us. *Let's go t' bed.* That was it though, that was half the problem, when things were difficult with us, I replaced intimacy with sex — the fuck and make-up habit I'd grown into but not out of. It made everything alright, alright for me and alright for her, but never for long enough.

I decided to speak instead of fall into the familiar trap. "Did y' know that he's out on bail f' being busted with a briefcase full 'f acid trips?"

"Who?"

"Cosmo."

"You're kidding!" She genuinely looked surprised.

"I'm not. Y' know, I can't help thinkin' the whole thing's weird the way I got pulled up at that time 'f night on a deserted road. The cop said he was chasin' another car 'n that I failed t' dip m' lights, so he turned 'round 'n chased me. Don't y' think that's a bit odd considerin' he was in a better position t' pull up the car that was headin' in the same direction as he was?"

"It does sound odd."

"There you guys are!"

I looked up to see Bruce striding across the garden towards us. I immediately tensed up.

"Hi, Bruce. How did it go?" asked Tania.

Sally appeared from the house, accompanied by Kim, and they made their way down to where we were sitting.

"It went badly. Does Sam know we were busted last night?" he asked, looking at me, even though the question was directed at Tania, who nodded silently.

"What the fuck happen'd, Sam?" There was no *Are y' alright, Sam? Jesus, mate, that must've been a horrendous experience. Christ! What the fuck's up with y' face?* It was all about him, and reluctantly, I began my story once again.

"Why did y' tell them where y' lived?" Bruce asked in disbelief.

"It never occurred t' me that y'd have the oil in the house."

"I didn't. I had it stashed in the van."

"Y' kiddin'…'n they found it in there! Did y' have it in the glovebox or somethin'?"

"No, it was well hidden in a panel. Look, y' sense 'f humour's startin' t' piss me right off," he snarled aggressively.

"Hey, look, I'm sorry. I didn't feel I had any choice. They beat me up real bad tryin' t' find out who m' supplier was. I didn't tell them, I just told them where I lived."

"Yeah, yeah, I get y' drift," he sarcastically interrupted.

"I didn't want them goin' 'round there in the middle 'f the night," I continued persistently. "It didn't take them long t' add it all up. I mean, look at the way they pulled me up last night. It was as though they were waitin' f' me in ambush."

"What do y' mean?" Bruce exclaimed.

"You think about it. Why would a cop turn 'round 'n chase me when he's already in pursuit of another vehicle, 'n just because I hadn't dipped m' lights?"

"It's a bloody fuck up whatever it is!" he commented.

Bruce had fire in his belly, a brooding side to him, simmering constantly below the surface. If he knew for sure I'd snitched on him, things would be considerably different. It didn't warrant thinking about, and I was grateful for small mercies.

"Did you get Cosmo to Canberra safely?" Sally suddenly asked. She looked tired and troubled, having been at the police station for several hours waiting for Bruce to be released, and had obviously been affected by the ordeal.

"Yeah, I did, thanks."

"Wasn't such a good idea, was it?" she continued.

"What do you mean?" Tania interrupted.

"Look what's happened as a result of it. If Sam hadn't taken him none of this would've come to pass." She stood there trembling, visibly upset, and the tears began to flow. Bruce didn't seem at all interested in consoling her. Tania stood up and put her arm around Sally, coercing her to sit down on the garden bench.

"Do y' think Cosmo tipped the cops off?" Bruce was staring at me with his intense brown eyes, his hands on his hips, as if his question were a demand I ought to satisfy. I shrugged my shoulders, as it was all I could do. It wasn't like I knew for sure.

In perfect timing, Kim arrived with a tray on which a coffee percolator, cups and some baking were arranged.

"You shouldn't have, Kim," said Tania, genuinely grateful.

"But I have, so you better drink up." She smiled warmly at me and I instantly felt more at ease. Tania poured the coffee, and everyone helped themselves to milk and sugar. Bruce was deep in thought, his forehead furrowed, his eyes held a worried, faraway gaze.

Sally's right. If I hadn't taken Cosmo t' Canberra ... Fuck them, fuck them all. Everyone wanted him gone. I did what no other dared. I sipped my coffee slowly, wondering if I should just borrow some money and drive across the border to Melbourne and catch a plane home. *Would they really come after me if I didn't report t' the station or show up f' m' day in court? Would I be tracked down by Interpol, extradited back t' Oz? Or would I be safe?* I dreaded making that phone call to my parents.

"We may as well go home 'n try 'n sort somethin' out," Bruce said, and stood up. "Come on, Sally, let's catch up on some sleep. Cheers f' the coffee, Kim. How're you two gettin' home?"

"We'll be right," I said. "I've got the car outside. Surprisingly, she still goes, even though the cunts left the lights on. The battery was flat when I got back t' pick it up."

"That's cops for y'." Bruce turned and walked off, waving his hand up by his head as if to swat a fly away. Sally fell in step behind him.

11

My Solicitor

I was sitting in a solicitor's office with a ruddy-faced man, feeling like a complete fool while listening to him as he exhaled more smoke into his already smoke-filled office.

"The fact is, son ..." *Where d' y' get off callin' me son, y' wanker.* "If it was illegal to smoke these things," he said, waving his cigarette in my face, "this packet would be in the bin just like that." He picked up his cigarette packet, and to emphasise his words, he chucked it into the bin beside his desk. His ashtray overflowed with fags, some stubbed out, others burnt to the butt, sitting there as one long, completely perfect length of ash. He inhaled heavily on his cigarette as he peered at me through his thick-rimmed glasses. He looked like he drank too much, his face was blotched with red spots, and his skin was transparent, with surface blood vessels on his nose and across both cheeks. It was only a matter of time before he croaked, as he was well on the way to a stroke or a massive heart attack.

He was right, though. Everything he put into his body was legal and my small addiction to dope had landed me severely in the proverbial shit. I believed him when he said he'd give up the fags tomorrow if it was law. He'd probably do it hard but not as hard as I might be doing it if found guilty. I'd heard a lot of bad shit about Australian jails — young guys like me, ripe for the picking by sexually frustrated, long-term, bad-fucker inmates; young guys being bent over handbasins in the ablution blocks and gang-banged by ten willing inmates in one session. It did little for my self-esteem as I listened to my solicitor's prognosis on drug-related incidents in this small, godforsaken rathole in the middle of New South Wales.

"So y' reckon m' chances are bad?"

"Let's not be so hasty in making assumptions here, my boy," Dennis responded. He reached for the ashtray and stubbed out his cigarette which had burned right down to the butt. He promptly reached for the cigarette packet and pulled out another. I detected a tremble in his hands as he removed the cigarette. I was probably keeping him from his early afternoon tipple. I couldn't help noticing he stocked a bit of a cabinet — all top-shelf bottles in an old-fashioned, walnut oak sideboard.

Don't hold back on my account. In fact, I'll happily join y'. I could do with a drop m'self, what with everything that's happened, a little tonic would go down quite nicely.

He'd lit his fag and was inhaling it deeply. "There is a problem in how much oil the police found, and they're taking it seriously, you see. You had more than the amount deemed *Possession*."

"I know, I know, 'n now they're goin' t' hit me with *Supply*."

"You've got it, kid. But if we can prove you weren't Supplying, you might just get off this whole thing with a slap across the wrist. The first thing you need to do is plead guilty on the grounds of naivety and stupidity."

"Plead guilty! I thought it was never a good idea t' plead guilty!"

Dennis blew smoke directly into my face. He was probably getting fucked off with me, the greenhorn with an opinion on the law.

"Let's face it, kid, you got caught red-handed, they've got the shit to prove it." He leaned back in his chair and inhaled deeply, looking bored with the whole prospect of defending some young punk from across the ditch. Tania's parents had rung him to ask if he could help me. I had no option but to see him. Without legal representation I'd be well fucked.

I'd been to a local doctor who agreed with me that my scalp was swollen and my face bruised. The swelling could only be caused by the pulling of hair and a beating. When I asked him if he would write a report, he wanted to know why I needed one. I told him the swelling was a result of police brutality and that was the end of any potential report, with the doctor running scared and washing his hands of the whole matter. *Bloody wimp! I won't be relying on you t' save the world. What the fuck's wrong with people these days? Whatever happened t' help thy neighbour?*

* * *

My day in the Magistrates' Court arrived along with Bruce's, and the presiding magistrate looked as animated as a squashed centipede while he listened to all the defendants' misdemeanours. When it was my turn, the police prosecutor read out the offence: "Samuel John Gorzman, you have been found in Possession of a Class B drug, being determined as hashish oil. The volume which you were found to be in Possession of constitutes the charge of Supply."

"How does the defendant plead?" asked the magistrate, making the first gesture of interest as he peered over the top of his horn-rimmed spectacles to survey me. He didn't have a wig on, nor did the lawyers. Apparently, the lower courts had done away with it. Wigs only appeared in the higher courts these days. Nonetheless, the magistrate looked old, conservative and grim. I didn't like him.

"Guilty, Your Honour, but there are mitigating circumstances that I would like to present," announced Dennis. All I could hear was the word 'guilty' reverberating in my head.

"You must realise that a date will need to be set for a hearing, Mr Greenwood?"

"I do, Your Honour," he replied, turning his head and catching my eye enough to offer a wink as though he was enjoying the whole thing. Dennis requested I be released until the hearing date on the condition I continue to report to the police station every day, before midday, until the hearing.

"Does the prosecution have any problem with this?" asked the magistrate, peering over his spectacles again, this time to scrutinise the police prosecutor.

"None, Your Honour," replied the prosecutor, whom I'd not seen at the police station before.

Afterwards, once outside, Dennis fumbled in his coat pockets for his cigarettes as though his life depended on it. When he got his cigarette lit and inhaled, he was able to speak.

"So that's step one out of the way, Samuel. Now we need to present a case at the next hearing. Come up to my office soon and we'll talk more." He took another deep drag on his cigarette, shook my hand, then walked briskly off down the main street of Wodyn in the direction of his office. I stood there contemplating whether I'd hitch back to Yaringa now or get a snack in town first.

12

Tania's Parents

I should've been grateful for their help and I suppose I was in a way, except being dependent on their goodwill wasn't a position I wanted to be in. Tania and I had nowhere else to go after we mutually agreed it was impossible to continue living with Bruce and Sally in the house on the inlet. I had to confess my situation to Tania's parents, which was a shock for them, but they came on board and we moved into the caravan parked on a strip of grass parallel to the driveway.

What a fuck up they were, both raging alcoholics and chain-smokers. It made me wonder if something about this town drove people to drink. The facial features of every older couple I'd come across showed severe signs of excess drinking. To be fair, most of them were friends of Tania's parents. I had nothing against drinking, being partial to a tipple myself, and didn't mind a cold one after a hard day, or a nice glass of Cabernet Sauvignon with dinner and a medium-rare fillet steak with potato mash and a red wine jus. Of course, it's true — one drink can lead to a few, but it's a bit different when you're running a business in town.

Both Ted and his wife, Val, looked as though they were ripe for kicking the bucket. He spent most of his time propped up at the breakfast bar, drinking whisky and smoking in a fashion Dennis Greenwood would be proud of. If he wasn't at the breakfast bar, he was down the road at the bowling club with a fag in his mouth, a whisky in one hand, and the other pumping the poker machine. Val usually followed him over, which was a relief. She was a bit of a whiner with one of those classic, nasal Ozzie twangs. She had an opinion on everything, a know-it-all who knew fuck all, who got her knowledge from the local newspaper, and who listened to the equally average local radio station that broadcasted all the latest cheesy pop hits. Between listening to her and the local radio station, it was easy to become agitated. It was a constant effort to keep up my manners and show my appreciation.

* * *

Tania and I drifted further apart over the winter, to the point that things were tense between us, and even more so since I'd arrived back from the ski fields. I got the feeling she wasn't overly pleased to see me return, even though the arrangement we had was to meet back in Yaringa at the end of the season. Things can change rather easily in a short period of time when you're apart, the testosterone starts surging through the body like a junkie who's just injected. Up in the Snowy Mountains, I'd been happily having it off with whomever was up for it, and I had a feeling Tania might have been doing the same. She must've attracted the eye of one of the local boys, or perhaps she'd hit on him, as she was a bit of a flirt and horny as all hell. I couldn't really blame her, three months was a long time, and we'd only seen each other once or twice during that time. The worst thing was, I knew, I just *knew* something was going on.

One evening, after dinner with Val and Ted, Tania wanted to take me up to the local pub. I was happy to go, anything to escape Val's penetrating voice, as I could feel a headache coming on. I was a bit overeager getting out of my chair, knocking it backwards to the floor, and consequently receiving the full barrage from Val.

"Those were my mother's! Antiques, you know. You ought to be more careful. If it were your property, you wouldn't be treating it that way, would you!"

"Shut up, Mum. He didn't mean to," snapped Tania. Val was like that most of the time and she was always on at Ted. No wonder the poor bugger drank every night.

"Sorry, Val, I'll be more careful next time," I said. *Shut the fuck up, woman! I've been away three months 'n in five fuckin' minutes y' petty, whiney voice is already doin' m' bloody head in!*

13

The Local

At the pub there were a couple of people I'd met earlier when we first arrived in town, before we took the caravan up the mountain. They were all seated around a large table. I shook the hands of a couple of the guys and pecked their girlfriends on the cheek, performing all the pleasantries of meet and greet. Yaringa was a town full of cocksure surfers, and the whole coast was considered a Mecca of brilliant surf beaches. Surfers were not a breed of people I had ever warmed to, but I made the effort because I wasn't a snob.

Back home, I'd had a bad experience one night when I was at a party. I was talking about surfing with a guy who became all animated about it, and before I knew it, he had his photo albums out and was showing me the different places in the world he'd surfed, like he'd just found his long-lost surfing mate. When he asked me where I'd surfed, I said, "I've only surfed 'round here, 'n I'd hardly call it surfin'."

He immediately went all septic on me, accusing me of leading him along, how he'd just wasted his time showing me his photo album, how he thought we were kindred spirits. Then he slammed his album shut and disappeared with it into the crowded lounge.

"Fuck you too, buddy, 'n y' mother 'n sisters," I muttered under my breath. He must've heard me. He spun around and came back, but I was ready for him, expecting him to deck me one. He just stood there in my face, trembling with anger, trying to control his twisted mouth. "Just cos I'm not much 'f a surfer doesn't mean I don't appreciate y' photos," I said defiantly. He turned and walked off again.

"Idiot!" he yelled. Everyone stared at me, as if it were my fault he'd gone to find his mummy. Since then, I'd developed a bit of an attitude towards surfers, although most of the ones around the Yaringa area were alright, dead keen on hitting the waves at any given opportunity, and they smoked a shitload of weed.

We bought drinks at the bar and found a couple of spare seats at the end of the table, where I made small talk and sipped my beer. I watched with curiosity as a guy walked into the bar and Tania's eyes gravitated to him. I noticed his eyes meet hers, then he caught sight of me, as if he knew who I was, and looked away quickly, too quickly for me not to think anything of it.

"Do you want another drink, Sam?" Tania yelled from across the table. I lifted my glass and she nodded in acknowledgement when she saw I'd barely touched my beer. She'd sculled hers, no doubt dying to get up to the bar and talk with the guy whose dick she'd been sucking in my absence. She arrived at the bar without showing too much direct interest in him. I watched casually as his eyes followed her. He was leaning against a wooden pillar with a circular bench around it, as if it were his territory. Tania's head turned his way and a smile spread across her face, reciprocated by him. I'd busted them, him looking all cool as he sipped his beer and Tania's eyes glazing over like they did when she was happy, smiling profusely. She craned her neck and glanced over at me. I purposely averted my gaze. Drink in hand, she made her way between punters queuing for a drink to where this guy, who'd not shifted from his position, was standing. In my mind an image flashed of him plundering Tania on our bed, and for a moment I felt an irritation rising in my body. I wondered whether she'd left me up the mountain so she could carry on with him.

* * *

At the snowfields, Tania had told me conditions were too cold for her. She wasn't interested in working in the pizzeria any more, and the only other option was bar work, but she'd convinced me that she wouldn't cope with the smoky atmosphere as she suffered from asthma. *Strange, it doesn't seem t' be botherin' her t'night.* I hadn't wanted to go back to the coast with her, since I'd scored a job on the ski lifts and needed the cash.

"What the fuck am I goin' t' do back in Yaringa? It's a tinpot town. If y' not int' milkin' cows, there's no work!" I'd said. Well, I could've learnt to surf properly instead. I'd done a bit back home, but I was an amateur compared to the other guys in town. They lived and breathed it. When they weren't in the water, they were making surfboards in their backyards. "You can go back if y' want, but I ain't comin'," I'd told her straight.

"But I need you, Sam," she'd whined, perhaps not so convincingly.

"Look, it's only f' a couple 'f months, 'n the season will soon be over."

She had sat there at the table in the café, looking all pensive as she sipped on her cinnamon-topped cappuccino. When she moved the cup away from her mouth, her nose had frothy milk perched on its tip. She had smiled at me, and in that moment she had looked so incredibly sexy that I leaned forward and licked the milk off her nose. She had grabbed my head and had pulled me towards her, sticking her tongue down my throat as our mouths met. Tania had stood, grasped my hand and had led me out of the café into a shared foyer. I eagerly followed her toward the women's toilets. There had been no holding back, she was all over me like a rash as I shut the door behind us. I had fumbled with the buttons on her top to find her ample mounds of breast, all plump and firm, her nipples hardening as I squeezed them. She had my fly down and was rustling with my boxers. She had found what she was searching for.

* * *

As I sat watching her, so animated in the company of this guy who still hadn't moved from his pillar of support, I wondered for how long she had missed me, if she had missed me at all. I began to think the whole farewell-sex scenario we'd shared had been a well-acted performance on her part. She came back to sit at our table, looking pleased and slightly smug. "Who's the bloke?" I asked casually.

"Just a local boy I've known since high school days." She did her wriggle thing on the seat that she did when she was uncomfortable about something.

"What … an old flame?" I asked, knowing full well he was currently stoking her fire.

"What's with the fifty questions?" she asked, getting all snarky yet trying to maintain her composure.

"You know me … always curious."

She forced a smile and rubbed my knee. "Darling, you've got an overactive imagination."

"That's what m' old man use' t' say when I was a kid."

I hung about for another drink then decided I'd had enough. Tania was up on the dance floor shaking it with the rest of the pub goers. I watched them gyrating, all hot and sweaty in close confinement, everyone well on the way to becoming fuck-faced if they weren't already. There were a few there just for the dancing, but most were simply performing a mass mating dance, all boozed up to help them lose their inhibitions just so they could get it on with somebody. A lottery of

95

hopeful desperadoes. Some would go home alone and empty, dejected and disappointed, with only one thing guaranteed: a great big bloody hangover in the morning. Others would hit the jackpot and experience a few moments of pleasure. I was grateful I was not one of those hopefuls. I reached out and touched the arm of Shannon, a quiet, red-headed girl sitting beside me, not drop-dead gorgeous, but with a great body.

She turned to me and smiled. "Not into dancing, Sam?"

"Not t'night. Could y' do me a favour 'n tell Tania I'm headin' home? I'm a bit shagged."

"No problem." She smiled sweetly.

"I'll see y' then," I said, getting up out of my chair. Shannon nodded and smiled some more.

It was a relief to get outside, away from the smoky den and its sweaty, damp heat generated by all the bodies. As I walked, I pulled my tobacco from my back pocket and rolled a smoke. I needed something to calm my mind and rolling a cigarette did it better than most things. This simple act could be so soothing, ultimately more satisfying than the smoking of it. I never smoked the cigarettes down very far, usually six or eight puffs and I was ready to put it out. I'd get hassled for wasting so much of a perfectly good smoke. Most of my mates were seriously addicted to nicotine and smoked like chimneys. I finished building my smoke and lit it, inhaling deeper than usual, and as I walked and smoked, I realised there was nothing for me to look forward to.

Going back to Tania's parents' home was about as attractive as doing needles with an HIV-positive junkie, but there was nowhere else to go. I sat on a wooden bench on the hill just down from the pub, puffing on a smoke as I contemplated my situation. *How the fuck's m' chain-smokin', desk-bound, pen-pushin' solicitor, who signs wills 'n processes property title transfers, 'n who only appears in court t' defend drunk drivers, ever goin' t' get an out-of-towner from 'cross the ditch, like me, out 'f the deep fuckin' hole I'm in?*

14

Turning Tide

There was no work in the area, unemployment was at an all-time high, so Tania and I signed up for the de facto benefit. It wasn't ideal to be on welfare, but at least we didn't have to scrape together rent. Bruce and Sally had moved out of the house on the inlet, opting to stay with his brother who had a house in town. I was relieved not to be living with them, as Bruce wasn't pleasant to be around, constantly re-enacting the night he got busted.

Bruce and I were both up shit creek without a paddle, except he was further upstream with barbed wire wrapped around him. He persistently hounded me for giving the cops the address. "Y' should've known they'd find the stash if y' gave them the address," he told me more than once.

Bruce was older than me. He'd been around the block a few times and I hadn't even been halfway round. In my mind, though, I was eighteen going on thirty. The reality was I'd barely been out of school five minutes and I thought I was *the man*, all wise and worldly, afraid of nothing and ready for anything life threw at me, cocksure and confident until the night my world came crumbling down around my head.

Bruce intimidated me with his anxiety, even openly threatened me. He told me repeatedly that this whole thing was bigger than him and me, and that *those people* who supplied him with the hash oil were big

97

time, and if they got wind of what was going on down here, I could expect them to pull me out of my bed in the middle of the night, strap bricks to my body, and toss me off some bridge into a lagoon where the fish would feed off my rotting carcass. At night I'd wake drenched in sweat from a recurring dream of being tossed from a bridge, heavily strapped with bricks, breaking through the surface of the water, then slowly sinking to the bottom. I'd be gasping for air and thrashing around in my duvet, then experience great relief that I'd awoken.

It was an ongoing challenge living with Tania's parents. Every evening I was exposed to her mother's unbearable voice, so I became accustomed to joining Ted for a whisky at the breakfast bar. He'd tell me about his day at work and I'd feign listening, nodding in the right places and adding a few one-syllable affirmations, my mind often faraway, bordering on depression. Tania was going out more regularly and I was convinced she was having an affair with Rob from the pub. In some ways I would have preferred her to say it was over between us and leave me to my own devices. The problem was I needed the support of her parents to get me through the court case. I needed their roof over my head and their food on the table.

Tania and I weren't getting on at all, she bitched and moaned about living with her parents, about the lack of money, and about me.

"You're forever moping around the house not doing anything. Why don't you get out and look for a job? Anything's got to be better than sitting around here all day!"

"What? Live on a dairy farm? What farmer's goin' t' employ me knowin' that I'm charged with supplyin' drugs? Besides, cows 'n me don't cut it together! I've been there, done that, 'n y' know what? I ain't doing it! Oh, 'n besides cows, there's no work in this poxy town!"

"Fuck you! You're fuckin' useless! Look at you! You can't even dress properly!" I was wearing only my underwear which I often did, and I'd never heard her bitch about it before. Tania stormed out of the house, slamming the door behind her, yelling expletives all the way down the drive to the car. I heard the car door slam, the engine cough into life, and the sound of a squealing gearbox reversing fast out of the drive. I didn't see her for the rest of the day. *Fuck y', y' fuckin' bitch, good riddance. Go t' Rob 'n fuck y' brains out. See if I care.*

Now I was alone in the house with her brother, Tim, who was around the place but may as well not have been. He'd been released from the loony bin a few days ago, and no one in the family had spoken of him prior to his homecoming. Tania mentioned him in passing when we first got together, told me how her brother used to be a brilliant all-round sportsman and was clever academically until he went off the rails. Now he was off his trolley on powerful medication and just sat in one of the La-Z-Boys all day with the television on. Apparently, he'd been committed to the bin for staking out the houses of local women. The cops arrested him one night and the next day a local shrink did a psychiatric report on him, and he was committed by order of the court. Consequently, the drugs he was forced to take seriously fucked him up. He'd only been in the hospital for six months and was already a shadow of his former self. Tim's body was all hunched and his movements slow and difficult, a thirty-year-old trapped in the body of a seventy-year-old. Before he was committed, he was one of the top surfers in the area. At times, Tim still had a slight sparkle in his eyes and a very cheeky grin on his face, perhaps the drugs were really good. He often stared intensely at me, as if he were trying to figure me out.

It was a hot day and by noon the heat was unbearable. "Fancy a swim, Tim?" I asked, not expecting much of a response as I went to fetch a towel and my board shorts. To my surprise, he wrenched himself out of the armchair he permanently occupied and was in the hot-water cupboard searching for a towel. "So y' comin', huh?" I asked. He looked at me as though I was stupid and held the towel up in reply. "Cool," I said, trying to be enthusiastic.

"It will be," he mumbled.

We slowly meandered down to the beach. Tim's movements resembled the painful shuffles of someone afflicted with arthritis. We eventually arrived at the beach near the surf club, where we were supposed to swim, but the flags weren't up; it wasn't the holiday season yet. There was moderate surf. Some days the waves fair pounded the beach and other days it was like a mill pond. There were a few people in the water and a sprinkle of others sunbathing. I came to the water's edge and tested the temperature with my left foot. It was a little cooler than I expected, but I was so hot and desperate for a swim that I didn't care. I walked out and dived under the first wave that threatened to swamp me.

Tim was wading out slowly, each step calculated, painful. Eventually he had no choice, as the sea became deeper — he needed to take the wave or be taken by it. He came out the other side looking like a drowned rat with his ZZ Top-style beard all washed out, revealing a beaming smile. It was the first time I'd seen a genuine smile on his face. We bodysurfed a few waves together before heading back to shore where I spread my towel out and lay down in the sand. Tim dried himself briefly and headed back to the house. When I returned home, he was lying on the back lawn getting a few rays of sun on his body. There was a downstairs shower at the rear of the garage, and I used it to wash the sand and saltwater off my body.

Dressed in nothing but shorts after my shower, I headed upstairs and flopped into one of the armchairs, feeling almost as hot as before I'd gone swimming. I flicked the telly on and reclined in my chair. *Reckon I can handle summer if it's just Tim 'n me.* Tim wandered in, slumped into the armchair in the corner opposite me, and sat there staring at the telly in silence.

Right now, Tania 'n Rob'll be fuckin' each other's brains out. Although I didn't care much for my relationship with Tania, the idea of her and Rob getting it on was making me angry and *Days of our Lives* was doing nothing for my dark mood. I got up and stormed out of the house back down to the beach and sat in the sand, watching the waves pounding the shore with unrelenting force, totally in my own world, not noticing anybody around me.

15

Mum & Oma

Mum and Oma arrived to attend the court hearing that would decide my fate. I tried to convince them not to waste their time and money, but they wouldn't have a bar of it. Secretly, I was relieved to have their moral support. Mum was anxious the entire time they were here. She'd never been in a situation like this before, nor had she travelled outside of New Zealand before, and was way out of her comfort zone. Oma was different. She'd lived through the Second World War in the Netherlands. She'd travelled on ships to the far side of the world and given birth to her first two children on a coffee plantation in Southern Java, hence she was better equipped for life's dramas and complexities.

Tim and I drove to Wodyn in his car to pick them up at the bus stop. They'd flown from Christchurch to Sydney, from where they caught the train and then the bus south to Wodyn. They came armed with embraces and messages wishing us well from across the ditch. I was curious to see how Mum and Oma would cope with Val and Ted. Neither woman was big on the drinks front. One glass of bubbly and Mum was up onstage performing, doing things I never thought she was capable of, while Oma was moderate and controlled in most aspects of her life. I imagined Ted coming home, breaking out the gin, wanting to pour everyone stiff drinks and toast the moment. He'd get his drink down as quickly as possible and rapidly pour himself another, trying to control his trembling hands as he struggled to complete the pour.

Ted and Val arrived home late that afternoon, looking rather bedraggled after a long hot day in a stuffy building. Ted resisted the cabinet until I had introduced everyone. As I imagined, once the formalities were over, he clapped his hands together, announcing it was time for refreshments. "So … what would you ladies like to drink? I've got everything top-shelf you could imagine. Or perhaps you would like a glass of wine?" His hands were clasped together in anticipation, with a broad smile filling his ruddy face.

"Have you got brandy?" Mum asked, looking uncomfortable and apprehensive.

"Have I got brandy?" Ted chortled as he went to the cabinet. "Do you take that with ginger ale or perhaps Coke?" The smile was stuck to his face as he held his gaze on my mother.

"Ginger ale would be lovely, thanks," Mum replied, putting her hands together between her knees. I was expecting her to rub them in the way she often did when she was nervous or excited.

"Ginger ale it is then! And what about you, Helena?" he asked, eyeing Oma expectantly.

"If it's alright with you, I would like a cup of tea. I think I'd collapse if I had anything stronger."

"Of course you can have a cup of tea," chimed in Val. "Why don't you have a seat in one of the La-Z-Boys and put your feet up for a bit?"

"That's very kind, but I've been sitting on the bus all day so it's actually very good to be standing."

"Of course it is." Val pouted. "How silly of me! How do you have your tea, dear?"

"Medium strength with a dash of milk, thank you."

Val disappeared into the kitchen and Tim sat in the corner in his usual chair, silently observing, his eyes sparkling but his face sad. *Maybe he's the only sane one here.*

There was an uncomfortable silence as Ted poured the drinks and Val filled the kettle in the kitchen.

"So how was the trip?" Ted broke the silence.

"Long and tiring but nice to see the Australian countryside," replied Oma, all matter-of-fact. Mum still looked slightly fazed and shuffled uncomfortably on the couch, pushing the fabric of her dress about on her thighs.

"Mum, y' look exhausted," I said. She forced a smile at me, looking intensely into my eyes as if trying to ascertain if I was alright. I knew that look well. Mum wasn't an obvious worrier, but she shied away from any possibility of danger. She avoided taking risks and frequently condemned my father for doing so. Now she was here, with her mother-in-law, trying to rescue me, her son, from a stint inside an Ozzie prison. There was no guarantee of success, but I was grateful for their presence and eternally hopeful that some good was going to come of them appearing in court with me in a few days' time. Ted waited on my mum, bringing the glass of brandy to her. He then raised his own glass in a welcoming gesture before greedily gulping several mouthfuls.

"May the gods be smiling on us in the days to come," he toasted.

"Hear, hear," Oma responded, gingerly raising her cup of tea, then sipping cautiously.

We were disturbed by the sound of the front door opening and shutting, then moments later Tania appeared in the doorway, putting on a big smile for my mother as she rushed to greet her. *She's prob'bly come from Rob's place.* She hadn't been home for a couple of days, claimed she needed space, said she was going to stay with a friend. I doubted her but was beyond caring.

Mum looked pleased to see Tania as she'd become familiar with her during the time we stayed in Christchurch. Oma didn't really know her, but they had met a couple of times when we were picking apples together. Tania embraced Mum, then Oma.

"Where have you been, Tania?" Val demanded, interrupting the polite greetings.

Tania stared at her with a withering look that suggested *it's none of your fucking business!* She calmly replied, "I thought you knew, Mum. I've been staying with a friend."

"You said you were going to be back today."

"So here I am, just as I said."

Ted poured himself another Scotch. Normally he'd have knocked off two or three by now. *He must be dyin' t' duck down the road 'n pump a few gold ones int' the casino machines at the bowlin' club, 'n forget about the troubles under 'is own roof.* Small talk kicked in about the trip over, the weather, and what spring was like back in New Zealand.

* * *

Val had knocked up a casserole the night before, so all she had to do was turn the oven on when she came home. She was the ultimate stress merchant in the kitchen, it didn't bear witnessing. Nonetheless, she served up a grand-looking meal. We all sat around the large dining table, eating and drinking as the small talk continued. Tim fed his face silently. He hadn't said a word and wasn't likely to. Ted bravely entered into the deeper issues surrounding the arrival of Mum and Oma, which had been avoided until now.

"So…tomorrow you can meet my solicitor friend who's representing Sam in court. He thinks it will help to have you both present, and to provide a few written references from family and employers."

"Yes, we've got all that ready. What do you think the chances are of it all being sorted out in this court hearing?" asked Mum.

Ted thought for a moment before answering. "There are never any guarantees in life. It really depends on a whole lot of variables ..." He paused for a moment as though gathering his thoughts or probing for the right words to use. "It's perhaps wise to expect the worst and hope for the best." He picked up his glass of red wine and raised it. He liked a good tipple of wine with his meal as much as he liked a Scotch beforehand. "I'd like to welcome you here and hope for a good outcome. Here's to our good health! Cheers!" We all raised our glasses.

"Where there is a will, I'd like to say, there is always a way," Oma offered optimistically as we all clinked glasses. "So, things are fairly grim for Sam?" Oma was never one for beating around the bush.

Ted looked put out, almost choking on the wine he'd just quaffed. "I wouldn't go so far as to say that. I just don't want you to be disappointed if this isn't resolved in a few days' time. Drug offences are treated seriously in New South Wales."

"But I thought we had a case based on the fact he's young and has been taken advantage of," queried my mum, looking deeply concerned.

"Yes, we do, but like I say, that depends on how the police present their case and how the magistrate views it," replied Ted.

"You see, in New South Wales," Tania butted in, "the police like to come down on young offenders fairly harshly. Their philosophy is to scare the hell out of them once in the hope they won't do it again."

Like y're a fuckin' expert, Tania!

"Then we should all go to bed tonight and pray," Oma responded. I couldn't tell if she was serious or not.

"Yes, I suppose we should," agreed Ted. Mum looked alarmed. "Who's for another drink?" Ted asked, waving the wine bottle around as if it was going to solve all the problems of the world.

Mum and Oma went to bed early. Ted and Val had probably scared them off with their constant drinking and smoking. Tania and I retired to the caravan, leaving Tim to watch telly on his own. I lay awake worrying about Mum and Oma, then I worried about what I'd do if things weren't resolved in the coming days. Tania lay next to me sleeping, her tight warm arse against my thigh. Not so long ago, I would have struggled to resist the temptation to ravage her, but the revelation of her fling with Rob had erased any feelings I might still have had for her. Sleep eluded me, so I resorted to having a wank, and just as I was about to cum, I stuck my dick between the back of her thighs and came in spasms. Instant relief, sleep followed.

* * *

I awoke early, slipping out of bed silently so as not to disturb Tania, then dressed and walked down to the beach. There were a few people out walking their dogs, trying to get rid of their middle-age spread. A steamy mist rose off the sea and nice, even waves rolled in, smashing into white foam on the golden sand. The sun sat like a large ball, suspended just above the horizon. It was going to be a hot day. I strolled along the beach for a while trying to gather my thoughts. Life had been so sweet until now. *Now m' future's at the mercy 'f a magistrate presidin' in a courtroom, makin' decisions f' society based on written laws. In Australia, they called the Magistrates' Court 'The Court of Petty Sessions' until 1971. I wonder how petty my offence's goin' t' be in the eyes 'f the magistrate?*

I arrived back at the house to find Oma and Ted sitting at the table, drinking tea. Ted was already smoking a cigarette, looking like the day had spat him out before it had even started.

"Mornin'," I said.

"Morning," Ted responded, taking another drag on his cigarette.

107

"Good morning, grandson. Did you sleep well?"

"Pretty good," I lied. "What about y'self?"

"Good, considering the unfamiliar environment."

"That's good. Is Mum up?" I helped myself to cereal in the kitchen. I liked muesli, it made me feel healthy, like I was looking after at least one aspect of my life.

"She's in the shower," replied Oma.

"We were going to give you all a ride to the solicitor this morning, but I realise you will all need to get back somehow, so I suggest you take Tim's car," said Ted. "You should escort them, Sam, so you can introduce them to Dennis.

Dennis, m' chain-smoking solicitor who explains away illegal activity 'n temptation in one wave 'f 'is cigarette. God knows what Mum 'n Oma will think 'f him. Although Ted had assured me that he was a good friend and the best solicitor in town.

"Good morning, Sam." Mum entered the kitchen dressed and ready to meet the day.

"Mornin', Mum," I said as I gave her a hug. Usually, she was like a stiff board, never comfortable with physical closeness, but this morning she surprised me with her warm embrace.

"There's tea in the pot," announced Ted as he lit up another cigarette and reached for his cup.

Mum didn't look impressed with him lighting up. "Thank you."

"These are all the cereals," I said, opening a cupboard to reveal an array of cereals.

"I'll just have what you're having, thanks, Sam."

"Sure, I'll make it up. You just sit down with Oma."

Val was next to appear on the scene, all made-up with lipstick and various cosmetics she'd packed onto her face in an attempt to hide the wrinkles. Val puckered her lips as she entered the kitchen, trying to get the lipstick to spread evenly. "Is there any tea left in the pot? I suppose it's all been drunk," she whined.

"There's hot water in the jug and the teapot might just need a bit of a top up. It's been in demand this morning," Ted responded in an even voice.

"Couldn't you have kept an eye on it and done it for me?"

"If you didn't spend so long in front of the mirror, you wouldn't have to worry about the teapot being empty!" The amount of time she spent doing herself up every morning drove Ted mad. He was a man constantly waiting on his woman, and there wasn't much love between them any more.

"At least I care about how I present myself!" Val turned to me. "Are you accompanying your mother and Oma into town?"

"I might," I said, knowing I'd get a bite.

"I think you should! They've come all this way especially for you and they need looking after."

No fuckin' kiddin'! I might just sit back with Tim, smoke a few pipes 'n watch the cricket.

I took Mum her muesli then sat down next to her and ate my own. Conversation didn't come easily at the breakfast table that morning.

* * *

We all left the house at the same time but in separate cars. Tim was letting me use his Hemi Valiant at will, so long as I kept the tank in fuel. I pulled up in the main street of Wodyn and parked the car.

"I've got t' report t' the police," I told Mum and Oma.

"We'll wait for you in the car," Mum stated.

"You'll bake in here. Why don't y' get out 'n have a look at the shops?"

"We'll be alright, thanks," she said firmly.

"Suit y'self," I said, getting out of the car. "I'll be a minute or two." I closed the car's door and walked down the road to the police station where I found the old sarge on duty.

He stared down his spectacles at me and frowned. "Oh, it's you," he said, immediately tensing up as though I was a major threat that had entered the building.

"Y' should be use' t' me by now. I come in every day, but maybe not f' much longer, eh? And what a relief it'll be not seeing y' ugly mug any more."

"You fuckin' cheeky cunt."

"Y' should watch y' language, officer. It's not very becomin' 'f a man 'f your stature."

"I should give y' a fuckin' hidin'," he said, lifting the hinged part of the bench that allowed him to come out into the foyer. Just then the door opened and Harry, the officer who had pulled me over the night I was busted, came through the door.

As he caught sight of me, he smiled. "Gidday, Sam. How y' gettin' on?"

"What would you care?" the sarge asked, glaring at Harry. "He just gave me some lip. He's a smart fuckin' punk."

"Y' prob'bly deserved it," Harry said, nudging him with his elbow.

"Humpf!" the sarge grunted as he turned and walked out of the room.

"So seriously, how y' gettin' on?" Harry asked, smiling some more, looking me right in the eye.

"Why y' askin'? I don't understand why y'd care."

"I just do. It's m' nature."

"It didn't seem like y' nature the night y' took me in, or have y' forgott'n what you 'n that psycho Frank put me through? Can y' sign me off, please, so I can get out 'f here."

"That was just routine investigation tactics."

"Funny, but I don't think so. Now can I sign?"

Harry reached for the report pad and placed it on the bench. Dating it, he handed me the pen and I scribbled my name down, slammed the pen on the counter and walked out feeling irritated. *Why the fuck would Harry care about how I'm doin'?* I stormed back down the street to find Mum and Oma sitting on a street bench under the shade of a Moreton Bay fig tree, not far from the car. The temperature had risen dramatically.

We made our way down the street to Dennis's office where we were greeted by his receptionist, a young woman probably not much older than me. She was dressed in a red mini skirt that struggled to contain her arse, and a tight-fitting white blouse that beautifully pronounced the fullness of her breasts and the outline of her nipples. She smiled as we came in. "Have a seat. Dennis is expecting you. He'll be with you shortly."

"Thanks," I said, beaming a smile back at her. We obediently sat down. I positioned myself between Mum and Oma, neither of whom seemed to have much to say. Mum was anxious and Oma was really feeling the heat, so we sat in silence waiting for Dennis. The silence became unbearable. I flicked through one of the glossy magazines on the coffee table, glancing up occasionally to gaze lustfully at the gorgeous receptionist.

Finally, Dennis's office door opened, and a well-dressed, middle-aged female client emerged through a haze of smoke. "We'll be in touch," Dennis said, and he handed his receptionist a folder.

"So you must be Sam's mother and grandmother," Dennis said, turning to face us. He reached out and shook Mum's hand. "Dennis Greenwood."

"Celia … Celia Gorzman." Mum limply shook his hand.

"Pleased to meet you. And you must be …"

"Helena Gorzman," Oma finished his sentence, looking impatient and slightly irritated.

"Why don't you all step into my office." He made a gesture with his hand to usher us in.

There were two chairs in front of his desk and another to the left of the desk, against the wall. I let Mum and Oma sit in the former, while I sat in the latter. His office was as disorganised and messy as the last time I was in it — the ashtray still overflowed with cigarette butts, his bookshelves remained higgledy-piggledy, and the air stank badly of stale smoke. Mum was obviously unimpressed. *Don't judge a book by its cover, Mum.*

Dennis was compelled to tell his cigarette story again. Mum and Oma obediently nodded as if in agreement. He explained how he would present the argument in court that I was young and naive, that this was my first brush with the law, that they were here to take me home, and that it was unlikely I would reoffend. It all sounded logical and sensible, but he did emphasise that it would come down to how the magistrate viewed such an offence on the day. "There are no certainties in life besides taxes and death. We just have to do our best and hope for the best. Did you bring the character references with you?"

"Yes," said Mum, reaching into her bag and handing him a fat brown A4 envelope which he took and placed on his dishevelled desk while his other hand reached for a cigarette.

"Excuse me, do you mind not smoking that until we're finished in here? My lungs are very sensitive," said Oma, putting a hand to her chest and smiling warmly at Dennis.

He pulled the cigarette from his mouth and stuttered an apology. "I ... I ... I'm sorry, I thought we were done." He awkwardly placed his cigarette in the ashtray with all the other stubbed out butts and looked uncomfortable as he slowly raised his eyes to engage Mum and Oma. "Are there any questions?"

"What if the magistrate doesn't see it our way ... I mean, your way?" Mum asked.

"Then there aren't many options, I'm afraid. He can sentence Sam to whatever he's entitled to as a magistrate, but he'd normally set down a hearing date. Or he can let him off with a warning and a fine. Or ..." he hesitated, "or he can refer Sam to the District Court, which is a higher court, presided over by a judge."

"So there's no guarantee it'll all be over after tomorrow," Mum said, frowning.

"That's the reality," Dennis replied, shrugging his shoulders and looking gravely at Mum. "But we have a good chance."

"Thank you for your help. We'll see you in the Magistrates' Court tomorrow morning at ten," Mum said, lifting herself up out of the chair. Oma followed suit and I remained silent, like a mute ghost, simply observing. Dennis stood and ushered us out, putting his hand on my shoulder as I followed Mum and Oma out of the room.

"Chin up, Sam," he said. "Tomorrow, with a bit of luck, you just might be on your way home."

I actually liked Dennis, he'd been kind enough to help me, and he was doing it free of charge. He told me he wouldn't take a fee for his services because he had children my age, and if they ever got into bother somewhere else in the world, he hoped someone would do the same for them. He might not be the flashiest lawyer in the business, but he had his heart in the right place and seemed to know a thing or two.

* * *

We left the office and walked down the main street to a coffee shop. Oma was parched and needed a cup of tea, and I was more than happy to take some time out. We ordered tea and a snack, two scones and a doughnut, which the waitress brought over on a tray. She was a young woman, probably not long out of school, and rather large. Her tight-fitting T-shirt didn't do her any favours, highlighting the rolls of blubber above her hips and on her stomach. I watched her, intrigued by how it was possible for someone so young to become so overweight. *Anythin' t' distract me from the tragedy 'f m' own life. Must be her parents' shop. Surely no one would give a woman of her size a job waitin' on people. Not meaning to be prejudiced, but it's quite a tight space t' operate behind the counter.*

As I sat there eating my doughnut, an older woman appeared from the back of the shop. She was even larger than the girl, waddling her way to the counter to place another tray of sandwiches in the glass display cabinet. Her appearance confirmed my theory that it was a family business. The sight of her mother fondling the sandwiches with her fat, fleshy hands almost caused me to gag on my doughnut. Just when I thought I'd seen it all, the door to the café opened and a black-and-white checkered stomach appeared, followed by a man's body. With the entrance of the stomach-with-legs, the overweight family was complete. The man was too old to be her brother, although it could've been Cousin Barry who'd waddled his way from down the street to have some lunch. I watched him walk behind the counter. He almost needed a wheelbarrow to carry his stomach around. He stopped to talk to the girl before disappearing out the back where the other woman was baking.

All this went seemingly unnoticed by Mum and Oma as they sipped soothing mouthfuls of tea between bites on their scones.

"What do you think will happen tomorrow, Sam?" Mum asked.

"I dunno, Mum. It's not in my hands," I said, shrugging my shoulders. "But if y' want the honest truth, I'm hoping it's all done 'n dusted t'morrow, although I'm not a hundred per cent confident about it. I've just got t' face the music, and I hope the magistrate's name is Bruce."

"Why's that, Sam?" Mum asked earnestly.

"Let 'im loose, Bruce," I said, knowing she wouldn't get it.

"That's a good one, Sam," Oma said, laughing lightly.

"Thank God someone has a sense 'f humour 'round here."

"I bought some clothes for you to wear tomorrow. They should fit okay. You don't look as if you've changed weight or grown at all," announced Mum.

"No, don't think I have. Thanks, Mum." I hated new clothes that weren't a casual style, always feeling overdressed and awkward, as if I stuck out in a crowd. "We should finish our tea 'n go, eh? It's gettin' too hot t' be in town." I'd had enough of looking at fat people. I needed to get back to the beach and have a swim.

"What's Tim's situation, Sam?" Mum asked out of the blue as I was getting out of my chair. I sank back down.

"He's on medication, Mum. The cops put him in the loony bin f' being a naughty boy. The local shrink decided he was unbalanced 'n needed treatment."

"What did he do?" she asked, genuinely curious.

"Apparently he had a penchant f' a couple of young women. Followed 'em home in 'is car 'n sat outside their houses. Stuff like that. Whipped the odd bit 'f lingerie off clotheslines. Someone got scared 'n rang the cops. Complained they were being stalked and felt unsafe. So they took 'im in 'n got the shrink t' assess 'im. Sounds like the cops convinced the shrink t' write up a report sayin' he was unstable, 'n so they committed him. Now the women in the community are safe again 'n can sleep at night while Tim's pumped full 'f drugs t' keep 'im subdued."

"You sound cynical, Sam," said Mum.

"Some say it was a necessary procedure, 'n others say there was nothin' in it. Anyway, he's so drugged up now he's harmless as a butterfly. The nurse comes 'round to medicate him once a fortnight, so he doesn't b'come too lucid."

"That's terrible," said Oma, doing that *tssk, tssk* thing with her mouth.

"Yeah, I reckon so too, but what can y' do? Hey, I like him. He's good company, though he doesn't talk much, but he kind 'f listens. We get on in a funny sort 'f a way just by doin' things t'gether."

Oma and Mum nodded thoughtfully, but they both had faraway expressions in their eyes. Tomorrow was looming large in the scale of things.

16

Court Hearing

Mum took the suit from her case that night and got me to try it on. She had bought my suit on sale at Ballantynes, a massive middle-of-the-road department store in the heart of Christchurch. The jacket and trousers were dark chocolate brown, the shirt a creamy hue, and the tie a mustard brown that didn't match anything. I hated the suit but had to concede that it did make me look young, innocent and conservative, and that would surely be to my advantage.

I'd shaved my beard off for my first appearance in court, which was for Bruce's hearing, and I intended to do so again. Bruce's hearing had been deferred to another date because the police prosecutor felt it wasn't right for both hearings to be held at the same time. The fact that I'd pleaded guilty, and he'd pleaded not guilty, might have had something to do with it.

When I arrived at court with Mum and Oma, we were all well dressed for the occasion. Dennis met us on the court steps, complimented me on my attire and explained that the defendants sit outside the courtroom until called. He suggested Mum and Oma go inside and take a seat so they would be in the courtroom when I was called up. He ushered them in while I sat outside with all the undesirable urchins of Wodyn. Not one single person had made any effort to dress differently to how they normally would in their everyday lives. *Am I in deeper shit than they are? How come none 'f them thought t' change their clothes?* The wait was excruciating and long, with so many offenders to wade through. Most of them were drink drive, theft, or assault charges, and most of the offenders were unemployed whites or Aboriginals. They were a motley bunch and I felt out of place.

Finally, my name was called. I was ushered in, feeling self-conscious in my suit, with Mum and Oma watching proceedings from the seating gallery. The bailiff read the charge and the magistrate asked, "How does the defendant plead?" Dennis looked at me, urging me to speak.

"Guilty, Your Honour," I managed to force from my mouth. My tongue had stuck to my palate, which was parched and dry like an old buzzard's. *Please God, let it be all over after today.*

"Your Honour," Dennis said. "There is a case to be heard of how this situation came about."

"Thank you, Mr Greenwood, I am aware of that, hence this hearing. Tell us what it is you have to share." The magistrate appeared serious, his spectacles sat halfway down the bridge of his beak-like nose, his hair was greying and parted to one side, and his eyes looked mean and piercing, showing no sign of compassion or emotion.

"Your Honour, this young man fell into unfortunate circumstances since he arrived in this country from New Zealand, and made connections with the wrong people, not so much by choice, but more by fate."

Shit! Why the fuck does he need t' emphasise I'm from New Zealand! That might be 'nough 'f a reason t' convict me on the spot. I hope the magistrate isn't a fan 'f cricket or rugby. He might have more reason than usual t' take exception, the way New Zealand's been takin' it t' the Ozzies lately in both codes.

Dennis continued to play all the violin strings as he built his story of my misfortune. It was an impressive piece of storytelling. I played my own small part by remaining in a state of overacted remorse. "I conclude, Your Honour, that this young man fell prey to the influences of older men through naivety and a desire to fit in. I suggest there is not a criminal bone in his body, just perhaps a large dose of stupidity. We would do this young man more justice by sending him home with his family," Dennis continued, gesturing to Mum and Oma, "than by locking him up for years to come."

Midnight Express came hurtling to mind. An image appeared in my head of Billy Hayes standing before the judge in the Turkish court of law. The magistrate spoke only Turkish, offering Billy no chance of understanding what he was saying as he sentenced him.

Dennis finished his presentation, handed the magistrate the collection of references my mother had brought with her, and sat down. The magistrate glanced through the references then peered over his glasses perched low on his nose, looking directly at me.

"It is my belief," said the judge finally, in his deep, droll voice, "that this is a serious offence and an indictable one at that. Therefore, I feel it is out of my jurisdiction to hear this case. I hereby refer this case to the District Court when it resides here next." He banged his gavel down on his desk. "The court will take a ten-minute recess," he announced as he pushed his chair back and stood up, looking like a high priest in his black gown.

My face sank into my hands and I peered through my fingers, like a child might, at Dennis, who looked at me with obvious disappointment on his face. He'd done his best. I turned and looked over at Mum, who had tears running down her face, with Oma consoling her. We left the courthouse and stood outside on the steps with Dennis, who apologised profusely to Mum for the outcome, even though it wasn't his fault. He explained that the District Court sat only every six months in rural areas, and it wouldn't be residing in Wodyn again until February, having only just sat here a month or so ago. He also went on to say the case was out of his league now, and that we would be better off to hire a barrister.

"I know someone very good in Sydney, but he won't be cheap," he announced, rubbing the top of his balding head as if it might help his thought process.

"We'll manage to find the money," Mum said.

"Thank you, Dennis, for everything you've done," said Oma, acknowledging him by extending her hand which he took and shook gently.

"I've been more than happy to do this. I don't like seeing young people's foolishness resulting in time inside. That's the last road any young man needs to go down."

"We can't thank you enough," said Mum, offering her hand too. "We are greatly indebted to you and will be in touch about the services of your barrister friend." She broke down crying, trying to utter a few words, something about not wanting to leave me here on my own. Oma tried to console her, assuring her I wouldn't be on my own for Christmas. *God knows why she's so worried about me havin' Christmas on m' own, that's the least 'f m' worries.*

* * *

I walked down the main street of Wodyn with my grieving mother while consoling Oma, feeling like the whole thing was a surreal nightmare that I would wake from any moment. But there was no waking from it as we continued to walk. We arrived at Tim's Valiant. I started up the engine and carefully manoeuvred out of the park and onto the road. Mum and Oma discussed what they thought needed to happen as I drove us back to Yaringa. I didn't have much to say, since I was too preoccupied with my own thoughts, trapped in my mind. I thought about being in prison, imagining the handbasin scenario, and about how Bruce would react to the latest development. The sun was high in the sky, beating down on the road, causing waves of heat to rise off the tar-seal.

We pulled up in the drive, half-baked from the intensity of the sun in the hot car. Mum and Oma were in need of lunch, and I needed to strip off my suit and wash the day away. Soon I was heading for the beach. There was a good swell coming in, with an onshore breeze holding the waves up nicely so they broke evenly. I wasn't much of a surfer, but I loved bodysurfing. Tim had taken me out a few times on the longboards from the clubhouse, and I'd caught a few good waves on them but preferred to bodysurf, even though I was inclined to get dumped rather badly. I'd come up spitting saltwater, gasping for air and shaking sand from my earholes.

Tim was down on the beach sunbathing.

"Good day f' pervin'," I said, sitting down beside him. "They didn't let me off with a slapped wrist. They're sending me t' the District Court. Doesn't sound good t' me. Sounds fuckin' ominous, actually."

"Not good at all," Tim responded in a matter-of-fact tone.

"Thanks! That's just what I needed t' hear right now!" I headed for the water feeling irked.

"You said it first!"

I ignored him and dived into a wave that was threatening to break. I emerged on the other side of the wall of water, turning to admire its bubbling white froth, the only remnant of its existence, and then it was gone, replaced by another wave and another. I liked the backs of waves as they curved and peaked blue, sparkling and brilliant, before they broke with the wind blowing spray off their tips. A good-size wave came along, and I timed my swim to keep ahead of it, knowing it would pick me up and I'd drop down its face as it peaked. It was an exhilarating feeling to free-fall down a wave, and this one was large enough to allow me to manoeuvre. I could lean my body right and I'd go to the right, or I could change my weight to the left and I'd go left. The sea helped soothe my thoughts as I caught wave after wave, trying to free my mind.

* * *

Dinner that night was a sombre affair. No one had anticipated that my case would be taken to a higher level, although deep down, we all knew it was a possibility.

"I'm going back to New Zealand," Tania announced suddenly, above all the other voices at the table. Conversation stopped and cutlery ceased to clang on plates, except for Tim, who continued eating as if nothing had been said.

"Would you like to repeat that, dear?" Val asked.

"You heard me, Mum. I'm going back to New Zealand. I've thought about it and it strikes me as the best option. I'm not happy here and I can't handle all this shit that's going on. I feel caught in the middle between Bruce and Sam. I'm in an awkward situation."

"What's awkward about it, dear?"

"Oh, come on, Mum, can't you see? I've got Bruce saying shit like if Sam talks or gives evidence against him, he can't guarantee his safety."

"Really? We should call the police, shouldn't we, Ted?"

"I imagine the police are already aware of the potential threat," he replied as he put whisky to his lips and gulped down the remaining contents.

Here we go … Christ, Tania, of course you'd have t' one up the situation just at a time I'm feelin' m' most vulnerable. Well, yeah, y' know what? Y' can fuck off back t' NZ. In fact, it's a better idea than I'd have given y' credit for. At least I won't have t' deal with all the other shit y're up to.

"I think it's a very sensible idea, Tania," said Mum, joining in the conversation as if somehow reading my thoughts. "I wouldn't want to be in your situation either. You can live with us until you work out what you want to do."

"I think it's the right idea too. I don't see any point in you being stuck here with this going on," said Ted, joining in.

"Ted, what are you saying!" screeched Val.

"Just that I think Tania would be better off somewhere else while all this is happening."

"I can't believe you're saying this, Ted," she whined.

"We can have a holiday over there at Christmas. I've always wanted to see New Zealand," Ted enthused.

"I have a proposal too." Oma entered the conversation.

"Fire away," said Ted, taking another slug of his whisky.

"If it is alright … and Sam would like it, I thought my husband and I could come here for Christmas. That way Sam wouldn't have to be alone."

"I don't see why not. Do you, Val?"

"Ahh, it's all a bit sudden, this whole …"

"So you agree then?" Ted asked. "It's all settled. We just need to work out a bit of an itinerary."

"You can all make your own plans but I'm going back to New Zealand. That's final," Tania said. She stood up and left the table, taking her plate with her to the kitchen.

Tania slept in the caravan with me that night, she seemed almost happy to do so. Perhaps things had gone sour with Rob, or she was just celebrating getting out of the place and felt she could give me one final farewell. We shook and rocked the caravan in a test of endurance. Yet somehow it felt like my nose was being rubbed that little bit further into my own shit. She was taking my family escort home, a trip originally intended for me. In truth, I was relieved she was going. I didn't fancy having her around for the next few months while I waited for the District Court to come to town.

In Wodyn, two days later, I felt perfectly calm, almost happy to wave Tania off on the bus at the start of their journey to Sydney. Mum wept as she kissed and hugged me goodbye. Oma gave me her blessing, she seemed so calm, even under difficult circumstances. Tania embraced me, hugging me tightly as though she was never going to see me again. *Does she know somethin' I don't? Ah well, at least she's out 'f my hair.* A vivid image of Bruce throwing me off a bridge with bricks lashed to my body flashed in my mind. I shivered.

Tania held me even tighter and whispered, "Relax, baby, no one's going to hurt you." She pulled away. Tears welled up in her eyes as she turned and climbed aboard the bus. She found her seat next to the window, behind Mum and Oma, and looked out at me, tears cascading down her cheeks as the floodgates opened. I stood there feeling completely numb. The bus pulled out from the kerb. I was the only one there to wave it off. Tania's emotional performance was brilliant, the tears still flowing as she held her face up to the window. Mum and Oma waved, their motions synchronised like a morbid Punch and Judy act, both holding back tears in a bid to be brave. Then it was a blur of unfamiliar faces passing before the bus was gone, leaving a cloud of black diesel fumes behind that shrouded me as if I'd gone up in a puff of smoke.

17

Slow Days

Tim and I had some dope seedlings growing in seed pots in the back garden, concealed behind shrubs, and they were ready to be transplanted in the wild. Tim had an old plot of land he hadn't used for a year or two. That's where we headed with his plants. It was a drive of a few kilometres up the coast before we turned off, going up a dirt road. We drove a few more kilometres towards the beach, where Tim pulled up in a parking area. He didn't seem bothered about leaving the car there in full view.

"No one comes down this road 'cept f' surfies," he mumbled as he opened the boot and handed me several seedling pots. It wasn't going to be a crop that would make us rich, being intended more for personal use, but it would keep us well supplied for a few months. The irony was that by the time the plants matured, I would either be in prison or winging my way back to New Zealand. I was playing with fire and I knew it.

We walked through the bush for about ten minutes. There were swarms of bugs and flies hovering around, and the heat was intense. Tim almost stood on a brown snake basking in the sun, all subdued and sleepy from an overdose of warmth. I could've been racing Tim back to Wodyn for an antidote, having to explain why we were in the bush. The snake barely noticed us, only raising its head briefly before coiling up to take in more sun. Tim finally stopped in front of a shade fence, the only indication that a plot of land existed. It looked a bit tired but nothing we couldn't tighten up. There was a spade and watering can in one corner of the plot left there from previous years. We must've spent an hour turning the soil then digging small holes with our hands. We took the seedlings, placed them in the ground, and pushed soil around them before compacting it to make a nice, tight fit. We had about fifteen plants in the ground by the time we'd finished, then we tightened up the fence before going back to the car for containers of water to give the seedlings a good soaking.

As we drove off the dirt road and onto the sealed road back to Yaringa, I stiffened when a police car cruised past.

"That put the frighteners up y', didn't it," Tim said, sniggering psychotically.

"I must be absolutely crazy plantin' a dope crop with a loony tune while I'm already in a whole lot 'f shit. If I get caught f' this, I'll be put away … end 'f story." A tingle went up my spine as I contemplated the prospect of being charged for another drug offence. Gone would be my ability to plead naivety and ignorance, suddenly I'd look like a seasoned drug dealer, and they'd be throwing the book at me. I vowed then and there that I wouldn't be coming back to water or harvest any plants. Tim would have to do it on his own.

A week later I was carrying in containers of water with Tim. "I really must be mad creepin' through the bush doin' this shit!"

"You said it, not me," was Tim's dry reply. I was paranoid — fearful of stepping on a snake, and forever expecting the cops to be waiting in hiding, ready to ambush us. We made it to the plot without incident, all sweaty and puffed from struggling with the weight of the water. The plants looked a bit wilted as they'd taken a real blast from the sun. It was one of the hottest summers on record. A serious drought was going down in the area, and farmers were desperate for rain. It was little wonder our seedlings were struggling.

* * *

Summer was intensifying and I was becoming increasingly bored with the repetition of my days. Most mornings when I got up, I'd take a run down the beach then a quick swim in the sea. If there were a few waves, I'd bodysurf for a bit longer. After a swim, it was back to the house to shower, then breakfast upstairs. Ted and Val were usually gone by the time I made it back, part of my plan. Hanging around with them in the mornings was as morbid as attending a funeral. Tim never showed his head before ten in the morning. After breakfast I'd read awhile, then head into town, which usually involved hitching because I couldn't afford the petrol for Tim's car. I'd walk up to the main road to hitch a ride. I never got the same ride twice, even though I was out there at the same time every day, which surprised me considering I had the same daily routine for close on four months. I'd always get a ride within minutes. No one treated me like a leper. I didn't know how much the community knew about me, probably not much.

In Wodyn I'd report to the police station, so they'd know I hadn't done a disappearing act. Usually, I had to deal with the sarge, who was consistently an arsehole with his derogatory comments, which I was used to by now and I could let his snide remarks go over my head. After reporting to the police, I'd often have a cup of tea and read the paper at the coffee shop I had taken Mum and Oma to, the one with the fat, friendly chick working behind the counter, wearing the tight T-shirt showing all her rolls of fat. If I didn't have a cup of tea in town, I'd get straight back on the road to Yaringa since Wodyn was a depressing place. *It's hard t' put m' finger on it, there's just some*

Hitching back was the same, I'd never have to wait long before someone gave me a ride to Yaringa. People were friendly and mostly easy-going in these parts, though I never felt as trusting as I did back home in the countryside. I'd unwittingly developed a sense of distrust that made me wary of people, a paranoia that had contaminated me since I'd been done over by the cops. When I went out to see bands play at local village halls, the people that frequented those places seemed so out of this world, it felt strangely creepy. I was probably smoking too much dope, which contributed to my already over-imaginative mind. Once back in Yaringa, it was entirely up to me how I spent the rest of the day. Mostly I'd read or go down to the beach to cool off in the sea, but it was usually too hot to stay there for long. I'd end up like a boiled lobster.

18

The Company of Strangers

The year was coming to a close. It was just before the Christmas of 1980, and I was on my way back from Wodyn after having reported to the police. I was counting down the days until Oma and Opa arrived to spend Christmas with me. They were coming for three weeks, and I was excited in the knowledge that Val and Ted were going to New Zealand for a month and that Tim was going too, so I'd get a break from all three of them. I walked off a side street onto the main road to Yaringa, imagining the prospect, and I casually put my thumb out to the sound of an approaching car. A brown Holden Premier station wagon pulled up beside me, its engine idling throatily. A guy with an impressive mop of frizzy brown hair and wearing round, steel-rimmed glasses, much like John Lennon's, stuck his head out the passenger window. *God bless John Lennon. Some psycho shot him dead last week!*

"Where y' off to, mate?"

"Yaringa."

"Us too. Jump in," he said, before twisting and turning to reach the lock on the rear door. I opened the door and climbed into the back seat.

The driver had long, blond permed hair, a cross between Rod Stewart and John Farnham, with a distinctively long, sharp nose and a refined-looking face.

"Y' live 'round this way?" the driver asked, looking at me in his rear-view mirror.

"Sort 'f," I replied.

"Either y' do, or y' don't," said the passenger-seat guy with the frizzy mop of hair as he turned to face me, beaming like a Cheshire cat.

"Where y' from?" the driver asked.

"New Zealand," I replied casually.

"Get the fuck out 'f here! We're Kiwis too," exclaimed the frizz nut excitedly.

"Thought I detected a Kiwi accent." The permed-haired driver was nodding enthusiastically like one of those dogs that people have on the dashboard of their car, with the head that bobs spontaneously to the slightest bit of motion.

"Y' havin' me on. Y' sound like true dinkum Ozzies t' me."

"Yeah well, that's cos we've been over here too long. We've got our vowels all fucked up," the perm nut replied.

"So, y' live in Ozzie?"

"Yep," Perm Nut reiterated, still nodding his head like the dog on the dash.

"Whereabouts do y' live?"

"Would y' believe ... Woolongong," replied the frizz nut, seeming embarrassed.

"What the hell are y' guys doin' in Woolongong? Isn't it suppose' t' be hell, the industrial capital 'f Australia?"

"Yep," said Perm Nut who just kept that head going like he was at an AC/DC concert.

"We're electricians 'n the money's good there," explained Frizz Nut.

"Hey, it means we're handy t' the coast 'n we can take trips like this, 'n the money's so much better than back home."

"Hey, I'm convinced!" I said, throwing up my hands all animated.

"Anyway, what gives you the right to hang out in such a great place?" asked Perm Nut.

"It's a long story."

"One of those, eh?" It was uncanny the way he maintained eye contact in the mirror.

"Yeah, it's a bit like that. If y' don't mind, I'll abstain from tellin' it right now."

"That's cool."

We were approaching Yaringa and the coast became visible. The guys started going all goo and gaa over the beauty of the coastline and its golden beaches and amazing rocky outcrops.

"Where are you guys plannin' on stayin'? Y' look like y've got all the gear?" I couldn't help noticing the back of the car was fully equipped for camping.

"We thought y' were puttin' us up," Frizz Nut said, turning to me and winking.

"I'd love t' but I'm stayin' at m' girlfriend's parents' place 'n they're not the most hospitable people y' likely t' come across."

"Yeah … we understand. I's only pullin' y' leg. We can camp wherever, just point us in the right direction."

We were right in the middle of the village now, and Perm Nut pulled up to the kerb. I was thinking I'd like to spend some more time with these guys.

"Look, I'll show y' a good campin' ground, 'n how about once y' set up we go f' a beer at the local. It's not a bad kind of place."

"Sounds cool, dude," enthused Perm Nut as Frizz Nut nodded in unison. They seemed like genuine guys, and it was the first time since being up in the mountains that I had felt genuinely relaxed in the company of others.

We drove to the better of the two holiday parks. There wasn't much between them, but the one I chose was handier to the shops, had a view out to sea, and was nicely laid out amongst the eucalyptus trees that dotted the park. They checked in at the reception desk and the guy in the office marked out on a map where their tent site was. I stayed and helped them unpack their tent.

"So what's y' name? I'm Stu," said Frizz Nut, "and this is Mal." He gestured to Perm Nut. "A couple of ex-pat Kiwis. How do y' like that! Of all the people we see on the road we pick up a Kiwi. What are the fuckin' odds 'f that, eh?" he exclaimed, laughing heartily.

"I'm Sam," I said, grinning and shaking hands. *My names suit y' better, but I'll keep that one under m' hat. I now declare you Frizz Nut 'n Perm Nut.*

"Nice one, Sam," said Stu, releasing my hand.

"Yeah, good one, Sam," chipped in Mal. "Let's get this tent up, eh, so we can fuck off 'n have a beer. I want t' see this local 'f yours."

Between the three of us the tent was up in no time, their blow-up beds inflated, sleeping bags placed on top, and all their cooking gear set up. In a flash we were back in the Holden heading to the local.

* * *

The Yaringa pub commanded a sweeping view of the bay and was set on the hill, tucked away from the rest of the village. It was a magnificent spot. Stu bought the first round, and we found a table outside on the deck, looking out to sea.

"Now this is what y' call livin'!" announced Mal as he sat down and took in the view.

"Damn right," responded Stu, clinking his glass against Mal's, then mine.

"Slainte," I said.

"Slainte!" Mal and Stu chorused. We gulped down mouthfuls of cold beer simultaneously, as though nothing in the world tasted better, and the moment felt perfect in its simplicity.

"So, Sam. How come y' get t' live in paradise?" Stu asked.

"Like I said, it's a long story. Do y' really want t' know?"

"Try us, we're all ears. We'll let y' know if y' boring us," joked Mal.

I took a deep breath and reluctantly launched into my story. I was pleasantly surprised by their willingness to listen without interrupting me.

"So there y' have it," I finished. "Be y' own judge."

"That's one whacko story," commented Stu.

"Don't mind me askin', but why didn't y' just do a big bunk t' Victoria 'n fly out 'f Melbourne 'n back t' NZ?" Mal asked.

"It did cross m' mind more than once, but I thought they might make a big deal out of it. I dunno … they could extradite me back here if they wanted t'. I just didn't know whether it was worth it. S'pose I didn't want t' worsen m' chances 'f gettin' off."

"But y' haven't gotten off, have y'? I mean, look, y've pleaded guilty 'n they'll prob'bly throw the book at y'!" said Mal, like a dog with a bone.

"Steady on, Mal," said Stu, staring daggers at him.

"Hey," Mal continued, shrugging his shoulders. "Y' know what the New South Wales cops are like."

"Yeah, but it's out 'f their hands now. It's with the courts," I reasoned.

"That's what I mean, they're all kangarooed 'round here. It's all scratchin' each other's backs type of shit. Y' know what I mean?" Mal said, looking at me as if I should know.

"Look, I've got a good lawyer 'n he's getting me a barrister f' the trial.

Apparently, he specialises in drug cases. Hey, I'm not the big fish here, just the young punk caught in the wrong place at the wrong time, if y' get m' drift!"

"Yeah, but it sounds like there are some big fish out there. The cops might use y' t' get to them."

"Maybe," I said. "Anyway, I've made up m' mind 'n I'm seein' it out. I'm too deep in it 'n I've been t' court twice already, so I'm in the system now. Maybe if I'd abandoned ship right at the start, I'd've felt okay about it."

"Right! Who's up for another drink?" Mal stood and grabbed our empty glasses.

"Too right," replied Stu, winking at me.

"Cheers, Mal," I said, smiling awkwardly.

"Back in a minute then," he said, walking off with the glasses in hand.

"Don't be bothered by him," Stu said, once Mal was out of earshot. "He hates the law 'n thinks the whole system here's corrupt. It probably is, but if y've got a good lawyer 'n the cops aren't goin' for y', then y' should be fine. We ain't experts on the law. It's just what we've observed. We smoke weed too, 'n know the New South Wales cops've got a rep f' singlin' out pot smokers. They're also known t' be bloody corrupt, though not as bad as the Queensland cops."

"Yeah," I know. "They say the Queensland cops are the worst." I tried to smile, but doubt was invading my mind. The discussion with Mal unnerved me more than I was willing to admit.

Mal turned up with three glasses of overflowing beer. "Rescue that glass f' me, would y', Sam." He had all three clustered between his hands in a triangle, and the single glass at the front was clearly slipping out of his fingers.

"No sweat." I saved it in the nick of time as it slipped a few more centimetres down his fingers.

"Here's t' you, Sam, 'n y' court case. Bring on that Sydney barrister!"

Stu announced. "He'll sort y' out." We clashed our glasses together enthusiastically and slurped back more beer. As we did so, a couple of attractive blonde girls with glasses of wine cooler sat down at the table next to ours. One was tall, like a beanpole, the other a little shorter. Both had great figures.

"Aft'rnoon, ladies," said Mal, raising his glass, smiling broadly.

"Hi," they chorused simultaneously, smiling and giggling awkwardly.

"So, y're from 'round here?"

"Just on holiday," the beanpole said, shooting him her best smile. Her face was dotted in acne, unsuccessfully disguised with make-up, but she had a nice smile and piercing green eyes.

Mal continued with his questions. "So where y' both from?"

"Albany," replied the beanpole.

"That's a long way t' come for a holiday," responded Mal.

"Our families come here every Christmas," said the shorter one, speaking for the first time.

"Do they? They've picked just about the best spot on the south coast, haven't they, boys?" said Mal, looking to us for encouragement.

"Whereabouts are you boys from?" the shorter one asked. She was softer spoken. I was unable to take my eyes off her. She was bloody gorgeous.

"We're all from New Zealand originally, but I live here, 'n these guys live in Woolongong," I answered without hesitation.

"New Zealand," said the beanpole. "I hear it's really beautiful over there. I've never been but I'd love to go."

"Sure, it's beautiful in its own way but so is Australia. I mean look at this," I said, gesturing towards the bay. "This is some 'f the most amazing coastline I've seen."

"The seasoned traveller speaks!" quipped Stu.

I sipped my beer, peering over the top of my glass at Mal as he continued with his attempt to wow the girls. I swallowed the dregs in my glass and stood up.

"My round, folks! Three more beers, 'n can I get anythin' f' the ladies?"

"No thanks," said the beanpole.

"Come on, don't be shy. It's not every day I buy drinks."

"Alright then," said the shorter one.

"Done, two wine coolers f' the ladies."

When I returned with a tray full of drinks, the girls were sitting at our table. Mal and Stu were taking it in turns to tell a funny story and the girls were laughing at every second word. I was impressed that they had made inroads, considering I'd only been at the bar five minutes. I placed the tray on the table and handed out the drinks. The shorter one gave me a melting smile as I passed her cooler across the table. I had the pleasure of shuffling myself onto the bench seat next to her where our knees touched and neither of us pulled away.

"Slainte," I said, raising my glass. Glasses were raised in unison and there was a chorus of "Slainte!"

Stu introduced me to the girls. "Sam, this is Claudia —" he nodded his head toward the beanpole "— and this is Erika." Mal had rapidly worked his magic on Claudia. She seemed very taken by him, laughing and smiling at everything he said. Erika was more reserved and much prettier, with an irresistible demeanour. Turns out they were staying with Erika's parents at the same motor camp as Mal and Stu. We finished our drinks, and I reluctantly asked the guys to drop me off at the house. Dinner would be ready soon and Val got tetchy if I didn't show up. It wasn't worth the hassle to be late.

***

Inside the house it was the usual scene: Ted at the breakfast bar, knocking back his umpteenth whisky; Val's shrill voice penetrating all available ears; the smell of cigarette smoke permeating the air; the drone of the telly in the background screening *Sale of the Century*, with Tim firmly planted in his La-Z-Boy.

"Hi," I said, sticking my head in the kitchen. Ted poured me a whisky, which I gratefully accepted as I plonked myself down on the bar stool beside him.

"Cheers, Ted," I said, raising the amber liquid to my lips. We talked about their trip to New Zealand, only two days away now. They'd fly to Sydney and from there to Christchurch, where they'd stay with my parents for a few days, before travelling to see Tania in her new place, then they'd travel round the South Island together.

"What's the summer like? Is it hot? Not as hot as here, I suppose. Does it get cold at this time of the year? Will we need winter clothing? Tell us some good places to visit besides Queenstown, Sam." And so it went with Ted's questions, the same ones he had asked a few days ago, and last week, and the week before that.

After dinner I excused myself, saying I was going for a walk on the beach. The air outside was still sweltering, like a fan oven set on high, even with the sun now low in the sky glowing like a huge orange ball suspended in mid-air. Cockatoos screeched in the eucalyptus trees as they danced from branch to branch. Occasionally one would fly out and circle the tree with white wings spread wide. A lone kookaburra perched on a lower branch laughed as I walked by. I passed the bowling club, where Ted would end up within the hour, already full of patrons. It was the most frequented premises in the bay. I crossed the road to the motor camp and made my way between caravans and tents to Stu and Mal's site.

As I approached, I noticed the two sitting outside their tent, and

I was happy to see that Claudia and Erika were with them.

"Hey, it's Sam!" Stu cried out as I came closer.

"Hi, guys," I said, trying to be casual.

"Fancy a beer, Sam?" Mal was reaching into a red Esky.

"Sure, why not?"

"Fosters is all we've got," he said, tossing me a can.

"Perfect." I caught it and cautiously pulled the tab back, hoping it wasn't going to blow all over me as Mal watched in anticipation. Sure enough, it blew everywhere, and some froth landed on Erika's beautifully exposed leg. She was wearing the shortest of shorts. I impulsively went to rub it off, apologising profusely, then realised I was taking liberties by rubbing the beer off her leg, but felt relieved when she didn't seem to mind in the slightest. Mal and Stu roared with laughter, entertained by the smallest of practical jokes.

"Sorry, I knew it was goin' t' blow everywhere. I just didn't expect it t' reach that far," I said to Erika.

"I think you've got it all off now," she said, smiling cheekily.

We sat there drinking and talking well into the night. The campground went quiet as most people turned in, our voices the only sound cutting through the night's stillness.

"We should head down t' the beach 'n light a fire," I suggested, hoping someone might be interested.

"Mate, y're full 'f good ideas, aren't y'?" said Stu. "I'm up f' it."

"I don't know … think I might just have 'nother drink here 'n turn in," responded Mal, reaching into the Esky for another can of Fosters, instantly opening it and putting it to his lips.

"I like fires on the beach. I'd like to come down," said Erika in her soft voice.

"Are you coming down, Claudia?" Erika asked.

Claudia took a moment to respond, staring at the ground before replying. She looked up and calmly announced, "Think I'm going to stay here."

I wasn't surprised, having witnessed the chemistry that had been going on between Mal and her since they first clapped eyes on each other. Mal had worked overtime to make an impression on her. I half expected Erika to change her mind.

"Right then," I said, standing up. "Let's get down t' the beach."

Erika, Stu and I slinked our way in silence through the campground, then stumbled through the growth and small dunes onto the beach. A half-moon gleamed on the dark sea, spilling a beam of light from far out in the bay all the way to the shore, like a powerful flashlight. We began gathering driftwood from the high-water mark, along with spindly bits of dry tinder and twigs. Our job was made a whole lot easier by the moonlight, and soon we had built a fire that was ready to light. I removed a lighter from my pocket and ignited it amongst the tinder bushes, which instantly crackled and popped above my lighter's flame, quickly setting the material ablaze. As the smaller bits of kindling caught alight, we added bigger pieces until we had a raging fire. The yellow and orange flames licked at the night, sending thousands of small sparks up into the air.

Stu magically extracted a couple of Fosters from one of the pockets of his hoody, handing one to me and another to Erika. He pulled a third one out of the other pocket and cracked it.

"Great fire, Sam," he said, toasting the flames before slurping back his beer.

"Cheers." As I sipped, I watched Erika out of the corner of my eye and noticed her looking directly at me, her eyes dancing with the reflection of the flames. It was obvious Stu was interested in Erika too. Why wouldn't he be? She was well worth the interest, and I had no reason to begrudge him that. She handled herself well, not playing any games as far as I could detect, and I had a distinct sense that she preferred me.

Stu suddenly stood up, stretched his arms above his head, and let out a loud groan. "I think that's it f' me, I'm headin' f' the sack. What about you folks?" All I could see was the reflection of the fire in the lenses of his glasses, so I couldn't read his face at all, even with the moon out it was too dark, and we'd let the fire die right down to small flames.

"I think I'll watch the fire die out," I replied as casually as I could, feeling excited by the prospect of his departure. "I'm quite enjoying being down on the beach, still … don't often do this."

"Me too," Erika chimed in. I was gobsmacked, half expecting her to leave with Stu and return to her parents' campsite. I wanted to fist-pump the air. How sick was that, and for such a small victory.

"Right then. Guess I'll see y's in the morrow somewhere. Adios."

"Night," I replied. "See y' tomorrow."

He walked off showing no sign of disappointment, sand squelching underfoot as he trudged into the dark, eaten up slowly by the night.

I sat there with Erika, mesmerised by the sound of his fading footsteps, gazing into the small flames that remained of the fire.

"Just the two 'f us now," I said, stating the obvious then feeling really stupid.

"Wish I'd brought a rug down, I'm feeling really cold," said Erika. She threw me with the unexpected immediacy and suggestion of her words. I got up, gathered more wood and built the fire up. "I thought you were going to watch the fire burn down?" She giggled self-consciously as I sat back down next to her.

"I was but I thought y' were cold." She shuffled her bum across the small distance between us until she was right beside me, and she put her arm around me, pulling herself in even closer. Her forwardness surprised me. Nonetheless, I impulsively wrapped my arm around her, pulling her into me. I looked at her face and into her eyes. They were large and full of anticipation. Our lips met, lightly at first, then with greater urgency, kissing each other as though our lives depended on it. Teeth gnashed against teeth as we bruised our lips. Her tongue found its way to the back of my throat and my own tongue lacerated her tonsils with equal force. In no time my hand became bold enough to venture beneath her tight top, and I wasn't disappointed by the feel of her breasts — soft but firm with wonderful, erect nipples, begging to be kissed. We were half-naked now. I could feel the flames warming my exposed flesh. I could feel the warmth and softness of Erika's skin, the smoothness of her thighs. I found her mound as she pushed it up against the palm of my hand, my fingers finding her irresistible wetness, which in turn increased my hardness. Erika's hand seemed to find me with great ease as she removed my shorts, exposing my arse to the fire. She slipped me inside her. The sensation was a joy worth crying out for as she groaned with her own pleasure. As her crying out increased, I was convinced that the whole township could hear us. I exploded inside her with a shudder and a trembling of my body that I'd not felt before, and although I wanted to be responsible and pull out, I was compelled to stay. Some other force had taken over and I was hovering above, watching. I could hear my own crying out joining with hers as she climaxed, her cries matching mine. Spent, we lay there in each other's arms as if we'd been lovers for some time.

I awoke to the sun blazing down on us, cocooned in each other's bodies, still half-naked. I heard a dog bark and looked up to see a woman walking our way with a dog bounding at her side, expectantly waiting for her to throw the stick. Erika hadn't stirred. She was sleeping, peacefully snuggled up against my chest. I lay there with my face propped up on my hand, watching the woman and dog moving closer, thinking it was amazing the difference a day could make. The dog barked again, causing

Erika to stir, then wake.. She lay there, taking in her surroundings, then suddenly sat up, looking petrified. She reached for her jeans and began pulling them on.

"My parents are going to kill me! I'm in trouble. I'm in trouble," she kept muttering as she kissed me briefly before standing up. "I'll see you round," and she was gone, running off down the beach in the direction of the motor camp.

You stupid idiot, Sam. Of course she needed t' be back in the mornin'. I pulled my own clothes back on and lay there, soaking up the warmth of the sun, reflecting on the night, feeling warm and fuzzy inside. Right now, nothing could destroy the beautiful feeling inside me.

* * *

I arrived back at the house to find Ted and Val waiting outside with their suitcases. Ted's mate, John, from the bowling club, was taking them to the airport.

"There you are! Where on earth have you been? You know we're leaving today," Ted said, agitated and gasping on his cigarette.

"Sorry," I mumbled.

"We've got problems. Tim doesn't want to come on the plane."

"He won't come out of his room," Val whined. Ted stood there, dragging heavily on his cigarette.

"Well, he'll have t' stay then, won't he, or you'll miss y' plane," I stated.

"But he's meant to be coming with us," Val whined some more.

"Alright, I'll go 'n see what I can do." I didn't expect to achieve much, but I had a better chance than either of them.

I found Tim in bed, hiding under the covers. "What's the problem, Tim?"

"No problem," came his muffled reply.

"Y' mum 'n dad are outside waitin' f' y'."

"Not goin'." He rolled over, pulling the bed covers even tighter around him.

"Why don't y' come out so I can see y' … then I can hear y' properly, 'n we can talk about this better. If y' really want t' stay, y' can."

"Come on, Tim!" Val's shrill voice carried up to his room. "John's waiting to take us to the airport. We'll miss our damn plane if you don't come now."

Who'd want t' go on holiday with that voice? I'd be beggin' Tim f' his medication if I had t' cope with four weeks 'f that. I could do with some right now.

"I'm not comin'," came his voice from below the blankets.

"Don't y' want t' see Tania?"

"No!" Tim shouted. I opened the window and called out, "He says he's not comin'. I think y'd better go."

"That's just ridiculous," hissed Val. "We've paid for his tickets and he's all packed."

"Well, he ain't goin' t' come unless y' carry 'im, 'n he might put up a fight. They won't let y' on the plane with him resistin', will they?"

"Come on, Val, let's go. Sam's right, we can't force him. If he's changed his mind, then that's just the way it is. You know he's not well." Ted flicked his cigarette butt into the garden and took Val by the arm, coercing her into the car.

"He'll be fine with me," I called out in reassurance.

Ted waved as he climbed in next to Val. John was already sitting in the car, wisely keeping out of the whole affair. He started the engine, clunked it into reverse and backed out of the driveway. I stood at the window giving one last wave and the car was gone.

"Y' can come out now. They're gone, no one t' hassle y' f' a month 'cept me."

"Don't want t' come out."

"Suit y' self, the cricket's on at ten. New Zealand versus Australia. Reckon we'll give y' a run f' y' money."

"Bullshit." The duvet was thrown back and his hairy face appeared, grinning wildly like a deranged monkey.

"I'm starvin'," I said. "Want some breakfast?"

In the kitchen I made myself a bowl of cereal then went to sit in the lounge and flicked the telly on. The cricket hadn't started yet. There was an infomercial on, so I changed to another channel only to be confronted by a similar infomercial. That was enough for me to switch the telly off altogether. I sat there eating my cereal, thinking of Erika, wondering if she'd gotten in trouble with her parents. The door opened and Tim walked in. He plonked himself down in his favourite armchair without saying a word. A smug smile spread across his face, just visible beneath his big, hairy beard.

"Y' seem pleased with y'self. Didn't y' want t' go t' New Zealand? It's a great place, y' know."

"Not when I'm hangin' out with m' olds, it ain't."

"Well, I guess that's the truth. I can't imagine travellin' with 'em either, not y' mother anyway. But y'll have t' b'have y'self here. I've got zero tolerance f' bad behaviour."

"Yeah right! Who's the one that's in the shit!"

"Hey! That's a bit b'low the belt." Tim made a snorting noise, a cross between a distorted laugh and a snigger.

I finished my cereal and switched the telly back on. Cricket commentator Richie Benaud was on, discussing the pitch and how it would play. The captains hadn't come out to do the toss yet, so it was all up in the air who was going to bat first.

"I'm goin' f' a swim," I announced to Tim.

"Not hot enough f' me," Tim mumbled under his beard.

Once out of the house, I ducked into the garage downstairs, put on my swimming shorts and grabbed my towel. I passed the bowling club. The greenskeeper, whom I'd only ever waved to but never spoken to, was out rolling the greens in preparation for the oldies' afternoon bowls session. I raised my hand and waved. He waved back as if we were long-time friends. I continued to the beach, thinking how odd it was that one could be so familiar with someone on one level but never bother to take it any further. I decided that next time we passed close by, I'd say hello and stop for a chat.

On the beach there were many people baking in the sun, while others were in the water swimming between the yellow-and-red flags put out by the surf lifesavers. I scanned the beach for any sign of Mal, Stu or Erika, to no avail. Disappointed, I dropped my towel in the sand and went down to the water, wading out through broken surf. I dived into a breaking wave and came up on the other side, clutching myself as though I'd just dived into ice cubes. Strange how the water could be so cold sometimes, even in the middle of summer. The surf was breaking beautifully with a nice, even swell of about two metres. I caught the next good-looking wave, which broke perfectly as I raced halfway down before angling my body across to the right, the way it was naturally breaking, then I cut back to the left before going straight ahead. That's when I noticed Claudia in the water, so I let the wave carry me in. Just as I was getting close to her, I dived under so that I could surprise her from below by grabbing her legs. She jumped and hopped and thrashed about before I came up for air to the sounds of her scream.

"Hi, it's me … I thought y' look'd like y' need'd a hand t' get under."

"Bastard! That wasn't funny at all."

"From where I'm standin' it's real funny."

"I thought y' were havin' an epileptic fit, like a shark had got a grip on y'," Mal spouted, appearing from nowhere, then falling backwards into the water, playing the jester.

Claudia laughed loudly, then turned to me. "What did you and Erika get up to?"

"Me 'n Erika? What d' y' mean?"

"Last night … She's grounded for the rest of the day because she didn't make it home last night. Her dad woke early this morning and found her bed empty, unslept in."

"Well, didn't she say she slept in your tent?"

"She tried that. The trouble is that her father woke me up to see if Erika was with me."

"Y' been up t' no good, Sam?" Mal chipped in, giving me a wind-up.

"Nothin' you haven't been up t'," I replied, an involuntary grin spreading across my face.

"That doesn't leave a lot t' the imagination, does it?" He pushed me backwards and dramatically I fell into a breaking wave. I left Mal and Claudia on the beach, eating each other's mouths off, feeling annoyed with myself because Erika and I had fallen asleep on the beach.

* * *

Upstairs, Tim was in his armchair, sitting poker-faced, glued to the telly.

"How long's it been goin'?" I asked.

"Half an hour," he replied, quite matter-of-fact. Australia were batting and still without loss of a wicket. Worse though, was that they'd piled on quite a few runs in the short time they'd been in.

"Jesus, that's an ominous start," I remarked. Tim said nothing, as if the silence was comment enough. I went to the kitchen and made myself four pieces of toast, two with vegemite, two with jam.

"Want a cup 'f tea?" I yelled to Tim.

"Yes, thanks."

I took the cups of tea into the lounge and put Tim's on the side table next to his easy chair. I placed mine on the side table next to my easy chair. The chairs and side tables were matching, one was Val's and the other Ted's, but they hardly used them, being more interested in sitting around the breakfast bar drinking.

"Where's my toast?" asked Tim, glaring at me.

"I'm not y' fuckin' servant, so the sooner y' understand that the better off we'll be for the next few weeks!"

"Keep y' pants on. Y' were making toast anyway, I just thought y' could've offered."

"Like I said, I don't want t' start any bad habits. Y'll end up expectin' toast 'n tea every mornin', and next minute y'll want it in bed."

"Don't expect me t' bring y' treats when y' locked up 'n they throw away the key. Those Ozzie crims like a bit 'f Kiwi bacon on the side."

I was across the floor and on him before he knew what had struck. He put his arms up to fend me off but was too slow. I dragged him out of his chair and onto the floor. In the act of pulling him out of his chair, I fell backwards, finding myself on the floor with Tim on top of me, pulling hard on my hair. I was cursing him, and he was mumbling stuff I couldn't understand. I tried to muscle him off me without success, as he was stronger than I'd expected; his muscle mass hadn't turned to jelly yet. I settled for his beard, which had become quite long and dense, a statement he was making to piss Val off — the more she commented on it, the more he took pleasure in growing it. I was grateful though, as it gave me something to hang onto. We were like a couple of girls having a catfight. I kept pulling at his beard in the hope he'd let go, and he kept pulling my hair knowing it was the only chance he had of keeping things even. With one almighty effort I managed to roll him off me, but he still wouldn't let go of my hair.

"This is fuckin' stupid!" I yelled. "Look, I'll let go 'f y' beard if y' let go 'f m' hair."

Suddenly I could hear the animated voice of a commentator on the telly: "He's gone! Clean bowled by Hadlee … that's a very good wicket!"

The news prompted Tim to loosen his grip and allow me to move away from him. I was panting heavily from the exertion and the adrenalin running through me. Tim slowly pulled his body off the floor. I slumped back into my chair and watched him make his way back to his. We sat there watching the cricket for the next couple of hours without saying a word.

As the temperature rose, it became unbearable, even indoors. I had to leave for another swim. I'd lost interest in the cricket. The Kiwis had managed to haul the Ozzies back a bit, but the score looked like a difficult one to overtake. I succeeded in talking Tim into coming down to the beach with me, slightly regretting that I'd flown off the handle, that I'd not been able to take a bit of his verbal flack. At least he was interacting with me. I should've been grateful.

19

Billie

Tim shuffled his legs along the road to the beach, looking every bit the arthritic old man. Only closer inspection would reveal his youth. The heat rose off the asphalt in hazy waves as if the air were melting. It was crowded on the beach. People had spilled out of their houses, caravans and tents to cool off. As I surveyed the scene, I spotted Stu and Mal sunning themselves, not ten metres from us.

"Bloody hot enough, ain't it?" I said, sneaking up behind them.

"Eh?" Stu turned in surprise. "Oh hey … yeah." He was looking directly at Tim as if he were a freak.

"This is Tim," I said. "I live with him 'n 'is parents."

"Oh, right. How's it goin'?" Stu offered his hand which Tim limply shook.

"Hey, Tim, I'm Mal." Tim reached across Stu and repeated the limp handshake.

"The girls are in the water," Mal said, nodding towards the sea. I scanned the water for a glimpse of them, making out two blonde-headed bodies amidst the many others jumping in the waves. "That's where we're heading. Too hot t' sit on the beach," Mal added.

I dumped my towel and gestured for Tim to do the same, then I headed to the water. He traipsed after me. I waded through the shallows until it was deep enough to dive in and swiftly made my way to Erika and Claudia. Erika caught sight of me and waved exuberantly.

"Hello," she said, looking radiant in the golden sunlight. Without hesitation, she came right up to me and kissed me fair on the lips.

"Did y' get int' trouble over last night?" I asked, looking around, half expecting Tim to bob up in the water next to me.

"Hi, Sam," Claudia said, swimming over to us.

"Hi, Claudia. How are y?"

"Good thanks. Think I'm going to get out, I'll leave you two to it." She grinned at Erika and waded back through the surf towards the beach.

"I'll be up soon," Erika called after her. "It was nothing too serious," she said, turning back to me and putting her arms around my neck. "Dad's quite strict and particular, he's German you see. He grounded me for breaking the rules, then today as it got hotter, he softened up, letting me come down the beach with Claudia to swim … and I was hoping I'd see you down here." She kissed me then pulled away. "Who's y' friend?" She nodded towards Tim, hovering in the sea close by.

"Oh, that's Tim, he's the son 'f the family I live with. They've gone on holiday t' New Zealand 'n left 'im here with me. Sounds strange, doesn't it?"

"Yes," she said, nodding her head.

"Well, y' see, he was committed t' a mental hospital 'cause some people thought he was unstable. Perhaps he is, but I don't think so. He's drugged up t' the eyeballs now, so I wouldn't know. I didn't know 'im before … I've only known 'im in this state." I didn't want to reveal the full truth of Tim's story.

"Oh … sounds complicated."

"He's a good guy. I like 'im, harmless as a fly … well, almost." I smiled. Tim had drifted over so I introduced him. "Tim, this is Erika. Erika, Tim."

"Hi, Tim, pleased to meet you," she said, smiling warmly.

"Nice t' meet y' too," responded Tim, all polite and articulate. Usually, he muttered something undecipherable under his breath. The three of us walked out of the water together to sit on the beach with the others.

"Cool drinks at our house," I proposed, "and the bonus is the cricket's on!"

"The cricket! Fuck, is it? Thought it was t'morrow," said Stu. "I'm in." He looked to Mal who was busy snogging Claudia. "Guess it'll be just me." He shrugged his shoulders nonchalantly.

"I'm in too," piped Erika quickly.

"Right then, let's get out 'f this heat."

"Where y'all goin'?" asked Mal all of a sudden, having disentangled his lips from Claudia's.

"Cool drinks 'n cricket at Sam 'n Tim's," said Stu. "Y' were too busy feedin' y' face t' notice."

"Sounds like the best idea I've heard all day," Mal said.

"Really? Thought y' had far more interestin' things planned," Stu quipped sarcastically.

* * *

Tim had already started back to the house. I led everyone across the hot bitumen road and down the side of the bowling club, the green now dotted with bowlers all dressed up in their whites, pitching their balls down the green towards the jack. Back at the house, I offered our guests the opportunity to take showers downstairs, but no one was interested, so I skipped my ritual and led them upstairs. It was difficult to tell whether Tim was happy to have guests or not, his face characteristically devoid of emotion. He switched the telly back on. New Zealand were batting. We hadn't been in long and the score was fifteen without loss. The lounge was a good size, seating everyone comfortably.

I left them there and went into the kitchen to forage for drinks. Fortunately, the fridge was well provisioned with food, juice and beer. Val must've been worried that I'd starve, or more likely, she wanted to create a good impression for Oma and Opa, though they weren't due for a few days yet. I pulled a large carton of juice out of the fridge, found ice cubes in the freezer, and a set of matching glasses in the cupboard. I threw a couple of cubes of ice in each glass and poured the juice in, which crackled and popped as the ice rose to the surface.

I was almost done when Erika came in with a wry smile on her face. "Aren't you the perfect host?"

"Have I overlooked somethin'?"

"Maybe ..."

"There's biscuits 'n crackers in the cupb—" Erika suddenly put a finger to my lips then replaced her finger with her lips.

"Where's that bloody cold drink, Sam? I'm parched as an old buzzard," Stu called out, causing Erika to pull away.

"It's comin'!" I called back, annoyed, not wanting to end the moment. She looked at me and shrugged, then picked up two of the glasses and marched into the lounge.

We sat in the lounge all afternoon, Claudia curled up on the couch with Mal looking like he had a permanent hard-on as she continually massaged the inside of his thigh. Stu talked about skydiving, obviously trying to impress Erika, who was giving him her full attention. Tim remained transfixed by the telly, semi-reclined in his easy chair, seemingly uninterested in anything that was going on around him, yet I was quite certain that he wasn't missing a beat. Erika was telling Stu how she loved flying and wanted to be an air hostess. Stu was telling her that it would be a great career because she'd get to see so much of the world.

I stood and sauntered back to the kitchen. I was bored and wanted everyone to leave so I could have Erika all to myself. I opened the fridge and gazed into it, not really knowing what I was looking for. I decided to go downstairs and have my shower. Just as I was about to head out the back door, there was a loud, repetitive knock on the front door. I wasn't expecting anyone and most of Ted and Val's friends knew they were away for a few weeks. I opened the door to find Billie's face grinning at me.

"Made it down at last," he said, offering a hand, which I grasped affectionately, feeling surprised but pleased to see him.

"I don't fuckin' believe it!"

"Y' better," he replied, grinning from ear to ear. "Aren't y' goin' t' ask me in?"

"Course I am … come in, come in. I've got visitors at the moment, so come 'n meet them." I guided him into the lounge. "Everyone, this is a mate 'f mine, Billie. We worked together up the mountain durin' the ski season."

"Hi, Billie. Stu's m' name."

"Howdy," responded Billie, reaching out a hand.

"Mal. Pleased t' meet y'," Mal said, getting off the couch to shake his hand.

"Likewise," said Billie.

"I'm Erika."

"Nice name, Erika."

"And I'm Claudia."

"And that's Tim," I said, pointing to him sitting in the corner in the easy chair. Billie went over and shook his hand.

"Hey, Tim."

"Fancy a drink?" I asked.

"Bit early in the day f' me," he said.

"I meant a cup 'f tea, or a juice?"

"Yeah, a cup 'f tea'd be great."

"Whereabouts have y' come from, Billie?" asked Stu, the most social of the bunch.

"I drove down from Cooma. It's up on the tablelands on the way t' the Snowy Mountains. M' sister lives up there near Nimmitabel."

"What do y' do up there?"

"A bit 'f this … a bit 'f that. I suppose y' could call me a wheeler 'n dealer. Ain't that right, Sammy?" He slapped me on the back waiting for my reply.

"Yep, that's right, Billie," I said, cringing, hoping he wasn't going to reveal his true colours.

Billie was a good man with a big heart who hobbled when he walked from contracting polio while he was inside. He pulled his trouser leg up once and showed me the steel brace that supported the outside of his leg all the way up to his knee. The brace was connected to his boot, which had a built-up inner sole.

"Where's that cup 'f tea y' were offerin' me?" he asked.

"Comin' right up." Billie followed me into the kitchen and sat in Ted's spot at the breakfast bar.

"Those girls are right pretty, Sam. I hope y' gettin' a piece 'f the action," he whispered, winking at me. I smiled as I filled the kettle with water and switched it on.

"I drove past the prison y'll probably be endin' up in. It's quite handy t' my place, so I'll be able t' come 'n visit y'."

"Keep it down! The girls don't know about that stuff … 'n besides, I ain't goin' t' prison."

"Then it's time they did know. What y' hidin' from? Are y' worried they won't like y' anymore, worried y' won't be able t' pork that nice-lookin' Erika?"

"Her parents are German."

"What's that suppose' t' mean?" he asked, taking a bite of an apple he'd snaffled from the fruit bowl.

"I dunno …"

"So can we do a pipe in here?" He pulled out a pouch from his shirt pocket and opened it to reveal a small wooden pipe. "Brings back memories, eh? All those chilly months up the mountains. Eh, boy? Christ, I've never felt the cold like I did up there. I'm use' t' the tropics. But I must say, I had a bloody good time." He extracted himself from the bar stool and stood in the archway to the lounge. "Anyone for a pipe?" He waved the pipe in the air above his head as if he were taunting a small child.

"I'll be in," I heard Stu say.

"Count me in," Mal said.

"What about you girls?" Billie persisted.

"I'd like to try," said Erika quietly.

"I guess I'll try too," Claudia chimed in.

"Well, Tim? It is Tim, isn't it?" He glanced at me for confirmation. "That leaves you. Are y' goin' t' be the odd man out?" Tim mumbled something indecipherable. "Everyone's in then!" Billie returned to the breakfast bar looking as pleased as Punch and began preparing the pipe. I was concerned that Tim was going to participate, the last thing I needed was him going nuts.

"You're not goin' t' get those girls stoned with y' weed, are y'? They'll be on their backs f' a week!" I said.

"That wouldn't be so bad now." Billie laughed, winking at me.

Billie entered the lounge with the packed pipe. I followed and stood in the archway watching.

"Ladies first," he said, handing it to Erika. She put it to her mouth. Billie flicked his lighter on and held the flame above the pipe. She drew her breath in, and the flame was sucked down into the bowl of the pipe. "I reckon y' got the lot," said Billie, sounding impressed.

He took the pipe from her as she continued to hold the smoke in and went back to the kitchen bar to repack it. Erika slowly blew the smoke out, like a professional. He returned and gave the pipe to Claudia who took it without hesitation, putting it to her mouth. Billie went through his ritual again. Eventually we all had some and everyone was in the lounge smashed off their nut, talking about the most insignificant shit, laughter filling the room.

The cricket was still playing on the telly, although we'd turned the sound off long ago. Tim was sitting in his easy chair, not participating, just being there, with the same emotionless expression on his face. *I wonder if the dope affects him? It must play havoc with his mind. He must be thinkin' all sorts of weird shit right now. I bet he'd like t' have his way with one 'f the girls.* Tim was looking at the girls with glazed eyes, shadowed beneath his bushy eyebrows.

"Fancy a walk?" Billie muttered in my ear. I was sprawled on the floor next to him. Erika had taken the liberty of snuggling up behind me, and I could feel her thighs warming the backs of mine. I was reluctant to move, but Billie had come down specially to see me.

"Sure," I replied. "Though it's still pretty hot out there."

"Don't mind the heat. I'm use' t' it from livin' in Darwin."

"We can always go t' the pub if it gets too hot," I said.

"I'm known t' be partial to a schooner or three, y' know," said Billie as I reluctantly disentangled myself from Erika and stood up. I felt quite lethargic from the smoke and my legs were like jelly.

"You're all welcome t' stay," I said. "Might catch y's later, eh?"

* * *

Billie hobbled beside me along my usual path to the beach. As we were about to cross the road, a VW Kombi pulled up in front of us. It was Bruce.

"Hey, Sam, how's it?"

"Not bad," I replied. "This is a friend 'f mine, Billie. Billie, meet Bruce."

"Gidday, Bruce," Billie said, thrusting his arm through the window. "Nice Kombi y' got here. What is it, seventy-six or earlier?"

"It's a seventy-four. Yeah, it's pretty good … well decked out … eighteen-hundred engine."

"Really! I didn't know they made an eighteen hundred."

"Yeah. Hey, nice seein' you guys, but I got t' get goin'. Sam, we should catch up soon. Y' know where I am."

"Sure." He roared off down the road and we crossed to the beach.

"Haven't we met before?" Billie asked.

"Y' might've. He was up the mountain f' a weekend sellin' his wares 'n skiing on my pass. He would've had a session in the lodge with us. In fact, I know he did, but I can't remember if y' were there or not."

We sat at the edge of the beach under the shade of a large tree. The sun was ridiculously hot, but people still crowded the beach near the surf club. Guys were out in the water on boards, catching waves, and girls lay topless on their towels working on their tans. We sat there admiring the variety of shapes and sizes on display.

"So how's he been since y' dobbed 'im in?" Billie asked.

"What?" I elbowed him in the ribs. He pushed me away with his oversized hand and grinned at me.

"I told y' I went past where they'll be sendin' y' on my way down here, didn't I?" He said casually. "I'll take y' f' a drive past there if y' like."

"Thanks very much! Charmin' support, aren't y'?"

"Seriously, what's the story with this Bruce character? Has he made any threats against y'?"

"No, not really. Just that if I do anythin' that points the finger beyond him, he'll be comin' after me. Or more to the point, he reckons 'they'll' be comin' after me."

"Who's 'they'?" Billie enquired.

"His suppliers, I guess."

"So he's been gettin' his oil off someone up in Sydney, I s'pose? He wouldn't want them knowin' he's been busted. He's probably hopin' that he's far 'nough away that no one will read about what's happen'd t' him. I'd say he's fairly harmless, just wants t' keep the heat on y'. Y' can pretty much guarantee he's not told the guys he's dealin' with up there about any 'f this. My guess is that he's cool'd it with them for now … isn't buyin' any more shit off them."

"So y' don't think he's goin' t' do a hit on me, not goin' t' tie bricks t' me 'n drop me off some bridge int' a bottomless river?" I said, feeling all anxious and paranoid.

"He might … but I doubt it." Billie grinned and whacked me gently around the back of the head. "Fancy a cold one up at the local?"

"Why not," I replied. We walked across the beach through the sea of eye candy, making a closer inspection of the topless beauties basking in the sun, frying themselves with baby oil, all for the sake of a tan. Billie made hard work of hobbling in the sand, ensuring the view would last longer.

* * *

Billie stayed for a couple of nights, during which time I didn't see the others much. I found his company reassuring. He knew my greatest fear was winding up in prison, and he made light of my predicament. I needed that. He left the morning Oma and Opa were due to arrive.

"Worse comes t' worse 'n y' still 'round after the trial, I'll come 'n visit y'. Y'll be just up the road then. I'll bring y' a case 'f Vaseline."

"Y're fuckin' good t' me, aren't y'!" He embraced me with his incredibly strong arms, got in his car, tooted, and was gone. I stood there waving as an emptiness washed over me, my future as uncertain as the wind.

I went into the basement garage, grabbed my towel, and walked down to the beach for a swim. There I spotted Erika and Claudia sunning themselves in the same fashion as all the other girls — topless and oiled up.

"Hey," I said, dropping into the golden sand beside Erika.

"Hey," she said sitting up. "Where's your friend?"

"Which one?"

"Billie," said Erika.

"He's gone, left just now f' Cooma."

"You seem upset."

"S'pose I am a bit."

"Stu and Mal told us about your situation yesterday."

"Did they now …"

"Why didn't you talk to me about it?" Erika asked.

"I didn't want y' t' think the worst 'f me."

"But I don't. I think it's terrible what happened. I want to be able to help you. I just don't know how."

"That's great!" I snapped as I stood up and stripped off my T-shirt. I stomped my way down the beach with determined strides, wading through the water up to my waist before diving in. *What right do Stu 'n Mal have t' go tellin' others about m' fuck'n situation! Least 'f all Erika!* I stayed in the water for what seemed like an eternity, catching wave after wave, trying to get rid of my anger.

I saw Erika enter the water and make her way out to me. I wanted to maintain my annoyance but knew I couldn't since she actually seemed to care about me. I caught a wave and rode it to her. Jumping up and grabbing her, I pulled her down into the next wave, where we resurfaced together in the bubbling white foam. She hit me softly, then hugged me with great intensity. We stood there embracing, kissing passionately as the waves buffeted us. Eventually we made it back to our beach towels and lay down, letting the heat of the sun dry us off.

"It's too hot f' me," I said, unable to endure the heat anymore. "I'm goin' back t' the house. Want t' come?"

"Yes. Claudia, I'm going back with Sam," she announced.

"Okay," Claudia said, not moving from where she lay. "Have fun."

* * *

The main road was a constant stream of traffic with people arriving to spend the day at the beach or set up camp. We passed the bowling club where the greenskeeper was on his automated roller going up and down the green once more, preparing the ground for the afternoon bowling tournament. At the house, I eagerly led Erika into the garage where I tossed my towel on a bathroom hook. "I need a shower. Want t' have one with me?"

"Sure," she said, smiling her sweet smile. I stepped into the shower and turned the setting to get the temperature just right, holding my hand under the spray of water to test it. The shower had a large, old-fashioned, round nozzle that hung right over the middle of the shower floor. It had great pressure and I often prolonged my shower, just dreaming away. Not this time, though. I took Erika's hand and gently pulled her in with me.

She clasped me around the waist and drew me to her. Instantly we were at each other's mouths. I clumsily untied her bikini top and let it drop to the shower floor to reveal her breasts. I needed to taste them and placed the nipple of one in my mouth, causing her to sensuously arch her back in pleasure. My hand travelled down the front of her bikini brief and my fingers excitedly entered her. She pulled away and tugged at my swimming shorts until she had them off my waist, then she fell to her knees and took me in her mouth. Before long I came with one big explosion, bracing myself against the wall of the shower as my knees buckled. The shower continued its flow of warm water, washing over us as Erika rose to her feet, rising to kiss me. I could taste me in her mouth. I could feel her desire. I removed her bikini brief, sliding it down her thighs, letting it drop carelessly. I worked several fingers inside her, and she gasped as I built her up. It didn't take me long to get her full repertoire of moans, by which time I had rediscovered my own desire and eased her gently up against the shower wall, lifting her high enough so I could slip inside. She came within a few short thrusts, her excitement bringing me to another climax. Spent, we stood beneath the shower, holding each other tight as the water cascaded over us.

"I never want t' let y' go, my love," I said.

After a while, we emerged from the shower. I had to get ready to report to the station and to pick up Oma and Opa who were arriving on the late afternoon bus as the last stage of their journey from Sydney. They were catching the train to Nowra, then continuing by bus to Wodyn. I'd arranged with the police station to report in during the early afternoon on this particular day.

"Does that mean I won't be able to come around any more?" Erika asked.

"No 'f course not. Why do y' say that?"

"You know, grandparents are funny about that sort of thing. Mine are anyway."

"Really? Well don't y' worry, cos mine aren't."

"Okay, I'll see you later then." We kissed, gently at first, then urgently as if hoping to extract something out of the kiss to take away. Erika had tears running down her cheeks.

"What's the matter, babe?"

"Nothing," she said, wiping the tears away with the back of her hand. "I'm just being silly. Everything's going to be alright for you, isn't it?"

20

Oma & Opa

I borrowed Tim's Valiant to collect Oma and Opa at the bus stop. First, I drove Erika back to the motor camp, where she kissed me quickly and was gone. I watched her run between the rows of caravans. She was the most beautiful girl I'd ever had the pleasure of being with. It was a relief to be able to drive into town instead of relying on my usual hitching. This way, I would have some time to myself before meeting Oma and Opa.

I dropped by the cop shop to report in. Harry emerged when I rang the bell at reception.

"Sam, how y' gettin' on?" He seemed genuine in his enquiry, yet I struggled to respect him as he had done nothing to protect me from Frank and the sarge that fateful night of my arrest.

"Alright," I replied coyly.

Harry leaned forward on the desk and beckoned me to come closer. I leaned in warily. "I'd like you t' come 'round t' my place for a chat 'n t' meet my wife."

"Why?"

"Shh," he whispered, putting a finger to his lips.

"Are y' pullin' m' leg or what?"

"I'm serious," he said.

"I don't think so."

"Look, it'd be in y' best interest t' do this."

"Why?"

"Trust me," he said, giving me his stare.

"Trust you!" I sniggered. "On what grounds, Harry?"

"Please, just trust me … come around," he persisted, maintaining his stare.

"When?"

"Tonight," Harry replied as he scribbled his address on a piece of paper. "Come after dinner. Eight o'clock or 'round about."

"We'll see," I sighed, accepting the piece of paper and slipping it into my pocket.

Who the fuck does he think I am? Thinks I'm just gonna come 'round cos he says it's a good idea? How the fuck can I get away? Oma and Opa've just arrived. He's got to be deluded! I turned and walked out of the building and down the road towards my favourite coffee shop.

I ordered a pot of tea and an asparagus roll, then sat down at a table by the window. Harry's request was seriously bugging me. I sat there trying to understand why he wanted me to come to his house and meet his wife. Life had been going in a positive direction lately, and this new spin on things made me anxious. *Fuck you, Harry! Fuck you 'n y' far-flung ideas.* I managed to stretch out my pot of tea to three cups and read the newspaper, a boring local rag called *The Wodyn Times* that had so little news it had even splashed my arrest across the front page several months earlier. Fortunately, I hadn't been to court at that stage, so my name had been suppressed. I sat and did the crossword until it was time to meet the bus, and just three clues short of finishing, I tore out the page and folded it neatly to fit in my pocket. I thanked the pretty-looking fat chick whose name still eluded me.

"Y're welcome, darlin'," she drawled. "See y' next time." She smiled too much for my liking, but at least she was a happy fat chick.

"Guess y' will," I said dryly. Once or twice a week I would stop in at the coffee shop to break the monotony of coming into town. Most of the time I'd order a pot of tea and a cheese scone, the only two things worth having unless there were asparagus rolls.

* * *

There was no bus station or depot as such, just a designated park on one of the side streets off the main street of Wodyn in a central part of town. The bus was just pulling up as I arrived. I parked the car a short distance away, walked over and stood near the doorway, waiting for my grandparents to exit. I hadn't noticed them as I walked past the bus's windows, and I hoped they hadn't missed the bus connection from Nowra. Eventually they appeared, almost the last off the bus, looking tired for their efforts. Oma greeted me with a warm embrace and looked deeply into my eyes, scanning for signs of my state of being. Her grey-blue eyes were dancing, smiling at me more than her lips, and her wrinkled, weathered face looked soft and full of character.

"We're here now, Sam. Christmas will be good," she assured herself as much as me.

"Sam! It's good to see you," Opa said, reaching out to embrace me and slapping me firmly on the back. "I know it's not the best of circumstances in which we meet, but you seem to be bearing up. Look at you, you're looking healthy, huh?"

"It's the sun and sea, Opa," I said, laughing.

"Yes, yes. I'm looking forward to seeing this bit of coast you live on."

We made small talk while waiting for the baggage to be unloaded. Two well-travelled suitcases appeared, and I picked up both, one in each hand to balance the weight, and led Oma and Opa to the car.

"Nice car, Sam," said Opa. "Is it yours?"

"No," I replied, lifting one of the cases into the boot. "Although I wish it were. I've got an old Holden, but it's crapped out now."

"Holden's are a good car too."

"When they're going, they are. The engine came off the mounts on mine 'n I just don't have the money t' fix it."

"That's too bad," Opa commented.

I closed the boot and opened the door to the front passenger seat for Oma, much to Opa's obvious disappointment, but she knew it was more important to him to sit upfront.

"I think I'm more suited to the back seat, Sam," she said, smiling at me. I opened the back door for her. "Why, thank you, young man," she said, still smiling. Opa was already sitting happily in the front seat as I clambered in on the driver's side.

"Do you have enough food for dinner, Sam?" asked Oma.

"We've got plenty. Val left the fridge 'n cupboards full b'fore they flew out, although it might not be the type 'f food you're accustomed t' eatin'."

"We'll get by," she said. "Perhaps we could come back into town sometime in the next few days. Is that possible? We are really too tired to shop now."

"I don't see it being a problem. Tim should be okay about me borrowin' the car." I started the engine and drove away from the kerb, then down onto the main road.

"It's very beautiful country around here," said Opa, gesturing at the view in front of us — eucalyptus-covered hills, undulating fenced-off farmland, and low-lying areas of pasture.

"Yup, I s'pose it is. I'm so use' t' seein' it every day I guess I've begun t' take it f granted."

"Never take the forests for granted! Look what they've done back home." Opa was a great lover of the outdoors and the native forests of New Zealand. He was infuriated by the amount of native forest that had been milled since his arrival in New Zealand in 1950. He'd instilled his passion in my father, and my father had instilled it in me.

"I think that a lot 'f what y' see along the coast in New South Wales is protected as national parks these days," I reassured him.

"That's good to hear, huh."

The sparkling turquoise sea became visible on the horizon as we descended on the far side of a substantial hill.

"They call that hill we just drove over a mountain," I quipped.

"Ha! How crazy," Opa responded.

"Now this is a view I like," I declared as we approached Yaringa and the coastline spread before us. "I like the bush, but ultimately, I prefer the coast, and it doesn't get much better than this."

"Huh. Fantastic… beautiful," Opa drawled. I drove through the village down the hill to the house.

"I'll get the suitcases," I said, opening my door and clambering out. I opened the boot and heaved their cases out one by one. "That's where I sleep." I nodded at the caravan. "It's cosy 'n I like being away from the house. Come on, I'll show y' the house 'n get y' settled in. I'll cook dinner t'night."

"That sounds good to me," said Oma. "I feel very tired after the journey. Actually, if it's alright with you, Sam, I may take a small nap before dinner."

"Of course y' can." I was struggling up the stairs with the suitcases and had to surrender one to Opa.

"Not so easy going up, huh," Opa stated.

Once inside the main part of the house, we ambled down the hall to their designated bedroom. They seemed pleased with the room. The afternoon sun was beaming in through the west-facing window.

"Lovely, thank you, Sam." Oma took my face in her hands, pulled me down to her height and kissed me on the forehead. "The blessing for you, my grandson."

"Thank you." I was embarrassed now, and I felt tears welling up in my eyes, it was so special to have them here. "Do y' mind comin' down t' the lounge so I can introduce Opa t' Tim?"

"Tim?" Oma said, looking vaguely disturbed. "I thought he was travelling to New Zealand with his parents to see Tania."

"He was," I said, nodding in agreement. "But at the last minute he refused t' go. What could we do?" I shrugged my shoulders. "I tried t' talk him into it, told him he'd regret it. He wouldn't budge, didn't care. His mum was driving him mad, he said. We couldn't force him int' the cab. So here he is. He's been with me f' the last few days, 'n we've been having a fine old time."

Oma shrugged, looking slightly perturbed. "I guess it's not an issue. Well, we'll just have to get by as it is."

I led them back down the hallway and into the lounge where Tim was sitting in his La-Z-Boy watching the telly.

"Tim, I'd like y' t' say hello t' m' Oma whom y've met already."

"Hello again, Tim," Oma said, stepping forward and offering her hand.

Tim painfully extracted himself from the chair and stood awkwardly. "Nice t' see y' again," he said in a low, gruff voice, taking her hand and shaking it.

"Thank you, and you too, Tim." Oma pulled her hand away and turned towards Opa, gesturing. "This is my husband, Theo."

"Hello, Tim," Opa said, thrusting his hand towards him.

"Welcome t' Yaringa," Tim said, taking his hand and looking him straight in the eye.

"Well, I think I'll leave you folks t' have a nap 'n sort y'selves out while I cook some kai." I headed for the kitchen, opened the fridge, pulled out vegetables and cut them up, then found an onion to dice, along with garlic. But there was no meat, which might be an issue for Opa. I decided there should be meat on the menu for their first night.

I'd be pushed to make the butcher; it was near closing time and most of the shops shut bang on the dong at five in the afternoon. I arrived just as the butcher was taking in his 'Open' sign.

"Can I get a few steak fillets?" I asked, trailing him into the shop and helping him with the door so he could get his sign in.

"People like you who leave it until the last minute ruin my day," he grumbled.

"Yeah, I know. It's tough being in business, isn't it?"

"Damn right. What kind of steak are you after? It's all in the chiller."

"Whatever y' recommend. I'm doin' a stir fry, so somethin' lean, I guess. Oh, 'n enough f' four people."

"I've got just the thing," he said, raising a finger to the air. He disappeared into the walk-in chiller and returned with some nice-looking meat on a piece of white paper, which he tossed on the scales. "That'll be a fiver for you and to anyone else it'd be free." He allowed himself a smile and removed the meat from the scales, wrapping it in brown paper. I handed him a five-dollar note and took the package of meat.

"See you soon … and don't leave it so late next time." He winked as he closed the shop door behind me.

* * *

I was back in the Valiant and down the road I drove past the motor camp, then decided I'd drop in briefly, driving around to where Stu and Mal were camped. They were sitting outside in their chairs, sipping on some cold ones and looking like a couple of cool cats.

"Hey, Sam! Haven't seen y' f' a few days," called out Stu.

"Yeah, I know. Been gettin' ready f' the grandparents' arrival."

"Y' got y' grandparents here, dude?" said Mal, looking horrified.

"Yeah, I have, but they're cool. They're about the coolest grandparents y'll ever meet."

"Did I say somethin'?" He put his hands in the air in protest.

"No, it was just the way y' looked," I said. "You guys should come 'round soon 'n meet them. I think y'd like them."

"I'm up f' it," said Stu.

"Yeah man, count me in," Mal chimed in. "Maybe the girls could come too."

"Speakin' 'f which," I said, "if y' see them, can y' tell Erika I won't be able t' see her tonight with them havin' just arrived 'n al?."

"No worries. I'll pass it on. Claudia should be over shortly. Erika is usually with her if she's not with you," Mal responded.

"Cheers, got t' go. See y' soon." I jumped back in the car and drove off.

* * *

There was no sign of Oma or Opa at home. Back in the kitchen I put a pot of rice on to boil and set about cutting the steak into slithers. As I sliced it, my encounter with Harry at the police station replayed in my mind.

I want y' t' come 'round t' my place f' a chat 'n t' meet m' wife. The words reverberated like a stuck record. *Is he fuckin' with m' mind? Is it a set-up? Is he f' real?* It didn't make sense, but I was curious enough to want to go, and I didn't see what I had to lose. *Nothing ventured, nothing gained,* Cosmo would say as we would ride the chairlift. *Where's that fuck'r now?* It was going to be tricky to go out and leave Oma and Opa alone on their first night.

I finished cutting the steak into thin, even strips. There was nothing further to do until the rice was close to ready. I had a large frying pan

on one of the front plates for the vegetables, and a smaller one on
the other front plate for the steak. The plan was to get the vegetables
going, start the steak off in the other pan, then toss the two together.
I found a bottle of red wine in Ted's booze stash and popped the cork,
hoping he wouldn't mind. I gathered wine glasses from the cupboard,
found cloth napkins in one of the drawers and added them to the table
to complete the setting.

"What have you been up to, Sam?" Oma made me jump.

"Hey, a special occasion deserves a special setting, don't y' think?"

"Indeed, it does. Can I do anything to help?"

"Well, not really, it's all done. I just have t' finish the cookin'."

I wandered back into the kitchen and checked the rice which looked
ready, so I turned it off to let it steam with the lid on. I switched on the
element under the large pan and poured in a small amount of oil, then
I swept the onions and the garlic off the chopping board and into the
pan, letting them cook for a few minutes before adding the vegetables.
I switched the second element on for the steak.

"Would y' like a drink 'f somethin', Oma?" I called out.

"A cup of tea would be lovely. Oh, and Theo will have a sherry if
there's any."

"Bound t' be sherry in Ted's elaborate cabinet," I said, more to
myself than to her. I showed her where Ted's cabinet was then filled
the kettle with water and switched it on. The other pan was hot
enough now and once the meat seared, I added soya and oyster sauce.
The kettle boiled and I chucked a tea bag into a cup before filling it
with boiling water, knowing Oma wouldn't be impressed; it wasn't
her idea of a real cup of tea. "Here's y' tea," I offered, adding a small
drop of milk.

"Lovely. Thank you, Sam."

"Have it at the table if y' like, dinner's almost ready t' be served."

"Yoo-hoo, you two! Dinner's ready," Oma called out.

I tipped the steak in with the vegetables and stirred it well. I brought the large frying pan to the table on a breadboard so that everyone could serve themselves. I found a table mat to put the rice pot on and placed that on the table too.

"You've excelled yourself, Sam," said Oma.

"It's one 'f the few things I know how t' do well. It's pretty easy. Anybody fancy a glass 'f red wine?"

"You have red wine? You live like a king here," proclaimed Opa. "A glass would be very good, thank you."

If there was plenty of food and drink, Opa always thought one was well off. He passed his empty sherry glass to me which I half filled and passed back.

"Oma, a glass 'f wine f' you?"

"Just a very small one. Oh, that's plenty!" I'd barely covered the bottom of her glass.

"Tim?" I asked, brandishing the bottle at him. "Are y' interested in a glass?" He had his mouth full already and tried to speak, but it was undecipherable, so I poured him a glass anyway, then filled my own. "Bon appetite!" I said, raising my glass. "Here's t' an enjoyable couple 'f weeks."

"This is good, Sam," Opa said, his mouth full and glass of wine in hand to wash it down. We all tucked in.

After the meal, when all the dishes were done and it seemed Oma and Opa were still quite tired from the journey, I mentioned I was going for a walk on the beach.

"I would very much like to see the beach, huh," said Opa. My plan was backfiring on me. "But tonight, I think I just need to go to bed," he added. "Perhaps we can walk down there tomorrow morning, Sam."

"That's a date," I said, smiling in agreement. "Before breakfast or after?"

21

Harry's Place

I walked along the road parallel to the beach. From my pocket I extracted the address Harry had given me at the police station. *The day feels like it's goin' on f' ever ... And I must be crazy doing this now.* As I walked the street looking for Harry's letterbox number, I grew increasingly anxious and paranoid. *Don't be a daft cunt, Sam! Y' don't need to be doin' this.* I continued despite an overwhelming desire to turn and run. I stood outside the house, staring at the number on the letterbox, when Harry appeared from nowhere.

"I thought y' weren't goin' t' come," he said. "I'm glad y' could make it." He was out of uniform and looked like any normal Joe Blow, completely unthreatening.

"M' grandparents arrived t'day, so I had t' pick them up 'n settle them in. It's true, though. I almost didn't come. I don't understand why y' doin' this ... it doesn't make sense."

"Come inside, meet m' wife 'n have a drink." Harry coerced me toward the house. I felt like I was in a scene from a bizarre movie.

"Why would y' wife want t' meet me? I'm a criminal in y'r eyes, so I'm even more so in hers."

"I know how it seems, Sam, but not everything is black and white. There are shades of grey. Not everything is as it seems."

"M' whole life's one big grey area at the moment," I replied. He laughed heartily, opened the front door and gestured for me to enter.

Theirs was a fairly ordinary, suburban-looking house on the outside, but the inside was a total contrast. The space was well laid out and painted in soft pastel colours. There was an array of interesting artwork on the walls and the smell of home cooking permeated the air. A tall, attractive, olive-skinned woman appeared before me like a magnificent vision, radiating the warmest of smiles.

"Hello. You must be Sam," the vision said in what sounded like a faint Italian accent. She reached out and clasped my hand with both of hers. "I'm Sarah and I'm very pleased to meet you." Her eyes looked into mine with genuine warmth and a strange recognition, as though she already knew me.

"Yes … I … I'm pleased t' meet y' too," I managed to say. "I mean, yes … I'm Sam … I'm pleased t' meet y' too." She laughed lightly and released my hand.

"Why don't you two sit in the lounge and I'll organise some drinks. How does beer sound, Harry?" she asked, walking with poise to the kitchen.

"Great, honey."

Harry led me into the lounge where I sat down in one of the armchairs. Harry sat in the chair opposite. I still felt uncomfortable, like a freak in someone else's show. I wanted to run a million kilometres away. Instead I talked nervously. "Nice place y've got y'selves here, Harry."

"Yeah, it's pretty good, but we've been thinkin' 'f sellin' up 'n movin' on."

Sarah came in with a tray of drinks and placed them on the coffee table. She handed a glass and a can of Fosters to me.

"Harry's leaving the police," Sarah said, out of the blue.

"He's what?"

"I hope you like Fosters, Sam," she said, ignoring my reaction.

"Fosters is good, thanks." She handed one to Harry then sat down on the couch with one herself. "What do y' mean Harry's leavin' the police?" I enquired again.

"Tell him, Harry. It's not up to me," Sarah said.

Harry shifted uncomfortably in his chair, popped the tab on his Fosters, poured the golden liquid into his glass, and waited a moment for it to settle before carrying on. "I suppose it was after we arrested you that night and the way you were treated. It got to me … y' see."

"Harry hates the police. He hates the hypocrisy," Sarah butted in.

"Who's tellin' the story, you or me?" Harry stared daggers at her.

"Sorry, darling."

Harry continued: "I hate the good cop, bad cop scenario, but it's how the whole system works! I'm sick 'f people like Frank 'n the ol' sergeant. Fellini's alright, but he plays the game too by gettin' the likes 'f Frank 'n me t' soft'n up suspects, just as we did with you."

"So why are y' tellin' me all this?" I asked.

Harry leaned forward in his chair. "It's simple really. I made m' decision after the night we arrested y'. It'd been buildin' in me before that, though, 'n I guess y' were the straw that broke the camel's back, so t' speak. I realised that y' weren't some evil force at work in the world, just a young guy caught in a big spiderweb. It's been hard t' deal with the whole incident knowin' I treated y' like a piece 'f shit … like a criminal that should be locked away. There are plenty 'f bad arses out there, don't get me wrong, 'n they deserve what they get, but there is so much other shit that goes on. Some 'f the guys I work with just live f' situations like we had with you that night."

"Like Frank 'n the sarge," I interrupted. "But I still don't understand why y'd want t' confess all this t' me. What difference is it goin' t' make t' the trouble I'm in? Ease the guilt y' seem t' have f' arresting me?"

"I just need t'," he said, then cleared his throat as if there was something that required dislodging. "Y' see, I care … I care about what happens t' y', 'n I want t' be able t' tell y' that."

I looked at Sarah who was looking at Harry as if willing him to continue. She was a strong-looking woman with refined features and a rare natural elegance. There was something about her easy disposition that really drew me in. She must've been in her mid-thirties, with dark straight hair that fell to just below her shoulders. Her hazel eyes sparkled warmth and her mouth seemed to be fixed in a subtle smile that made me feel at ease. The blouse she wore hugged her torso, accentuating her breasts and revealing her cleavage where the top two buttons were undone. She wore a floral skirt that rode up her legs to reveal her thighs; she had the legs for it. I wondered why she was with Harry and concluded that they had probably been sweethearts at high school. Harry took another sip of his beer and sighed. There were signs in his appearance that he was once a handsome man. Now his chin was double and his neck a bit jowly. He'd developed a slight pot belly too, probably from sitting in police cars and at desks for too long. The beers and barbeques hadn't helped either.

"Would you like another beer, Sam?" Sarah was poised to get up.

"No, I won't, thanks. I should really get back. I feel bad sneaking out on m' grandparents. It's their first night here."

"Okay. We'd like to have you over for dinner sometime so you can meet the kids," responded Sarah.

"Maybe," I said vaguely. "Harry what y' goin' t' do if y' leave the police force?" I changed the subject.

"I've always wanted m' own business," he replied, his eyes lighting up for the first time since I'd arrived. "I don't know what yet, but that's the next step. Either a business or retrain in somethin'."

"Sounds good," I said. "I think y' brave wantin' t' make a change 'n being prepared t' do somethin' about it. My father was never particularly happy with what he did, but he seemed afraid t' make the change. Maybe it's harder when y've got four kids. He was stuck in a bind that wasn't easy t' get out 'f, but even now that I've left home, I don't see him talkin' 'f change."

"Perhaps he felt it was too late t' be changin'," said Harry as he stood up. "Thanks f' comin' t' visit. I'm sure it wasn't an easy decision t' make."

I was pleasantly surprised by his words. I pushed up out of the sunken armchair I'd made myself at home in. Sarah was also standing now, and I went to shake her hand. "It was nice meetin' y', Sarah." She moved gracefully past my hand, put her arms around me and kissed me on the cheek. I stood there feeling awkward as Harry looked on, seemingly unperturbed by her gesture.

"Bye, Sam. Harry will let you know what day for dinner. Actually, why don't we just decide on a day now. How about Saturday night, one week from today?"

"Saturday's no good," I replied quickly, thinking that there might be something on at the pub and I'd rather be hanging out with Erika since she wasn't going to be around for long.

"Then what about Sunday?"

"Ahh … Sunday's okay," I replied with some hesitancy.

"It's arranged then," she said, looking pleased. "We'll look forward to seeing you on Sunday!"

Harry shuffled his way to the door with me and we walked up the drive together.

"So the big question I have t' ask y' is — How long can I look forward t' being in prison for?" I said.

"It ain't goin' t' happ'n, Sam."

"How can y' say that with such certainty? I mean, after all, y' don't make the decision; y' just present the case. It's all there in black 'n white,

Harry. I was caught red-handed, arrested 'n charged. Y' don't have any influence on a judge's decision, do y'?"

Harry kicked at a stone on the driveway as if it were a soccer ball being driven into the back of a net. "Ultimately y' right, but as the arresting officer I can influence the police prosecutor, who in turn can influence the judge. Y've just got t' trust me on this, Sam."

"Oh, I see, some sort 'f blind faith. Maybe I'll get two years instead 'f three or somethin' like that, 'n y' won't need t' feel guilty any more!" I said sarcastically.

"Some faith is better than no faith," Harry responded.

"Y' know, I might've been bett'r off listenin' t' m' father's advice."

"What was that, Sam?"

"He told me t' drive across the border to Melbourne 'n t' jump on a plane home. He reckoned that y'd never bother t' follow up m' case, me being so young 'n just a pawn in the whole equation. With so many other serious crimes goin' on, he reckon'd it'd be consider'd a waste of resources t' bother with me. Oh, 'n of course, there's no passport required between here 'n New Zealand for citizens of either country."

"Yes, y' could've, but y' still here, so y' didn't. But y' still could if y' really wanted t'. Y' must've seen some merit in facin' the music b'cause it's prob'bly true, most people in your position would've skipp'd the country." Harry shot me one of his intense, police looks. "Why d' y' think I invit'd y' 'round here t'night?"

"T' ease y' conscience."

He suddenly grabbed me by both arms just below the shoulders and shook me. "Conscience aside, Sam! I happ'n t' care about what happens to y'. I don't want t' see a nice young man like y'self wind up in one 'f our prisons where y'll potentially come out hardened 'n broken. I told y' I'm gettin' out, 'n you've been the final catalyst f' that. I'm grateful f' that reminder, I'm grateful y' came int' m' life that night."

"I'm not Jesus Christ y' saviour, Harry."

"Take it from me, Sam, I'll be doin' everythin' I can t' see y' stay outside, 'n I admire y' guts f' stickin' 'round 'n facin' the music."

"Stupidity more like it!" I shrugged his hands off, glared fiercely at him and walked off. "Might see y' Sunday, Harry!"

"I hope so." His words hung in the air. I half expected more words to follow, but nothing came.

* * *

I kicked the same stone Harry had kicked into the middle of the road, but I kicked it so hard it hurt my toe. I wanted to cry out but didn't. I knew Harry would still be watching me. I should've been feeling better, much better, because Harry cared about my situation. It was ironic that the person who cared was the person who had put me in the situation in the first place. It felt like Harry was befriending me to purge his own guilt. Meanwhile, I'm supposed to trust him and believe that at the end of it all I'll be able to walk away unscathed. Where was the guarantee of that?

I slipped across the road and down a dirt track leading to the beach, where I dropped down on the sand. I sat and watched the waves roll in, breaking in nice even sets, a slight breeze whipping their tops off, sending a misty spray into the evening air. My thoughts consumed me.

The old man'll be comin' out f' the final day in court, 'n a barrister'll be comin' down from Sydney. He's a mate 'f Dennis's, 'n specialises in criminal law, renowned f' gettin' people out 'f difficult situations. M' life feels like it's hangin' by a thread, precariously in the balance. On the one hand, I might end up in prison gettin' butt fuck'd daily over a handbasin, on the other hand I've got Harry — the long arm 'f the law 'n beyond reproach. By some cruel twist 'f fate, Harry pulled me up on a lonely stretch 'f road in the middle 'f the night. The actions he played out that night with Frank, led t' sleepless nights for him 'n a feelin' that something's amiss in his life. One night as he slept beside his beautiful wife, he awoke from a bad dream, saturated in sweat. Perhaps it was a reoccurring dream that nagged away at his conscience in much the same way I dreamt 'f Bruce. Bruce with his sinister cronies tyin' bricks t' me 'n tossin' me off a bridge int' deep water t' drown. I bet Harry's bad dreams haunt him in much the same way mine stalks at the edges 'f m' mind, growin' in paranoia. Somethin' must've shifted in Harry as he became consumed with it, consumed with the guilt that he could be responsible f' puttin' a man 'f eighteen years behind bars. Knowin' the predatory nature 'f men in prisons, it must've become too much f' him t' shoulder. Sarah, havin' t' put up with his frequent night sweats 'n buildin' anxiety, must've encouraged him t' do somethin' about it.

And so I concluded that Harry inviting me around to their house was probably based on his wife's encouragement. If he could somehow change the outcome of his deeds, starting from the night he arrested me, he'd be able to leave the police force and move on without waking at night to his recurring dream and nagging conscience. It was all too fucking bizarre!

* * *

It was dusk by the time I walked past the motor camp. The sun had dropped behind the hills, creating a dark-blue hue on the land. The sky was a pinky red, and several cockatoos squawked from trees above. I needed another beer, so decided to swing by Stu and Mal's site, hoping that Erika and Claudia would be hanging out with them. Sure enough, as I approached, I could see Erika sitting in a camp chair outside the tent with Stu and Mal, tinnies of Fosters in hand. Claudia was sitting on Mal's knee like some inseparable parrot a pirate might have. Stu was on his throne, looking fully content as he inhaled on a rolly. Erika, sipping on her wine cooler, appeared pleased to see me.

"Hey! We'd almost given up on seein' y' t'night. Help y'self to a cold one," said Stu as he gestured to the esky.

"Thanks, don't mind if I do," I said, reaching in and pulling one out, as cold as the ice it lay in. I popped the tab and guzzled back as much as I could in one go without snorting it out my nose.

"Thirsty work havin' the grandparents t' stay," Stu teased.

"No, not at all … just haven't had a beer f' a while. I really needed that. There's always something refreshing about the first few mouthfuls, don't y' reckon?"

"I reckon the whole damn lot's refreshing," mused Stu. "Y' better have another, Sam, that barely touched the sides."

"Don't mind if I do," I said, reaching into the esky again. I peeled the tab on another, and having guzzled the top off it, I sat down beside Erika. She instantly reached for me and pulled herself in close.

Over the past few days, I had often wanted to tell her how much I liked her, but the words never came out, remaining jumbled in my mind, as if they would be insignificant or reveal a weakness in me. It seemed easier to keep her at arm's length and not show too much emotion, making it less painful when it came time for her to leave. For Erika, I imagined it would be easier; she would have distractions — university enrolment, her holiday to talk about with friends, social events to attend. In no time at all she would be reabsorbed into her familiar world, her holiday and our fleeting intimacy a distant memory. There was no certainty in my future other than reporting to the police daily and waiting for my day in court.

"Hey, Sam, what y' doin' f' Christmas Day?" asked Stu.

"What's that?" I asked, emerging from my thoughts, aware that Erika was holding me unusually tight.

"Jesus, y're away on another planet tonight, aren't y', mate! I said what y' doin' f' Christmas Day?"

"Oh … Don't know, hadn't giv'n it much thought. I s'pose Oma will cook up a feed, 'n I'll give her a hand."

"Sounds good," Stu said.

"What about you guys?"

"I guess we'll have some damper or camp bread 'f some sort, 'n a couple 'f sausages with tomato sauce," replied Stu.

"Fuck that," said Mal.

"So what are you proposin'?"

"I thought we could go out f' lunch somewhere," said Mal.

"Yeah right! We'll go t' the Park Royal or the Sebel Town House, will we? Mal y're full 'f shit." We all laughed.

"There must be somewhere we can go," Mal said, maintaining his deadpan look.

Stu sighed deeply. "This isn't Sydney, Mal. It's not even Woolongong. It's the middle 'f fuckin' nowhere, 'n I'd say that even the bowling club will be shut f' the day."

"Come on, Stu. The bowling club not open on Christmas Day! Where's y' sense 'f reality?" Mal replied.

"They'll probably have a tournament in the afternoon," I said.

"See?" said Mal, enthusiastically.

"He's pulling y' leg, y' daft cock," Stu said.

The girls were trying to suppress their amusement at the situation and Stu was on the verge of cracking up.

"Why don't y's come t' my place f' Christmas dinner?" I said, opening my big mouth.

"Are y' serious?" Stu leaned forward on his throne. "We could buy the turkey 'n help stuff it, 'n bring some bubbly as a contribution. That'd be fuckin' great, wouldn't it, Mal?"

"What about y' grandparents?" Mal asked. "They wouldn't want us all round there, would they? We'd be too raucous. We might give them a heart attack or somethin'."

"Not likely, Mal. Y' don't know them. Strange as it might seem t' make this observation, but my grandparents aren't y' average grandparents."

"That's very deep, even profound f' this time 'f night, Sam," Mal said, laughing, obviously quite drunk now. No one else was amused, only Claudia had a bit of a smile on her face. She probably felt obliged to show some amusement at his efforts.

"Do you think we would be able to come too?" Erika asked.

"Of course," I said, a little surprised that my place would be such a popular venue for Christmas Day. "But what about y' parents, they won't agree t' that, will they?"

"I'll work on them," she said, squeezing me tighter.

"You'd be surprised how well Erika has her parents wrapped around her little finger, even though they do seem to be the strictest parents in the world," Claudia said. "What do you want us to bring?"

"I'll talk with the grandparents 'n let y' know t'morrow."

"Who's for another can?" Stu was leaning into the esky, fossicking for beer. Without waiting for a reply, he tossed one straight at me. I had to stretch to catch it before it hit the ground, rendered useless. He fired another one at Mal. The girls continued sipping their everlasting wine coolers.

"I think I'm goin' t' head home," I said, then kissed Erika gently on the lips.

"Can I come with you?" she whispered hopefully.

"Course y' can." I wasn't about to decline her warm body in bed next to mine. I stood, pulling her up with me. "See y'all in the morrow."

"Right then," said Stu, raising his can in a toast. "Let us know if it's a goer."

"Y' can bet on that."

Back at the caravan all extraneous thoughts were abandoned as Erika and I set about removing each other's clothes with urgency, kissing hard, wanting each other with a desperation that couldn't be satisfied. In no time I was inside her, riding her hard on all fours, like an Apache escaping the Union Cavalry, and yet when I was fully spent, I still wanted to ride her. But all my passion was consumed on an emotional level, all feelings of warmth were gone, and strangely, but to my relief, Erika didn't seem to notice as she cried out, and I realised she was having her own moment of self-indulgence.

In that moment I saw us as separate individuals, gaining pleasure from one another, rather than as two merged beings, in union together. I pulled away and collapsed on the bed beside her, looking searchingly into her eyes. She looked euphoric and in love, I felt cold and distant. The strange state I was in meant I could've been having sex with anyone, that she was not special. *My walls are crumblin'... I dunno how t' cope any more.* I held her gaze, desperately wanting her to see that I felt the same as she did, whereas all I felt was my own sense of emptiness. Erika was all I dreamt of in a girl, yet now that I had her lying beside me, I felt strangely suffocated. A sense of unworthiness washed over me, creating a desire to sabotage the only good thing that had happened to me recently, and I didn't understand where these feelings were coming from.

"I love you, Sam," Erika whispered in my right ear. Instead of saying anything, I squeezed her tighter and she snuggled in until she couldn't get any closer without merging into my body. I knew the feeling she had, I'd had it myself on occasion, usually after making love. It came from the heart and was expressed with the body.

"Why d' y' love me?" I asked her.

"Because you're beautiful. You're different from any other boyfriend I've ever had. You seem to be yourself all the time. I watch you and see you as somebody who doesn't pretend to be someone they're not."

"Yeah, well right now I don't feel like I know m'self at all."

"We all have moments like that. I never felt I knew myself ... until I met you!" She climbed on top of me all playful and smiling, and she tried to tickle me. I grabbed her arms and rolled her off me, pinning her to the bed, placing my knees on her biceps, tickling her waist until she was begging for mercy. Eventually I relented, bending forward and kissing her gently. The kiss turned into a lingering, explorative one that aroused my loins again and led me back to the warmth between her legs. It was strange now to observe myself being gentle and loving. A softness had washed over me, and I was able to look at her and feel my emotions as we rose to climax together.

22

Tim

I awoke the following morning reaching for Erika. My hands groped all the way across the bed without finding her, and I sat up to see if she was curled up somewhere else. She must've left in the small hours of the morning so her parents wouldn't find her missing when they rose for the day. I curled up in a ball and lay there thinking about my visit to Harry's place. Weird though it was, I decided to play along with his request to visit on Sunday in the hope that it would turn out to my advantage. Besides, I was intrigued now that he'd invited me into his family. His exotic wife had surprised me, and I was curious about the part she played in the scheme of things.

I showered in the basement to wash away the residue of the previous day, and then went upstairs only to find Oma and Opa already up and eating breakfast at the dining table.

"Good morning, grandson," said Oma. "Did you sleep well?"

"Like a baby," I replied, sitting down at the table to join them.

"What are your plans for today, Sam?" Opa asked. "I would like to take that walk on the beach."

"Well, I've got t' go int' Wodyn at some stage t' report t' the constabulary, but other than that I'm free."

"Huh, the what?" he asked, cupping an ear with a hand as if it would help him hear better.

"The police, Theo. Sam has to report to the police daily," explained Oma. He nodded as if understanding.

"Oh …'n we should shop f' Christmas, for Christmas dinner, I mean. Don't worry about presents. And while I'm on the subject, I was wonderin' … I've got a couple 'f friends over at the campin' ground. Would y' mind if they came f' dinner on the day?"

"If that's what you want, Sam, I don't see why not," replied Oma, looking to Opa for some response. He didn't appear to hear. "Sam's invited some friends for Christmas dinner, Theo," she stated slowly and loudly.

"Oh good. I look forward to meeting them," he replied, nodding.

"They're good people, you'll really like them, 'n they're curious t' meet y'. I told them you're very cool grandparents, so now they're intrigued."

"I love it that you're not embarrassed by us," Oma replied, looking amused.

"Why should I be?"

* * *

The sea was the tamest it had been in days. Small waves lapped the beach in constant repetition, making it difficult to believe that two days ago there had been a metre swell from the south-east, pounding the beach with wild surf. As we walked north along the beach towards the lagoon, I explained to Opa that most young people in and around the area surfed.

"It's the normal Ozzie thing t' do. If y' live near the coast, y' surf. Most beaches have good surf, not every day but most 'f the time."

"Do you surf, Sam?" he asked.

"Me? Sometimes. Tim's got a spare board, so I have a bit 'f a paddle, and I try t' catch a wave or two. It takes a bit 'f practise, and I probably don't do it enough."

We walked up the beach then back down to the surf club, Opa forever asking questions about the area, which I endeavoured to answer. By the time we got back to the house, I was relieved to escape his unrelenting questioning. I half expected him to dredge up how I happened to get involved with drugs. I knew what he'd say: *How is it that an intelligent and talented young man like yourself, can be foolish enough to get involved with something as stupid as drugs? For a start, they're bad for you, and then they're illegal, so why would you bother?* It would be difficult to come up with an intelligent answer, so I was grateful he didn't ask. Yet I knew it wouldn't be long before I would get the lecture. Dad's well-intended advice to me when I was at high school came to mind: *When you're at a party and someone tells you to drink up or have another drink, just tip it out the window when they're not looking. That way you can always have a glass in your hand and know that you haven't drunk too much.*

Along with drink, there was the common practice of smoking marijuana, which had initially been a social curiosity for me, but then developed into a cool, mind-altering thing to do. As a result, I became fascinated with the stuff. By eighteen, I was a regular consumer of dope, but that didn't mean waking to it in the morning like a seasoned cigarette smoker. Take the likes of my lawyer, Dennis, for instance, who probably didn't get out of bed until he'd had a couple of cigarettes. Put into context, I didn't see myself as an addict or even remotely close to being one. If I couldn't get my hands on any dope, I wasn't going to fret, break out in a sweat or have withdrawals the way I imagined Dennis would if cigarettes were outlawed tomorrow. *I'd give up just like that!* he'd assured me as he tossed his packet of cigarettes in the wastepaper basket.

* * *

Tim drove us into town, offering no explanation as to his motivation other than it was his car and he felt like a drive. It was probably a good thing he was getting out of the house because he didn't do it much besides his daily walk to the beach for a swim. Maybe by the time the fortnight came around for the rural nurse's visit to administer his medication, the effects of the previous dose were starting to wear off, and he began to feel more like his normal self. I noticed that he would become more sociable toward the end of the two-week cycle and seemed a whole lot more relaxed within himself. He could even hold an extended conversation.

I laughed to myself as we travelled to Wodyn that day. What a scene! Tim, the local nutter, driving us to town to shop for Christmas dinner, and Oma and Opa over here to ensure I didn't have Christmas on my own. And here we all were, driving into town with an undermedicated, possibly delusional schizophrenic, our lives in his hands. He could drive us into the oncoming logging truck if he chose to. In fact, one was looming on the straight stretch of road ahead, getting closer every second, and for one brief moment I thought Tim was going to do just that as he swerved to avoid a large wombat that had appeared on the edge of the road.

Oma cried out in alarm, uttering something in Dutch.

"What was that, Helena?" asked Opa, oblivious to the event, preoccupied with the scenery and not really interested in anything else. Oma was still clutching my arm in the back seat, and I was wishing my mind were less imaginative.

We arrived safely at the one and only supermarket in Wodyn. Tim waited in the car while we shopped. By the time we got to the checkout, the trolley was loaded up with a turkey, a leg of ham, new potatoes, an assortment of other fresh vegetables, cream, milk, juice, cheeses, nuts, potato chips, and the first berry fruits of the season. The checkout girl raced our produce across the barcode reader. It blimped and beeped as

I stood there admiring her breasts, overly large in comparison to the rest of her body. I even caught Opa eyeing them up. It was amusing to see he still appreciated the finer things in life. Oma paid, and I smiled as I shuffled past the young woman, trying to avert my gaze. She beamed me a lovely smile as I picked up several full bags of shopping.

"Might see y' in the Yaringa pub sometime," I involuntarily said. "They have bands out there on Thursdays 'n Fridays, y' know."

"I know." Her voice soft and sexy. "I often go there. I've even seen you there."

"Really?" I was surprised I hadn't noticed her. "Well ... might see y' out there next time."

Christ! It's happenin' t' me now. I could like someone a lot, but then I could still easily have sex with some other girl. That was all it had to be — sex! My dick had a mind of its own, it thought and operated separately to anything vaguely resembling my rational mind. *Ha, ha! Is that how my penis got its name, 'Dick'?* My dick was another entity, and it liked to please itself whenever the opportunity presented itself. *What a dick!*

I opened the boot of the car and with Opa's aid, we put the trolley load of shopping in while Oma stood close by, instructing us as to what we needed to handle carefully.

"Fancy a cup 'f tea before we head back? That place I took y' to with Mum," I said, looking at Oma.

"That sounds like a nice idea. I feel parched after all the shopping. Cup 'f tea, Theo?" Oma raised her voice; he was quite deaf in one ear.

"Hmm?" he grunted, raising his hand to his left ear, cupping it as if to catch something.

"Tea?"

"Mmm, tea? What ... here in town?"

"Yes."

"Good, huh."

I nodded, slammed the boot shut and we all piled back into the car. Tim had the music up loud. It was Van Morrison's 'Angelou'.

"We'd like t' go f' a cup 'f tea at the coffee shop," I said to Tim, raising my voice above the music. He stretched his arm across the dashboard and turned the music down. I repeated myself. He nodded, started the engine, and gently negotiated his way out of the car park.

The police had no right t' arrest him, let alone take him f' a psychiatric evaluation. Outrageous! Like puttin' the cart before the horse, like being found guilty 'f a crime without havin' committed one. What happened t' 'innocent until proven guilty'? There's nothin' fuckin' democratic about the allegations made against Tim. Maybe his other piece 'f thinkin' anatomy, the one called Dick, like mine, had overruled his rational mind. Could happen t' anyone!

Tim came in for tea, just to keep me guessing. Just when I thought he was as antisocial as he could be, he'd turn around and be the opposite. There were only a couple of people in the coffee shop — an elderly lady I'd seen there before, having her morning tea, and a younger woman, dressed formally as though she might be a secretary, engrossed in a *Dolly* magazine. I encouraged Oma and Opa to take a seat while I ordered.

Tim seemed to know the fat chick behind the counter. "Where've y' been hidin'?" she asked.

"In the loony bin," he replied deadpan. She burst out laughing.

"What's so funny?" asked Tim.

"You, y' such a kidder."

"Am I? Can I have a chocolate milkshake, 'n one 'f those." He pointed to a sandwich in the cabinet.

"The ham sandwich?"

"Yeah … if that's what it is."

"Tea today?" She asked me, forcing a smile that refused to form on her lips, obviously still uncomfortable after her attempt to be friendly with Tim.

He must've come here in the past, or perhaps they knew each other at school, or Tim use' t' give her one after school in the bike shed, or maybe it was at a party after they'd both drunk too much. She must've been in better condition then. Workin' in her parents' shop has taken its toll on her physique. Too many opportunities t' down a pastry or a cheeky sticky bun!

"Tea f' three 'n somethin' nice t' have with it. Those Anzac biscuits look good. How about three 'f those." I pointed to the jar.

"Sure," she said as she expertly picked the jar up and removed the lid. With a pair of tongs, she plucked the Anzac biscuits out one by one, placing them on a plate. I watched her heaving breasts as she brought the teapot and milk jug to the counter and realised she had caught me in action. "Somethin' else y' fancy or will that be all?" she asked coyly.

"Not at the moment," I said, suddenly feeling acutely self-conscious.

"Just say if y' want anythin' else. That'll be eleven dollars all up, thanks."

The rest of the morning was uneventful. Tim dropped me at the police station to report in. I half expected to see Harry at reception, waiting to ask if I cared to join him and his colleagues for a round of golf over the weekend, but there was a young constable behind the reception desk, obviously a new recruit. He was friendly enough, pulling out the report book and getting me to sign.

* * *

Tim pulled up in the driveway at home, clambered out of the car, opened the boot and took a load of grocery bags up to the house. His enthusiasm astounded me. I pulled the rest of the grocery bags out, dividing them between Opa and myself. By the time we emptied the bags, the fridge was jam-packed with food. We could barely close the door.

"Think I'll go f' a swim," I announced. "Anybody else up f' it?"

"What a good idea. A swim before lunch could be just the tonic," enthused Oma. "Are you going to swim, Theo?"

"Hmm?" He was distracted and hadn't heard a word, engrossed in packing his pipe with tobacco.

"A swim, Theo! Down to the beach!" she said loudly.

"Yes, it's too hot to do much else. I'll just finish packing my pipe and I'll smoke it down on the beach after we've had a swim."

We found a spot directly in front of the surf club. Between the flags the area was packed with bathers and swimmers, while the rest of the beach was deserted.

"Why don't we go further down the beach away from the crowd?" Opa asked, keen to be away from the masses.

"We can if y' want, but they say it's not safe to swim 'cept up this end. It's more sheltered 'n you've got the surf lifesavers at this time 'f year."

"I think we should swim here, Theo," Oma said. "They have flags for a reason. I didn't come over here to witness you being dragged out to sea."

"Let's get in the water!" I said impatiently. We dumped our towels and belongings in a pile and walked down to the sea. A metre-high swell was coming into the bay, breaking perfectly to the right. "Good f' bodysurfin', Opa!" I yelled as I dived into the cool water.

There were a few surfers out just to the left of the flags. As we floated in the water, I noticed one of the surfers was Tim, and on a longboard. I pointed him out to Opa who then wanted to go back to the house and get the camera to take some photos. Tim looked slightly stiff on his board, but he caught a beautiful wave and rode it nicely, pulling out just before it broke into white tumbling foam. I saw Oma in the distance, floating on her back, prominent with her lime green bathing cap, toes poking up just above the surface of the water, and looking relaxed and serene. I bodysurfed a few waves before boredom set in, and I decided to return to shore.

My mind was on Erika as I waded from the water, scanning the beach in the hope I might spy her. Oma and Opa emerged from the sea and we headed back to our spot together. I picked up my towel to spread out on the sand.

"We're not staying, Sam," announced Oma. "The sun's too strong. You be careful you don't get burnt lying there."

"Actually, Helena, I might stay and have my pipe. I'll come back for some lunch after."

"Okay, good idea. See you back at the house." She trudged off with her belongings, golden sand squeaking underfoot.

"Tim's good on that board, huh," Opa said as he placed the pipe in his mouth, clamping down on it with his teeth.

"He used t' be the top surfer in this area before he was put in the loony bin."

"Really? And if you don't mind me asking, Sam, what was he put in the mental hospital for?"

"A couple 'f local women complained t' the police that he was stalkin' them," I began.

"Was he?"

"That's open f debate. What constitutes stalkin'? It's not a reason t' put someone in the loony bin. Some local shrink wrote a report sayin' he was a danger t' the community 'n himself. Bang! He's arrested 'n dragged off … medicated 'n zombified."

"Huh. So if he was stalking those women, maybe worse was to come," Opa said between clamped teeth as he worked on his pipe, sucking hard. The flame from his match sat above the bowl while great wafts of smoke billowed out the side of his mouth.

"Yeah, well … from where I'm sittin', there was only one side 'f the story told, 'n so the democratic system which we live in failed him. Y' see, just because we know someone has the potential t' commit a crime doesn't allow us t' pre-empt their action 'n lock them up on the basis that they might offend. We don't know for sure that someone will commit a crime. We all have that potential, every single one 'f us. If a crime hasn't been committed, we can only take precautions t' prevent it. That's the way our society is structured and that's how the law is, 'n in my opinion, how it should be."

"I see what you're saying, Sam," Opa responded, deep in thought, more smoke billowing from the side of his mouth.

"Look at me," I continued. "I got caught red-handed, 'n even though I thought what I did was harmless 'n insignificant, in the frame 'f things the law saw it differently 'n treated it so. I've been arrested 'n charged based on the evidence found on me. In the eyes 'f the law I committed a crime 'n was charged accordingly."

"And you're saying that Tim had not been?" Opa asked, taking his pipe out of his mouth and blowing a long plume of smoke into the air.

"Exactly."

"You've got a point, Sam," he conceded, pointing the stem of his pipe at me for emphasis.

"What I don't understand is why his parents just accepted the whole thing, 'n no questions asked," I said.

"Perhaps they felt their hands were tied, perhaps they didn't know what they could do."

"Maybe."

Tim was out of the water and heading to the surf club with the longboard when he saw us, and he came and sat down beside Opa, puffing loudly from his exertion.

"You're pretty handy on that board, Tim," Opa said admiringly.

"I haven't done it f' a while, so it's a bit 'f a challenge. I'm a bit stiff but it was nice t' get out on the water 'n get a feel f' it again. Gentle waves 'n this larger board," Tim said, tapping it gently, "really helps me get m' balance back."

"Why does the longer board help?" Opa asked.

"Cos the board's so long 'n broad, it's more stable on the water than a small one."

"Yes, that makes sense. But I remember that when surfing first became big, all the boards were long like this one, weren't they?"

"Yeah, that's right, Malibu boards. I s'pose it's the same with anythin', as they became aware 'f the dynamics 'n surfing became more popular, the boards became shorter cos they're more aerodynamic 'n manoeuvrable on the wave. Guys started doin' more 'n more tricks 'n whatnot. That's the way with technology, isn't it?"

"Yes, I suppose it is," said Opa, tapping his pipe in his hand to remove the ash. "Are you two coming up for some lunch? I'm heading back to the house," he announced, getting up.

"I'll be with y' 'n a minute," I said.

"I've got t' take this board back, then I'll be up," Tim replied.

"I'll see you back there then," said Opa.

"Y' will," I said.

Tim stood, then stooped back down to pick up his board and headed off. I fell into step beside him.

"I've never really seen y' surfin' like that before. Y' looked pretty damn good out there."

"Yeah, like I say, if m' knees weren't so fuck'd, I'd be able t' go a whole lot better."

"Would y' teach me t' surf properly?"

He walked to a rack where all the boards were stored and slid his board in alongside another. He took his towel from the rail on the wall and hung it on his shoulder, turning to me.

"Reckon I might be able t' do that."

"Would I be able t' borrow one of those boards?"

"We'd have t' see about that," he said, grinning at me through his Amish beard, his face all animated.

* * *

Back at the house Oma had lunch laid out on the table in a similar fashion to what she'd do at home. She and Opa had already started eating.

"Sorry, we couldn't wait," she apologised. "We were absolutely ravenous. Come, sit down and eat. Tim, your beach is beautiful!"

"Yeah, it's pretty popular in the summer. The locals get pissed about that."

"Someone was tellin' me the town doubles in population at this time 'f year," I said.

"Really?" said Opa, who'd just stuffed half a sandwich in his face.

There was a knock at the door.

"Who could that be?" I asked, getting up to answer it.

"That girl y've been seein'," teased Tim.

I got to the door and saw it was the nurse who administered Tim's medication. My heart sank. I wanted to tell her that he was so much better, that I'd never seen him looking this happy since I'd been here. I wanted to tell her that he didn't need to be medicated any more. I wanted to tell her to fuck off! But it wasn't her job to assess whether he was improving; her job was to administer the drug. If I told her to go away, we'd probably end up with Frank on the doorstep to put Tim back in the loony bin.

I reluctantly let her in, showed her to the lounge, and went to tell Tim. He must've sensed her, knew she was coming, as he was already up out of his chair and heading for the lounge. I smiled weakly at him

197

as he passed. His eyes were impassive, showing no indication of how he might be feeling.

"Who was that at the door, Sam?" Oma asked as I sat back down at the table.

"Tim's nurse," I replied dejectedly.

"Hmm," grunted Opa, feeling like he was missing out on something, instantly cupping his right hand around the back of his ear.

"And what does she want?" Oma asked.

"She's here t' give him his medication." *So that he remains a zombie.* Feeling agitated, I added, "Look, I don't think now is a good time t' be talkin' about this."

"Hmm?" Opa was leaning in closer, still unable to get the gist of what I was saying. Oma uttered something in Dutch, which prompted him to pull his hand away from his ear like a scolded child, and he carried on eating his lunch with his head down.

I heard the screen door opening, then shutting. Tim was shuffling his way back into the dining room. He sat himself down at his unfinished plate of food. There was silence for a while as we ate, only the clatter of cutlery on crockery could be heard.

"How do you want to do the food for tomorrow, Sam?" Oma broke the silence as she placed her cutlery neatly down on her plate.

"I s'pose we need t' start the turkey off pretty early so it can cook slowly, the rest can be prepped ready t' go. It's all pretty straightforward," I replied.

"I'll make a Christmas pudding," said Oma.

"Wow! Have y' got a recipe?"

"Yes, it's the one your mother gave me."

* * *

After lunch I stacked the dishes in the dishwasher, while Oma and Opa went off for their afternoon nap. Tim blobbed in his easy chair to watch the telly, and I joined him once I got the dishes out of the way.

"What's it like after y' take the medication? Do y' notice a difference?"

"Course I do. My whole body feels slowed down ... everythin' is like in slow motion. It's like m' brain's instructions f' m' body's movements are delayed. I'm permanently unco— same with thoughts 'n speech, everythin' is slowed, delayed. Y' must've noticed ..." His voice trailed off into space and he stared blankly at the telly.

"Yeah, I've noticed. Y' describe the effects 'f the drug well because that's exactly how y' seem t' me. Before I knew what was wrong with y', I thought y' were maybe some kind 'f genius. Y' know, a meticulous, methodical thinker 'n mover, like the stereotypical mad professor."

"Better than being a zombie," he chuckled.

23

Dick

I left Tim watching the cricket in his zombie-like state and, stepping out of the house into a wall of heat, I went in search of Erika. The beach was still choked with swimmers and bathers herded between the flags. I dumped my towel and was about to peel off my T-shirt when a voice called out, "Hi, Sam." I turned around to see Harry's wife sunbathing topless, her olive skin glistening with oil.

"Hi. How are y'? I asked hesitantly. "Didn't expect t' see y' down here."

"It is a public beach and it's such a scorching day."

"Yeah, 'f course it is," I stuttered.

"I take it you were about to have a swim?" she said.

"Yeah, kind 'f. I was actually lookin' f' some people, but it's so hot I think I need another swim. I dunno how y' can sunbathe in this heat."

"I guess it's like anything, Sam, you get used to it. I understand in New Zealand it's very cold in the winter, and you get used to the cold, don't you?"

"Yeah, I see y' point."

"Would you mind if I joined you?" Sarah asked out of the blue.

"Join me? What do y' mean?"

"Swimming, silly," she said, starting to get up.

"Oh, sorry. No 'f course not, please do."

She stood without covering her breasts, as though it was the most natural thing in the world and walked down the beach beside me. With every step I became more and more self-conscious, aware that the whole world might be watching. *Look! There goes that young drug dealer with Harry's wife! He's got a bloody cheek, hasn't he? Harry's gonna fuckin' kill him! Isn't that Sam about to get in the water? Look over there, Erika ... With that topless woman. I think he's two-timing you, Erika.*

Sarah dived straight into the first wave and came up smiling, pushing her long dark hair out of her face, waiting expectantly for me to join her. I dived into the next wave, emerging on the other side into frothing white turbulence, right beside her. Without warning she threw herself at me, trying to pull me down in the water. I succumbed to her need to dunk me by submissively sinking below the surface. *Is she just a playful, exuberant woman who isn't embarrassed t' be herself, or is she playin' some kind 'f game with me?*

I didn't stay in long, hoping to make the walk up the beach back to my towel on my own. No such luck. She came out of the water behind me, exclaiming that I was too young to be so serious.

"Yeah well, if y' husband hadn't been such an arsehole the night he pulled me up I might feel a bit lighter. And being seen on the beach with you half-naked isn't a comf'table feelin'!" I snapped at her.

"Why, Sam?"

"Go figure!"

"Oh Sam! How can you say Harry's an arsehole after how he was with you the other night?"

Pull y'self together, Sam. Y' want t' get off this fuckin' offence or what?
"Y're right. I'm sorry, I'm just a bit wound up 'n self-conscious being seen on the beach with you half-naked."

"Half-naked?" She laughed lightly. "Yes, I suppose I am. But look around you, Sam, so are almost all the other women on the beach."

I didn't want to look round, I didn't want to be any more obvious than I already was, and I didn't want to be patronised. "Y're right." I just wanted her to shut up. "I'm just feelin' paranoid cos y're Harry's wife."

"Oh, you poor thing," she murmured, leaning into me. All I could feel was her breast pressing into my arm. "Tell you what, Sam. Why don't you come back to my place for a cold drink and we can talk more about this?"

"I don't think so, not right now. Anyway, I've got things I need t' do this arvo."

"Really, like what? Sam, you should relax a little. I was only being supportive. That's why I was suggesting you come back home for a nice cold drink. I think it would be good to talk some more."

"Well, maybe. I can't cope with this heat any more."

* * *

Sarah opened the front door to her house and ushered me in. I walked in feeling like a real sneak, as if I were jeopardising any chance of freedom.

"Feel better now that we're out of the public eye?" she enquired.

"Not really," I said.

"For heaven's sake, Sam. Why not?"

"I feel like I'm sneakin' 'round b'hind Harry's back."

"Sam, he'd be happy to know you're here. It's not like we're in bed fucking!" The coarseness of her words made me shudder. "Never heard a woman use the word 'fuck' before, Sam?"

"No, it's not that."

"Oh, I see. You fancy me. I never realised! How very foolish of me. We better sort this out right now." I didn't like her tone of voice. She came up to me and stood facing me, too close for comfort. I could feel the steamy warmth of her breath, its sweetness like rose water, fuelling

202

my desire, disturbing me even more. "You're a good-looking man, Sam, but I'm married with two kids and a husband whom I love very much. He's so riddled with guilt for having arrested you." She was full of contradictions.

"He was only doin' his job," I said, feeling pathetic.

"I suppose." She reached for my waist and pulled at the tie in my board shorts.

"What're y' doin'?" I asked meekly.

"What does it look like?" she whispered. After a brief struggle with the tightness of the tie, wet from swimming, she managed to undo it, slipping her hand inside. I knew that if I didn't pull back now, my desire would overrule any remaining rational sense I had, and my protuberance would develop a mind of its own, operating under the name of Dick. My shorts were now at my ankles and Sarah dropped to her knees. I was on the verge of surrendering. *What the fuck are y' doin', Sam? Y're really gonna fuck this up if y' carry on with this shit!* Panic surged to the fore as Sarah was about to take me in her mouth. Everything seemed to be happening in slow motion — her lips ready to envelop Dick, her hands pulling my arse in.

I jumped back. "No!" I cried out. "No, I can't do this."

"Why not, Sam? You really do need to relax."

"I just can't. I keep thinkin' 'f Harry," I said, a half-truth.

"I thought you'd want me."

"Oh, I do ... but I don't. Look, if y' love Harry so much, why are y' doin' this?"

"Sam, you've a lot to learn about women." She lunged at me, my shorts still around my ankles and Dick still showing signs of interest.

"No!" I cried, raising my arms in protest.

She looked up at me with surprise, her eyes all forlorn. "What are you afraid of, Sam?"

"Everything!" I bent down and pulled up my shorts.

She grabbed me by the hand. "Come with me."

"Where are we going?"

We came to an open door and she tried to pull me through the doorway. There was a double bed in the room, with matching side tables and trendy white lamps on either side of the bed. The walls were covered with insipid, patterned wallpaper, a throw-back from the seventies. I looked at the bed, thinking that I had the perfect opportunity to fuck Harry's wife. It was still very tempting, and it felt like there would be some redemption in doing so. *Harry, y've got such a beautiful wife. How'd y' swing that? It's the uniform, isn't it, Harry?* Sarah tried dragging me further into the room, but I wasn't budging at all.

"You're weird, Sam," Sarah said.

"It's been said before."

Sarah began undressing. The voyeur in me wanted to see her naked. Her sarong fell gracefully to the floor, and she undid her bikini top from the back, then pulled the bikini brief off her waist down over her thighs. From there they dropped to her ankles. She fell backwards onto the waterbed, and absorbed into its motion, she lay there on her side, propping her head on her hand to gaze at me with a sultry look.

Don't do it, Sam, don't do it. Y' better than that. Think 'f Erika.

Then Dick spoke. *F' fuck's sake, Sam! What's with all this ditherin' 'round? She's gaggin' f' it. Stop moralisin'. Do it! Harry deserves it.*

I wanted to believe this was the first time she'd behaved this way, that I'd stirred something special in her, that I was intriguing to her. Maybe Harry's story about me had created a fantasy in her mind. On the dresser I saw a wedding photo of Sarah and Harry. I walked up to it, and wanting to take a closer look, I picked it up to inspect their faces.

"Y' made a good-lookin' couple on y' wedding day. Y're both so happy lookin'."

"Put it back, Sam, and come here!" she demanded, then softened. "Please, Sam, come here."

"I don't understand why y' want to do this. Are you unhappy?"

"No! Not at all."

"Then why are y' doing this?"

"Because I can," she said, creating motion on the waterbed.

"That seems like a strange reason. Y' don't think y'd hurt Harry if y' went through with this?" I asked, placing the photo back on the dresser.

"He'll never know." She was becoming fidgety. "Is it a crime to be attracted to you?"

"It will be in Harry's eyes … and in the eyes 'f God. Even if Harry doesn't know, somethin' won't feel right, which he might not equate t' us fuckin', but somethin' won't feel right. There'll be this unspoken discomfort circulatin' in y' relationship."

"Sam, you're talking nonsense. People do this sort of thing all the time. I've got friends doing it. That doesn't mean we love our husbands any less. It's just that once you've been married awhile something extra seems necessary," she replied, as if it absolved the situation.

"Bullshit! Why be in a relationship if that's what y' need t' do?"

"Spice of life, Sam."

She was off the bed and coming towards me. It would've been easy to give in to her, to take her right there and then. *Take that Harry, y' cunt!* Instead, I stepped out of the room into the hallway.

"I'm goin', Sarah. Thanks f' the cold drink," I said, backing down the hallway.

"You're a freak, Sam!"

"I know but put y'self in my shoes. If Harry caught me with you, I'd be history. I'll let m'self out. See y' 'round."

* * *

I headed back toward the beach, feeling perplexed by the contradictory images of Sarah in my mind. The first was of the night I met her as Harry's wife — a charming, warm, supportive woman with a certain charisma. Bumping into her on the beach, though, revealed a different side of her personality — a flirtatious nature that disturbed me from the moment we swam in the ocean. I'd been crazy to return to her house, to fool around with a cop's wife, in my situation, was madness. It alarmed me how close I'd come to allowing myself to indulge my alter ego. Even though I desired her, I needed to keep Dick in check.

Looking down the beach I could see hordes of people dotted like red ants between the flags. In that moment I felt a certain sense of freedom and individuality, separate from the masses. *People are so rule abidin', such conformists. Not that I'm an anarchist goin' 'round breakin' the law all the time. People want t' be seen with the masses, doin' what everyone else is doing. We really are like sheep!*

I made my way through the sheep in the hope that I might spot Erika. It felt like forever since I'd seen her. It was probably just as well I couldn't find her, as I was in no state of mind to be with her. I headed back to the house alone and showered, washing the afternoon down the plughole. Freshened, I went upstairs where Tim was still glued to the telly, watching the same one-day cricket match between Australia and New Zealand.

"Better than watching wallpaper peel, huh?"

"What?" he asked.

"Y' know, wallpaper … the stuff on the walls," I said, pointing to the wall. "It's all around y'."

"What's with you?" Tim grunted.

24

Christmas

Christmas Day arrived relatively unannounced and low key except for the fact that I was in the kitchen helping Oma stuff the turkey. I had my fist in its cavity, holding on to one of its legs so that I could give it a good ramming. That way the stuffing would be packed in nicely. I carefully worked the stuffed turkey into an oven bag that Oma was holding open. It was going to be a tight fit being such a monster of a bird. Once we'd manipulated the turkey into the bag, I tied it off with the provided twist-tie, and laid it in the roasting dish, then slid the whole thing into the oven. I set the oven temperature for 180 degrees Celsius. It was going to take all morning to cook.

With the turkey out of the way, I knocked up a special breakfast of scrambled eggs, bacon and toast while Tim cracked a bottle of bubbly. We felt like we were the cat's whiskers, and Opa thought he was in heaven, going on and on about how good breakfast was with grunts and groans of appreciation every time he swallowed another mouthful. We didn't buy one another presents, as I had no money to speak of and hadn't received gifts from Oma and Opa since I was about ten years old. Oma did produce a parcel from Mum and Dad, which I unwrapped eagerly. It was full of necessities such as underwear, T-shirts, a couple of pairs of shorts, and a few Christmas treats. It was nice of Mum to be so thoughtful.

* * *

Later in the morning, with the turkey in the oven and the vegetables prepped, we all sauntered down to the beach for a swim. It was yet another balmy summer's day and the beach was packed. *I guess if y' campin' 'n y' don't have the facilities t' put on a good old traditional roast turkey, what better way t' spend y' day than on the beach, 'n then maybe whip out the barbie later on 'n knock-up a bit 'f sizzle with a few beers 'n wine. After all, that's the Ozzie way.* We were all in the water together, Oma floating on her back in calmer waters while Opa braved it further out with Tim and me, attempting to catch the odd wave.

Suddenly someone was on my back, their hands were covering my eyes and I was supposed to guess who it was. I could feel their chest pushing into my back and the length of their body against mine. I took the hands away from my eyes and grasped them as I spun around.

"Merry Christmas," Erika beamed, then kissed me.

"Merry Christmas, babe," I replied, beaming my own smile. I liked it that Erika was so into me. I liked the feeling that she wanted me so much. I held her tightly in the water, feeling warm and fuzzy, enjoying the moment.

"That's m' grandfather," I said, pointing to him as he caught another innocuous wave which carried him the small distance between us. "Opa!" I shouted. He looked up disorientated, then smiled when he saw me standing there. He came towards us looking rather pleased with himself.

"I think I'm getting the hang of it, Sam."

"I think y' might be."

"And who's this pretty young lady?" he asked, blatantly admiring her.

"Erika, meet m' grandfather, Theo."

"Hi, Theo." Her face went all red and she couldn't look at him.

"Erika is comin' f Christmas dinner."

"Hmm ... Good, huh," he said, his automatic reply. "I'm going to get out now. So I'll see you later on." He waded through the water and onto the beach where Oma was drying herself.

"Guess I'd better get going too so that dinner is ready on time." Erika latched onto me like a limpet, kissing me long and lingeringly. Eventually I managed to extract myself from her arms. "I could handle a bit more 'f that later on," I whispered.

"You'll have to play your cards right," she said, grinning stupidly at me.

* * *

The house was pungent with the aroma of turkey. After making sure everything was under control in the kitchen, I went down to the basement and showered, enjoying the fine spray of hot water that hit me like softened needles as it broke up on impact, cascading down my body. I stood in the shower far too long, as though the water was purifying my body, washing my soul clean.

Upstairs I found Oma adding the finishing touches to a large bowl of salad.

"Sam, I've put the potatoes in the oven, but I just wasn't sure about the kumara. I imagine it doesn't need as long, does it?"

"I guess not. Mum always puts it in a bit later."

"We'll do that then, shall we?"

"Sounds good t' me. Do we still want peas?" I opened the freezer door at the bottom of the fridge, pulled out the bag of frozen peas and slapped them on the bench top, the way a fishmonger would treat a fish at the market.

Oma jumped. "Heavens, boy! What are you doing?"

"Being dramatic." I grinned, cutting the top of the bag open with scissors, and pouring the peas into a saucepan. "That should do it."

"Sam, what drinks shall we have on the table?" Opa came into the kitchen, all freshened up. His abundant grey hair was swept back in a part to one side, his beard looked as though it had been trimmed, his face was tanned and weathered from years out in the sun. His features were quite refined, distinctively European. He was a handsome man for his age.

"Well, I suppose we should be traditional, so let's start with champagne," I said. Opa fossicked in the cupboard and found a mixture of champagne and wine glasses, which he dotted round the table.

"Who would like a wee aperitif now?" Opa looked at Oma and I expectantly, his eyes begging us to say yes.

"Why not?" I said, feeling like I could do with one to relax me a bit before the onslaught of the masses. As if on cue, the doorbell rang. "I guess that'll be our dinner guests," I said. "Yes, I'll definitely have an aperitif. Looks like y' might have a few more t' pour."

I walked through the lounge to the hallway, past Tim in his usual seat with the telly on. "Why don't we have a bit 'f ambient music, Tim?" No reply. "I take it that was a yes?"

I opened the door and there they all were in their finest beach attire.

"Come in, come in." I gestured with my hand, stepping aside to allow them through as I ushered them into the lounge. "Y'all know Tim."

"Hi, Tim," said Erika, waving as if he were far away.

There was a staggered chorus of "Hi, Tim."

"Come and meet m' grandparents," I said, leading them into the dining room only to be headed off at the pass as Oma and Opa appeared expectantly.

"Well, here we are. This is m' Oma Helena 'n m' Opa Theo."

Oma was the first to step forward, reaching for Erika's hand, not to shake it, but to hold it as she always did when meeting someone for the first time.

"This is Erika," I said.

Oma smiled warmly at her. "Pleased to meet you, Erika."

And so we continued through the formality of introductions.

"What would everyone like to drink?" asked Opa. "That is, assuming everyone wants a drink."

"A tinny would be grand," suggested Stu.

"Hmm," responded Opa.

"A tinny, Opa," I chimed in loudly, winking at Stu.

"What's a tinny?" He looked confused. His forehead screwed up in a line of wrinkled frowns.

"A tinny's what an Ozzie calls a can 'f beer," I replied.

"Oh, I see," he said, and laughed.

"And it better be cold," I added. He'd already turned, heading for the fridge. "Y'd better get several 'f those. His mate Mal drinks 'em as well, 'n I think I'll have the same," I said loudly.

Oma was in the kitchen attending to the saucepans on the stove, in between trying to hold a conversation with the girls. Mal had sauntered into the lounge to watch telly with Tim.

"I think you'll need to attend to the turkey soon, Sam," said Oma.

Opa was in the midst of pouring his own tinny into a glass and was talking to Stu who was sipping on his beer.

"I see you ladies don't have drinks yet. Opa, what's the story, pouring y'self a drink b'fore attendin' t' the ladies?" I asked cheekily.

"I got a little distracted," he stuttered, quickly putting his glass back down.

"It's alright, I'll sort them out. So … what will it be ladies? Champagne or wine?" I asked.

"Champagne," Claudia replied.

"Of course," I said. "Oma, a glass 'f champagne f' you too?"

"Yes please, Sam. Then I really think you should attend to the turkey."

"Gobble, gobble, gobble." I danced around the room like a crazy turkey, all the time looking at Erika. I popped the champagne cork and as it rocketed to the roof the girls squealed with delight. I poured the fizzing liquid into their glasses and one for myself.

"Now, Sam. You need to check the turkey!" Oma insisted impatiently.

"Okay. Please excuse me ladies." They giggled and sauntered off into the lounge.

The turkey was ready. The meat was falling away nicely from the bone, and in no time I had stripped it to its carcass, producing a serving plate full of steaming white meat. We sat down to a table overflowing with food — roasted vegetables, green peas with fresh mint and melting butter, broccoli, baby potatoes, a tossed salad, ham sliced off the bone, and of course, the plate full of roast turkey. Everyone managed to squeeze around the table and plates of food were passed in all directions as everyone marvelled at the mouth-watering array of food. Christmas was an excuse for excess.

Dinner was a success. The food was enjoyed, conversation was light and easy, and no one drank too much. Tim was on his best behaviour, and despite having been recently medicated, he engaged in conversation. Everyone ate too much and still there was food left over. The ham and turkey would feed us for the rest of the week, by which time I'd never want to see another slice of either.

"Who would like some Christmas pudding?" Oma asked. We all groaned. I rubbed my stomach.

"I don't think I could at the moment," I replied. My comment gave licence for everyone else to decline except for Opa, who seemed eager to continue with dessert.

"I'd love t' try some later, Helena," Stu said politely, and the others nodded in agreement. We adjourned to the lounge and sprawled ourselves out on the couches, beached like whales waiting for the tide to come in and ease our distress. Oma and Opa excused themselves for their afternoon nap. We sat around talking and drinking more champagne until someone suggested a swim might be a good idea.

* * *

Every mother, father, child, and their dog must've had the same thought. The beach was crammed full of sunbathers, and swimmers were packed in between the swimming flags fluttering in the afternoon's offshore breeze. I didn't fancy squeezing in amidst all the sun worshippers, glistening like well-oiled meat on the barbie. I imagined a giant pair of tongs swooping out of the sky and turning them all over to roast the other side.

"What do y' think 'f goin' further down the beach away from all this?" Stu asked us all.

"Suits me," I replied. The others murmured in agreement. We trudged through the hot sand, moving a few hundred metres further down the beach, away from the maddening crowd. I spread my towel out and flopped onto my stomach to absorb the heat of the sun. It would have been easy to nod off with a belly full of turkey and a bladder full of champagne and to wake up an hour later cooked like a lobster, skin redder than red. It didn't take much for my fair skin to fire up.

"Hey, that was an awesome dinner, Sam. Your Oma did a real good job," said Erika.

"Yeah, she did. It was a combined effort though, her 'n me. I like cookin', always have."

"It's a great skill to have," said Erika. "That turkey was the nicest I've ever tasted, not that we have turkey very often."

"Yeah? Well, cheers. I think I've got t' go f' a swim before I explode," I announced, standing up and stretching.

213

"Y' what?" Mal asked, looking at me like I was nuts.

"Never mind." Erika and I walked down to the sea hand in hand.

She's such a beautiful lookin' girl. What's her attraction t' me? I would've thought I'd be too rough 'round the edges f' her. She's like m' dream goddess 'f a woman. What's it goin' t' be like when they're all gone? I wonder how I'll cope on my own t' face m' demons?

The sea had warmed dramatically over the past few weeks, influenced by warm currents circulating the coast from the north. It was refreshing to be in the water, but a few moments out and the heat of the sun made me want to return home to be under shelter.

"I'm goin' back t' the house," I said. The others opted to stay, except for Erika, who was eager to come with me and I was more than happy for her to do so.

"I'm going to miss you when I go home," she said out of the blue as we walked along the beach.

"Y'll be fine once y' get back int' the swing 'f things. It'll be just another mem'rable holiday y' had in Yaringa."

"No, it won't!" she cried, hurt showing in her eyes. "It won't be just like any other memorable holiday. How could it be now that I've met you? Going home and getting into the swing of things will be that much harder now. I know it's crazy, but I love you, Sam!"

I didn't want to hear those words. They penetrated my core like a hot knife slicing through butter.

"Whoa," I said, putting up my hands as though trying to halt a horse that had just bolted. "Y' shouldn't've gone sayin' that, don't complicate y' life. I might be goin' somewhere undesirable soon. Y' know it isn't a good look t' be in love with a criminal. Not at your age, Erika. I mean waitin' f' me t' do time, it ain't good. What'll y' friends think? What'll y' parents say?"

"I don't care what any of them think! Besides, I don't need them to know. And another thing."

"What?"

"You haven't been sentenced yet. I thought the law was that you're innocent until proven guilty."

"Well, I'll be pleading guilty cos I am. It's the circumstances under which I'm guilty that might save me from goin' inside. The operative word is 'might'."

Erika was frowning at me. "If you want to give up and believe that, then that'll be your lot. I refuse to think that!" she blurted out.

"But I dunno what's goin' t' happen t' me. I'm just lookin' at things kind 'f practically, y' know. That's one 'f the possibilities, 'n I have t' be prepar'd f' that scenario," I continued.

"Haven't you ever heard of the power of positive thinking? There's a good book, it's by Norman Pearce and it's called *The Power of Positive Thinking*. You should read it. One of my teachers gave it to me. I can send it to you if you like," she insisted.

"Sure," I replied, hoping we could steer the conversation down a different path. She'd become overly passionate about my dilemma, and her words were starting to bug me in the same way a teacher's lecture might. *I should be appreciative 'f everythin' she's sayin', but I'm not!* I could feel the cynicism in me, welling up unreasonably, my whole being wanting to lash out at anything authoritative, anybody telling me how I should be or what I should be doing. *She's not in my situation. She doesn't know what it feels like. She's rationalisin' from a place 'f ignorance, based on a dangerous word: 'hope'. God talks about hope 'n prayer ... everyone's always hopin' f' somethin'.*

We walked and talked our way back to the house as if we'd not noticed the steps it had taken to get there. The walk reminded me of when I was a kid of about four and I'd been to the shops around the corner from our house to buy sweets with some money I'd acquired from a great aunt. As I was coming out of the shop, I felt something underneath my foot, simultaneously a dog barked, making me jump. When I looked at the dog, I saw it only had three legs, and I looked around for the fourth leg, thinking that I'd stood on it, causing the leg to fall off. I ran home terrified of what I'd done, and it wasn't until later that I realised I hadn't injured the dog as it was already missing a leg. Now one of those surreal moments occurred again, where it felt as if Erika and I had just floated home. Anything could've happened around me and I wouldn't have noticed.

* * *

We entered the caravan, and I kicked off my jandals as we sat down on the bed and looked at each other awkwardly. Erika appeared so mournful, but all I could think about was how great she looked in her bikini. Her skin glowed from the remnants of baby oil, accentuating the firmness of her stomach. The towel draped around her waist covered her legs down to her knees, and I wanted to slip my hand up her leg and feel her quiver as I gently made my way up to her bikini bottom. I felt a rising in my board shorts, aware that it wouldn't be long before she'd notice. She moved in close and gazed into my eyes, still looking somewhat downcast but increasingly less so as she edged closer, and her skin touched mine. I put my arms around her and held her, resisting my own needs to meet hers.

Her lips found mine, gently pushing against them, touching and pulling away, then touching again as if undecided whether she wanted to kiss me. Each time she pulled away, I pulled her back, encouraging her until she upped the tempo. Soft kisses became harder as her tongue searched my mouth endlessly. There was no room to reciprocate, so I responded by slipping my hand underneath her towel, up the inside of her thighs. She gasped softly into my ear, her senses heightened, and my own level of control wavering as I found my way inside her bikini brief. My hand moved over her soft mound, reaching eagerly inside her, and she raised her pelvis to greet the sensation, pulling me tight to her, our mouths locked in passion. I resisted her need to have me inside her, preferring to build her to a climax we could share. I worked several fingers inside her, and she writhed all over the bed as though she had an itch that couldn't be scratched. I moved down her torso, kissing her breasts, my mouth desiring her nipples. Aware of how sensitive she was, I lingered long enough for her to want more before taking my tongue down her midriff, below her navel and down one thigh, coming back up the other thigh to the place she so longed for me to be. She totally surrendered to the experience. I worked on her softly, building up to more vigorous strokes that had her moaning loudly. Her moaning grew more primal; her pelvis rose higher and higher in her quest for euphoria. I felt her reaching that point of no return, and I moved quickly up her body finding her face then her mouth and pushed my tongue inside. She clamped down on it, and at the same time I slipped my firmness between her thighs. I felt her passion rising and she called out, *"God! Yes. Oh God, yes! Oh God! No, no, no! Please ... Oh God, yes!"*

Her cries were joined by my own outpouring. "Oh fuck ... Oh Jesus ... Oh baby ... Oh yeah!" And when there were no more words to utter, we collapsed into each other, holding on tight, wanting the moment to last.

* * *

I awoke with a start to someone knocking on the door of the caravan.

"Yoo-hoo, Sam. Are you in there?" It was Oma. I was dripping in sweat with Erika still tangled around me like a rag doll. She stirred to life.

I'd been immersed in an endless nightmare. Bruce had tied bricks to me and was about to push me off a bridge into a deep, dark river, where my body wouldn't be discovered for a long time. He was laughing like the devil at how easy it was to dispose of me.

There was another knock on the door. "Sam, are you there?"

"Yes, I'm just wakin' up," I replied, slightly irritated and not feeling very with it yet.

"I was wondering where you were, that's all. Opa and I are going for a swim, then we thought it would be time for some supper."

"Okay, I'll see y' f' supper."

Erika was awake now, and she snuggled tight into me like a limpet on a rock.

"What's going on, baby?" she mumbled, her eyes still closed.

"M' grandparents are off t' the beach f' a swim."

"Your grandparents are very cool. I wish they were mine. Hey! How come you're sweating all over?"

"I was havin' a bad dream when Oma knocked on the door 'n woke me."

"What kind of bad dream?" She propped her head up in her hand, resting her elbow on the bed, looking at me expectantly.

"Just one 'f those bad dreams where y're fallin' off a cliff 'n y' fallin', fallin', fallin', 'n y' wonder if y' ever goin' t' wake up," I lied.

"And you did," she said, snuggling into me. "Those kinds of dreams are really scary, aren't they? I always wonder what would happen if I didn't wake up and hit the ground."

"Some people say y' die if y' don't wake up."

"Really?" She looked surprised.

"Truly."

* * *

Erika left to be with her parents for the remainder of Christmas Day. Although I wasn't hungry in the slightest, I soon found myself in the house at the table, gazing vaguely at leftovers.

"That was a successful dinner, Sam," stated Oma, looking pleased.

"Yeah, I s'pose it was," I said, feeling melancholy all of a sudden.

"Is something the matter, Sam?" asked Oma.

"Did you have a good day?" Opa asked, as though he hadn't heard any of the conversation.

"No, nothing is really the matter … guess I'm a bit tired. Mostly it's been a great day. Thanks for being here. I guess I'm goin' t' miss everyone when they're gone. You'll all be goin' soon 'n I've still got a couple 'f months till I appear in court. It seems t' be takin' forever."

"What's that, Sam?" Opa asked, cupping his hand to his left ear, hoping to capture my words.

"Yes, I can understand that's going to be difficult for you, Sam," Oma said, looking intensely at me, genuine concern etched in her eyes.

"What's the problem, Helena?" Opa still had his hand cupped to his ear, determined to be in on the conversation. *It must be a pain in the butt f' him. The poor bugger, he only hears snippets 'f what's being said. He never gets the complete picture.* Oma uttered something in Dutch, and he mumbled something back before continuing with his meal.

All the while Tim remained focused on his meal, not revealing any interest in what was going on. I could feel my eyes welling up in the corners and tried to suppress the inevitable overflow. Hot tears poured down my face, falling off my cheeks, landing in splatters on the table. I stood up, pushed my chair away with the backs of my knees and walked out.

"Where are you going, boy? Sit down and finish your meal!" Opa shouted. I didn't reply. I detested being called 'boy'. I walked to the front door and down the stairs into the caravan. Inside I threw myself onto the bed dramatically and lay there, tears spilling onto the sheet, the smell of Erika on my pillow as I buried my head and cried in great heaving sobs.

I must've fallen asleep again because I was awoken by a knock on the door. I stirred slowly, not sure if I wanted to face anyone. My immediate thought was that it was Erika.

"May I come in, Sam?" It was Oma's soft, even voice. I got up without saying anything and unlocked the door. Oma's tiny stature greeted me in the frame of the doorway, like a guardian angel sent from heaven. "May I come in?" she asked again.

"Of course," I said, suddenly aware that I must've looked a right mess. She gave me her hand so I could assist her to step up into the caravan, and she embraced me warmly.

"Come … Let's sit down and talk for a bit," she said. I gestured to the table, which stood between two bench-type seats built into either side of the caravan, designed to fold down into a bed. Oma sat and patted the seat to suggest that I come and sit next to her. Like an obedient dog with its tail between its legs, I came towards her and sat down, bowing my head, feeling ashamed to be seen this way. She put her hand on my back and rubbed it gently. After what seemed like an eternity of silence, she spoke.

"I realise it will be hard for you, Sam, when we have all left. But remember that Ted and Val will be back, and your father will arrive a few days before your court hearing."

I nodded my head, knowing she was only trying to highlight the positive in what was a negative situation. "I'll be alright. I'm just havin' a moment 'f feelin' empty 'n alone. When I was a kid, I use t' feel the same sense 'f anxiety late on a Sunday when the weekend was over, and it was almost time t' go back t' school. Everything seem'd t' go quiet on a Sunday afternoon 'n I'd feel all blue and melancholy, like the world was about t' end. I just want'd t' curl up in a ball on m' bed 'n fall asleep, dreamin' I was somewhere else."

Oma sat listening, nodding occasionally without saying anything.

"That's when I got int' readin'. It was like an escape from all my depressing feelings. Did y' know that Dad thought I should go across the border t' Victoria 'n catch a plane home from Melbourne? He said the authorities wouldn't care about a small fish like me. But I feel I need t' sort this out, face the music 'n take what they dish out t' me."

"You're very brave, Sam. I have to say I admire the way you've been coping with all of this. You seem very strong within yourself."

"I don't always feel strong, but I do feel that I need t' stay here 'n sort this all out so I can move on. I'm sorry I've put y' through this."

"Things happen and what's done is done. You can move on from this and use the experience to grow." Oma was so full of wisdom. She had the ability to find the right words to put things in perspective. "I'll leave you now to be with yourself."

We embraced and as we separated, she put her hands on either side of my face, pulled my head down towards her and kissed me on the forehead. "Know that you are blessed, and that everything will turn out for the best."

25

New Year's Eve

New Year's Eve arrived. It wouldn't be long now before all my friends packed up and went home, and I was making the most of the last few days. We planned the evening so that Oma and Opa wouldn't feel excluded. The Christmas Day crowd returned to our lounge, this time for a game of charades. Oma loved games and suggested we play some to make the evening more engaging.

I'd made an 'oliebollen' mix for later on. It was a traditional Dutch doughnut that had apple, raisins and spices mixed into the dough, which was dropped in dollops into hot oil, cooked briefly until brown, then removed and drained, and finally rolled in icing sugar and stacked on a plate to serve. I loved them and considered oliebollen to be far tastier than any traditional American doughnuts. I had placed the mixture on the bench so the yeast could activate, creating airy and light doughnuts. Traditionally, they're cooked just before midnight and enjoyed with coffee or mulled red wine. Only thing was, we weren't going to be home at midnight. We'd arranged to go to the local pub an hour before midnight, where most locals and campers of our age would see in the New Year.

Charades proved to be a runaway success with everyone in hysterics over some of the antics and actions required to enact the selected movie or novel. We split into two teams — Erika, Stu, Oma and me on one team, with Claudia, Mal, Opa and Tim on the other. I never expected Tim to participate. Ironically, he got right into acting out *One Flew Over the Cuckoo's Nest*, making a real show of being a cuckoo, but it wasn't until he changed from being completely nuts to being a kookaburra that we finally got what he was trying to be. I was doubled up on the couch watching his performance, happy that he'd come so far out of himself. When I initially raised the subject of having my friends over for New Year's Eve and Oma suggested charades, I eyed her sceptically, wondering how the others would feel. It reeked of a blue-rinse brigade's knitters evening, followed by a light supper. To my surprise, no one screwed up their face, in fact they took to it faster than ducks to water. Oma flashed me a wry smile as the evening kicked off with full participation. It was impossible to halt the charge or stop for knitters' aperitifs.

Erika joined me in the kitchen, curiously watching the dollops of oliebollen mix I was dropping into the hot cooking oil. The oil formed frenzied bubbles around the mix, like hungry enzymes in a laundry detergent commercial. As they browned, I removed the balls with tongs and placed them on a plate lined with a paper towel to soak up the excess oil.

"Can I try one?" Erika asked.

"Yes, of course, but first y' need t' roll it in icing sugar," I replied.

"Why's that?"

"Cos that's how they're served." I reached into the cupboard and extracted a bag of icing sugar which I handed to Erika. "That cupboard by y' leg," I said, nodding my head in the other direction, "should have a shallow dish that'll be good f' rollin' them in."

"A shallow dish for rolling them in," she repeated, mocking me with her big smile. "You sound like you're on some cooking show."

"Oh yeah, I will be one day."

"Yeah right," said Stu, walking in and interrupting our banter. "So these are oliebollen, eh?" he asked, eyeing them up.

"You can't have one until I've rolled them in icing sugar," Erika stated smugly.

"Is that so?" Stu said.

"Yes, it is."

"Damn right. Stu, y' can get glasses ready f' the mulled wine."

"Can I now? And where would I find them?" He began opening cupboards and peering into them.

"Not down there, in that one directly above y'."

He opened the cupboard to reveal a fine array of wine, highball and whisky glasses. Ted was well stocked in this department.

"Ah, yes. How silly 'f me not t' realise they'd be in here." Stu removed the wine glasses and lined them up on the bench.

"Mmm, that's delicious."

I looked at Erika to see she'd taken a bite out of a freshly rolled oliebollen.

"Hey!" I cried.

"Sorry, it was too much to resist." She began to laugh; it was infectious.

"Here give me some 'f that," I joked as I reached for it. She pulled her hand away from me, holding the oliebollen high out of my reach.

I was watching her looking pleased with herself when Stu, who was standing behind her, suddenly snatched it from her grasp, quickly putting it to his mouth and taking a bite.

"Mmm, I see what y' mean."

"Give it back!" Erika demanded, looking mortified.

"Catch, Sam!" cried Stu, throwing the oliebollen at me. I caught it and rammed what was left in my mouth.

"Mmm, very tasty," I mumbled through my full mouth.

"You two are cheeky blighters," announced Erika, as if it was a revelation.

"But not half as cheeky as you, eh?" said Stu. "That was one damn fine Dutch doughnut, Sam."

"Well, we're almost done here. Got all those glasses ready, Stu?" I pulled a tray out from beside the oven and handed it to him.

"That's the story," he said.

"We need a jug to pour the mulled wine into," Erika said as she began opening cupboard doors in search of one, clambering through cluttered cupboards seldom ventured into.

"This might do the trick!" she proclaimed, waving around a seventies-style German ceramic jug.

"Yep, that'll do perfectly," I responded.

"I'll just pour hot water into the jug first to warm it up," said Erika.

"Good thinkin', Ninety-Nine."

"What?" She looked at me weirdly.

"Maxwell Smart," said Stu.

"What?" Erika was looking at us both as if we had lost the plot.

"Have you never seen the TV show *Get Smart*?" I asked.

"No," replied Erika, looking concerned.

"Well, I'll be damned. Maxwell Smart is a secret agent, Agent Eighty-Six, and Agent Ninety-Nine, a woman, is his partner. Maxwell Smart always says the line: 'Good thinkin', Ninety-Nine'," I explained.

"Agent Ninety-Nine's not only his partner, she's also his really sexy wife, 'n she's always savin' his arse when he fucks up. She's the brains of the operation. Maxwell Smart is dumber than dumb," added Stu.

"You guys are too much sometimes," she stated, looking bemused.

"No, you're just not with the programme," said Stu.

"Watch it, Stu! I'm the one with a jug full of hot wine," she said, pouring the last of the mulled wine from the saucepan into the jug.

"Right, let's get int' the lounge with all of this," I intervened, picking up the plate of oliebollen.

"Right then!" Erika ceremoniously led the way holding the tray with the wine and glasses. Stu and I followed obediently, with oliebollen and paper serviettes.

"Wow, look at this! You've done well," exclaimed Oma.

"Mmm," was all that came from Opa's mouth as he salivated, leaning forward on his seat in anticipation.

Mal and Claudia were on the couch, inseparable as usual, like a couple of beavers, and Tim had retreated to his armchair, sitting there like a silent king on his throne.

Here I was in a tiny seaside village in southern New South Wales with my ex-girlfriend's psychotic brother, four people on holiday in Yaringa whom I'd befriended in a short space of time, and my grandparents who'd flown in from New Zealand because Oma insisted I not spend Christmas alone.

"A toast!" announced Stu, who had passed a glass of mulled wine to everyone as quickly as Erika had been able to pour it. "Firstly, here's to Sam. You're a great bloke 'n we'll be sorry t' leave y' knowin' what you've got t' face. So chin up 'n good luck. We'll all be thinkin' of y'. Everything's goin' t' work out just fine."

"I'll drink t' that," Mal said, joining in and raising his glass.

"To Sam," Erika raised her glass, tears pooling in her eyes.

"To Sam!" they chorused, raising their glasses.

"Damn fine mulled wine," commented Stu.

"Y' can thank Oma f' that. She made it. I just heated it up," I said. Stu raised his glass to Oma who responded by raising her own and smiling. "I'd like t' say thank you, everybody," I said, standing and raising my voice to interrupt. "I'd like t' toast y'all." I cast my eyes over all of them one by one, including Tim. "Y've b'come good friends 'n a great distraction over the last few weeks. Happy New Year t' all of y'. I hope 1981 is a bloody good one! And …" I added, turning to Oma and Opa sitting together on the couch, "I'd like t' thank m' grandparents f' comin' out here 'n makin' Christmas special."

"F' he's a jolly good fellow," Stu started, and everyone burst into song, completing the verses.

"Right," I shouted above the racket. "You've got t' try an oliebollen or I'll be offended!"

"They're bloody good. I tried one in the kitchen earlier." Stu picked the plate up and passed it to Opa, whose eyes lit up like the Christmas tree as the plate hovered in front of him.

"Mmm, what have we here, huh? Thank you." He picked one up, looking it over before he put it to his mouth, and took a bite. The rest of us swooped on the plate like gannets diving on a school of fish.

"If I could just say a small thing," said Oma as we all hoed into the oliebollen. "It's been a pleasure to meet all of you young people and to have you up here for Christmas Day, and again this evening. It's been good for Theo and me, and made a big difference for Sam."

"I'll miss Sam very much. Don't know how I'm going to be able to leave him," blurted Erika. "We go back home in few days, and I'm not looking forward to it at all." Tears were forming in the corners of her eyes. "Sorry." She buried her face in Claudia's shoulder.

"We'll all miss y', Sam," proclaimed Mal, who never said much.

"Yeah well, thanks guys, but let's eat up 'n enjoy the night. It's a bit depressin' t' dwell on this. It's been great havin' y'all here, but right now I'd rather forget about the fact y'all are goin' home soon."

"Hey, it must be time t' head up t' the pub," Mal said, looking at his watch. "It's almost eleven, time t' party!"

The guys wished Oma and Opa a Happy New Year, kissing Oma on the cheek and shaking hands with Opa.

It came my turn to kiss Oma goodnight, and she whispered in my ear, "Not too much drink, son. Enjoy yourself and be sensible."

"I'll see y' in the mornin'," I said, ignoring her comment.

"Happy New Year, Sam," said Opa, embracing me before I made for the door. "Your friends are nice. Have a good night with them. Good oliebollen, huh?"

"Thanks, Opa. See y' later."

* * *

I was free. Even though the night had been fun, it wasn't quite the same staying with the oldies when there was entertainment at the pub. The world felt electric as we walked the short distance to the pub, singing 'Auld Lang Syne'. We sang it badly, stumbling over the words and only really doing justice to the chorus, feeling jolly from the drinks we'd consumed back at the house.

As we approached the pub, we could hear the band playing a Split Enz cover, and we all joined in on the chorus, singing and jumping up and down, shaking our heads madly. There was no cover charge and no bouncers on the door for a change. Holidaymakers outnumbered locals 4-to-1, whereas in the off-season it was just the locals shaking their booties. Everyone seemed very drunk as the band continued pumping out its covers. Erika was clinging to me, she seemed afraid we'd become separated. We waded through the sea of bodies to the bar and caught the eye of the barman who nodded and took my order. He didn't look like a happy man tonight.

"Bit busy for y', Don?" I asked in jest.

"Son, 'bit' ain't the word. It's like a fuckin' Chinese market in here t'night. No one knows if they're comin' or goin'."

"Looks a bit that way." I took the wine coolers, passed them to

Erika, and juggled the beers myself. Carrying four glasses was no easy feat. Fortunately, Mal spied me and rescued a couple from my hand. I handed Tim his beer, wondering how it would affect his medication, hoping he wouldn't pour too much down his throat. I'd never seen him indulge before and wasn't interested in keeping an eye on him tonight.

"Cheers then," said Mal, raising his glass. Our glasses clashed together, beer cascading over the sides, and we swilled greedily as if we'd just returned from the Sahara Desert. "That barely touched the sides, must be my round," Mal said as he headed for the bar.

"Dance with me," Erika whispered in my ear. I grasped her hand and led her to the dance floor. It wasn't really my thing to dance in an environment like this. I hated crowded dance floors where all you could do was shuffle your feet, and if you accidentally banged into some bloke's girlfriend, you'd get shoved across the floor. There was the potential for a punch up, which often became a brawl. I'd seen it all before. We shuffled our way through a Dire Straits song, followed by The Police's hit 'Message in a Bottle' which I loved. Erika moved in, wrapped her arms around my neck and held onto me for the rest of the song. When the song was over, I peeled her arms away from around my neck only to see she was crying again.

"Sorry, it's just that I can't stop worrying about leaving you. What's going to happen?"

"Come on, let's get off the dance floor. See if we can't get a seat somewhere."

We found the guys and Claudia pretty much where we'd left them, still standing drinking their schooners.

Claudia's become Mal's appendage. She smiles 'n seems inoffensive, but she rarely says a fuckin' word. She's a birdbrain, a bore... And she's right int' Mal, 'n he seems t' love her t' bits. Neither 'f them talk a lot, so maybe they suit each other really well, or perhaps that's what love does t' some people. Turns them int' happy, lovin', fuckin' zombies.

***

Opa and I went walking on the beach one day and ended up going a lot further than expected, deciding to venture around the rocks at the far end of Yaringa Beach to see if we could reach the next bay. We were halfway around, taking it fairly easy as Opa wasn't the steadiest on his feet. We had just negotiated a large, awkward rock and there in front of us, tucked slightly into the cliff face, was Mal with his trousers down around his ankles and Claudia's head bobbing furiously in front of him, like a goose's head does when you get too close. Mal was oblivious to us at first, but when he spotted us, he didn't pull away or push Claudia off.

"Don't mind us!" I called out. Claudia stopped briefly to see what was going on, leaving Mal momentarily exposed.

"That was an unexpected encounter," said Opa, laughing as we retreated back around the rocks toward the beach. I couldn't stop laughing at his casual comment.

***

"Y'r beer 'n Erika's drink are on the table," Mal said, spitting beer in my face as he gestured to the table behind him.

"Come 'n sit down," I said to Erika, leading her to the table and pulling the seat out for her. I sat on the seat beside her. She'd stopped crying but tears still streaked her face. I noticed Claudia looking vaguely concerned for a few seconds, flashing one of her brainless smiles. Erika smiled meekly back at her before looking to me and reaching for her drink. She skulled her wine cooler as if hoping it would give some relief. I automatically reached for my beer, taking a large gulp, then another. It tasted so good I almost downed the whole lot while Erika stared mournfully at me.

"Let's go outside 'n get some fresh air," I suggested.

"No," she said, shaking her head adamantly. "I'll be alright. Sorry, I didn't mean to ruin your evening."

"Y' haven't. So y' don't need t' worry thinkin' y' have. Okay?"

"Must be my turn t' refuel," said Stu, arriving at the table. "Drink up, son. It's not a fuckin' tea party." I skulled the remaining two mouthfuls in the bottom of my glass and slammed it on the table. "That's m' man." He whisked the glasses away and headed for the bar.

Erika didn't appear to be pulling herself together and the drink was only making her mood worse. "Y' sure y' don't want t' come outside f' a wee bit 'f fresh air?"

"I'm sure."

"I'm just goin' t' have a slash," I said, getting up. I headed to the men's toilet.

I stood at the urinal getting some relief when a pair of feet stepped up onto the stainless-steel footplate.

"Havin' a good night?" I asked without looking at who I was talking to. I was in bliss, staring up at the ceiling, as guys often do when they're taking a slash.

"Sam, m' man. Haven't seen y' f' fuckin' ages! Where the hell've y' been hidin'?" I recoiled at the sound of the voice and didn't need to look to know who was speaking.

"Don't believe I have, Bruce. I'm still right here in Yaringa," I said, trying to sound laid back, even though my heart had jumped into my mouth and my knees were going weak.

"Right here in Yaringa, eh?"

I'd shaken and zipped my fly ready to walk out. "Yep, what about y'self?"

"What about m'self?"

"Well, haven't seen y' round either. Have y' been away?"

"Away, eh? Y' some kind of detective these days, Sam?" He turned to me as he finished, forcing the zip the last bit as if it'd jammed. I was relieved it wasn't his dick that had jammed. I didn't need him any angrier than he already seemed.

He came towards me with a menacing look in his eyes, the kind of stare I knew I had to hold, and as he came closer, I noticed his left eyebrow having a muscle spasm. I often got the same spasm in my upper lip, usually when I was upset about something. Instead of staring him directly in the eye, I concentrated my attention on his twitching eyebrow so that I didn't have to endure the full force of his intimidating stare.

Without warning there was a hand on my throat, and I was slammed up against the wall. Men came and went from the bathroom, looking at us strangely and passing us awkwardly. No one asked me if I was alright or offered me assistance.

"Listen, Sam! I don't need y' cocky little quips, just remember who we're up against. The powers that be could arrange t' have bricks strapped t' y' 'n have y' tossed into some deep, dark river before y've had a chance t' blink an eye. So remember what side y' bread's buttered on — no plea bargains, no givin' evidence. Got it? Y' life won't be worth livin' if y' haven't!"

"Got it, Bruce." I felt his grip on my throat ease, and I noticed the twitching eyebrow had ceased.

"Don't forget who got us int' this mess. Y've got a responsibility t' get us out."

"With all due respect, Bruce, y' need t' accept y' mate Cosmo has been the perpetrator of our demise. If y' hadn't given Cosmo drugs t' travel t' Canberra with, 'n if y'd stashed y' supply better, we might not be in the shit. Fuck! It's all hearsay 'n hindsight. The reality is nothin' is gonna change our situation. I've accepted m' day in court 'n what might be, 'n y' need t' do the same, Bruce. But y're not somebody who's goin' t' take notice 'f y' own shortcomings, are y'? And y're ev'n less likely t' admit them."

His hand tightened on my neck again. "If there's any hint that y' might be goin' soft cock on me, I'll personally come down on y' like a ton 'f bricks. Y' got that, Sam?"

"Yeah, I've got that."

"Oh, 'n pardon the pun."

"What pun, Bruce?"

"Ton 'f bricks! Get it, Sammy?" He laughed wildly like a hyena. "Y' know, Sam, y' too fuckin' serious f' m' likin'." He released his grip as the door to the toilet opened and a punter staggered in, well cut and trying to find his zip.

"Hey, boys. Y' havin' a good night?"

"Fuckin' great, mate," replied Bruce as he stepped away from me.

"That's the fuckin' ticket," slurred the punter as he found relief at the urinal.

I walked out of the bathroom with Bruce to the sound of The Cure's 'Seventeen Seconds', and Erika came into view, still sitting at the table, with the boys standing, beer glasses half empty, stomping their feet to the music. I didn't want to be here any more.

"Y' should come 'n visit sometime, Sam. We need t' stay 'n touch, y' know, stick together over this," Bruce said.

An image appeared in my mind of us sharing a cell in the prison that Billie teased me about, saying that's where I'd end up, and I shuddered at the thought. I'd have to listen to his accusing rantings from dawn till dusk and take a regular beating. There was no way I was going to prison with him. I'd do whatever it took to avoid that prospect.

"I will Bruce." *Get me out o' here!*

"Y' will what?"

"I'll stay in touch," I shouted in his ear, having no intention of doing so.

"See y' soon." He slapped me on the back as if we were mates, then he was gone, another silhouette in the crowd, backlit by the stage lights.

* * *

I sat down next to Erika. She looked better than when I'd left her. "Who was the man you came out of the toilets with?" she asked.

"Just an acquaintance."

"He looked angry with you."

"Well, he wasn't. He looks like that all the time. Y' know, one of those people that looks annoyed even when they aren't," I lied, not wanting to discuss it.

She leaned into me and kissed me on the neck, then moved up my neck to my ear, kissing and blowing in it, and I could feel emotion welling up in my chest, my eyes filling with tears. *Come on, let's go home. Let's get the fuck out 'f this dump. Let's go back t' the caravan.*

A siren suddenly blared obnoxiously. *Fuck, there must be a fire! How the fuck are we goin' t' get out 'f her?* I was just about to grab Erika and head for the door when the siren died and there was a chorus of voices counting down. "Ten, nine, eight, seven, six, five, four, three, two … Happy New Year!"

Everyone was hugging and kissing. They had the opportunity to hug the sexiest guy or girl close to them on the dance floor or at the table next to them, count how many kisses they got, which ones lingered on their lips and which ones might lead them to the bedroom. Wasted, they'll wake up the next morning with only sketchy details of the night before, but they'd be feeling happy because they awoke in someone's bed, or with someone in their bed, or they'd be bummed because they hadn't. Either way, the likely outcome would be an epic hangover that required a gentle day of doing as little as possible.

"Happy New Year to you, babe." Erika kissed me.

"Come on, Erika, my turn." Claudia aggressively broke us up. "I want to see what this hunk of yours is like at kissing." She winked at Erika then turned her attention to me. Grabbing the back of my head, she pulled me towards her, forcing her tongue inside my mouth and lingered too long. I tried to pull away, but although she'd downed a few too many wine coolers, she seemed to know exactly what she was doing.

"Mmm, you taste good, Sam." Erika looked unfazed, as if she'd seen it all before.

"Couldn't you come and live in Albany?" Erika asked me.

"Y' don't want t' go fallin' in love with me, Erika. Y' don't know what's goin' t' happen t' me. Y've got school 'n friends t' go back t', 'n y' whole life ahead 'f y'. Y've got t' forget about me when y' go home." She glared at me, a look I'd not seen before. Then she was on her feet and heading for the door.

I sat there and contemplated whether to follow her. Tim arrived with another round of drinks. Mal and Stu were grinning at me like Cheshire cats.

"Where's the good lady gone?" Mal asked.

"Fresh air," I said.

"Bit 'f domestic bliss already?" Tim slammed a beer down on the table next to me and caught my stare. I tried to guess what sort of state he was in, and noticed he seemed more sober than the rest of us despite his cocktail of medication and alcohol.

"Where's Erika gone, Sam?" Claudia slurred, lurching over me.

"Outside gettin' some fresh air."

"What's she doing out there? It's not like her to be outside alone. Shall I check on her?"

"Please y'self." She did, heading with drink and all for the main doors.

"Y've really got a way with the women tonight," Mal quipped.

"Y' don't know what the fuck's goin' on. Y're so engrossed in y' own wee schoolgirl holiday romance, how could y' know?" I snarled.

"Come on, boys. Let's keep New Year's Eve seemly, the way it should be," Stu interrupted. "There's no need t' wind Sam up, Mal. He's got enough on his plate without it."

"Yeah, yeah. Sam, let's forget about it. Drink up," responded Mal reluctantly.

"Sure, f'gott'n already." I picked up my schooner and drank, watching Mal over the lip of my glass as he guzzled back his beer. He slammed his glass down on the table, empty.

"Your round when y' ready, Sam," he said smiling. It was hard to tell if he'd let go of our previous spat or was saving it up for another moment. I gave him the benefit of the doubt. He'd always been friendly enough and welcoming when I visited their campsite. We'd just not clicked in the same way Stu and I had.

"I'm up on the dance floor f' a bit," Stu said as I departed for the bar.

"Right," I nodded.

"There's a babe up there I've had m' eyes on!" he shouted, competing with the volume of the band.

"Go f' it," I yelled back.

"Yeah, Stu, go f' it," bawled Mal, wanting to get in on the act. Tim remained his silent self. I shuffled to the bar feeling somewhat depleted by how the evening had unfolded.

Bumping into Bruce and offending Erika had put a damper on the evening. I was feeling drunk and empty. A heavy feeling of melancholy enveloped me, and I couldn't fight it. I was slipping into a state of depression, and although it was only momentary, I was struggling to shake it off. Like thunder clouds that arrived on the horizon, bringing inevitable rain, the melancholy could rapidly spiral into darkness.

"What'll it be, Sam?" Brigitte, the barmaid, asked. I'd made it to the front of the queue without even noticing. "Y' don't look s' good, y' sure y' should still be drinkin'?"

"Sure, I'm sure, I've got nothin' t' lose."

"Happy New Year! Want me t' see y' home after?" She reached across the bar, grabbed my face with her hands, and pulled me the rest of the way over the bar counter so our lips met. She had her tongue inside my mouth quicker than a lizard, then pulled away just as quickly. "So what'll it be, Sam? Same as before or what?"

"Yeah, same as b'fore." I watched her as she poured the beers. She was a voluptuous girl with great-looking breasts that were overly accentuated in her black singlet.

"Take a photograph, Sam. It lasts longer 'n y' can jack off when it takes y' fancy."

"Hey, I'm sorry. I didn't realise I was starin'."

"Everybody does it, so why should y' be any different. Men! They're just interested in m' tits or m' arse. They never take the time t' notice me."

"Have y' thought about …"

"How much fuckin' longer are y' goin' t' be, mate? There's a bunch 'f thirsty punters behind y'. Save y' chat up lines f' some other time!" some guy slurred behind me.

I ignored him. I was going to suggest she look at changing her clothing if she didn't like men looking at her the way they did. Normally I'd have plenty to say to the oaf who'd interrupted me, but lucky for him, or me, I wasn't interested in going down that track tonight, too many other things were on my mind.

"Almost done, mate," I replied. Brigitte finished pouring the last glass.

"Not before time," he quipped.

"Need a tray, honey?" She didn't wait for an answer, whipping one out from under the bar and placing the glasses on top in lightning fashion. I handed her a twenty-dollar note, hoping it would cover everything.

Back at the table, Mal and Tim were draining their glasses, Erika and Claudia were nowhere to be seen, and Stu was still on the dance floor gyrating next to a random woman. I placed the tray on the table and picked up the two wine coolers with one hand and my schooner with the other.

"I'm goin' outside t' find the girls." I departed without waiting for a response. Mal mumbled something, but I was out of earshot and unable to decipher what he'd said., No doubt it was one of his usual witty one-liners that everyone laughed at except me.

* * *

Outside there were a few drunken hotel goers sitting around on car bonnets drinking their tinnies. Some were well pissed, stumbling around talking to themselves, and there were a couple who were really hammered, giving it their best shot to throw up their ring pieces on the grassy verge at the side of the road. I didn't expect to find Erika and Claudia out here amidst this mayhem.

A chick in skimpy clothing suddenly lurched at me. "Happy New Year, baby," she drawled, stretching her words out. "Got a kiss f' me, y' big hunk." If I'd wanted someone like her, it would have been my lucky night. Her great heaving breasts wanted to burst out of her half-undone blouse, and her skirt was so short it was hard to understand why she bothered wearing one. I sidestepped her, not wanting to spill my drinks. She fell harmlessly onto the grass verge, unable to pull out of her committed lurch towards me. "Y' uptight prick," she shouted into the night, dragging the words out in an echo. "It'll be your loss!"

I made my way around to the deck that ran off the public bar. A lot of people drank there during the day to catch the sun and admire the view of the coast. To my surprise, all the tables were full of drunk punters smoking and drinking beneath the stars and the half-moon beaming across the bay. I spotted Erika and Claudia in a corner and made my way over.

As I approached, Claudia lashed out. "You sure know how to upset a girl, don't you, Sam!"

"Hey, I was only tryin' t' be realistic about the situation. It wasn't m' intention t' upset y', Erika." Erika looked up to meet my gaze, her cheeks were streaked with tears again.

"It's okay, Sam. I know," she sniffled. "It's just that it was painful to hear you saying that I shouldn't worry about you, cos I've got all these feelings for you."

"I know," I said gently.

"Where there is a will, there is a way."

"Perhaps there is. I'm just havin' trouble seein' it right now. I'm tryin' t' endure the wait till m' court hearin'. Y' don't know what it's like not knowin' whether I'm goin' t' prison in a few months or not. I've got a mate who drives me past the prison jokin' that's where I'll be soon. I guess it's good t' make light 'f it, but I have t' admit it gets t' me, not knowin' what lies ahead." They were both staring at me with compassion in their eyes.

"Please come back with us when we go home. I'm sure Dad would give you a ride. That would be an easy way of getting to Victoria," pleaded Erika.

"Yeah, Sam why don't you come back with us?" Claudia suggested as though a lightbulb had been turned on. "How can you lose? It's not like you're going to end up on a wanted list. You're a little fish in a big pond, right? If you disappear and they can't find you, they're not exactly going to cast a wider net, are they?"

What the fuck's gott'n int' Claudia? I've never heard her string so many words together. "You don't know that," I replied.

"Surely it's better to risk getting out of here than face the prospect of prison. Please, Sam, think about coming back with us," Erika pleaded.

"Okay, I'll think about it." I took a long sip on my beer and waited to see what their reactions would be. I knew escaping in this way wouldn't work. I always thought of the worst-case scenario, of being caught red-handed at the airport as I checked through Customs. *Midnight Express* sat too vividly in the back of my mind.

"You're so infuriatingly stubborn, Sam!" yelled Erika.

She pushed her wine cooler away and stood up, looking annoyed. "I'm going back."

"Back where, Erika?" Claudia asked.

"The tent. Are you coming?"

"I don't think so, Mal's still inside partying. I'll be awhile yet."

Erika looked sulky and agitated as she stared me down. "Guess I'll just head back on my own."

"Sam! Why don't you walk her home?" demanded Claudia.

"I think I'm goin' t' have another beer," I said cautiously. I wasn't up for Erika's moodiness, and I thought she'd be better off with some time to herself. I knew I would be.

"I don't need anyone to walk me back, thanks very much! I'm perfectly capable of finding my own way."

"Suit yourself," said Claudia, picking up her empty glass as she stood and moved away from the table back towards the bar. "I'll see you in the morning."

"Goodnight, Erika," I said, standing and reaching out to hug her, but she turned away.

"Perhaps you're right. I've been stupid. It might be best if we forget about each other. I'll just get on with my life. You obviously don't feel the same way about me," she said, not looking me in the eye, her expression hiding in the shadows.

"That's pretty harsh, Erika. Y' know damn well how I feel about y'!"

"Do I? You told me to forget about you when I told you how much I was in love with you."

"Oh, for Chrissake, Erika! That's cos I don't want t' see y' gettin' hurt. How can I tell y' that I love y' 'n put y' through all the torment, all the angst that will follow once y' go back home?"

"That's why I want you to come back with me."

"Y' know I can't."

"You can! You just won't! You don't love me!" She pushed past me and stormed off.

"Erika! Erika, come back! Why are y' doin' this?"

Everyone on the balcony was looking at me. Erika kept walking, not even looking back to see if I was coming after her.

"Y're being unreasonable, Erika!" I shouted.

"You are!" she shrieked as she crossed the road.

"Go get her, man! That's what she wants y' t' do," some random guy called out.

"Maybe, maybe not," I replied. "Not m' style anyway." I picked my beer up off the table, gulping the last of it back.

* * *

I walked back inside to find the table we had been drinking at deserted. A brief glimpse around the room revealed Stu, Claudia and Mal on the dance floor. I didn't expect to see Tim up there and searched the room, but I couldn't see him. I half expected to see him up at the bar ordering another round, but he wasn't there either. I freaked for a moment, wondering where he might be, then just when I thought I should do a bit of a search for him, he stumbled out of the toilets. Before he caught sight of me, I made a beeline for the bar. I wasn't about to encourage him to have another one. I nudged my way forward through the punters and found myself face to face with Brigitte again.

"Same as usual, Sam?"

"Yeah, just the one."

"Goin' t' Pete's party after this?" she asked as she deftly poured my glass.

"Didn't know he was havin' one, but now that I do, maybe I will."

"Might see y' there then." Brigitte smiled, looking pleased with herself.

"Yeah, y' might."

She slammed the beer down on the counter, the froth flowing down the side. "That one's on the house," she oozed.

I beamed. "That's very kind of the house."

At the table I found Tim with his arm around some woman, giving her the full snog. It was quite a moment to appreciate, and I knew I wouldn't need to concern myself with him any more. I could slink off, even risk sneaking into Erika's tent. As I pondered my options and watched the gyrating bodies on the dance floor, the music suddenly stopped.

The barman announced over a microphone, "The bar's now closed!"

I glanced at the large clock on the wall, and saw it was two o'clock in the morning, no surprise they were shutting down. I sucked heavily on my beer as the guys approached from the dance floor, Claudia wrapped around Mal, and Stu looking smitten with some leggy, long-haired brunette he'd managed to impress with his moves.

"Where's Erika?" Claudia slurred drunkenly.

"She decided t' go back t' camp. She wasn't much up f' partyin' any more."

"Shame y' couldn't — Ouch!" Claudia dug Mal fair in the ribs to stop him saying anything.

She quickly added her own commentary, "She was tired anyway 'n not feeling great, so I'm not surprised she's gone back."

"Well, whatever. But it's true, she's pissed off with me, Mal. I'm a stubborn prick sometimes," I conceded.

"All good with me, Sam," Mal said, shrugging his shoulders.

"Hey, there's a party at the house 'f one 'f the locals. Anybody up f' it?" I asked. Their enthusiasm was as pitiful as a squashed centipede. "It's cool, I'm goin' anyway," I announced loudly.

"We might tag along if that's alright," said Stu, clutching his new-found love around her waist. "Anna meet Sam. Sam, Anna."

"Nice t' meet y'." I reached out to shake her hand.

"Nice to meet you too, Sam," she said, shaking my hand limply and forcing a smile.

"Right then! We'll need some beers," I said, feeling pissed and wanting more. "I'll sort that out 'n be back in a mo'."

"Don't worry about us, Sam, we're goin' back t' the camp," Mal said, grinning his Cheshire cat smile. "See y' tomorrow, eh, f' a bit 'f a fry-up. Midday, shall we say?" Mal cast his eye around for approval.

"Sounds good," responded Stu, nodding overenthusiastically.

"We'll see y' then." I turned and walked off in the direction of the bar. Brigitte was busy cleaning up, going like a cut cat to get out of the place.

As I approached, she shot me a smile. "Let me guess," she said, going all serious again. "Y' want a slab 'f Fosters t' take back t' camp with y' new-found buddies." The sarcasm in her voice was unappealing.

"Maybe." I paused a second for dramatic effect. "And then again, maybe not. I'm goin' t' Pete's party, actually." I observed her wry smile. She couldn't suppress her delight.

"Are you? So am I. Want t' wait while I finish cleaning down this poxy bar?"

"Maybe. How long y' gonna be?"

"Another ten I reckon."

"Alright then but do us a favour."

"What's that?" she asked, all curious like a kid who's about to be rewarded for doing something right.

"Give me that slab 'f Fosters," I said, flashing her a pleading smile.

"Oh yeah, right." She blushed and disappeared into the walk-in chiller, returning shortly with a slab that she flung wildly onto the bar. "That's twenty f' that."

I handed her a crisp twenty-dollar note and swooped up the slab. "See y' outside, Brigitte. Don't be too long."

Slab of Fosters in arm, I headed outside. I spotted Tim climbing into a taxi with the woman he'd been snogging inside at the table. I watched them drive off, amazed and pleased he was taken care of for the night. Other drunk punters were getting into cars or lurching on the pavement, too out of it to know what they were doing. I made my way around to the balcony, deciding I was going to have a Fosters while I waited for Brigitte. I came to an abrupt halt on the balcony.

Stu was standing at the end of a table with his pants down. The woman, Anna, was laid out on the table, skirt pulled up around her waist, legs apart, crying, "Fuck me, Stu! Fuck me hard!"

He moved in on her, and I turned back the way I'd come, departing the scene to the sound of her constant cries. "Harder! Oh yeah, baby, that's it. Oh yeah. Ohh baby!"

Stu had been hanging out for sex since he'd arrived here. He'd had eyes on Erika and missed out. Tonight he'd found someone equally hungry for sex, and I hoped for his sake he could fuck her hard enough as her cries continued into the night air.

I sat down on the steps in front of the pub, pulled a tinny out, cracked the tab and gulped back the amber liquid. It tasted good, though I needed it like a hole in the head. Most of the punters had dispersed by now and the only sound in the still night was Anna as she reached another climax. As her cries became more intense, I decided I didn't need to be around when the publican came out with his shotgun to see who was being murdered. In a split second I made up my mind, picked up my slab of beers, got to my feet and started walking down the road.

As I began walking, a voiced called out, "Oi! Wait up!" It was Brigitte. "I thought we had a deal." I spun round to face her. She had a denim jacket on and a bottle of something under her arm.

"We did. I'm sorry but I couldn't hang around any longer." Just then there was an almighty scream that pierced the night.

"Jesus, what in hell's that? Sounds like it's comin' from the pub. We'd better go take a look," Brigitte said, somewhat alarmed.

"No! I don't think so. I know who it is 'n it's not what y' think. Besides y' boss is bound t' have heard it. Let him deal with it," I said, grabbing her by the arm and encouraging her to keep walking. She took it as an opportunity to hold my hand. I pulled away. "Look, Brigitte, I don't think I'll go t' the party. I'm feelin' pretty out 'f it. Think I'm just gonna head home 'n crash."

"That's cool, I'm pretty pooped too. I could maybe come back with y'," she suggested coyly.

"Maybe, but maybe not. Look, I'm seein' someone, so it wouldn't be very cool, would it?"

"Y've always got an excuse. Are y' interest'd in me or not? Y' actin' like y' are."

I stopped and faced her. "Look …" I started. We stopped by a stand of old trees near the cliff overlooking the bay. "Here, sit down 'n have a beer."

Brigitte sat on one of the old tree stumps remaining from trees that'd been cut down years before. They'd become a safety hazard in the wind. She took the beer I handed to her, opened it quickly and slurped.

"I'm sorry, Brigitte. I didn't realise I'd given y' any wrong ideas."

"Oh, come on, Sam. Every time y're up at the bar y're pervin' at m' tits!"

I cracked a can for myself. Gulping it down I almost choked on it. "Well, maybe if y' didn't wear such revealin' tops I'd be less likely t' stare. I mean, come on, Brigitte, it's a natural phenomenon. Guys will stare at a great-lookin' pair 'f tits. Y' must be okay with it or y' wouldn't wear such revealin' clothin'."

"See! So y' do look at them."

"Well 'f course, but that doesn't mean I instantly want t' get with y'." She gulped some more of her beer. "But I thought y' liked me?"

"I do!"

"So what's the problem?" she demanded.

"There isn't one from my point of view."

"Right then, let's go back t' y' place." She tossed her can and was up off the tree stump, grabbing at my hand.

"Whoa, whoa, whoa!" I said, as I dug my heels in and pulled her towards me, which she took as a sign to wrap herself around me. Pulling herself up close, she reached up and stuck her tongue in my mouth. Her body pressed firmly against me, and I wondered why I was bothering to resist, but I pushed her away nevertheless. "That isn't what I had in mind. I've already told y' that this isn't happenin'."

"Oh, come on, Sam, y' know y' want it."

"No, Brigitte, I don't. Now go! Leave me! Go t' y' party. There's bound t' be someone who takes y' fancy there." I started to walk away. She followed.

"Sam, y' can't just leave me at this time 'f night. Not on New Year's Eve."

"I can! I just did. Goodnight!" I started walking again, pulling another beer from the slab under my arm. I managed to crack the tab one-handed, get it to my mouth and guzzle. I was well drunk now and had no taste for the beer. It was simply from force of habit that I continued to drink, a throwback to my school days when you were encouraged to 'drink till y' drop' — that's what everyone did.

"Hey, Sam, I can't go back t' town." Brigitte had caught up with me and was tugging on my arm, pleading. "I can't drive m' car, I've been sipping on wine coolers all night. It's too bloody risky on New Year's Eve. There'll be cops everywhere."

"Well, perhaps y' should've thought that one out before y' started on the wine coolers." I felt no sympathy for her.

"Ohh, come on, Sam, it's New Year's Eve!"

"Y' were plannin' on going t' the party, so y' must've made plans t' stay somewhere." The slab under my arm was becoming uncomfortable, and I had to swap it to my other arm.

"No, I wasn't. I thought tonight might be m' lucky night."

"It still might be if y' get there soon."

"Why are y' such a prick, Sam?"

"Because I can be!" We had made it down the hill and weren't far from my caravan.

"Look, y' goin' t' have t' go now, Brigitte. Go t' the party."

"It'll be dead 'n over by now." She started crying in big sobs. "Why don't y' like me, Sam?"

"But I do, Brigitte." She was in full emotional flight.

"All y' ever see is m' tits, never me. You're all the same, you're all just a pack 'f arseholes with one thing on y' mind." Her voice rapidly rose in volume, and I was worried she would wake the neighbours.

"Hey, calm down. It's alright." I grabbed her and gave her a quick hug, hoping to appease her.

"Get away from me!" she yelled as she pushed me away.

"Okay, okay," I said, raising my arms in the air in truce. "Look, I'm goin' t' m' caravan. There's a spare bed there 'n y're welcome t' use it. There're a few blankets that should keep y' warm, but it's pretty warm anyway, so y'll be fine."

"Fuck y' bed! Fuck y' blankets!"

"Suit y'self. Goodnight."

"No, it's not a good night!" She was walking behind me again. It was turning into a really bad night.

"Oh, come on, it's not so bad." I stopped and tried again to put my arms around her. This time she didn't resist. "So, are y' goin' t' accept m' invitation 'n stay the night on the spare bed?"

"I s'pose, if that's all that's on offer, it'll have t' do," she conceded.

"Come on then." I started walking with my arm still around her, and she fell into step with me. I was relieved that she'd calmed down and wasn't waking the neighbourhood.

The caravan door's squeaky hinges seemed more pronounced than ever as I opened the door. I held my breath, half expecting Oma's face to appear at a window, or hear her voice calling out into the night. I ushered Brigitte in, and following behind her, I closed the door as it squeaked its way shut. I fumbled for the light switch, and quickly dumped the slab of remaining Fosters on the table. I turned on the reading lamp beside my bed so I could turn the main light off.

"There, that's better," I said.

"This is a great caravan, the way y' got it set up," Brigitte said, suddenly all perky.

"Y' think so?" I never really thought it was particularly homely. To me it was a bed to sleep in and a place to escape from the world. I had a few books on the shelf and some posters on the wall. There was a bit of snack food on the table, and I'd managed to get hold of a couple of reading lamps. My clothing was strewn around the place. To me it just looked like anyone's bedroom.

"That's y' bed f' the night," I said, pointing to the bed at the end of the caravan. "And this is mine." I patted the one before us. "And now it's bedtime."

"Think I'll sleep with you," she said mischievously.

"No, y' won't! The agreement was y' can stay but y' sleep in y' own bed, not mine. That's y' bed over there."

"Oh, come on, Sam. I don't believe y' not horny." She started to remove her clothing.

"No."

"Just a little bit horny?" She was undressing right next to me. I quickly kicked my shoes off, dropped my trousers, whipped my T-shirt off, and dived under my duvet while Brigitte floundered with her bra. "Jesus, Sam, that was quick." She tried lifting my duvet but I rolled into it so she couldn't get in.

"Brigitte, for fuck's sake get int' the other bed. Otherwise, y' goin' t' have t' go."

"But I want t' sleep with y'!"

"Well, it ain't goin' t' happen."

"Come on, Sam."

I sat up to face her. She was naked in front of me, her breasts were absolutely huge, but not saggy like I thought they'd be out of her bra — they were outstanding.

"Y're not sleepin' with me, Brigitte!" I rasped, trying to maintain eye contact with her face and not her breasts. She wasn't really overweight, just big boned, solid like a swimmer or a weightlifter, but more glamorous, with beautiful olive skin. I was simultaneously tempted and annoyed that she'd manipulated her way this far.

"Couldn't we just have a cuddle f' a minute, 'n then I'll pop into m' bed," she pleaded. with her expectant, puppy eyes. She was unrelenting.

"Y're sleepin' over there 'n that's that. Fuckin' end 'f story! Goodnight!"

"I can't believe that y' don't like me." She was sniffling and pathetic again. "I feel so embarrassed standin' here in front 'f y' like this, all naked and rejected."

"F' fuck's sake, Brigitte, y' haven't been rejected cos I never wanted y' in the first place. Now *please* go t' bed!" I said, my voice raised as I physically attempted to guide her towards the bed.

"I can't. I'm too upset. Why do y' find me ugly?"

"I don't! Just cos we aren't goin' t' sleep together doesn't mean y' ugly."

"I'm cold," she sobbed. "I just need a cuddle. I promise nothin' will happen."

"No! I promise nothin' will happen," I sighed. "Y' can get in m' bed till y' warm up, then y' can get in y' bed, 'n y're not gettin' in till y' put some clothes on."

"I will, I will," she mumbled happily. I heard her rustling then felt the duvet being pulled back as she climbed in beside me. She snuggled into me. I could feel the warmth of her body, her breasts pushed into my back, and her hand move over my stomach as she pulled herself in closer. "Thanks, Sam, I feel much better now," she whispered close to my ear. "All I wanted was t' be close t' y'."

"Well, that's not what I wanted, but if it keeps y' happy, then so be it."

"Why are y' so harsh with me, Sam?"

"I'm not harsh on y'. It's you that's harsh on y'self. Y're the one that wants me, not the other way 'round, so it's disappointing for y' to hear me say I'm not int'rested and that I've got a girlfriend. Y're very persistent, but it exposes y' t' rejection."

"Jesus, y' talk some shit, don't y'? Studied psychology or what?"

"No, y' asked me a question." Her hand was roving down towards my boxers. I felt aroused being so close, and I grabbed her hand before it was too late. "We had a deal, remember? Y' could warm up in here then go t' y' own bed. There was nothing extra in that deal."

"Oh, come on, Sam, it's all free. Y' can't tell me y' don't want it."

"I can. I just did."

"This is fuckin' ridiculous!" She sat up, exasperated.

"To you it is. To me it's not. Look, lie down 'n be happy t' snuggle up 'n go t' sleep."

"But I can't be happy unless y' fuck me."

"That ain't happenin'. Fuckin' y' won't make y' happy, y've got t' make y'self happy."

"Obviously!" She rolled over in a huff, exposing her back to me.

"I'm sorry, Brigitte. Y' know y' would've been better off not subjectin' y'self t' this."

"Go t' sleep, Sam."

I said nothing more and rolled away until I was hard up against the caravan wall.

* * *

I was dreaming that I was about to cum in a woman's mouth. I was groaning like it was the real thing, and then I was cumming in one massive explosion that wasn't going to stop, and next, the mouth was gone. I could feel someone moving up my body and the soft flesh of breasts on my torso. I realised my dream wasn't a dream — it was Brigitte moving up my body, about to lie on top of me so she could take me between her legs.

"Are y' awake, Sam," she whispered as she reached my face and kissed my left ear. "I thought that might wake y' up. A nice dream, don't y' think?"

I was so shocked I didn't know whether to be angry or happy for the experience. Instead, I pretended to still be asleep, making a few small movements and grunting, suggesting I was still rousing from sleep. Brigitte was trying to get me hard again so she could have me. She obviously never took no for an answer and didn't have any respect for the word at all. She'd just violated my body while I was sleeping. If the tables were turned, and I'd done what she'd just done to me, I'd probably be guilty of sexual assault.

"What the fuck? What are y' doin' on top 'f me, Brigitte?" I rolled her off, somewhat reluctantly, as I'd become highly aroused by now and would've loved to have my way with her. But I wasn't going to give her the pleasure of thinking she'd conquered me with her persistence, taking me while I was in a deep sleep. No way did I want her claiming victory.

"What's y' problem? I just gave y' a blow job. So yummy, Sam."

"That was by default! Y' fuckin' took advantage 'f me while I was sleepin'! I thought I was havin' a wet dream. It wasn't till I awoke I realised what was happenin', and even then, I still wasn't sure what was going on till y' whispered in m' ear."

"Y' bastard!"

"No! Y're the bitch f' doin' it. We had an agreement, and y' violated it."

"I can't believe y're sayin' this!"

"Look, all y' can see is that because I've rejected y' physically, I don't like y', that I'm not attracted to y'. So just bloody listen! I think y're great, y're good lookin', 'n y've got plenty going for y'. It's not my fault that y're attracted t' me, or that y' think y' should be able t' have me. The reality is I'm goin' out with someone else 'n I'm good with that."

"Fuck her 'n fuck you!" She was out of bed and pulling on her knickers, then she found her bra and struggled to get it on. "I'm out 'f here. You're a prick, Sam. A selfish fuckin' prick's what y' are. Y're a fuckin' weird bastard!"

"Hey, Brigitte, I'm the one who said y' shouldn't come back with me, but y' wouldn't let up. Y' found a way 'f gettin' what y' wanted, didn't y'?"

"Fuck you, Sam." She picked up her bag. "I'll find m' own way out, thanks!" She opened the door and stepped out, slamming it as she went. I listened to her loudly scuff her way down the drive, then silence engulfed me. I lay there dazed, reflecting on the surreal situation that had unfolded in the last twelve hours.

<h1 style="text-align:center">26</h1>

Fallout

I eventually managed to peel myself out of bed, throw my board shorts on, pick up a towel, and walk down to the beach. Already the day was heating up and a haze rose off the pavement, cars were coming and going to the shops, and plenty of people were out and about. They were inescapable now as the season was in full swing. The sea was relatively flat with small sets of waves rolling in and breaking on the shore. The odd surfer dotted the back break-line but mostly it was swimmers trying to cool off. Just as I lay down in the sand to relax, a voice called out, "Sam!"

"Hello, Sarah," I said, trying to look surprised and pleased simultaneously, while cringing inside. "Happy New Year."

She was sitting topless on her towel, her two children playing with their buckets and spades in the sand beside her.

"Happy New Year to you, too. This is Sophie and Daniel." The children squinted into the sun to get a look at me. The boy looked about eight years old, and the girl about six. "Say hi to Sam, kids."

"Hello, Sam," they responded in unison.

"Do I get a New Year's kiss?" Sarah demanded.

"Well, I s'pose I …"

"Come and sit with us." She patted the sand next to her as if she were beckoning a dog.

Picking up my towel, I moved the few metres to sit beside her. I felt self-conscious and uncomfortable, forever paranoid someone on the beach was watching. Part of the fear was that it would get back to Bruce, then I'd have him giving me the full interrogation.

What the fuck d' y' think y' doin', Sam? Hangin' out with a cop's wife on the beach? Y' think that's goin' t' give y' brownie points come D-Day? I'm sure Harry's really wrapped t' know y've been tryin' t' seduce his wife. Yeah, she's got a bit 'f a history f' gettin' herself int' positions she shouldn't, if y' get m' drift. That's right, she likes a bit extra to what she's already got. My syndicate already wants y' out 'f the picture, Sam.

"Where's that kiss you promised me?"

"Look, Sarah, if y' don't mind, I don't really think it's appropriate f' me to be sittin' here on the beach next to y', let alone me kissin' y' in broad daylight, no offence intended."

"Oh, come on, Sam, you're just being paranoid and neurotic. It's the New Year, everybody does it. It's traditional."

"Not with the arrestin' officer's wife, it's not!" How I hadn't noticed her before I lay down in the sand was beyond me, but I guess my head was a little foggy from overindulging the night before, and all the carrying on with Brigitte had completely fucked me up. "How's Harry by the way? Did he have last night off?"

"No, not likely, Sam. Another one of the joys of being married to a cop. Harry seems to work every bloody holiday there is. Part and parcel of being in a small town, I guess. I'm telling you, if he doesn't leave the job" — she lowered her voice to a whisper so her kids wouldn't hear — "then I'll be leaving him."

"Y're kiddin' me, right?" She shook her head from side to side.

"I thought you two had a good thing goin' on. I'm startin' t' understand somethin' about y' that until now I didn't."

"What's that, Sam?"

"Well, y' know ..."

"Mummy, can we go in the water now? It's too hot," asked Sophie as she stared intensely at me.

"In a minute, honey. Wow, look at those castles you've built!"

"It's too hot, Mummy."

"Just a minute, Sophie," she said firmly. Sophie started beating her upside-down bucket with her spade like a drum roll.

"Look, I'm goin' t' head back up t' the house. Y' daughter's right, it's too hot."

"Aren't you going to come in the water with us?"

"I don't think so."

"Oh, come on, Sam."

"Look, no offence, but I just don't need the profile. Y' see, there are certain people who would like t' see me dead," I told her, thinking of Bruce at the pub last night. "And this ain't helpin' m' cause. Y're a very nice woman, 'n you 'n Harry've been good t' me, but y've got t' understand m' predicament." I stood, picked up my towel and shook the sand off it. Sarah stood too. She really was a remarkably good-looking woman. One temptation after another was being put before me, and before I could react, she'd kissed me on the cheek in front of her kids and the entire beach.

"See you Sunday, Sam. Come on, kids, let's go and cool off," she said, taking them both by the hand and sauntering down the beach to the sea.

* * *

I walked in through the front door of the house and into the kitchen to find Oma and Opa at the table eating what I initially thought was breakfast, before realising it was actually lunch.

"Where have you been, boy?" shouted Opa. "Your Oma's been worried sick." He aggressively sawed at the sausage of salami on the breadboard, waiting for my answer.

"I've been down at the beach swimmin'."

"But why didn't you come up and say good morning first? We haven't seen you since last night … and where's Tim?"

"In his bedroom I s'pose." I'd forgotten all about Tim. My mind flashed back to the night before and the image of him getting into a car with the girl he'd been snogging.

"It's almost noon, Sam," said Oma.

"Shit! I mean crikey. Is it? I haven't been t' town yet! I've got t' run. I need t' report."

"Sam, when you come back, we need to talk," Oma said with a look of concern. "We're too old to be worrying about you going out, worrying about where you are the next day. Opa went down to your caravan and when he found you weren't there, we became worried."

"It's a small town, Oma. It's safe, everyone knows everyone."

"Well, look at what's already happened to you, Sam."

"I've got t' go. Talk soon, eh?"

Their disappointment in my behaviour wasn't worth debating at this point. I needed to get to town fast. It was the first time I'd forgotten to report, and I was dead worried about who might be on duty and how they'd view it. I bolted down the internal stairs to the garage. Tim usually left the keys in the Valiant and I was relieved to find them there now. I gunned the engine and it immediately burst into life. As I turned onto the main beach road, Erika appeared, clambering over the roadside railing from the motor camp, dressed in shorts that were far too short, and a white V-necked T-shirt. My heart skipped a beat, and I was momentarily tempted to pretend I hadn't seen her and keep driving, but I knew she'd spotted me, so I pulled up beside her. There were a bunch of teenage guys sitting on the railing, giving her the once-over. I could hardly blame them. That's what I would've been doing too, if I'd just noticed her for the first time. She opened the car's door and stuck her head in.

"Hi. I was just on my way to see you," she said. "Where are you off to?"

"I'm late. I slept in 'n I've got t' report t' the cop shop. Want t' join me?"

She hesitated for a second then nodded, climbed in and pulled the door shut behind her. The jaws of the guys sitting on the rail fence dropped in unison as I drove off with her. Van Morrison's album *Moondance* was playing through the rear speakers. He was singing 'Come Running'. I pumped up the volume for emphasis as the Valiant powered up the hill towards Yaringa village.

As I drove up the hill and turned right onto the main road to Wodyn, there was an awkward silence. So much had happened in the twelve hours or so since Erika had walked away from me at the pub, and I was still in a sort of surreal, dream space.

"You're not saying much," said Erika, breaking the silence.

"No, I guess not. I'm not really sure what t' say after last night," I said tentatively.

"I'd like to say I'm sorry," she responded.

"What for?" I glanced at her sideways. She looked pretty miserable. I hadn't seen her this way before. "Are y' okay?" I wanted to pull over and give her a hug, hold her tight, but I was already running late for my reporting deadline.

"I'm sorry for being unrealistic and for not understanding your situation. I agree it would be better for you to stay and see it through. I was being selfish and unreasonable to think that you would agree to my proposal. It was such a rash idea."

"Hey, don't be silly. It's perfectly understandable for y' t' have that kind 'f idea. Why wouldn't y' want t' offer y' help 'n see me come back with y', 'n y' know I'd like nothin' more than t' be able t', but I just have t' see this through. Maybe after it's all been sorted out ..."

"You see, it's just that ..." She hesitated then started again. "You see it's just that I've never felt this way about a guy before, so it's all a bit overwhelming having such strong feelings for you. I love you, Sam."

My eyes were misting over. I didn't want her to see that I was holding back tears and was relieved that I was driving. I didn't want to have to hold her gaze. We were almost in town and I was having trouble remaining dry-eyed. I could feel a teardrop forming in the corner of my left eye, welling up, poised to fall, then it rolled freely down my cheek, followed by another and another. My right eye joined in and I had tear after tear spilling down my cheeks. I don't know whether Erika even noticed, since she was staring straight ahead as she spoke about her feelings, as if she were searching deeply for each word.

I couldn't enter the cop shop looking as though I'd been crying like a baby. They'd wind me up about that, so I pulled over onto a grassy verge. The car came to an abrupt stop. I was a bit heavy-footed on the brakes.

"Why have we stopped here?" Erika turned to face me and saw my tear-streaked face for the first time. "What's the matter?" she asked, appearing alarmed.

"It's you, it's the words y' said t' me. I've never been spoken t' like that before. I've never really had someone have strong feelings f' me."

She undid her seatbelt and moved across the seat. Taking my face in her hands, she looked me straight in the eyes and said, "I do love you, Sam." Then she kissed me so beautifully I felt like I was a movie star acting out a scene that had been played over and over before.

"I love you too, Erika," I said, pulling away to look at her. She grabbed me and kissed me again, then pulled away.

"Don't you have to get to the police station?"

"Yes, but I'm already late."

"Then let's not make you any later."

I gunned the Valiant back into life and pulled out onto the road to travel the short distance to the police station.

"Won't be a minute," I said, getting out of the car. I walked into the station feeling anxious about who might be on duty.

* * *

Inside there were still Christmas decorations around the reception area. I rang the bell, and the door opened. My heart sank as Frank appeared.

"Good morning," I said, all chipper.

"Is it?" snarled Frank. "I think y' might find mornin' has b'come afternoon. Y're late!"

"Come on, cut me some slack."

"Y' know y' reportin' time is nine in the morning till noon."

"Yeah, but it's not even one o'clock yet, 'n it's New Year's Day," I pleaded.

Frank weaved the fingers of both his hands together, then he turned them inside out and stretched his arms out fully in front of him. Next, he raised his arms towards the ceiling, at the same time arching his back slightly and yawning. As he lowered his arms, he spouted out the conditions of my bail.

"It was agreed in court that y'd report t' the police station at the times I've just quoted. Failure t' do so could result in y' being taken int' custody."

"*Could* ... doesn't that apply only if I've blatantly abused those conditions, like if I've absconded or something equally as serious?" I blurted it out without thinking.

Frank leaned forward on the counter and with his finger he signalled me to come closer. He kept signalling until I was only a few centimetres away from his face.

"Listen arsehole, I'll be the judge 'f that. Y're in no situation t' be tellin' me how serious y' breach is. *Got it!*" I sighed and nodded.

The door behind Frank opened and Harry appeared. "What's goin' on here, Frank?"

"Einstein here has breached his reportin' time, hasn't he? That could result in another court appearance 'n some custody time."

Harry glanced at the clock. "It's only just gone one o'clock, Frank. "That's a breach that doesn't really warrant any action. Besides, it was New Year's Eve last night, everybody's goin' t' be behind the eight ball today."

"Be it on your head, Harry."

"Just make a note 'f it in the book, sayin' he was issued a warnin'."

"You can do it," Frank grunted. "Y've been warned, kid. Pull y' neck in and no more slip-ups." I nodded obediently as Frank turned and stomped out of the room, slamming the office door behind him.

"Don't worry about him, he's just hot air," Harry said. I nodded again, not believing it. Frank was far more than hot air.

"Can I go now?"

"Sure. How've things been?"

"Fine. Look, I need t' go. I've got someone waitin' f' me."

Harry started to say something, but I was already out the door.

"Bye," I called out, heading back to the car and Erika.

"Is everything alright?" Erika asked.

"Yeah. Since I was late t' report, one 'f the cops reprimanded me. He likes t' give me grief at any given opportunity. Come on, let's get out 'f here."

Erika hopped back in the passenger's seat while I pulled myself in behind the wheel, turned the engine on, and made a U-turn.

"It must be a real pain having to do that every day," Erika said.

"Damn right it is. At first, I really resented it, then I just accepted it as part 'f what I have t' do t' get out 'f here. Usually, I hitch into town cos I ain't got the money t' put petrol in Tim's car. He wasn't round this mornin', so I just took it."

"I missed you last night," Erika said softly.

"Well, y' seemed pretty upset with me last night, and I didn't see any point in tryin' t' sort it out. We'd all had a skinful, so it wasn't goin' t' go anywhere. But y're here now."

"Did you miss me, Sam?"

I leaned forward on the steering wheel with my elbows resting on the bottom part of the wheel. "Course I did. Look, this isn't easy f' me either, Erika. That's why I was sayin' what I was sayin' about how y' should just carry on once you get home. I mean, y' can't expect too much cos we don't know what's goin' t' happen t' me. I care about y', I love y', 'n at the same time I don't really know what love is."

"It's a feeling."

"I know, but there're lots of feelings that can be confused with love, aren't there?"

"What do you mean?"

As we came to a junction in the road, I impulsively swung right, taking the road that led to a small coastal lagoon.

"Where are we going, Sam?"

"It's a surprise, y'll see." I drove the stretch of road around the lagoon, passing the occasional house. Eucalyptus trees grew on the slopes down to the water's edge, obscuring the view, and kangaroos could be seen here and there in the clearings at dawn and dusk. We came to a small, run-down house near the end of the road, and I pulled up in front of it.

"What are we doing here?" Erika asked.

"This is m' secret wee hideaway."

"What?"

"Just that."

"But who owns it?"

"Tim. Why the hundred questions? Does y' mind always operate in overdrive?"

She punched me affectionately and smiled. It was the first time I'd seen her smile since last night's drama at the pub, and she looked radiant in her moment of happiness.

"Come on," I said, opening the car door and getting out.

"I'm coming!" she said, clambering across the front seat. She jumped out beside me and we started walking hand in hand. We crossed the road and made our way down through the eucalyptus to the lagoon.

"Hadn't we better watch out for snakes?" Erika asked.

"Nah, they're all asleep. It's too hot t' be slitherin' 'round."

"You're crazy, Sam."

"That's true."

We reached the lagoon's edge, where there was a large rock that looked just right for sitting on. I climbed up onto it and pulled Erika up after me.

"See, it's so nice 'n peaceful here. There's hardly anyone here compared with Yaringa. Y' know, I get so sick 'f all the people being 'round, it's like a fuckin' circus. All those people come t' the campin' grounds on the coast with their caravans 'n tents, parked up next t' each other, with their TV aerials 'n all the mod cons f' their caravans. It's just another suburbia they've created f' themselves. Even when I was a kid 'n stayed with m' grandparents in their caravan with their motorboat 'n all that stuff, I thought it was peculiar the way everybody crammed in next t' each other."

"Yes, but Sam, they're on holiday. They want to come to a nice beach and relax, and they need facilities for their children, not everybody has the luxury of being able to live in a coastal village. Jobs are mainly in the urban areas, unless you're a farmer or a small business owner. We've been studying urban versus rural economies in geography at school."

"Yeah, I understand what y' sayin'. Don't mind me, I can go on a rant sometimes 'n don't know when t' pull m' neck in. Anyway, I just wanted t' bring y' here cos it's nice 'n peaceful."

Erika reached out and pulled me in close, her eyes looking intensely into mine, and she succeeded in melting my sternness. She found my lips with hers and kissed me ever so softly.

"You're a beautiful man, Sam," she whispered, kissing me again before pulling away. "I should be getting back."

"Oh, come on … stay a bit longer," I pleaded. "Look, I haven't even shown y' inside the house." I grabbed her hands and pulled her up. I wanted her all to myself, to pretend that the rest of the world didn't exist right now.

"Sam, you've got no idea what my parents are like. They are quite strict and worry easily."

"It's daytime 'n we've only been gone an hour or so. What are y' so worried about?"

"Yes, but I told them I would be at your place, not going off in a car with you somewhere."

"Come on." I wasn't about to let her win. We walked back up the slope through the trees to the road. "Christ! I thought I was fitter than that," I said, panting with my hands on my knees. Erika was standing upright, taking in deep breaths.

"Amazing that such a small climb can make you puff that much," she agreed.

"Come on," I said, grabbing her by the hand again.

She followed me without protest. Strangely, the front door was unlocked, and the key wasn't in its hiding place under the rock near the entrance. I turned the handle and swung the door open, pulling Erika in after me.

"So this is it! This is where I come sometimes when I want t' escape," I lied. I'd only been here once with Tania when we'd stayed over and tried to rekindle the romance in our fucked-up relationship.

I turned to Erika and kissed her and began pulling her top up. Meeting no resistance, I was all over her breasts like a bee in a blossom tree as I coerced her to the couch and continued my exploration down her torso to her shorts, where I easily managed to find the press studs, undoing them in no time. Erika obliged as I removed her shorts and knickers. I was about to explore between her legs when there was a noise like a door opening and Erika tensed up. I pulled away and glanced around the room. No one was there. We looked at each other and shrugged. I slipped my pants down to my knees and found her warmth between her legs. She groaned, arching her back as she grabbed my face, tugging at my hair. She cried out with pleasure, and at the same time I thought I heard a toilet flushing, then a door opening, followed by soft, shuffling footsteps. I froze for a moment, undecided in my next move. Erika, though, was more decisive, reaching for her knickers and shorts and desperately pulling them on, prompting me to pull mine back up too. As I did so the door from the hallway opened and Tim came into view, looking like he'd just risen from the dead.

"What the fuck are you doin' here?" I exclaimed. I tried to stand so I could pull my pants all the way up.

"More t' the point, what the fuck are you two doin' here?" Tim demanded.

"Y' brought that woman y' were with last night back here, didn't y'?" I said, feeling amused.

"Might've," he said, grinning, touching his nose with a finger and tapping it. "Y'll never know."

Erika had managed to find her top and had pulled it on while hidden behind me.

"I'll meet you at the car," she said, walking out.

"See y' there in a minute."

"So ... thought y' could come here 'n get lucky. Sorry t' foil y' plans," he said disingenuously, still grinning.

"Where's the woman?" I asked.

"Fuck, I can't remember, must've been that cocktail 'f medication 'n alcohol I had last night," he mumbled through his beard. "No hang on ... now I know who y' mean. It's all flashin' back t' me like a bad dream. She must be the chick I found dead in m' bed when I woke this mornin'. I wondered how the fuck she got there, but I don't remember anythin' else."

He was beginning to freak me out. "Yeah, right," I said.

"No. Go on, take a look f' y'self." With his right arm he gestured towards the rooms down the hallway.

"Y're sick, Tim. Y' shouldn't be goin' off with women y' don't know while y' on that shit, 'n drinkin' too. That's just plain madness!" I started walking towards the rooms.

"So the doctors tell me."

I approached the room that had a partially open door and I pushed it inwards, concerned about what might be revealed. With the door fully open I could only see the end of the bed, so I had to stick my head further into the room to see the whole bed. As I did so, Tim broke into gruff laughter. I jumped back.

"Y' almost believed me, didn't y'?" he said, smirking.

"No," I lied. The bed was just a jumbled mess of sheets and a duvet.

"Oh, come on, Sam! Don't give me that shit! I can tell these things. I'm psychic, y' know."

"Y' should sleep with women more often, seems t' do y' the world 'f good," I said, slapping him on the back.

"Yeah, maybe. Would've been nice if she'd stayed the night."

"What do y' mean?"

"She made the taxi wait. She told the driver she wouldn't be long. We came inside 'n she had her clothes off in a matter of seconds, not that I was complainin'. She got to it immediately and came really quickly, jivin' that she didn't have all night, and asking when was I goin' t' cum. I faked it, and she said, 'Thanks, that's just what I needed.'" He chuckled. "She had her clothes back on 'n was out the door and int' the cab before I could even say 'fuck'!"

"What a crazy chick!"

"I'm not complainin'," he said, grinning wryly at me.

"Are y' comin' back with us then? I've got a confession t' make."

"I know. Y' borrowed m' car, didn't y'? How else were y' goin' t' get here?"

"I had t' report t' the cops 'n I woke up late."

"Just don't be makin' a habit 'f it. I'll be with y' in a minute." He trudged back to the bedroom.

* * *

We pulled into the caravan park and dropped Erika outside her parents' caravan. Her father was lounging in a deck chair, enjoying the sun and reading a book.

"See y' later f' a swim," I said to Erika.

"Alright then. Bye."

"See y' in a bit. Nice t' see y', Mr Mayer."

"For Chrissake, Sam, call me Hank, will you!"

"Righto, Hank it is. Oh, 'n by the way, this is m' friend Tim," I said.

"Hello, Tim," Hank said, waving from his deck chair.

"Gidday," Tim burbled through his beard.

I shifted the car's gear lever to 'D', and we gently accelerated down the lane toward the exit.

* * *

Back at the house, Oma and Opa were nowhere to be seen. Only then did I realise that I'd completely forgotten about Mal's fry-up, but I didn't care. Tim turned the telly on and flopped in the armchair to watch an afternoon soap. I heard a door bang closed in the hallway, then the toilet flush, and shortly after, the sound of a jug being filled in the kitchen.

Oma appeared. "Would you boys like a cup of tea?"

"That'd be great, thanks," I said.

"Tim?"

"Ah, umm … No thanks."

"Perhaps you might like to join us at the table when the tea's ready, Sam."

"Sure."

Opa stuck his head in the lounge to announce the tea was ready and I joined them in the dining room. Oma was pouring milk into the teacups, and there was a tray of biscuits and cake on the table. The teapot was covered in a brightly coloured, hand-knitted tea cosy.

"The tea just needs to draw a little more. Have some 'kooke', Sam," said Oma. Kooke is a simple Dutch spiced cake, delicious with a dollop of butter. I took a piece and bit into it, waiting for the lecture to begin. Opa cleared his throat, an obvious sign he was about to say something that wasn't easy for him to express.

"Mmm … Sam … we feel that last night didn't go well for us. You went off to the hotel and we never saw you until midday. Your Oma was worried sick all morning."

"Sam, we are here to support you at this time, but the respect needs to run both ways," interrupted Oma in a grave tone, sipping at her tea.

"But I came home last night 'n slept in the caravan!" I exclaimed. "I awoke earlier than expected, and it was so hot that I went straight t' the beach f' a swim. I bumped int' friends there 'n got distracted. I'm sorry I didn't come up t' the house first t' say good mornin', but nothin' bad happened. Why are y' so worried?"

"Sam, you've got to consider us. Do you know what it's like for us to be here?" Oma said.

"Well, I'm sorry, it just never occurred t' me that you'd be worried about me. Y' knew where I was 'n I thought that was enough information."

"We're only here for a few more days, Sam," she said.

I was feeling annoyed, but knew it wasn't worth debating any further. I had to admit, it probably wasn't easy for them. They were obviously more worried about my situation than I had previously realised. We sat and sipped our tea in awkward silence until Oma proposed we all go for a swim.

"Great idea," I sighed, grateful for the change in focus. Tim opted to stay in the coolness of the house, slouched in his armchair, communing with the TV. I grabbed a towel off the clothesline and strolled down to the beach with Oma and Opa.

* * *

For the next few days, the heat was unrelenting, plants wilted, and the lawn begged to be watered. It was always cooler in the house, and I made a point of being inside as much as possible, partly to escape the heat but also because I wanted to pay more attention to Oma and Opa in the few days remaining before they returned to New Zealand. I wanted them to see their experience here in a good light. They would be staying with my parents in Christchurch on their way home to the top of the South Island, and I didn't want them expressing concerns about me. Oma and Opa loved the sea and thought Yaringa a beautiful place. I knew they had enjoyed their stay and that New Year's Eve was the only blip that had truly disturbed them, apart from the obvious discomfort related to my ongoing predicament.

I managed to see Erika in the afternoons when Oma and Opa were having their nap, and she came over for dinner on their last evening in Yaringa. For their farewell meal, I bought some fresh, locally-caught fish off one of the boats. I set the table with Val's best cutlery and crockery to make it a special occasion, and Erika added the finishing touches with flowers from the garden. Tim was there, of course. He had become part of the family, and Oma and Opa had embraced him. I'd noticed of late that he was more personable, more conversational, a glimpse perhaps of the person he once was. Everyone loved the fish, and I had raided Ted's wine stash to find a nice bottle of red to complement the meal. By the end of the evening, I was feeling quite sad that they were leaving, aware that others would be leaving soon, too. Erika needed to get back to camp.

"Goodbye," Opa said, hugging her warmly. "We might see you in New Zealand one day, huh?"

"You just might." She beamed him a smile.

"Bless you," said Oma, taking her face in both hands and kissing her forehead in the same way she would mine. Oma had taken quite a shine to her, and they seemed to get on well.

* * *

I awoke the next morning with Erika wrapped around me. She had sneaked back after saying goodnight to her parents. She didn't usually stay the night for fear of being discovered, so I was surprised to find her still with me. As I untangled myself from her, she groaned, and I half expected her to sit bolt upright in shock, with the realisation she was still in my caravan. It was early and the only sound was the intermittent cacophony from cockatoos in nearby trees. Other than that, there was an eerie stillness as the world slowly woke to a new day. I stumbled into my shorts, pulled on a T-shirt, slipped my feet into thongs, and opened the caravan door. I stepped out onto the driveway and stretched my arms skywards, yawning at the same time. It was early for me.

Upstairs in the house, Opa was adding the final touches to their suitcases, packed and ready to go. Sitting in the passageway, he was writing out baggage tags for their destination.

"Mornin', Opa."

"Good morning, Sam. These are ready to go in the car," he said, indicating the suitcases.

"Right. I'll just grab a cup 'f tea." I wandered past him into the kitchen.

"Mornin', Oma."

"Good morning, grandson," she said, busily wiping down the bench. "Are you going to have breakfast with us?"

"Just a cup 'f tea will do me, thanks." She deftly poured milk from a jug into a cup then popped the tea strainer on the cup with one hand while lifting the pot with the other and pouring. "Thanks." I picked up the cup and sat down at the table. Opa joined me, his bowl of yoghurt and oats awaiting him.

"So, Sam, from today you'll be on your own again, huh?" he said.

"Yes, not so long t' go now. Six weeks or so, I think," I said, trying to calculate it in my head.

"Is it really that soon?" exclaimed Oma.

"Yep," I said, nodding.

"Keep your nose clean then, boy. You don't want to go adding fuel to your fire," Opa said, chuckling as if his comment were funny. "It's been good to be here with you, but I shall be happy to get back home." He shovelled in a mouthful of yoghurt and oats.

"Sam, you just have to be strong until your father gets here," said Oma.

Judgment day was looming and for the first time in a while, I felt an intense knotting in my stomach. I sipped the last of my tea and stood up.

"I'll be fine. The time will go quickly, 'n it'll be all over soon, one way or anoth'r. It's been great t' have y' here. I'll go 'n put the suitcases in the boot."

As I walked toward the Valiant with the suitcases, I realised I wasn't feeling so great. I would miss them. There was a certain feeling of security and comfort in having them here. Opa arrived at the car with their hand luggage.

"These can go in the boot with the cases if you want," he said.

"Y' may as well take them in the car. Pop them on the back seat so they're handy for y'."

"Yes, I suppose that's a good idea," he said, shuffling to the car door.

"Do you want me to pull the door shut, Sam?" Oma called from the balcony.

"Is that everything down here now?" I called back.

"Yes, it is."

"Righto, then," I said. "We may as well get goin'. Better early than late, eh?"

Oma shut the house's door and made her way down the stairs to the car.

"Helena, would you like the front seat?" Opa was standing at the car door, ready to give the seat to Oma if she so wished, although he was obviously anticipating she would decline.

"No, thank you. I'm perfectly happy in the back." He opened the rear door and gave her his hand to help her in, gently shutting the door behind her before getting into the front seat.

I drove Oma and Opa up the hill in the Valiant for the last time.

"You're fortunate to be living in such a beautiful place, Sam," said Oma. "It really is quite special around here."

"We almost moved here once," said Opa.

"What? To Yaringa?" I asked, surprised.

"No, Australia. When we emigrated from Holland, it came down to a choice between Australia and New Zealand."

"What clinched New Zealand?"

"We knew more people who had emigrated there."

"You sound like you have some regret that we didn't move here, Theo," said Oma.

"No, that's not true. How could I say that when I haven't seen anything of Australia apart from a few weeks in this beautiful place?" replied Opa. "Besides Helena, we have a very good life where we are, huh."

"We most definitely do," agreed Oma.

The sea was at our back now, and I turned inland onto the road to Wodyn, driving through a thinned-out forest of eucalyptus trees. We travelled in silence for a while, each with our own thoughts.

"Well, at least y're goin' t' have a great trip up the coast. It's such a stunning day," I said, breaking the silence.

"It seems that every day is a good day around here, Sam," said Oma. "I don't think we've seen more than a few clouds in the sky the whole time we've been here, certainly no rain."

"No, not a drop of rain, huh," Opa agreed. He loved to measure the rainfall back home and would document it in his diary for later reference. If he lived here, he'd have to document how many days in a row the sun shone and how high the temperature reached. "It's so dry round here, it's hard to believe it's a dairy farming area," he added.

"They've suffer'd drought conditions f' two years now. It's definitely a serious concern f' the farmers. Look, y' can see by the condition the cows are in," I said, pointing to where several cows stood in a paddock on the side of the road, their bony rib cages exposed, looking somewhat the worse for wear.

"Mmm. Shocking, huh," stated Opa, all serious.

In town I pulled up a few metres behind the bus. "Here we are. Next destination Sydney, folks."

"Thank you, Sam," said Opa, simultaneously opening his door and easing a leg out onto the pavement.

I turned to Oma, still in the back seat. "I've already said goodbye to y' once here, along with Mum. Doesn't seem that long ago. It's like déjà vu," I said sadly.

"Not long now until your father gets here, Sam," Oma replied, looking at me with her grave face and steely blue eyes that somehow showed her warmth and compassion beyond their grim intensity.

"I'll be alright, Oma," I assured her as well as myself. I felt strong, but beneath the surface there was a niggling feeling of uncertainty, the fear of the unknown eating away in my stomach.

"Of course you will be, Sam," she said with conviction. "You are a strong person, and you seem to cope with whatever comes up in your life. That is a gift to be cherished."

"Are you coming?" asked Opa, impatiently pointing at the bus. "The bus will be leaving soon." Oma reached for his hand and allowed herself to be assisted onto the pavement.

I got out of the car, made my way around to the boot, and removed their suitcases, placing them side by side on the pavement. There was also an old worn leather carry bag containing food and a thermos, wrapped in a tea towel, that Oma had prepared for the journey.

"I'll take that, thanks Sam," she said, reaching for it. The bag was never far from her side when she went on a journey, always full of food and drink for the trip ahead. I went to pick up the suitcases.

"You don't want to carry both of them, boy. You'll do yourself an injury," said Opa, stepping forward, not wanting to be seen empty-handed.

"Help y'self," I said. He did so, and we made our way to the bus, both looking comically lopsided.

"Look at the two of you!" Oma laughed. "You look like a couple of hunchbacks!"

"Huh? What was that you said, Helena?" Opa sounded bothered. His deafness had caused him to miss out on a moment of humour.

"I just said you look like a couple of hunchbacks carrying those cases," she repeated loudly, smiling at me.

"Oh," he grunted, not seeing the amusement in it.

After the bus driver had confirmed Oma and Opa's destination, their suitcases were loaded, and it was time for them to board.

Opa shook my hand then gave me a firm, brief hug. "Take care, Sam. I hope it all goes well."

"Likewise," I said, embracing him.

"We enjoyed our stay. Will you thank Ted and Val, huh?"

"Yeah, 'f course."

"Oh, and ahh … all the best with the court case."

"Thanks," I said, feeling something catch in my throat, raw emotion, and I just wanted to leave.

"So, grandson … We come, and now we go. Life works its mysteries every day." Oma reached up and took my face in her hands. "The blessing, my boy." She kissed me on my forehead. "*Hou je sterk*. Stay strong. It will be over in the twinkling of an eye and you will be back home with all of us again."

I was supposed to feel reassured; her hands still held my face. "I hope so." I wanted to believe her, as it was all I ever thought about most days.

"Judgment day will reveal all," I said. There were tears forming in the corners of her eyes. I had to go because I didn't want to be breaking down here beside the bus. "See y' soon in New Zealand," I said, leaning down to kiss her. "And have a great trip home."

She took Opa's hand, and they boarded the bus together while I stood watching their slight, stooped figures climb the steps of the bus. Oma glanced back briefly, then they were gone, swallowed up in the bus's interior behind tinted glass windows.

The tears came as I made my way back to the car. I couldn't get there fast enough. I sat in the car and sobbed, no longer able to hold back. The bus started up and blew a large cloud of black diesel smoke from its exhaust, straight in my direction. Seconds later it departed, and I was alone. I wanted to drive now, to drive and never return, to keep driving until I arrived somewhere else, far away, the temptation to run stronger now than it had ever been.

* * *

Before heading back to Yaringa, I needed to report to the police station, but I wasn't going there in my current state. I knew the coffee shop would be open, so I drove the short distance there. Entering the cool interior, I was greeted by the fat chick with the pretty face.

"Cup 'f tea, please, 'n one 'f those pies," I said.

"How are y'? Haven't seen y' in here f' a while."

"No, I haven't had the time."

"Have y' been t' the pub lately?"

"Only on New Year's Eve," I replied.

"I was there, too. Didn't see y'."

"No, didn't see you either. It was pretty crowded though."

I didn't really need the attention and the conversation was as boring as bat shit, but I was grateful for the cup of tea. Fortunately, another punter entered, and I went to sit in the corner as far away as possible from the counter, where I waited for my tea and pie. I picked up a magazine and pretended to read it. More people entered and another woman joined her at the counter to serve. The fat chick waddled over with a tray, wearing an overenthusiastic smile.

I dunno if I would be smilin' if I had the excess fat she's got. Although ... most large people seem quite jolly. I wonder if it's b'cause she's content 'n doesn't care? If she cared t' lose weight, she'd be quite an attractive girl. How do y' tell someone that? It must be hard t' lose weight ... better not t' put it on in the first place.

"Thank you," I said as she placed the tray down on the table.

"Y' welcome," she said, still standing at my table, clasping her hands nervously together. "Would y' go out on a date with me?" she blurted out. Her brave question took me by surprise, causing me to miss the teacup into which I'd begun to pour the tea, and I spilt it all over the saucer and table.

"Well, that's nice 'f y' t' ask, but right now I already have a girlfriend," I replied.

"Oh," she said, looking disappointed. "Sorry, I didn't realise." She looked completely deflated, yet somehow still maintained her smile. "I had t' ask. Sorry ... I didn't mean t' bother y'."

"You didn't. It's not a problem. I'm flattered."

"Great." She returned to the counter leaving me with my tea.

What is it about this place? I've been propositioned more times here than I have in m' whole life! I drank my tea and kept my head buried in the magazine between bites of pie. Half an hour must've passed, and I needed to get out of the coffee shop, out of Wodyn, and back to Yaringa.

She's definitely fat. Her tight black T-shirt doesn't help t' hide the fact that she's got a spare tyre on board. She's definitely pretty, too, with lovely eyes 'n nice long dark hair ... bit greasy though, probably diet related. If she put a halt t' the cream buns 'n went t' the gym f' a while, she'd scrub up real well. I went to the counter to pay.

"Is it my weight?" she asked as if she'd just read my mind. She handed me the change, maintaining eye contact.

"No," I replied, feeling caught out. "Like I said, I've already got a girlfriend."

"I know y' did, but y' see I just wanted t' make sure it wasn't m' weight." She maintained her smile. "Might see y' at the pub sometime."

"Y' might. See y' later," I said, pocketing the change.

27

Fucking Skirts in Small Towns

I reported to the police station without incident then headed off toward Yaringa. The day was still young but felt like it had been going on forever. I felt shagged. I just wanted to go back to my caravan and sleep. Halfway between Yaringa and Wodyn, on a straight stretch of road, I saw someone, dressed entirely in black, jumping up and down and waving manically. I recognised Brigitte and felt obliged to stop and pick her up.

"Thank God y' stopped! My car wouldn't start this morning 'n I've got t' get t' work," she said, opening the door and clambering in.

"What are y' doin' in the middle 'f nowhere?"

"Waitin' f you." She grinned. "Nah, someone gave me a lift as far as the turn off down the south coast 'n I thought it was bett'r th'n nothin'."

I accelerated out onto the road and just as quickly Brigitte moved across the seat.

"Had any good dreams lately?" She placed her hand on the inside of my thigh.

"I thought we discussed the lay 'f the land the other night," I said.

"We did, 'n it resulted in y' comin' in m' mouth."

"Fuck off! That was not by consent." I took her hand and pushed it back onto her own lap.

"That wasn't the impression I got."

Just as quickly her hand returned to my thigh, and there was no denying that part of me liked it very much. It was a difficult moment. On the one hand I had been caught off guard and didn't want any part of the action, and on the other hand, Dick was saying, *Yeah man, don't be daft, 'n give me a piece 'f the action!*

As if sensing my weakness, Brigitte deftly unzipped my fly, put her hand in my pants and removed my firmness.

"Y're so big f' a boy that doesn't want me. I'd love t' see what y're like when y're really excited." Her head disappeared below the dashboard, her lips engulfed me and there was nothing I could do. There was no way of stopping her. I was driving down the main road with nowhere to pull over and Dick was loving it.

Oh, yeah man, this is good! I can't believe you've deprived me 'f this f' so long, Sam. I had to concede she was good, effortlessly bobbing her head in my lap, working away with great skill. There was a side road just ahead, and I suddenly swerved the car up the road, sliding the back of the car around and just missing a eucalyptus tree as I fishtailed up the dirt road. The jolting ride cost Dick a few teeth marks but he seemed beyond caring, the euphoria of the moment was so good.

"What the fuck are y' doing, Sam? I just about bit it off!" she exclaimed, coming up for air and looking incredibly annoyed.

"Sorry." I decided enough is enough. A few hundred metres up the road I found a clearing to pull into. The perplexing thing was my mind was telling me this had to stop, but Dick still dictated the proceedings. There was no way I was going to unload in her mouth. I wanted the part of her that every man desired — many a fantasy had been imagined from the other side of the bar.

"Stop! I don't want t' blow yet!" I removed her mouth from Dick and brought her face up to meet mine. We mashed mouths and bumped teeth as the lust in us overrode anything resembling the rational. My hand opened the buttons on her blouse and forced her bra cups upwards. Her breasts spilled out, soft and tanned, ripe for devouring. I was all over them like a rash, nuzzling them, nipping them between my teeth, sucking them till they were hard as cherry stones. She groaned as if she ached, and the more she groaned, the more I was encouraged. Her back arched and she raised her buttocks off the seat, pulling her skirt up over her thighs. She began removing her knickers and as she did, I ran my hand up her thigh, finding her wetness.

"Let's get in the back," I said. She didn't need asking twice, clambering over with me as I removed my shorts and boxers. Brigitte wanted me in her mouth again. Instead I undid her bra and slipped her blouse off her shoulders, at the same time encouraging her to lie back. She was begging for me to be inside her. "Not yet," I whispered. I straddled her midriff so that Dick was below her cleavage, and I moved my way forward until I was firmly between her breasts. Brigitte cottoned on, pushing them tight together. "Some oil would help," I joked.

"Oh, y've done this before?" We built momentum and I worked one hand down between her thighs, her groaning changed to cries of pleasure. "Oh, y're good at this, Sam. Can't y' be inside me now?" I was so close to coming between her tits that it was going to be all over in a few seconds. "Sam, I want y' inside me now!" she gasped. But that wasn't going to happen. As I exploded between her breasts, I moved up to her face so she could taste me. She hadn't climaxed, but it felt as though she was close. While I was still hard, I moved down her and quickly slipped inside. I could feel myself going off the boil, so I pulled out and got her to turn over. She was on her hands and knees, her beautifully rounded arse in the air. I wasn't disappointed. She came quickly in loud, violent cries. "Fuck me, fuck me … Ooh, yeah!"

We lay sprawled in the back seat, saturated with sweat and juices. "You were fantastic," said Brigitte. "Everything I'd dreamt 'f. How do y' manage t' go f' so long?"

"Don't know."

"I'll have more 'f that any time, thank you." She kissed me gently on the lips then more firmly with her tongue doing an exploratory rove.

Suddenly Erika came to mind and guilt swamped me. "Don't y' have t' get to work?" I asked hopefully.

"Yeah, but we've got time." She kissed me, again reaching for my groin hoping to arouse me once more. Irritably I sat up, trying to contain my annoyance at my lack of willpower, but now I had a taste for it. With Erika gone before long, there would be no reason to avoid such temptation. There was something about having sex with no strings attached that felt liberating.

"We better get y' t' work, 'n I've got t' have this car back soon or Tim'll be gettin' agitated because I've had it f' so long." I reached for my clothes and began pulling on my boxers.

"Y' sure y' don't want t' go again?" Brigitte asked, kissing my arm.

"I'm sure. I want t' get this car back so I can use it again when I need t', 'n I'm sure y' boss won't be happy if y're late."

I dropped Brigitte off outside the pub. She wanted to kiss me goodbye, but I wasn't up for it. She got to peck me on the cheek and that was that.

"When do I see y' again?" she asked.

"Who says y' do?" Her face dropped, and I winked at her.

"Y're a real shit y' know." The smile returned to her face.

"It's been said b'fore. I'll see y' 'round." She slammed the door, and I accelerated out of the car park and headed down the hill towards home.

I opened the caravan door and to my relief Erika had gone. The bed was a mess — sheets tangled across its width, the duvet bunched up in one corner, and pillows propped at the head of the bed, suggesting she'd been sitting there reading before she left. I picked up a towel and took a shower, standing under the stream of water for an age, hoping to wash away Dick's sins. I wondered how I was going to face Erika since I wasn't very good at hiding things from others. My face read like a book.

A year ago, I'd smashed up my old man's VW Beetle. He owned a service station, and my brother and I worked there. We pumped fuel on the weekends to help him make some extra money because Dad always took the weekends off. I'd driven the car to the shop to buy a milkshake, and afterwards I continued around the block, any excuse for a spin. I must've taken the corner too fast and got the car going sideways. Although I hit the brakes, I failed to correct the skid and smashed into a brick wall. It put a huge ding in the front of the car and knocked the brick wall off its foundation. I was devastated, so much so I even thought about killing myself. The beach was just down the road, and I drove the damaged VW there while I contemplated walking into the ocean. The sea was wild that day, huge waves pounded the beach, and I would've been swept out to sea in no time. After standing for an age watching the waves, I changed my mind, deciding a better option was to run away. This was my intention until my brother talked me into going home with him.

At the dinner table that night I was so down and bummed out my father knew straight away something was up.

"Okay Sam, what's the problem?"

"What do you mean?" I asked meekly.

"Something's wrong. It's written all over that face of yours." He had it out of me in moments — the tears and the whole sob story poured out of me.

Now as I stood under the shower imagining my sins running down the drain, I hoped Erika would be less observant than my father.

I popped upstairs. It was the 13th of January and Erika would be leaving soon. Oma and Opa were gone now, and the house seemed strangely quiet. I found Tim in the lounge, sitting on his throne, with the telly going.

"I'm waiting f' the cricket t' come on. Did y' grandparents get away okay?"

"Yeah," I replied, still distracted by my thoughts.

"Nice folk."

"Mmm, they are," I mumbled. "Who's playing today?"

"Australia, New Zealand."

"Oh, and what's the standings overall?"

"New Zealand has t' beat India in their next game to get in the final with Australia."

"Oh shit. That's goin' t' be tight then."

"Yep."

I disappeared into the kitchen, made myself a bowl of cereal and a cup of coffee, then went back into the lounge to sit myself down in the empty armchair.

"So, who's goin' t' win?"

"Not you."

"Hah. Trust you. Oh, come on. The Indians are crap 'n y' know it." I shovelled in a mouthful of cereal, crunching my way through it.

"Erika was up here lookin' f' y'."

"What did she want?" I asked anxiously.

"How would I know?" Tim said, shrugging his shoulders.

"I just thought she might've said somethin'."

Tim said nothing in response as I crunched my way through another mouthful of cereal.

"She's a nice-lookin' girl, isn't she?"

"Yeah, she is," I said, looking sideways at him. "Keep y' hands off."

"I don't think y've got too much t' worry about there. She's only got eyes f' you."

I finished my cereal and gulped my coffee down. I didn't much feel like going out of the house, but the alternative was sitting there with Tim all day. I liked the cricket but being in his company in large doses was more than I could cope with at the moment.

* * *

A swim was the way to go, even though I'd probably see Erika, but there was no point in avoiding her. As I made my way to the beach, I managed to rationalise my behaviour, convincing myself that there was no future for Erika and me.

Yeah, it's an affair really, isn't it? One 'f those holiday flings that y' have in a resort town. Nice while it lasts but it's over when the holiday's over. That's what's gonna happen t' us when Erika goes home. I'll never see her again. We'll probably write f' a month, maybe two. Next minute we're a distant memory t' each other, and our lives will take different roads! I'd experienced it before with good mates when my family shifted towns because Dad got a promotion. My mates and I would write a couple of letters over a period of a month or two, I'd even go back some weekends and holidays to see them, then — *Goodnight, Nurse*, as the old man would say. *Lights out. All over, Rover.*

I crossed the road to the park by the surf club and slipped between the rails of the fence, making a beeline for the beach. *So ... it kind 'f makes sense that if Brigitte wants t' tango, I'll be up f' it. After all, I'm the one stuck in this fuckin' town waitin' f' punishment. Why shouldn't I have a few pleasures? Christ, is that Dick or me talkin'?*

"Sam, how are you?"

"Sarah … Hi. I'm good," I replied, somewhat startled. "How about you?"

"You're still coming for dinner on Sunday, aren't you?" she stated more than asked, placing her hand on my forearm as if that would help persuade me.

"Yes, I'll definitely be there. I wouldn't miss it f' the world, Sarah."

"Great." She leaned forward and kissed me on the lips, catching me off guard. "I'll look forward to it. I better attend to my children," she said, inclining her head towards the playground where her two children were playing on the swings. "See you Sunday," she said.

"I can't wait."

I squinted my eyes into the sun, scanning for any sign of Erika. I spread my towel on the sand and sat down, taking my T-shirt off to catch a bit of sun. Taking one more glance around the beach to assure myself Erika wasn't around, I lay back on my towel, placing my T-shirt over my face to keep the sun's brightness off my eyes.

A voice, very close and softly spoken, awoke me. I thought I must've been dreaming and rolled towards the voice without removing the T-shirt from my face.

"I've been waiting for you all morning! Where have you been?"

I stretched my arms. I could feel I was sunburnt.

"Must've fallen asleep f' quite a while," I said, peeling the T-shirt off my face and squinting to make out Erika against the brightness of the sun. "I came down here t' see if you 'n the others were here. I couldn't find any of y', so I lay down here thinkin' I'd have a swim 'n must've fallen asleep."

"You look burnt."

"Yeah."

"Serves you right for not looking harder. You know I'm going home in three days. I can't bear not being with you, knowing how little time there is to go."

"Yeah … I know. It's bloody hard." I pulled her in towards me and held her tight. She snuggled in close and I could feel her tears warm on my arm. "I don't want y' t' go, Erika. Waitin' f' D-Day with all you guys gone is goin' t' be bloody depressing." My words just increased her flood of tears. I didn't know what to do, as part of me had become numb to the idea of her leaving.

"Let's go back t' the caravan," I said.

"I can't," she said, looking up for the first time since she started crying. "We're going for a drive up the coast for the day. Dad says I've got to go because I haven't done anything with the family since we've been here."

"Well, do y' want me t' come with y'?"

"I couldn't expect you to come with my family for the day, they'd drive you mad."

"I don't think so. I've got a family too, 'n they'd drive y' mad. If y're allowed t' take me, I'll come with y'. I'm there, babe."

She was chuffed, snuggling in closer to me. She looked so beautiful in her vulnerable state that I reciprocated, and pulling her into me, I kissed her forehead.

"There won't be any question of *allowed*," she responded. "I'll just tell them that you're coming."

"Then it's a done deal, isn't it? Y' better go 'n tell them, 'n I better go 'n get a bit more respectable f' the ride."

I walked home and changed into some smarter-looking clothes while still maintaining a casual look. I brushed my hair, cleaned my teeth, and pulled several faces in the mirror to make sure I looked good, then I bolted upstairs to tell Tim I was going out with Erika and her family for the day. Tim was still in his La-Z-Boy, watching the cricket.

"What's the score?" I'd forgotten about the cricket and was starting to feel a bit bummed that I was going for a drive. With a bit of luck her dad might follow it on the radio in the car.

"Who cares? Y' goin' t' lose."

"Nah. Wait 'n see … it's not over till it's over." Tim probably wanted another wrestling session. *Next time I'll take that ZZ Top beard clean off his chin.*

"Whatever," he drawled, scratching at his groin. He'd probably caught something from the nymph he'd been with at the house on the lagoon.

"Okay, catch y' later, eh. Don't get too depressed when we beat y'." He gave me a raised finger, grinning as I walked out of the room.

* * *

Erika's dad, Hank, was very welcoming, he even seemed pleased to have me join them. Her mum was the same. We drove south to a coastal town of much larger proportions than Yaringa, and apparently the retirement capital of southern New South Wales.

Overall, the trip was nothing more than a dull, hot day out. Erika's parents seemed nice enough and didn't seem to mind me being with their daughter. Her twin sisters were friendly and intrigued by me. On the way back in the car, her mum asked questions about my family and where I lived, and if I had plans for a career. I told her my current plans involved travel, and I hoped that travelling would present me with some experience in life that would help me to know what I wanted to do.

I was grateful when we arrived back at their campsite. I was feeling claustrophobic. The twins were shouting at each other in the back seat next to me, and Erika's mother was starting to develop a whine in her voice, reminiscent of Val's.

"Thank you for the day," I said to Hank.

"You're welcome," Hank replied in his strong German accent as he shook my hand.

"We're going to have tea now. Why don't you stay?" Erika was looking at me pleadingly with her big, blue eyes which had hooked me in when I first met her.

"It's very kind 'f y', Hank. But I really should be gettin' back. There's a few things I need t' be doin'." I couldn't face sitting down with the whole family and being the centre of their attention. The day out had been enough.

"I'll see y' tomorrow, Erika, or y' can pop round after tea if y' want t'."

"I'll see," she mumbled, eyes down.

"And let's get t'gether with everyone on Saturday night," I suggested. "We need t' have a farewell party."

"Okay," she nodded in agreement.

"Okay, then. Bye," I said, walking off.

I walked through the caravan park feeling melancholy. Life had dealt me a raw deal just as I was coming to grips with being an adult.

* * *

Saturday night eventuated. It was like the early days with everyone back in the fold — Stu, Mal, Claudia, Erika, Tim and me, all sipping on tinnies, sitting and gazing into a small fire that wasn't meant to be. Fires had been banned on the beach, but we were so far down the stretch of sand that we felt safe from prying eyes. Stu's new girlfriend, the woman he had met at the pub on New Year's Eve, had left the day before. Her family holiday was over, and another senior high school girl had possibly lost her virginity in Yaringa.

How many girls had gone that way up 'n down the coast this summer? Strange …. all three 'f us ended up with high school girls. Although girls do usually go f' guys older than themselves. It's somethin' about them maturin' earlier than guys. I had a girlfriend at high school, though, 'n she was the same age as me. Funny that. I must've been one 'f those exceptional developers, mature beyond m' years. Ha ha ha. When I was pickin' apples in Motueka, no one could believe how young I was.

"So how's it been lately, Sam?" Stu asked, taking another sip from his tinny.

"Good," I lied.

"So we're all out 'f here soon 'cept you. How's that goin' t' be?" he asked.

"Fuckin' great! What do you think, Stu?" I barked, feeling annoyed.

"Hey, I was only askin' … didn't mean nothin' by it."

"I know. I fuckin' know." I could feel a lump growing in the back of my throat. "Obviously, things won't be quite the same when y'all have gone. I'll get by, though. I have t', don't I? Hey, I got by before y' were here, 'n I'll get by fine again when y're gone." I could feel Erika's hand tightening around my arm as her head leaned in on my shoulder.

"Of course y' will, Sam. It's still summer, 'n there's a heap 'f nice-lookin' babes 'round," Mal quipped.

"That's the last thing on m' mind," I said, squeezing Erika's hand.

Tim passed me a joint he'd rolled. He was happy smoking the stuff, and it didn't seem to impact negatively on his mental state. I took it and inhaled heavily, sucking it deep into my lungs, feeling the burning sensation as it went down. I held it in for several seconds before blowing out one long stream of smoke. I watched it disappear into the darkness as I offered the joint to Erika.

"It's y' last night, y' should have some," I tried to persuade her.

"No," she shook her head. Erika often refused to partake. She seemed afraid of losing control. There was a certain amount of letting go of the mind required if one was to experience dope.

"It'll open up y' mind 'n allow y' t' see the world a wee bit differently," I persisted gently.

"But I don't want to see it differently. I'm perfectly happy with it just the way it is."

"Fair enough, but y' might find it fun," I said.

"I'm having fun being here with you," she responded.

"Yeah, but y' might find it so much more fun … much more freeing."

"I might, and I might not, so I'm not going to."

"Sex is amazin' after y've had a smoke," I whispered in her ear.

"Sex should be amazing without a smoke," she whispered back.

"Oh, it is with you, babe. Don't y' worry 'bout that. But y' know it just adds a little somethin' that's hard t' explain without tryin' it."

"I'm not having any. End of story!" she snapped. "Look at the trouble it's got you into and you're still smoking it!"

These were hard words to hear but how right she was. I watched her gazing at the fire, flames flickering across her face.

"Y' know, if I wasn't in this predicament, we prob'bly would've never met," I whispered softly, my face close to hers. "I prob'bly wouldn't be here. I'd be up in Queensland, or some northern New South Wales beach, or back in New Zealand by now."

"I never thought of it like that. Just as well you smoke dope, you big dope," she said grinning, trying to tickle me around my ribs.

Opposites attract, don't they? We contrast well. Sitting stoned on the beach around the fire, with this realisation, made me feel that much closer to her. Erika really did feel deeply for me and tomorrow she was leaving, while I was staying to face the consequences of my actions. The last few months had already been a form of punishment. Waiting, waiting, not able to leave, reporting to the police station every day — these were a constant reminder of my situation. Erika snuggled in closer as if she were cold, even though the night was mild and we were near a fire.

"Can we go back to your caravan," she whispered in my ear.

"Sure, babe," I whispered back, kissing her on the cheek. "Just give me a minute."

"So, guys. When y' headin' out 'f this godforsaken slice 'f paradise?" I asked.

"Not sure, Sam. I'd've been happy t' leave a coupla days ago if it wasn't f' this love-struck bunny," replied Stu, pointing at Mal sitting on the other side of the fire, Claudia beside him.

"Prob'bly t'morrow or the next day. Not much point in hangin' 'round aft'r the girls've gone," Mal said.

"Shit, Mal, don't I do it f' y'," I responded.

"Afraid not, Sam."

I knew the guys would've been gone long ago if they hadn't met girls here.

"We've got another week b'fore we've got t' be back in Woolongong. We'll probably stop somewhere up the coast for a few nights."

"Will I see y' tomorrow b'fore these lovely ladies depart? B'cause right now I think we're goin' t' crash. Right, Erika?"

"Right, Sam," beamed Erika.

"Like I believe y'," said Stu. "Sure, let's meet at our tent f' a late mornin' fry-up. Y' up f' it, Mal?"

"Always, mate!"

"It's a done deal," I said, getting up and bringing Erika up with me. "Tim, y' walkin' back with us?"

"No. I'm good right here," he said, not looking up from the fire.

"Okay, I'll catch y'all tomorrow."

Arm in arm we walked down the beach towards the village, the lights on the hill acting as our lighthouse beacon. Erika tripped me up and I fell playfully to the ground, rolling in the sand, pretending I was hurt, and when she knelt to see if I was okay, I grabbed her and pulled her down and tickled the living daylights out of her. She begged for mercy as we rolled around in the dark, silhouetted by the almost-full moon. Then somehow, she was on top of me, tickling me and sitting on my chest, my arms pinned under her knees.

"I'll let you go if you say you'll come to Albany with me."

"Y' know I can't," I said, grinning at her.

"That's an unacceptable answer." She tickled me more.

"Mercy," I begged.

"So, Sam … What is it to be?" She stopped and looked all serious.

"Y' know the answer."

She began tickling me again, I squirmed, begging for mercy. When she stopped this time there were tears streaming down her face, and I tried to free my arms, but she wouldn't let me go. I could have muscled my way out, but I didn't want that.

"You're such a stubborn son of a bitch!" she sobbed. "I need you, Sam. You don't need to risk going to prison. I don't know what I'd do if they locked you up."

"They won't, babe."

"You don't know that for sure. Besides, with the hell they've put you through already, it's inevitable, isn't it?" She didn't mince words when there were just the two of us around.

"Hey, I dunno what the story's gonna be, but I know that everything'll work out," I said, trying to convince myself as much as her. "I know it in m' heart, 'n I'm goin' t' hold on t' that or I've got nothin'."

"You've got me."

"Right now I have, but y' gone t'morrow. How many weeks d' y' think it'll be till y' forget about me 'n y've got a new boyfriend?"

"Never, Sam. Never!" she cried, pounding my chest.

"Life's like that, Erika." She still had me pinned to the sand.

"I don't want another boyfriend. I'll wait for you, Sam."

"When I was fifteen, I had a girlfriend at high school whom I thought I was in love with. Near the end 'f the school year, her parents decided they were movin' t' another city, a city far away from the one we were living in. She was very upset 'n I was too." Erika leaned forward, rested her forearms on my chest, and stared at me intently. "We planned t' go on a summer campin' holiday 'n spend as much time t'gether as we possibly could before she left. When it came t' our campin' trip, though, m' parents wouldn't let me go."

"Why ever not?"

"They thought I'd get int' trouble, that I'd get m' girlfriend pregnant. Whatever. I don't exactly know."

"That's unfair."

"Yeah. So the campin' holiday didn't eventuate 'n I was very angry with m' parents. When school finished f' the year, we saw each other f' the first week 'n said our goodbyes at the end 'f that week. We were both pretty cut up, as it was the hardest thing in the world t' do. We promised t' write t' each other. I went on holiday with m' parents, still very angry with them. I hardly talked t' them f' a week or so, then somehow life took over again 'n I was almost back t' m' normal self. Sure, I thought about her 'n wondered what she was up to. But the thoughts became less 'n less. Sometimes she still pops int' m' mind in a curious way, but she never wrote 'n I never wrote. We never saw each other again."

"No! I don't believe you! That's not going to happen to us. We're different. Both of us are older than you were then," Erika stated passionately.

"I'm not sayin' that it'll happen, I was explainin' about separation 'n distance 'n lives in two different places. That's the reality 'f you goin' 'n me stayin'. It's not good, but it's not all bad either. I'm just sayin' that somehow life finds a way t' continue. Are y' goin' t' let me up?"

"Maybe," she said. "Will you come and see me once this is all over?"

"Of course I will," I said.

She removed her knees from my arms and leaned down and kissed me. "I want to stay the night with you," she whispered.

"Sure y' can, babe."

We stumbled into the caravan. Our hands immeadiately all over each other. Our mouths met in passion, and clothes disappeared from our bodies as if by magic. In moments we were on the bed, naked, wildly devouring each other. Erika placed me inside her, and there was an urgency and desperation in her I hadn't experienced before.

She cried out, "I love you, Sam. Make love to me like you've never done before."

Which I did, except it was not fast or furious like she may have desired. It was slow, long, lingering, full of touching, kissing and being close, skin on skin, sweaty from the heat of the night. I really allowed myself to feel the warmth and love between us, and somewhere amidst it all, there was an extended moment of euphoria as we both cried out in the darkness.

* * *

I awoke early the next morning to find we were still entangled in each other. Erika's arms were wrapped around me and one of her legs straddled my lower torso. I moved slightly to get a better view of her face, and as I did so she groaned and stretched. She looked beautiful in the rays of sunlight streaming through the window. I slipped my hand over her breasts and felt the stiffness in her nipples. Erika stirred then suddenly sat up.

"What's the time, Sam?"

"I dunno. Early, I think."

"What's early? As much as I'd like to stay forever, I'd better get back."

"Not now … please," I whispered. She climbed on top of me, the warmth of her body sensual against mine.

"I really do love you, Sam."

"I know y' do, Erika. I love you too." I held her in my arms, caressing her face and shoulders, inhaling her sweet smell, wishing this moment would never end.

It must've been a good half hour that we lay there before we were interrupted by a knock at the door, which caused us both to jump.

"Erika, are you in there?" It was Claudia. "If you are, your mum and dad are looking for you."

"I'll be there in five," Erika called out.

"Okay, I'll wait then. I told them you'd gone for a big walk with Sam to say goodbye before we go. I think they believed me."

Erika was already out of bed and pulling on her knickers.

"Sam, can I have a shower? I don't think I should go back like this. They might smell our sex on me."

"Yeah, 'f course y' can." I was impressed with how calm she was, her ability to think on her feet. She wrapped a towel around herself and was out the door. I heard her talking.

"I need a shower first, Claudia. Thanks for covering for me. Do you think they suspect anything?"

"Maybe your mum, but not your dad. Besides, he likes Sam. You know that. He thinks he's a real gentle …" Their voices faded.

I lay there wondering how I was going to treat the rest of the day and whether it was a good idea to go and say goodbye to Erika's family. The door opened and Erika was back from her shower. She flung off her towel and stepped quickly into her knickers before throwing on her jeans and T-shirt.

"I don't know about brunch with the other guys, Sam. It might not be a happening thing now. I doubt my folks will let me, now that I've already been away this morning, I'm sorry."

"Hey," I said, propping myself up on an elbow, "it's not a problem. If y' can, y' can, 'n if y' can't, y' can't. That's just the way it is, right? At least we had last night."

"You're so profound, you big goof. Will you come over in a little while?"

"Will it be safe? I don't want y' parents' wrath, y' know."

"I promise," she said, climbing onto the bed and kissing me.

"Come on, Erika!" Claudia called out. "If we go now there might be an opportunity to go to the fry-up before we leave."

"Coming!" she called out, recoiling from the bed like a serpent of rare grace and beauty. "See you soon." And she was gone.

* * *

In my own time I got up and made my way to the shower, staying under far too long as I dreamt of the night with Erika and how amazing it had been. As I stood there in my shower trance it suddenly dawned on me that it was Sunday. Tonight I was expected at Harry and Sarah's house. *Christ, not exactly what I need today!* I put my face under the full force of the shower spray, hoping the warm water would wash away my worries. I couldn't just pull out of dinner. I would never hear the end of it from either of them. Sarah's behaviour towards me made me nervous. *What's with her? She seemed like a good woman the evenin' I first met her. Since then, she's shown a very different side 'f herself, and I'm confused.* No matter what anyone said, I didn't really understand Harry's motivation for wanting to be personally involved with me. It made me nervous. I was a criminal in the eyes of the police, and he wanted to help me. It was too bizarre. I couldn't even talk to anyone about it. I shook my head as a shiver ran up my spine. I turned the shower off and grabbed a towel, then made my way back to the caravan to dress.

Upstairs in the house, Tim was already up and in his usual place, as permanent as the furniture he was sitting on.

"Mornin', Tim."

"Mornin'."

The telly was on, playing an infomercial. I walked into the kitchen, opened a cupboard and pulled out the jar of muesli Oma had made.

"Who won the cricket the other day?" I shouted, pouring muesli into a bowl.

"New Zealand by one run."

"No shit!" I exclaimed, pouring milk into my bowl. Grabbing a spoon out of the top draw, I rushed into the lounge. "So that must mean New Zealand play the Ozzies in the final, huh?"

"Yep, should be, but if India beats us then they would nudge you out."

"Nah, India hasn't got a chance. Y' know what?" I asked Tim.

"What?"

"I reckon we can whip y' Ozzie arses in the final!"

"We'll see," said Tim, all cool and cocky.

"Tim, I don't mean t' sound like y' nana or anythin', but why don't y' shave y' beard off? Y' look like y' should be livin' in Pennsylvania with those horse 'n cart people, you know the ones whose women wear those white bonnets. Or y' could audition f' ZZ Top."

"The people are Amish."

"Yeah, that's the ones."

"Y' really think I'm goin' t' listen t' your advice on how I look?"

"No, but I can only hope y' might take notice 'f a man who knows style. The ladies will really dig y' if y' don't have that beard."

"They didn't seem t' dig me before I had the beard. Look at the situation I'm in now, all because 'f a couple 'f girls."

Tim had a point. "What! So y' goin' t' let them get the better 'f y'? Ain't worth it, Tim. Y' can't just give up cos life tosses y' a bad experience," I ranted.

"Then let's see how y' fare when they lock you up," Tim said.

"Jesus, Tim that's a bit below the belt, ain't it?"

"Maybe, but it's what happened t' me, isn't it?!"

"True." I spooned muesli into my mouth silently, not really tasting it, then changed the subject. "Erika leaves t'day, as y' know, and I'm goin' t' have a swim then say goodbye. Hopefully, she's allowed t' come over t' the boys' camp f' the fry-up. Her parents couldn't find her this morning because she stayed with me last night."

"Ooh, the big last night. Did y' fuck her senseless?"

"Not quite senseless, Tim. I like m' girl t' have a brain," I replied as I wandered off to the kitchen with my empty bowl. "Might see y' over there, eh?"

* * *

I found a towel and my board shorts, slung them over my shoulder and headed down the road past the bowling club, which had a session in full play — all the oldies in whites down by the jack, checking out their last shot and planning their next attack. The day was cooking already and looking like it would only get hotter. All the gardens I passed were parched, suffering badly from the drought. I couldn't recall the last time it had rained, and each day was a repeat of the day before — clear blue skies accompanied by a very hot sun. The only thing that seemed to vary was the surf at the beach. Some days it was dead calm and other days there would be waves of one-to-one-and-a-half metres breaking evenly along the shore.

Down on the beach there wasn't much activity. Things were getting back to normal. The main group of holidaymakers were either heading home today or had already left in the past couple of days. I liked the beach with less people on it, so except for Erika's departure, I was happy about the exodus. There were the usual locals, along with a scattering of topless women getting their dosage of sun — thirty minutes and turn seemed to be the rule of thumb. I could almost set my watch to it. I wrapped a towel around my waist, whipped off my shorts, replaced them with my board shorts, and headed for the water.

Occasionally the sea had cold currents running, but most of the time it was of such a moderate temperature that there was no need to piss around in the shallows, and I usually dived straight in. This morning was no exception. I waded in up to my waist and dived into the first breaking wave. They were a good size, so I spent a while catching waves without having to look out for other swimmers or surfers. I loved the bigger waves that peaked really quickly. They were steeper before they broke, and when they did break, it was an instant drop down the front of the wave. The only drawback was that sometimes I'd get dumped badly onto the sea floor, and it could hurt like hell. I stayed in for half an hour or so for a good, old-fashioned workout, just the tonic to start the day. I needed to get cracking if I was going to fit Erika in and attend the fry-up. As I walked up the beach, I noticed someone waving at me, they were right in the line of my path and unavoidable. It was Brigitte.

"Hi, Sam. How's it hangin'?"

"A little t' the left today," I said, readjusting my shorts.

"Aren't you the wit." Brigitte looked good, nicely tanned with her magnificent breasts beckoning.

"Look, nice t' see y', but I've got t' go. I'm meant t' be somewhere five minutes ago."

"Hey, no problemo. What y' doin' later? Want t' meet?" she asked.

"Today's not really good f' me. I've got a lot on," I replied hesitantly.

"Are y' tryin' t' avoid me since the other day, now that y've had y' fix?"

"I thought it was the other way 'round," I teased. "Hey, got t' go, might catch y' soon, eh?"

"Yeah, well, don't make it too long, Sam. I'm already feelin' horny. I should hitch t' work more often, huh?" She chuckled. "Cos y' never know what might happen." I gave her a sideways glance and continued on my way.

***

Erika's campsite was no longer recognisable. The caravan was hitched to the back of the car, the awning had been pulled down, and her father was folding it up. The girls' tents were gone, and they were packing the last of their bags. Erika saw me and flashed a smile, which I returned.

"You folks don't muck around," I said, walking up to her father.

"No, Sam, we don't. When it's time to leave it's all about getting it done quickly so it doesn't feel like too much of a chore," said Hank.

I knelt down to help him with the final folding of the awning. "Has it been a good holiday?" I asked earnestly.

"Good morning, Sam," Erika's mother called out from behind the caravan where she was packing something away.

"Good morning!"

"Oh yes, a very good holiday," replied Hank. "Erika probably told you that we have been coming here ever since she was a small girl."

"Yes, she did say she'd been comin' here as long as she could remember. Erika's a great girl, 'n I'm sorry t' see y'all go. I'll miss Erika a lot."

Hank stopped bagging up the awning for a moment and looked me straight in the eye. "Sam, you are welcome to come and visit us any time. It's not all that far away, so keep it in mind."

"Thanks, I will."

* * *

I could smell Stu and Mal's fry-up before I could see it, great wafts of bacon and sausages drifting through the hedge as I approached their camp. Erika was sitting with Claudia, talking and laughing, both with wine coolers in their hands. Erika shot me one of her wonderful smiles, her golden hair shimmering in the sunlight. She glowed like an angel.

"So!" Mal said as he slapped me on the back before draping his arm over my shoulder. "How the fuck are we goin' t' get by without these lovely ladies in our lives?"

"Well, it ain't goin' t' be easy," I replied.

"I don't know about you, Sam, but it's been one 'f the best summers of my life," said Mal.

"Yeah, for you. But for me it's been the strangest summer. So many weird things've happen'd," I replied.

"Weird in what way?" enquired Stu.

"Well, y' know … gettin' busted, then you guys comin' along and pickin' me up on the side of the road, meetin' the girls, m' grandparents here f' Christmas … livin' with Tim 'n his parents. It's not somethin' I would've scripted three months ago."

"Yeah, of course. How could it not be weird when y' put it that way? With a bit 'f luck, Sam, it'll be over for y' in a short while."

"They could never lock you up, Sam. Such a lovely guy like yourself," Claudia chimed in.

"That's right, Sam," called out Stu, half concealed in smoke, turning bacon and sausages at the barbie. "Hey, guys, this is ready, so y' should come 'n get it. Is Tim comin', Sam?"

"Me thinks not, there's cricket on today."

"Why didn't y' drag him down here? There's so much food it's all going t' go t' the birds at this rate."

"Hey, I ain't his nana, 'n I'm not plannin' t' be anytime soon."

"Yeah, Stu, so leave it alone," said Mal as he served himself up a giant plate of eggs, sausages, bacon and tomatoes.

"I must say it's a bit 'f a shame if we aren't goin' t' see Tim again. He's come along alright since we've been here, don't y' think, Sam?" enquired Stu.

"Funny y' should say that. This very morning I was considering those sentiments myself."

"Speak 'f the devil! Look who's just wandered in," announced Mal, sitting down with his plate overflowing with food. "We were just talkin' about y', Tim. Y're conspicuous by your absence. Hey, y' better tuck in. Stu's worried that he's gone 'n cooked too much," Mal said as he shovelled a loaded fork of sausage and egg into his mouth.

"Smells good, just the kind 'f breakfast I like," responded Tim, stroking at his beard and admiring the spread on the barbeque.

"I'm glad y' made the effort, Tim. Don't y' go wastin' away in front 'f that telly once we're all gone. Y' should seriously get back in t' y' surfin' 'n take Sam with y'," said Stu encouragingly. "It'll be good f' both of y'."

"We might get int' it a bit more once we've thrashed you guys in the one-day cricket finals," Tim said smugly.

"Shit! Did we make it t' the finals?" asked Stu. "That means we must've beaten Oz in the last game."

"Yep, but y' still have a couple of games to go, though," answered Tim, methodically picking up a plate and piling food onto it like he hadn't eaten in weeks.

"Fuckin' fantastic," Stu said, forking a sausage into his mouth. "Sit down, Tim, there's a seat over there," he added, pointing with his fork to a seat beside Erika. "I'm just standing cos I need t' keep an eye on the barbie."

Tim sat down beside Erika and began to load refried potatoes into his mouth while attempting to engage her in conversation.

"So y're off home today, Erika," he stated more than asked.

"Yes," was Erika's monosyllabic reply.

"Looking forward t' it, are y?" Tim continued.

"No," she said, prodding her fork at a sausage, showing little interest in eating it.

Suddenly I felt strangely pleased Erika was leaving. I was grateful to have had her company for the summer and it had been fun, but as I sat there looking around at each of them, I realised I didn't mind that they were all departing, a strange contrast to my feelings from a few days prior.

"Tim, y' need a glass. You too, Sam." Stu had a bottle of cheap bubbly in his hand. "Come on, here y' go, guys." He tossed tumblers our way, then proceeded to walk around and fill them. "Right, everyone got a drink? I'd like t' make a toast to you, Sam. It's been an unusual 'n unexpected holiday f' Mal 'n me. We were plannin' to travel a lot further 'n would've if it had not been f' meetin' you. You so passionately introduced us t' Yaringa 'n welcom'd us int' y' world. The rest is a story in itself. So thanks, Sam, 'n t' you too, Tim. A toast t' Sam 'n Tim!" Stu cheered, raising his glass high in the air.

"A toast!" Claudia called out, raising her glass. "And could I just add that it's been one of the best, if not *the* best holiday Erika and I've ever had, and we've been coming here for years."

"Hey, you two've covered all the bases 'n left nothin' f' Erika or me t' say, but I'll say something anyway," Mal said. "It's been a blast, Sam, 'n I wouldn't've met Claudia if it wasn't f' you," Mal added, grinning one of his cheesy grins.

"Well, guys, thanks f' sayin' so, but y' know I get the last say. And I say that the river runs both ways. It's been a bloody great summer f' me too, despite the obvious weirdness. I'll miss y'all, so there. Cheers." I raised my glass.

"Cheers!" Our voices reverberated in unison.

Erika sat quietly, trying to hold back her tears but now they came, running freely down her face. An urgent need to leave suddenly overcame me. I wanted to get up and just go. I didn't want an extended, emotional farewell, and then I realised I had the perfect excuse to do so.

"And on that note folks, it's that time 'f the day. Unfortunately, I've got t' be in Wodyn t' report t' the local constabulary. Who wants to drive me there? We've got less than half an hour b'fore midday."

"Y' can borrow m' car," offered Tim, who still had half his breakfast on his plate as he plied his mouth with food.

"Thanks, Tim."

"It's been good, Sam," said Stu, giving me a bear hug. "You'll get through this," he murmured quietly before letting me go.

"Y're a top man, Sam, even if y're easy to wind up," Mal said.

"Cheers, Mal."

Claudia was standing too, waiting her turn to farewell me. She embraced me briefly and kissed me on the cheek. "Good luck, Sam."

"Thanks." It felt overwhelming to say goodbye to everyone, and yet the strongest feeling was still relief. Erika came to me. "Can I walk you to the car?" she asked softly.

"Of course. Ciao, everybody!" I called out.

Erika and I walked hand in hand back to the car.

"Are you alright?" Erika asked. "You seem very quiet."

"Sure, I am. Y' seem quiet too, even aloof," I replied.

"Yes, I suppose I am. I don't mean to be. It's just that leaving today means leaving you, Sam." She burst into tears. "It's going to be awful without you. I just know it is, and like you said, life goes on, but…" She took deep breaths between sobs.

"Y' know I don't feel that great t' see y'all leavin'. Just as well Tim ain't goin' anywhere."

"I can see you two now, in your matching armchairs, fighting over the television channels and winding each other up when the cricket's on," Erika mused.

There we were standing in the driveway, having an awkward moment. I reached out and pulled Erika in close. She responded by hugging me tightly.

"I won't ever forget you, Sam. I won't ever forget this summer. You're amazingly strong and brave, and I know in my heart it will all work out for you." I held her tight for a moment.

"Y're very special t' me too, Erika," I said, choking up, wondering how life would be with her gone. "I've got t' go or I'll be late, 'n y' know what the coppers're like down the station." I kissed her beautiful soft lips for the last time as our tears blended on the cheeks of our faces. "Ciao."

"Ciao. Please write to me, let me know how you're getting on. Here's my address." She pulled a piece of paper from the pocket of her shorts.

"I'll write to y'," I said, taking the piece of paper and putting it in my pocket. "I really have t' go, Erika."

"Then go."

I walked to the Valiant and found the keys above the visor. The engine roared to life and I backed out. Erika stood at the end of the drive presenting a brave smile that contradicted her tear-streaked face. She raised her hand as if to wave but simply held it there, without the motion. I swung the car out onto the road and waved, tooting the horn as I accelerated away from her.

I drove up the hill away from the sea, away from Erika, and as if by magic, a wave of relief swept over me; I was free again. I reached across the car seat, found a cassette and stuck it in the stereo player. The sound of Van Morrison's 'Angelou' filled the car.

* * *

I pulled up outside the police station, Van Morrison's music still blaring out of the rear speakers and coming to an abrupt end when I killed the engine. Inside the station there was an eerie stillness. I pressed the buzzer, hoping like hell Frank was having Sunday off. There was no response, so I pressed the buzzer again. A few seconds later the door opened, and I heard a voice.

"Alright, alright." Harry appeared through the door behind the counter. "Oh, it's only you," he exclaimed.

"Yeah, it's only me." I grinned.

"Hey, I didn't mean it like that. I'm here on m' own today, tryin' t' catch up with paperwork. I still don't understand why the magistrate made y' report here every day. I would've thought once or twice a week would've sufficed."

"Funny how seriously they take bustin' someone like me, considerin' there must be much bigger fish t' fry," I said, fishing.

"Yeah, well …" Harry was lost for words as he ticked me off in the logbook. "Oh, so don't forget dinner t'night. Sarah told me t' remind y'. She's got a real soft spot f' y'. She can't understand how the system can treat someone the way they've treated you. Someone as young as y'self, just out 'f high school 'n bang, one bad decision that might have a huge impact on y' life. I tell y', Sam, she thinks it's outrageous."

"Well, I feel very fortunate y' wife cares about people like me, I mean, people in my situation."

"Oh, 'n one more thing, Sam."

"What's that?"

Fuck! He knows! He knows his wife fancies me! He's goin' t' tell me if I lay a single finger on her he'll take me int' the forest 'n make me dig m' own grave. He'll put a gun t' m' head 'n pull the fuckin' trigger. Y' dead now, Sam. I'm shovellin' dirt on y' corpse ... I've buried y'. No one will ever find y'. Christ, I've been watchin' too much telly. I'm lettin' my imagination run away with me!

"Just remember that we are both anti-drugs, 'n the dealin' 'f them. If I wasn't, I wouldn't be in this job. But what I do believe is that young people like y'self, who get caught up in it without really knowing what they're doin' ... Well, we don't want t' see y' goin' inside f' one foolish moment in y' life, cos that's just creatin' another criminal mind. Y' understand where I'm comin' from, don't y', Sam?"

"I do, Harry," I replied, feeling greatly relieved.

"Hey!" he said, suddenly slapping the bench top with his hand and causing me to jump.

"We'll see y' tonight. I've got t' finish m' paperwork."

"Y' will. Thanks, Harry."

"For what?" He raised his hands in the air, turned and walked back through the door.

* * *

Driving home, I was full of thoughts about Harry and Sarah and their motive for wanting to help me. I continued to feel wary no matter what they said. Besides, Harry had arrested me in the first place.

How would Harry have dealt with the situation if Frank hadn't come t' the scene, all guns blazin'? Frank's arrival forced Harry's hand, he had t' play the game. It was his duty t' follow through, wasn't it? In the absence 'f Frank, some discretion could've been applied. Harry might've overlooked a body search. Frank's overbearin' tactics, 'n the night in police custody, accentuated m' situation, 'n Harry felt obliged t' play the game. P'haps the severity 'f the game brought home t' Harry the irony 'f his job. I'm sure Cosmo tipped them off 'bout me, purposely sending me back t' Yaringa with capsules from Bruce. Was Bruce in on m' being set up? What did he stand t' gain? He was stupid t' give Cosmo the capsules in the first place, his short-sightedness backfired badly. I'm the pawn that led t' Bruce, the bigger fish, the fish they hoped would lead to the biggest fish.

The night Harry busted me, other than his suspicious explanation for pulling me over, he appeared to be simply doing his job. He wasn't exactly pleasant to deal with, but he had to be cautious, matter-of-fact in his approach; he needed to maintain the upper hand. Even though I had a case full of hash oil capsules stuffed down my pants, I wasn't worried at all initially. If I'd been concerned while he was grunting and snorting as he searched my glovebox and under the front seats, I could've easily tossed them over the fence into the paddock, unnoticed in the darkness. He would've been none the wiser. It never occurred to me that it was going to be a problem as he rummaged around the front seat, doing what seemed like a fairly mandatory search. The only thing he found was the dried carrot Cosmo had carved into a chillum, which we'd used to smoke the hash oil.

It wasn't until the second set of blue lights flashed in the distance, growing closer by the second to become as large as life, with the vehicle skidding to a halt in the gravel, that the situation escalated. The vehicle's blue lights were still flashing as the door opened and that pair of black shiny boots stepped out onto the gravel, followed by legs and torso, and a head donned with a cap, then those purposeful strides as he crossed the road. Frank looked forever like he should've had a horse and a sheriff's badge as he strutted towards me. Harry was still scuttling around the front seat of the car. From the moment our eyes met, I knew I had a problem. Did it all happen by chance? Events seemed so well choreographed. The only thing unpredictable about this piece of theatre was what time I would arrive on that stretch of road, or whether I would arrive at all. As it was, I'd already had problems with the car, and I was close to calling it a night and staying over on the side of the road or going to a motel.

* * *

I was almost back in Yaringa. My thoughts and imagination had filled my head for most of the drive home. I felt pleased, having come to the conclusion that Harry was the full quid. He genuinely wanted to help me. I guessed that Sarah had been the perpetrator of his new-found altruism. The first night I'd visited them, I'd been struck by Sarah's presence. She had shown a genuine concern for how I was faring under the circumstances. What I didn't understand was how she could be so different the next time we met. Harry had approached me outside of work, and I had no doubt it would not be viewed well by his colleagues. In his profession, making someone's case personal would meet with disapproval. If he had approached a superior officer about his concerns, he surely would've been told to keep his nose out of it and let the court decide my fate.

The sight of Erika's family driving towards me, caravan in tow, all laden down and heading out of town, snapped me out of my thoughts. As we converged, their car horn tooted, and Erika's face appeared out the window along with her frantically waving arms. I tooted and waved back.

28

Sunday Dinner

I made my way to Harry and Sarah's house at five-thirty, bearing a bottle of wine I'd chosen from the local liquor store earlier in the afternoon. I knocked on the door and Sarah appeared.

"Sam, how are you? It's so good to see you again." She pecked me on the cheek.

"I'm good, thanks," I said self-consciously.

"Come in." She gestured with her hand and I brushed swiftly past her.

"I brought a bottle of wine," I said, handing it to her. "Thought it might go well with the meal, not that I have any idea what y're cookin'."

"That's very sweet of you, thank you so much," she said, taking it out of my hand as she led me into the kitchen. She was casually dressed but still looked like a million dollars in a floral-patterned blouse, unbuttoned just enough to reveal some of her cleavage, dark-blue body-hugging jeans, and open-toed stilettos.

"Where's Harry?"

"Oh, he rang just before you arrived, saying something had come up at work. He didn't know whether he would make it home for dinner, and he sends his apologies. That's life as a policeman for you, Sam," she said, placing the bottle of wine on the bench. "Now come and say hello to the children before they go to bed."

Sophie and Daniel were lounging on a couch in another room off the dining room. They were engrossed in the telly, eating what looked like home-made pizza.

"Sam's here, kids. Say hello, please."

"Hi, Sam," they said in unison, looking up briefly.

"When that programme finishes, I want you two in your pajamas, ready for bed. Okay?" There was no response as they sat there glued to the screen. "I said 'okay'," Sarah repeated firmly.

"Okay," they chorused back at her in a long whine.

I sat down next to Sophie. "So, what y' watchin'?" I asked.

"*Doctor Who*," she replied.

"*Doctor Who*, eh? That was m' favourite, too, when I was your age."

She turned and looked at me. She was interested now. "Really?" she asked, squinting her eyes as if trying to imagine me when I was little. "Do you like it when they travel in the phone box?"

"Oh yeah! That's the best part, isn't it? They never seem t' know where they're goin' t' end up," I replied..

"And the Daleks?" she asked.

"Yeah, they're very cool, too."

"It's quite scary, though," she said, looking seriously at me.

"I know, that's why it's so good. But it's all make-believe."

"That's what Mummy says, too."

The *Doctor Who* theme music came on and the credits started to roll.

"Come on, kids, that's it, pajamas on, please." They reluctantly got up off the couch and disappeared down the hallway.

"Nice kids y've got."

"Yeah, they're great," said Sarah, smiling warmly as she sat down beside me on the couch. "I'm sorry Harry might not be here tonight. He often misses out on putting the kids to bed. It's part of being a policeman in a small town. The work is so much more demanding, and the resources aren't there, whereas in the city the workload can be passed on to the next shift. It's another reason why Harry wants out."

"Yeah, I imagine at times it's a pretty thankless job. Wouldn't be my cup 'f tea or slice 'f bread, f' that matter."

Sarah stood up. "I'd better get these kids off to bed, won't be long. Would you like a beer or perhaps something else?"

"A beer would be great, but I'll get it. You see t' y' kids." I got up off the couch. Sarah was standing there, looking at me. "What's up?"

"I just think you're a very handsome young man."

"We aren't goin' down that road again, are we, Sarah?"

"Sam, why do you have to be so calculated? Why can't you just enjoy this moment?"

"If y' want t' talk about it, put the kids t' bed first, eh?"

"You don't understand, Sam," she said, grabbing hold of me as I moved to walk past her towards the kitchen. "I don't need you. I just really like you. I feel something for you, and I felt it before I even met you. The very first time Harry came home and told me about the evening he arrested you, I felt something for you."

"How can that be possible? Y' didn't even know me then." Her hand was still on my arm. I lifted it off and her arm fell to her side. "Perhaps I should be going. I expected t' be havin' dinner with both you 'n Harry, 'n now that he's not at home, I'm not so sure what I'm doin' here."

"There's no need to go, Sam. There's a perfectly good meal in the oven ready to be eaten. We can be adults about this. Stay and eat with me," she pleaded. "We can talk."

"Okay," I said, sounding like one of her children. She walked off down the hallway as I headed for the kitchen.

In the fridge I found a couple of bottles of bubbly and a row of Fosters, from which I grabbed a cold one. Peeling back the tab, I guzzled down as much beer as I could in one gulp. Something in the oven smelled really good and I realised I was ravenous. As I looked around the kitchen, which was immaculately kept, I noticed several photos on the fridge door. Closer inspection revealed that most of them were family snaps. There was one with Harry and Sarah in a restaurant, toasting champagne glasses and looking directly at the camera. Perhaps it was a celebration of their wedding anniversary because they both looked very happy. There was also a photo of Harry standing beside another guy, Harry beaming a big smile, but the other guy not looking as happy; his smile seemed forced. Harry was holding a trophy related to a shooting competition. As I looked closer, I realised the other guy was Frank, a younger Frank without the moustache. Harry must've beaten him to win the trophy. Perhaps Frank was the runner-up. There was another photo near that, one of Harry, Sarah, Frank and another woman. The unknown woman was probably Frank's wife or girlfriend. They were all smiling, and this time Frank's smile seemed genuine. Sarah appeared happy too, yet I thought neither Harry nor the unknown woman looked particularly cheerful even though they were smiling. Frank's arm was tight around Sarah's waist, they were very close physically — there was no distance at all between their torsos. Harry had his arm limply over the unknown woman's shoulder, and the woman's arm disappeared waist-high around the back of Harry.

"Oh, don't look at those photos. They're so old and shabby," said Sarah from across the room, startling me as she made her way to the kitchen.

"How long ago were they taken?" I enquired. She came up beside me, leaning forward to look at the photo I was pointing at.

"This one of the four of us was taken when I used to go out with Frank. It was a while ago when they were both at police college."

"Y' used t' go out with Frank?"

"Frank and Harry were good mates, had been since high school."

"Y' kiddin' me. What on earth inspired y' to go out with Frank?" I asked, intrigued.

"Frank was quite different when he was younger, but he always wanted to be in the police force." Her look altered and I could see sadness in her eyes. "He changed once he became a policeman."

"So how did you 'n Harry end up gettin' t'gether?"

"I walked in on Frank fucking Georgina in our bed. Georgina was Harry's girlfriend through most of high school. I left Frank there and then."

"My God … I'm sorry."

"What for? It worked out for the best. Frank had been changing rapidly since he joined the police, so it wasn't a hard decision for me to make. It was Harry who suffered, as he was much more cut up about Georgina than I was about Frank. He didn't believe me at first and told me I was making it up. When he confronted Georgina, she told him that she didn't love him anymore and was leaving him for Frank. Harry was shocked because he had no idea, and to make it worse for him, she moved in with Frank the day after I walked out."

"Are they still together?"

"No. Georgina died in a car accident some years ago now. Frank's never really gotten over it. He's not one to talk, so he just buries himself deeper in his work and blames the world for Georgina's death. He's an angry man with a lot of hurt in him."

"How does Harry manage t' work with Frank? I don't get it." I was mystified.

"Life is a strange thing, Sam. That's the beauty of being young, there's so much to experience and learn." I half expected her to make a move on me, justifying herself by saying it was all part of the experience. "I guess Harry still feels some sort of childhood loyalty to Frank," she continued. "They did, after all, grow up together. Don't you have friends who annoy you and drive you mad sometimes?"

"Yeah, I guess so," I conceded. "But y' best friend sleepin' with y' girlfriend, that's next level."

"Does that mean you abandon the friendship as soon as things don't go your way?" she asked.

"No, I see what y' mean, but do y' see what I mean? Guys don't easily forgive that kind 'f thing."

"Maybe, Sam, maybe not," she was looking intensely at me now and I felt uncomfortable.

"But I don't see how Harry could condone some 'f the things that Frank got up to the night they arrested me. Frank was totally out 'f order."

I moved away from the fridge, back to the couch. Sarah followed me.

"What do you think Harry has done by inviting you around here? He's been honest with you and tried to right a wrong in the best way he knows how. Do you know how much courage that takes? Harry made the unusual step of showing his hand to you. Cops don't do that sort of thing!" She clasped her hands together and walked back to the kitchen. I heard the oven door open and the sound of sizzling oil, followed by the distinctive smell of roast lamb and rosemary.

"You're right," I said, standing again. I walked back into the kitchen. "Harry's taken quite a risk approachin' me and for that I'm grateful," I lied. "But at the same time, y' can't blame me f' being a little suspicious. It's such an unusual thing t' do."

She had removed the roasting tray from the oven and was spooning juices over the meat to baste it. "What's there to be suspicious of, Sam?" She picked up a fork and deftly turned all the potatoes sitting in the oil, then put the fork down and put the roasting dish back in the oven.

Sarah turned to face me and looked directly into my eyes for an answer. I felt uncomfortable and averted my eyes, shifting my gaze to the floor like a naughty boy who's just been told off.

"Perhaps it's not Harry that I'm suspicious 'f. Maybe it's you." I looked up to meet her gaze.

"You've lost me now, Sam," she said, unflinching in her gaze, hands on her hips.

"Come on," I said sarcastically. She just stood there transfixed, as rigid as a mannequin. "Why did y' take me home that afternoon I saw y' at the beach … with the full intention 'f gettin' it on with me?"

"Look, Sam, there's nothing wrong with two consenting adults doing what they like together. It's true I wanted to have sex with you, and I thought you might like to with me. It was a spontaneous thing, an irrational moment. I didn't even know I was going to go down that road until you were here alone in the house with me, and my feelings took over."

"I don't mind that y're attracted t' me, y're a beautiful woman. It's Harry that I'm worried about. How would he feel about it? Imagine if he'd walked in on us that afternoon."

"He wouldn't have," she said, relaxing her posture. She removed her hands from her hips and averted her gaze.

"Y' could never be one hundred per cent certain 'f such things," I challenged her.

"Sam, you are so contrary sometimes." She moved back to the stove and turned on two of the elements.

"I don't mean t' be contrary," I insisted. "I just find it hard t' believe that it doesn't bother y' conscience havin' sex with me when y're married to Harry."

"We have an understanding," she responded.

"Sorry, I don't get it." I didn't want to get it.

"Harry and I have an arrangement that we … If we fancy someone, have a strong sexual attraction to them and the opportunity presents itself, then it's okay."

"What do y' mean?"

"It's okay to have sex with that person. We think it keeps our own relationship strong and stimulated."

"Really? Well, I've heard 'f that sort 'f thing goin' on in the sixties 'n early seventies durin' the peace, love 'n happiness era. I read a book called *Ringolevio* by Emmett Grogan, partly set in San Francisco in the Haight-Ashbury district. It was all about that kind 'f carryin' on. M' parents use' t' talk about friends 'f theirs experimentin' with that sort 'f thing, 'n from what I could gather, more often than not those relationships fell on the rocks."

"Harry and I are far from on the rocks. Our relationship is sound. When Harry retires from the police, I expect it will be even better." She was coming towards me with a seductive look glistening in her eyes. "What are you afraid of, Sam?"

"I told y'. Harry comin' home. You. I dunno … it's just too complex f' me to comprehend, Sarah."

"Look at me, Sam."

"I don't want t'." Her hand arrived under my chin and forced my head upwards so that I had to look at her. I closed my eyes.

"Just look at me, Sam. Just for a minute." I opened my eyes and there were her beautiful green eyes. I could smell her, she was so close, just a subtle scent. Not perfume, rather a female fragrance, the smell of her skin, the slight smell of her armpits. I breathed her in and felt intoxicated.

I placed my hand on hers and removed her hands. "Y're very beautiful, Sarah."

She took my hand, placed it upon her right cheek and held it there. I could feel the warmth and softness of her face, and I could feel a swelling in my loins that was growing by the second. She leaned her face forward and kissed me ever so gently on the lips. I could've eaten her lips right there and then. My swelling had become rock hard, and I knew if I didn't stop myself now, I wouldn't be able to. I pulled my hand away suddenly, stepping back dramatically at the same time.

"I'm sorry, Sarah. Y've got no idea how attracted t' y' I am, but this voice inside me just keeps sayin', 'Don't do it! Don't do it!' Sorry if I disappoint y'. I think it's best I go. Tell Harry I'm sorry but I wasn't feelin' well. Tell him whatever y' want t' tell him."

"There's no need to go, Sam," she said in a matter-of-fact manner. "Dinner is almost ready." Her eyes were so warm they mesmerised me. "I'm not going to force myself on you. Sit down and I'll get you a drink."

I hesitated for a moment then sat down obediently. She walked to the fridge and returned with a can of Fosters and a glass. Sitting down on the couch next to me, she opened the can of beer and poured it into the glass she'd placed on the coffee table in front of me. She picked up the glass and handed it to me. "You're a determined, stubborn man, aren't you? Quite a moralist for someone your age."

"Not really. Depends how y' look at somethin'. My idea 'f marriage is one 'f commitment 'n loyalty. Call me idealistic, but that's me."

"Harry and I have all that in our relationship. We don't hide the fact that we have sexual encounters with other people."

I thought of Erika and what her expectations in a relationship would be. "I've been seein' a girl who came here at the start 'f the holidays. She went home today."

"I didn't realise you had a girlfriend, Sam."

"Well why would y'? I've only just told y'."

"Yes, but I see you at the beach from time to time."

"True enough. She was campin' here with her family 'n a friend who came with them. They weren't always able t' get away, 'n I've got t' go int' Wodyn every day. So it wasn't like I was with her every giv'n moment 'f the day or night."

"Do you love her?"

"I didn't really allow myself t' love her. She was goin' back t' where she came from, 'n my future's uncertain. She's still at school too, final year 'f high school."

"I'm sorry, Sam."

"There's nothin' t' be sorry about. It was just one 'f those holiday flings that happen up 'n down the coast every summer, I imagine. If y' look around, y' can see young people pairin' off on the beach daily."

"I suppose you're right," Sarah said, looking thoughtful for a moment.

* * *

A beam of light flashed across the window. "That'll be Harry," Sarah said, pushing herself up off the couch. The door from the hallway opened and in walked Harry in full uniform, his gun still holstered on his right hip.

"Hi, folks, sorry I'm late. I thought I was never gonna get away."

"You're just in time, darling. I was about to serve up," Sarah called out from the kitchen. "I held off in the hope that you would get away soon."

"Sorry, Sam, somethin' came up at work." Harry looked towards Sarah as he spoke, as if his eyes were asking a question.

Harry must be in on Sarah's attempts t' seduce me, but what would his motive be f' wantin' that t' happen? It makes no sense, but what proof do I have? Y've got t' stop y'r imagination runnin' away with y', Sam.

"I'm just goin' t' get changed out of these clothes. Won't be long," he said, unbuckling his holster.

"Okay, honey," Sarah said as he departed the room.

"Sam, if you like you can open that bottle of wine you brought," Sarah called out. "Once I've carved this meat, I'll be ready to serve up."

"No prob," I said, feeling quite relaxed now. "Y' know I'm a bit 'f a dab hand at carvin' meat, so if y' want I could carve that f' y'," I said, walking into the kitchen.

"You're on. But first open that wine." She handed me a corkscrew and I inserted the screw into the top of the cork, hoping the cork wasn't going to crumble on me. I leveraged it out with surprising ease and poured the wine into three glasses set at the table.

"I read somewhere that the French usually decant their red wine," I said, filling the last glass and placing the remainder of the bottle on the table.

"It's true, they do."

"Ah, you've read that too?" I asked, coming back into the kitchen. I took up the carving knife and fork and began cutting the meat.

The knife was somewhat blunt, making it difficult to cut smoothly through the flesh, which looked tender and nicely cooked. Sarah was serving vegetables onto the plates.

"You really do carve a roast well, Sam," she commented, peering over my shoulder.

"Smells good, honey," Harry said as he entered the room.

"As soon as Sam's finished carving the meat, we can eat."

"Great! How's m' beautiful woman?" He came up behind her gently slipping his arms around her waist.

"Great," she replied, placing the saucepan down and turning to kiss him. I watched them out of the corner of my eye as I finished cutting the last of the roast.

"The meat's ready," I said.

Good, let's eat. I'm ravenous," Harry replied.

"The meat can be served at the table," Sarah said. "I'll just pour this gravy into a jug. If you'd like to take the plate of meat to the table, Sam, that will help me. Harry, you can take a couple of plates too."

I placed the plate of meat in the middle of the table while Harry set the two plates down. We stood there awkwardly, waiting for Sarah.

"Sit down you two," she said, arriving with the third plate and a jug of gravy. She pulled a chair out and sat down. Harry and I followed suit.

"Harry, can you say grace, please?" Sarah asked, smiling at him.

"Sure," he said, looking somewhat surprised but bowed his head dutifully. Sarah did the same.

It all seems a bit fuckin' weird to me. They don't strike me as Christian folk, certainly not the way Sarah's been carryin' on. Weird!

"Lord, for what we are about to receive we are truly thankful. May we receive your guidance during the coming weeks as Sam's court case approaches. Give us strength, Lord, and guide us all safely in the right direction. Amen."

"Amen," said Sarah.

"Amen," I mumbled self-consciously, reminded of dinner at my maternal grandparents' house, always having to say grace before eating.

"Help yourself, Sam," insisted Harry, pushing the plate of meat towards me. I served myself several slices of meat. "I found out today that the judge sittin' f' the next District Court is a reasonable sort 'f fella," announced Harry. I passed Harry the meat fork, which he took and hooked himself a couple of slices of juicy pink meat. "He's apparently a bit more liberal than some 'f the ones that sit down this way. A bit younger 'n new t' the job."

Harry pushed the meat off the fork with one of his fingers, then passed the fork to Sarah, licking his finger. "He's quite unlike some 'f the stiff ol' boys who throw the book at drug offenders. Not a lot 'f leniency shown by most 'f them. So that's a small bonus in y' favour, Sam," he added.

"I'm grateful t' know it. But I ain't gonna build m' hopes on a chance that some new, younger judge is gonna see better sense 'n let me off with a rap over the knuckles."

"Sam, Harry's just trying to give you some hope," Sarah chimed in, prodding the fork into a slice of meat and placing it delicately on her plate.

"Every day I hope … I hope that I'll wake from this nightmare, that I'll wake up in m' own bed back in New Zealand. I hoped earlier that the magistrate in the Magistrates' Court would see sense. He didn't! I'm still here, waitin' f' the District Court t' sit. It's hard t' get a job 'round here, and it's hard doin' nothin' most 'f the day. I'm grateful, Harry. I'm grateful f' the judge, and I'm grateful that y' care. Y've gone out 'f y' way t' show that. I'm surprised that y' would risk havin' contact with me, considerin' the circumstances," I ranted.

"Harry gave his six months' notice today. Didn't you, love," Sarah interrupted.

"What?" I was genuinely surprised.

"I did," he said, raising his glass. "And oh, did it feel good." He winked at me, smiling.

"A toast to Harry," said Sarah, raising her glass in response. I raised mine.

"To Harry." We clinked glasses and sipped our wine. "Does it feel right, Harry?" I asked, looking for any hint of remorse.

"I felt ten years younger from the moment I handed over that envelope with m' writt'n resignation," he replied with satisfaction.

"I'm so proud of you, darling," said Sarah.

* * *

The remainder of the evening was pleasant enough, spent drinking and eating. Sarah brought out dessert, a delicious apple tart accompanied by home-made vanilla ice cream. She was a great cook.

Perhaps they'll open a restaurant. Sarah could cook 'n Harry could be the waiter. Hands up, folks, or I'll shoot y'! Whoops, wrong line! Hands up, folks,

*who wants a drink? What, y' don't want one? Fuck y'... I'll blow y' fuckin'
nuts off!*

Several bottles of wine later and with a belly full of good food, I
announced that I should be getting home.

"No, Sam, you can't be walking home in your condition at this time
of night," responded Sarah.

"I'm only a short walk up the road. I'm not drivin', 'n it's not like I'm
in some big city full 'f dodgy characters. Seriously, I'll be fine, even if I
do stagger a wee bit."

"Harry, do something! He's far too drunk."

"You heard him, darlin', he'll be fine. If he wants t' go home, let him."

"The bed's made up in the spare room, Sam. Please stay."

"Then that decides it, Sam. Another beer?" said Harry, getting up
and making his way to the fridge.

Outside the world of the New South Wales Police Force, Harry
was a very different man, and I was beginning to like him. He returned
with two cans of beer and handed one to me as he slumped back on the
couch. I opened the can and gulped down several mouthfuls, feeling a
little uncomfortable about staying the night. I wondered if what Sarah
had told me was true, that she and Harry could do it with whomever
they pleased so long as it was purely sex. Sarah poured herself another
glass of wine, draining the last drops from the bottle. We'd drunk two
bottles between the three of us over dinner, so Sarah must've drunk the
third bottle entirely on her own. Since dinner, Harry and I had moved
on to beer and the couch.

"That's me f' the night," Harry said as he put his empty beer can on
the coffee table. "There's no rest f' the wicked." He winked at me. "Sam,
it was good that y' came round, we should do it again before y'r day in
court. In the meantime, don't spend y' days worryin' so much."

"Yeah, that'd be good. Look, I think I'll go. I prefer wakin' up in m' own bed." I gulped the remaining beer as fast as I could, then stood too quickly, tripping on the corner of the coffee table, but recovering in time to avoid falling on Sarah.

"Perhaps y' really should stay the night, Sam," responded Harry, laughing loudly.

"You definitely should, Sam," said Sarah.

"Okay, okay. I get the message."

"Goodnight, darlin'." Harry bent down and kissed Sarah on the cheek.

"Goodnight, sweetheart."

"Night, Harry," I said as he moved his large frame in the direction of the door.

"Night, Sam," he said, exiting the room.

"That was a pleasant evening," said Sarah as she adjusted herself to face me in the armchair which appeared to swallow her up.

"It was. Thanks f' cookin' such a delicious meal. It was great."

"Thank you," she looked pleased. "I enjoy cooking, especially when we have guests, then I make the effort to try some of the recipes that are neglected when I'm just cooking for the kids."

"Yeah. I s'pose it has t' be a lot simpler with kids. Although I seem t' remember eatin' anythin' as a kid. I always liked interestin' flavours."

"You are an exception to the rule, Sam."

"P'haps."

"I'm going to have another wine. Do you care for one?" Sarah asked, getting up from the armchair.

"No, I'm good thanks," I said, raising my hands in protest.

She fussed around in the kitchen looking for the corkscrew. Moments later there was the sound of the cork popping and glass on glass, then she was back in the lounge with more wine. She stood over me while she poured.

"I'll be offended if you don't join me," she stated as she finished pouring the glass, handing it to me.

"I really don't need another one, Sarah. I'm gonna head home," I said, standing up. "Goodnight." I could see the disappointment in her face as she attempted to say something.

"Thanks for the evening." I turned and walked to the door half expecting her to drag me back to the couch. In the hallway there was the sound of snoring — long, deep and loud. Harry was well and truly asleep. I opened the front door and quietly let myself out.

29

Awoke the Next Morning

I awoke the next morning to the sound of cockatoos making a racket in the trees above my caravan. I got up feeling deeply disturbed and walked down to the beach. It was still relatively early with hardly a soul about, just the way I liked it, much as it had been before Christmas. The waves weren't large, though big enough to bodysurf, and I caught a few. I emerged feeling refreshed and alert. I dried myself off and started to walk back to the house, deciding that I'd have breakfast and go into town early to get the daily reporting out of the way. I'd have to hitch as I didn't have enough money to put petrol in Tim's car, with the tank already close to empty the day before. Tim wasn't up yet, so I had the house to myself. I shuffled around the kitchen getting cereal and finding milk in the fridge. I doodled with my cereal as the events of the previous night ate away at me.

I walked up the hill to the village and out onto the main road to Wodyn. The sun was high, and the day was like any other in Yaringa — clear blue skies with a gentle onshore breeze whispering quietly through the eucalyptus trees that edged the side of the road. The odd squawk of a cockatoo overhead filled the otherwise still morning air. As I thumbed a ride, I could feel the heat of the sun warming the back of my head and neck, and I felt a sense of calm wash over me. A van pulled over to the side of the road just metres from where I was standing. I ran to the van and opened the door.

"Long time no see, Sam." It was Bruce.

"Yeah, Bruce," I said, trying to appear casual. "Are y' goin' t' Wodyn?" I stood in the gravel waiting for a response.

"Yeah, I am," he replied.

"Okay t' get a lift?"

"That's why I stopped, Sam."

I climbed in hoping my reluctance wasn't too obvious. Bruce looked like he'd just gotten out of bed after a week of binging — his hair unwashed and starting to knot into dreads, his clothes dirty as if they'd not seen a washing machine for weeks, all permeated with the stale smell of dope.

"So … how y' been keepin'?" I asked as I settled into the passenger seat.

"What would you care, Sammy?"

"Why wouldn't I?"

"Never see y' any more! How come I get the feelin' it's avoidance, Sam?"

"Well, I don't have a vehicle," I explained. "Since I moved t' Tania's parents' place, it's not so easy t' get 'round."

"How's Tania? I heard she's gone back t' New Zealand."

"She has. She couldn't bear it here any longer." I shifted my bum around, trying to get comfortable. The seat seemed to be missing some of its padding and the metal springs were pushing through the foam. "Being 'round her parents and the shit that's gone down, she just needed t' get away from it. Things deteriorated between us, so it was kind 'f a good thing 'n she wanted t' go. Her folks weren't happy about it, but what can y' do? At the end 'f the day, it's her choice. I never hear from her. I think she's still angry with me."

"Maybe. She always was a bit 'f a headcase," he said, laughing. "Anyway, what y' doin' in Wodyn?"

"Reportin'."

"Oh yeah. Y've got t' do that every day, don't y'? I'm only once a week." He laughed again, maniacally and loud. "Y' must be a bad bastard, Sam. Drugs or somethin', was it?" He laughed, and I said nothing. "Y' better not bleed anythin' to those motherfuckin' cops. Mum's the word, Sam! No fuckin' me around now!" He banged his hand on the steering wheel to reinforce what he was saying. "The whole thing's a fuck up, Sam! An inconvenient fuck up!" Mum's the word, Sam. Say it!" He hit the steering wheel again, wrenching on it and causing the van to swerve all over the road.

"Mum's the word," I muttered.

"Goddamn, Sam. Say it again, I can't hear y'!"

"Mum's the word," I said louder, with more conviction.

"That's right, 'n y' just gotta remember that, Sam, cos God help y' if y' fuck me over! Y' hear?" He took his eyes off the road to give me one of his snarling glares as the van veered over the white line into oncoming traffic.

"I ain't fuckin' with y', Bruce," I said loud and clear as he managed to steer the van back onto our side of the road in the nick of time.

"Then we understand each other. Want a pipe? There's one made up in the glovebox."

"No, I think I'll pass, thanks." I had no interest in getting stoned with Bruce.

"Thanks! What for? I didn't do anythin'" Bruce was on a rant. He didn't seem as together or as confident as I'd known him to be in the past.

"I've got t' report, so I'm not keen t' go in there smelling like I've just been smokin' weed."

"They'd never notice. They're all so fuckin' hopeless. They wouldn't know the smell 'f dope from the smell 'f tobacco."

"Maybe y' right, but I'm not gonna take that risk, Bruce."

"There is no risk, Sammy. No fuckin' risk at all. Y' fuckin' scared of them, aren't y?" He banged the steering wheel again, like an auctioneer banging a gavel to conclude a sale.

"I'm not scared 'f them, Bruce, I'm just not prepared t' rock the boat when it's not necessary."

"Ah, y've gone all soft cock on me."

"I ain't soft."

"Well, have a fuckin' pipe then."

I didn't like where the conversation was going, but I wasn't going to back down. I didn't want a pipe and I wasn't going to have one. I was relieved we were almost in Wodyn since I'd had enough of Bruce already.

"What y' doin' after the cop shop?"

"Going back again. Don't like Wodyn, nothin' t' do anyway." I wasn't going to tell him I'd probably go to the coffee shop for a cup of tea.

"I can give y' a lift back if y' want t' hang 'round while I pick up a few things. I'll probably be an hour or so."

We were almost at the police station and I didn't want him to drop me off outside. It wasn't going to help my case to be seen associating with Bruce.

"Look, do y' mind droppin' me off outside the barbers? I really need some tobacco before I go in there."

"No prob," he said and drove me around the corner, stopping outside the barbershop.

"Cheers," I said opening the door. "I'll see y'."

"Not if I see y' first. Y' know where I am," he said, giving me one of his intense stares.

"I do," I said, trying to hold his stare as I closed the door. I stood and watched the van pull away from the pavement, accelerating down the road and making that familiar throaty, jingly sound characteristic of VW motors.

* * *

Feeling unsettled, I turned and walked into the barbershop. I hadn't smoked for a while, but I'd scab the odd rolly off staff up the mountain, yet right now I felt like a smoke just to calm me down. Bruce came on all friendly most of the time, but since I'd seen him in the pub on New Year's Eve, I felt uncomfortable about him living in the same area. He wasn't stable any more. In his eyes I'd put him in the situation he was in, and it was true, to some degree I had.

"Can I help you?" The barber's voice brought me out of my thoughts. He was standing in front of me in his blue smock, a pair of scissors in hand.

"Yeah. Can I have a packet of Drum, thanks, 'n some blue Zig-Zags."

"Of course," he replied.

"Better have a lighter too." I handed him twenty dollars. "Nice one," I said. "Have a great day."

"And you."

"Thanks." I turned and walked out, in a hurry to open the tobacco.

Out on the street I ripped open the dark blue packet, tossing the cellophane in a nearby bin. As I walked, I rolled myself a smoke and decided that I needed a cup of tea. I hadn't had one this morning. Mentally, I didn't feel ready to report at the police station, and since I was early to town, I had a bit of time to kill. I opened the door of the coffee shop to be greeted by the fat chick who smiled broadly as she always did.

"Hello," she said, "how are you t'day? I haven't seen y' in here f' a while so … thought y' must've left town."

331

"No. No … I'm still here as y' can see. Just that the weather's been good out on the coast 'n I've been busy, I s'pose." I rustled in my pockets looking for my lighter to no avail.

"Need a light?" She picked up a box of matches from on top of the cash register and handed them to me.

"Ta."

"No problem. So what can I get y' today?"

"Well … definitely a pot 'f tea f' starters."

"Okay," she said as she pulled a small stainless-steel teapot out from under the bench and placed it on a tray on the counter.

"Got any 'sparagus rolls today?" I asked, peering into the glass cabinets.

"We should, in the sandwich cabinet."

"Okay. I must be goin' blind." On closer inspection I found them. They were covered by a slightly damp, white cotton cloth to stop them drying out. I removed two and put them on a plate.

"Been t' see any bands at the pub lately?" she asked as she filled the teapot with water from the Zip boiling water unit on the wall.

"Not recently," I replied, admiring the chocolate eclairs in the confectionery cabinet. They were coated in chocolate with cream oozing everywhere, looking awfully decadent and irresistible. I took one, put it on another plate, and carried both plates up to the counter where she had the tray with the tea ready.

"By the way, my name's Amanda," she said casually.

"Oh, I'm Sam," I said.

"Is that the lot then, Sam?"

"It is, thanks." I handed her the change from my pocket.

"Y've given me too much," she said, handing some of it back.

"Hey, that's a bonus," I said, dropping it into the tip jar next to the cup of teaspoons.

I took the tray of tea and plates of food to a table in a sunny spot near a window. There were no other customers yet. Amanda pottered around behind the counter, wiping down the bench and putting things in their right place. Her mum appeared with a large tray of pies, which Amanda proceeded to place in the pie warmer. I found her strangely intriguing.

She's a big girl but she moves gracefully. Some people might describe her as voluptuous, but I'd say she's fat. Her greatest asset is her face. It's plumper than most faces cos she's fat, but it's still a beautiful face.

"Are y' doin' much today?" she asked as she wiped the salt and pepper shakers.

"No, not really." I poured myself a cup of tea. It was a strong-looking brew. I wasn't a great fan of strong, stand-your-spoon-up tea, and fortunately, she'd given me a jug of hot water.

"So, y' just came int' town t' get a few things, did y?"

"Yeah, that's right." This time I poured only half a cup of the tea so I could dilute it with the hot water.

"Are y' goin' t' see the band at the pub tonight?"

"What band's that?" I took a sip of my tea. It was an improvement.

"Some band from Sydney called Midnight Oil. They're about t' put an album out. They're doin' a bit 'f a road tour between Sydney 'n Melbourne. The lead singer is mates with the singer in the cover band that usually plays at the pub on Friday nights."

"I wasn't plannin' on it. What about you?" I took another sip of my tea. It tasted pretty good really.

"Yeah, I'm goin'. I'm tryin' t' talk a friend in t' goin' too, but she's not so keen, y' know with it being a Monday night 'n all. But I think I'll go anyway."

I hadn't seen a band for a long time, and I began to wonder if it might be a good idea to go. It might take my mind off everything that was looming and relieve the intensity of my daily life. I took a bite of my chocolate eclair. *Fuckin' delicious! The crème anglaise is amazin'!*

"Great chocolate eclair," I said with my mouth half full.

"I made those," she said, looking pleased as Punch, puffing out her already ample chest.

"Well, they're very good. Y' could make money out of them. Sell them t' supermarkets 'n other coffee shops," I told her, taking another bite, careful not to lose any of the cream filling.

"I'll take that as a compliment then, shall I?"

Just then the door opened and a young woman about Amanda's age walked in.

"Hi, Mands," she said. "How's y' day goin'?" She was tall and dressed in tight-fitting black clothing that didn't really suit her as she was carrying too much weight in all the wrong places — around her arse, on her hips and waist.

"Good, thanks," Amanda replied, trying to clear her throat at the same time. I realised she was trying to discreetly point out that there was someone else in the shop besides herself.

"So, I'm on f' t'night. Y'll be hopin' that guy …"

"Would y' like another chocolate eclair, Sam?" Amanda called out abruptly.

"Ahh, thanks but no thanks. I've got t' dash after this one," I said, waving around the remains of the one I had in my hand.

Her friend spun around without any subtlety at all to see who Amanda was talking to. Her eyes met mine and fixed on me for several long seconds. She had a pretty face too, with bright red lipstick on her mouth and large blue eyes. Her hair was blonde, wavy and long. She wore too much make-up and would look better without it.

"Rose, this is Sam. Sam meet Rose," said Amanda.

"Hi, Sam."

I'd just shovelled in the last of my eclair and was having trouble responding, waving my hand around my mouth to gesture that it was full. It seemed to take forever to swallow the last mouthful.

"Hi, Rose," I eventually managed to say. "Amanda makes great chocolate eclairs, doesn't she?"

"You're tellin' the story. I wouldn't know ... I don't eat them," Rose replied. "But I'm sure she does, she's a wickedly good cook."

"Sam comes in here quite often," explained Amanda.

"Does he now?" She was still facing me and seemed intent on checking me out. "So what do y' do round these parts, Sam?"

"Ahh ... Well, not that much at the moment. Y' see, I'm not from these parts."

"What parts are y' from then?" She didn't muck around with the questions, and I didn't particularly feel like answering.

"Y'll have t' work that one out," I said, getting up to leave.

"Stop interrogatin' him, Rose," demanded Amanda, busying herself behind the counter.

"I'm just curious, Mands."

"Well, maybe y' shouldn't be so nosey sometimes. Y' know what happen'd t' the cat ..."

I stood up, deciding it was time to make an exit and pushed my chair back, causing it to scrape noisily on the linoleum.

"Might see y's t'night then."

"Might you now?" said Rose.

"Shut up, Rose."

I closed the door behind me and walked up the road to the police station.

* * *

As I approached the police station, I wondered whether Harry would be on duty, then realised he probably wouldn't be since he'd worked late the night before. Once inside, I rang the buzzer and stood waiting, tapping my fingers on the counter. The door opened and to my surprise Harry appeared.

"Hey, Harry. Didn't think y'd be in after workin' late last night."

"No, it doesn't work like that. If y' rostered on f' the day 'n somethin' comes up that's y' lot, y've got t' go 'n do it. The time gets added t' our annual leave but 'f course we never get extra leave. They never want t' bring in additional staff t' cover f' the time, so it gets added t' the followin' year's leave allocation. When I leave the police, I'll get a nice fat envelope f' all the extra time I've done in addition t' m' termination payout. It's another reason not t' be here any more, Sam. Oh, 'n sorry about being so late last night."

"Hey, it's fine. It was a great meal Sarah cooked," I said, half expecting him to say something about the state he found Sarah in on the couch when he got up this morning.

"Sarah had a sore head when she woke this mornin'. She doesn't usually drink that much, but she's incorrigible around you, Sam," said Harry, looking amused.

"Do y' think so?" I asked.

"Hey, I'm only havin' y' on."

The door opened to reveal the sarge. We looked each other up and down with equal loathing.

"Right. Well, I'll be seeing y' tomorrow," I said.

"He keepin' his nose clean, Harry?" The sarge asked, pulling a draw open in a cabinet and filing papers into it.

"Cleaner than some, Sarge," Harry said, winking at me. It was Harry's way of being on the level with me. The sarge grunted something indecipherable.

I nodded at Harry and walked out onto the street. I felt unsure what to do next, so I pulled my tobacco and papers out and rolled a cigarette. As I was doing so, Frank pulled up in front of me in a police car, and climbed out. He was immaculately dressed from head to foot: his boots shone like a mirror in the sun, his trousers and shirt looked hot off the dry-cleaners' press, and his moustache and sideburns were evenly manicured.

"That'll stunt y' growth, y' little runt," he said.

"And wankin' makes y' blind."

"What did y' say, y' smart prick?" He stopped in his tracks and came right up to my face. I could feel the warmth of his breath as he spoke.

"Got a light?" I asked, presenting my freshly-rolled smoke.

"I'm watchin' you very fuckin' closely. Don't y' go puttin' a foot wrong." His eyeballs enlarged as he spoke, and his moustache twitched on the right side.

"I'll be seein' y' then," I said as I found the lighter in my pocket and lit my rolly. He turned and walked off in a huff. "Y' fuckin' fascist cunt," I mumbled so softly he'd never hear it.

I was back on the main street in Wodyn, not wanting to hitch home yet. Life was feeling somewhat empty now that everyone had left. I wondered how Erika was getting on back home. It had only been a night, but for a moment I was tempted to hitch a ride up country to her place. Instead, I reached into my other pocket and pulled out my loose change. There was enough there for another pot of tea and maybe something to eat.

I opened the door to the coffee shop to find it buzzing, now full of the blue-rinse brigade in town to collect their pensions and treat themselves to tea and cake before all their utility bills sucked up what little money remained. They were all chattering amongst themselves in groups of twos and threes. Amanda looked surprised to see me.

"You've gotten busy," I said, walking up to the counter. She was making up a tray of tea.

"Yeah, Mondays are always like this from about eleven, 'n it doesn't really stop till we close. Anyway, what are y' doin' back here twice in one day?"

"I'm at a bit of a loose end 'n I don't have the car today, so I've got t' hitch back. I don't feel quite ready t' do that, so I thought I'd have another smoke, a pot 'f tea, 'n read y' paper if there's one floating 'round."

"Excuse me. I'll just take this out 'n I'll be right back," she said, picking up the tray in one hand and walking onto the floor with it.

"No problem. I'll just have a seat and when y've got time, would y' mind bringin' me a pot 'f tea?"

"No, of course not, silly," she said, grinning as she walked off.

"Cheers"

I went to sit down, collecting the newspaper off the magazine rack as I passed it. I sat and unfolded the paper to peruse the front page, but there wasn't anything that captured my eye. I lit my cigarette and sucked on it until the end started burning evenly. I drew the smoke into my lungs, then blew it out in a big sigh. The first inhalation was the best, the rest just habit. I turned to the back page and my eyes were instantly drawn to the headline: *Kiwis Go One Up in Best of 4.* I was excited and continued to read that the Kiwis had beaten the Ozzies in the first cricket final with overs to spare, surprising them with their aggressive approach. It was a rare occurrence to beat the Ozzies in cricket, whereas a win was expected in rugby. Tim would no doubt give me his blow-by-blow commentary when I got home. A tray landed on my table, bringing me out of the paper.

"Too much tea's bad for y'." I looked up. *So are those sticky buns y' scoff all day long, darlin'.*

"Not half as dangerous as those chocolate eclairs," I said, grinning.

"Y' really think they're the best y've had?"

"Without a doubt. They're dangerous f' sure."

"I told Dad what y' said, 'n he's decided t' approach a distributor 'n see if they'll take them."

"Now y' talkin'. I read somewhere that great things come from great ideas acted upon."

"I'll tell him that," she said, leaving my table to attend to someone at the counter.

I finished reading the very average local newspaper and decided it was time to get going. Amanda was busy with a customer, and she seemed quite onto it, running the counter on her own. Her parents seldom came out the front and when they did, it was usually to replenish something that had run low.

"I'd better pay f' that pot 'f tea," I said, approaching her at the counter.

"Don't worry about that one, it's on the house."

"Y' don't need t' do that."

"But I just have," she said, looking pleased about the fact.

"Well, I won't argue. Thanks 'n cheers. I best be goin' b'fore I'm tempted by one more 'f those eclairs."

"World famous in Wodyn," she grinned. "Might see y' tonight then. Rose 'n I'll be there about eight if y' want t' join us."

"Could be a possibility. See y' later," I said, walking out the door for the second time that morning.

* * *

I walked out of town and onto the main road to Yaringa. It was pretty much the middle of the day now and the sun was at its hottest. I was perspiring badly and hoped like hell the first car would pick me up. A vehicle approached in the distance and as it took on a more defined shape, I realised it was Bruce — the one ride I didn't desire but wasn't able to avoid. Now I was cursing my decision to take a second sitting of tea.

"Thought you'd be well gone by now," he said as I clambered into the passenger seat. He'd been smoking a joint. The van reeked of fresh smoke. I imagined Frank pulling us up on the side of the road to do a so-called routine check. The smell of smoke would be enough to whip him into a frenzy, and he'd have half the police force out in seconds, stripping the van down to find the source. Bruce probably had pounds of it stashed in the van, in the back under the bedding or in the mattress. *I'd be fucked. I'd be in the slammer for the next five years, and that'd be the end of me f' sure!*

"Want a smoke, Sam? There's plenty more where that came from, 'n it's nice shit too. Y' got no excuse this time."

"I don't think so. Not really in t' the shit since everything that's gone down," I lied.

"Ah, come on, harden up. Y' can't let the fuckin' establishment get y' down. That's like sayin' y' beaten. Here." He pulled a large bag out from under the seat and tossed it onto my lap, causing me to jolt, as if he'd tossed me a hot potato. "Take a look at that," he enthused.

"I can't believe y' carry this shit around with y'. If they bust y' f' more dope they'll throw the book at y', Bruce."

"That's right, Sam. The old reverse psychology. Y' see, that's what the cops'll be thinkin' too. Who in his right mind would drive round with a big bag 'f dope? Me, 'f course, but they'd be thinkin', not Bruce 'n not Sammy. They're already in hot water."

"Maybe, but is it worth the risk?"

"It's the principle 'f it, Sam. Now are y' gonna light one up or what?"

I stared at the bag for a minute, thinking how crazy it was. I didn't even feel like a smoke, not with Bruce, but it was a short trip back to the coast and then I'd be rid of him. I opened the bag and put my nose to it, taking a deep breath. A pungent, sweet smell filled my nostrils.

"Don't just smell it. That metal tin's already got several in it, ready t' go."

I took the old tobacco tin from the bag and opened it, revealing four neatly rolled joints. I picked one out, put the tin back in the bag, and handed it to Bruce.

"Y' can take a few buds if y' like."

"No thanks," I said as I reached for a lighter on the dashboard.

"Y're overreactin', Sam. The cops've got far more important things t' do than waste their time keepin' an eye on the likes 'f you 'n me. Their philosophy is that they've got us now, so there's no need t' spend more time on us."

I lit the joint and watched the flame ignite the paper, then sucked gently to get it burning evenly. Once I'd inhaled enough smoke, I passed the joint to Bruce and exhaled. Bruce took the joint and inhaled deeply.

"Trouble with you, Sam, is that f' a young guy y' think too much. Y're far too calculated," he stated, trying to hold the smoke in while talking, causing his voice to sound strained as if he were trying to have a shit.

"What makes y' say that?"

"Just somethin' I've observed."

"I don't feel that I'm calculated. Well, not very."

"Course y' are." He took another long, deep puff on the joint then passed it back to me. "Just the way y' had t' think about whether or not y' were goin' t' have a smoke." Smoke wafted out of his mouth as he spoke. "Take this mornin', f' instance. I picked y' up 'n took y' int' town. Y' didn't really need the tobacco, first up. Y' just didn't want t' be seen gettin' out 'f m' van outside the cop shop, did y'?" He didn't wait for an answer. "Y' also said y' were goin' straight back home cos y' didn't want t' ride back with me. Am I right or am I right?"

I was surprised that he'd made such an astute deduction. I wasn't really looking for a deep and meaningful discussion, but what could I say? "Well, there might be some truth in there if I think about it. But I don't think they're outright conscious decisions," I lied, blowing smoke out. "Want some more?" I asked, offering him the joint.

"No, not at the moment. Stick it in the ashtray f' now. *Oh shit!*" he exclaimed dramatically.

"What?"

"Cops are pullin' me over," he said, looking in his rear-view mirror as he slowed right down.

"Jesus, Bruce! They'll smell the shit on us. It's stinkin' the van out big time!"

"Wind y' window down," he said as he wound his down. "Just let me do the talkin', okay? Close that fuckin' ashtray so he can't see that joint or even bett'r, if y' can flick it out the window."

I was freaking out, as my worst nightmare was being realised. I grabbed the joint and dropped it out the window as Bruce pulled up onto a grassy verge.

"Keep cool, Sam." I wasn't feeling cool at all. My heart was in my mouth and I was cursing myself for having gotten into the van with Bruce.

"What's takin' him so long?" I asked, reluctant to turn around and draw more attention to ourselves.

Bruce grinned at me, a mad, sadistic grin, then burst into full-bodied laughter. I thought he'd flipped. I looked around to see where the cop was, half expecting Frank in my face at any second, but I couldn't see anyone. I twisted my body around further to see where the cop car was parked. I couldn't see one. Bruce was in total hysterics, doubled up, gasping for breath. I turned the other way and still there was no cop and no car to be seen. Then I realised Bruce had bluffed me. I was so angry, but his laughter was infectious, and I found myself laughing too. Bruce was doubled up in pain.

"I really got y' with that one, didn't I?"

"Did y' fuckin' what! I thought we were totally 'n utterly fuck'd, y' bastard."

Bruce started up the engine and headed back out onto the road. "See, Sam, y' need t' light'n up a bit. Life's too short t' be worryin' all the time!"

"Yeah, maybe y've got a point." I didn't feel like I worried all the time. Though I was certainly worried about going to prison, but I knew Bruce was too.

"Point taken?" He looked at me for acknowledgement.

"Point taken," I said. He grinned at me, and I felt stupid for being too serious. Bruce didn't seem so bad when he was like this.

We drove through Yaringa and stopped outside the bowling green.

"I'd invite y' 'round but I've got a bit on today, so maybe come 'round in the next few days, Sam," said Bruce.

"Okay, I'll do that. Thanks f' the lift, Bruce."

"Watch y' back," he said with a serious voice before breaking into laughter.

"Always." I grinned and shut the door. He drove away from the kerb, and I watched him disappear up the road. I didn't feel like going home, so I strolled down to the beach. Bruce's theatrics had sent me into a spin.

* * *

I flopped down on the sand not far from the flags and closed my eyes, feeling grateful to be alone. I must have drifted off into a stoned siesta because I awoke to a familiar voice.

"Hi, Sam!" I rubbed my eyes and looked in the direction of the voice. Brigitte was walking towards me in her black bikini, looking divine. She sat herself down in the sand beside me, giving me the full view of her fruits.

"What are y' doing down here?" she asked.

"Oh, not much. Lookin' f' you," I replied.

"So now that you've found me, what can I do f' y'?"

"I'm not sure," I said all coy, smiling at her as if she should know.

"I've got t' be at work in ten."

"Shame one of us didn't notice the other sooner," I responded. "I only just got here, had to go t' Wodyn."

"I've got t' go, Sammy," she reiterated, getting to her feet. "But hey, there's a band on tonight. Why don't y' come up 'n check it out. They're s'posed t' be really good."

"I just might do that," I said.

"See y' tonight then," she said.

"If y' lucky," I called out, watching her shapely arse wiggle its way down the beach.

It was hot, too hot to be doing very much. I needed a swim to cool down and wake up properly from my stoned sleep. I stripped down to my underwear, not caring if anyone noticed and strode down the beach, wading into the sea up to my waist before diving in. I bodysurfed a couple of waves then waded back out, all the while thinking it was a shame that Brigitte had gone to work. I needed the distraction. I picked my clothes up off the sand and headed home.

At the house I showered, standing under the spray for a long time, letting the water wash over me. Nothing mattered in that moment as water cascaded onto the shower floor, disappearing down the plughole. Eventually, I turned the shower off and dried myself. I didn't feel like being upstairs with Tim and the telly, exposed to the conversation or lack thereof, and opted for the quietness of my caravan. Inside I lay down on the bed, towel still wrapped around my waist, and picked up a book someone had given me. It was a Frederick Forsyth novel, *The Day of the Jackal*, a thriller which I thought was quite a cleverly-written yarn. I was four chapters in when I was interrupted by a sudden and loud banging on the caravan door. Startled, I recoiled, heart thumping.

"Get y' hand off y' cock 'n come f' a swim." It was Tim's voice. "Think I might go f' a surf up the coast f' a bit."

"Okay. Give me five, will y'?"

"If I must. But don't nancy about, time is short."

"Yeah, okay." I searched for shorts and struggled my way into them. There was another loud banging on the side of the caravan.

"Are y' comin' or what?"

"Comin'," I called out.

"In y' pants!" he called back. I pulled on a T-shirt and stepped out into the sunshine.

Tim was waiting in the car, listening to Van Morrison. Without saying a word, he backed down the drive and onto the road.

"Y' seem bothered about somethin'," Tim said as we drove up the coast north of Yaringa.

"Not really … How come y' ask?"

"Y' seem like somethin's been eatin' y' up these past few days."

"Well, I s'pose with Erika 'n the other guys leavin', it's left a bit 'f a void f' me."

"Just as well y've got me t' go surfin' with then!"

"I s'pose so, Tim."

We drove for what felt like an age. Finally, he slowed the car for a bend in the road and we turned up one of the numerous side roads that led down to the beaches along the coast. There were many remote beaches, and all the surfers knew them well. The road curved and wound through forests of eucalyptus trees and scrub down to one of these out-of-the-way beaches. There was a moderate swell rolling in evenly, breaking from left to right, with an offshore breeze holding the waves up nice and clean.

"Y' should be able t' handle this," Tim said, winking at me mischievously as he brought the car to a stop.

There was a family of kangaroos of various sizes grazing on the grass nearby, looking curiously at us, ears pricked for danger. We grabbed our wetsuits from the boot of the car and slipped them on, then removed our boards from the roof rack and strutted down to the beach. Tim always looked awkward when he walked, as if he needed to have a shit and was holding it in, but in comparison, once in the water he was graceful, like a seal. We walked out onto rocks at the end of the beach where we could get into the sea behind the waves, instead of battling them head on, doing duck dive after duck dive to get out past the breakers. Tim threw himself into the water, board and all, and paddled out effortlessly with strong even strokes. I followed, diving in and paddling furiously to catch up with him. He was already out in his waiting position, searching the horizon for the perfect set of waves. He soon picked a wave he liked, and lining it up, he paddled like crazy to catch its momentum. I saw him rising and dropping on the crest of the wave, flicking out of it the moment the wave began to collapse into foaming white water.

Now it was my turn. I'd drifted quite a way down the beach and the waves here seemed a lot bigger than they had from the shore. A nice, even set came in, and I picked one in the middle of the set, paddling with great fury to catch it at its peak. But I timed my paddle too late and was left floundering in the back spray of the wave. Another wave presented itself, and I started paddling earlier to time my run better. The wave picked me up, and I was flying down its face. I'd never caught a wave this steep or big before, so I decided it was time for the daredevil in me to come out. I went to my knees then quickly to my feet, and I was up racing down the face of the wave. I moved forward on the board to manoeuvre a turn, but moved too far forward, and the board nosedived into the wave, shooting out from under me. Surfacing out of the foaming wave, I looked around for my board, but it was nowhere to be seen. Unlike Tim, who had a leg rope attached to his board, I had none and was floundering in the middle of a set of breaking waves in a cumbersome wetsuit, without a board. I couldn't touch the bottom and was drifting down the beach, simultaneously being pulled out to sea by the current. In a panic, I tried swimming furiously. Tim was out the back of the waves and would possibly ride in soon. I hoped he would see me. *Just stay cool, Sam. Go with the flow 'f the current. Stay cool, Sam.*

I allowed myself to drift out to where the waves were peaking and caught the first wave that looked promising. Again, my first attempt was mistimed, but my second was good. I was on, riding the face of the wave for all I was worth. When it broke into white water, I stayed with it, and was carried in further on its momentum before coming to a standstill, but the undertow was determined to pull me backwards. My feet searched for the bottom, and just as I could feel the sand on tiptoes, the next wave turned to white water. I swam with it, pulling hard on each stroke as it carried me further ashore. I stood up quickly so I wouldn't be sucked out on the back of another breaking wave.

Tim passed me as he rode all the way in on a magnificent wave. Oblivious to my predicament, he headed back around the rocks out into the back water again. On dry land once more, I found my board washed up on the beach, and I traipsed several metres before dropping the board in the sand to unzip my wetsuit and free my arms. I sat there looking out at where I'd been a few minutes ago, wondering what might've been.

My eye was drawn to Tim frantically paddling to catch a huge wave, then he was on his feet riding it for all he was worth, looking a little stiff, like a cardboard cut-out, but he had great control. Watching him, I wondered what had flipped him over the edge, or had he truly flipped? His friends had distanced themselves from him, no one offered him any help, no one seemed to care. *No bastard stood up 'n said, "I'll help y', Tim."*

Did they? Now I seem t' be y' only social contact, y' only friend. As the wave died out, Tim dropped back down onto his board, letting the force of it carry him to the beach. He picked up his board and walked up the beach the way a cowboy might and sat down next to me.

"What happened t' you?" he asked, dropping his board down on the sand beside me and unzipping his wetsuit.

"I tried t' stand up, and managed that, so thought I'd have a bash at turnin'. Got too far forward 'n lost m' board cos I don't have a leg rope, do I? Thought I was a cooked goose f' a minute."

"But y' got in alright?"

"Yeah, not before I shit m' wetsuit," I joked.

On the way home, Van Morrison spilled out of the rear speakers, filling the space of an otherwise silent car journey.

"So y've already got someone new with y' in the caravan?" Tim asked as Van Morrison took a breather between songs.

"Say what?" I said, totally shocked.

"Y' heard me."

"Do y' want t' know somethin' really weird?" I said, raising my voice above the music.

"Not really. Y're weird enough already." Van Morrison gently accompanied our conversation: *In the month of May in the city of Paris…* *Angelou.* "Tell me anyway," Tim said after a moment.

"Nah! On second thoughts, don't think I can. Y' know, though, in all 'f m' life I've never had so many strange experiences with girls. They all seem t' want me. It's an unheralded moment in the history 'f m' life. At school it was always the jocks who got the girls, and I was just the funny man. I could make people laugh. I'd have girls 'n guys in stitches in the locker bays at lunchtime, but I've never really b'n int'rested in team sports. Not m' forte. I skied in winter 'n sailed in summer. They aren't popular sports."

"Aren't you the lucky one."

"The thing is, I dunno if it's all it's cracked up t' be. There's more fuckin' disadvantages than advantages, 'n at the same time, there's somethin' quite excitin' about it."

"So what's the problem then?"

"Well, f' a start, girls always want more, so it gets complicated, especially if y' don't want t' be tied up in a one-on-one situation."

"Erika?"

"Yeah, she's awesome. But I slept with Brigitte while Erika was here. It's a long story 'n it started on New Year's Eve."

"Y' livin' dangerously with Brigitte. She's a fuckin' headcase."

Tim slowed down as he came into the limited speed zone of Yaringa. A police car passed. Harry was driving. "Y' didn't wave," jibed Tim.

The next minute Brigitte was walking across the road, heading in the direction of the bowling club.

"Are y' expectin' a visitor?" Tim asked.

"Shit. No! She isn't, is she?"

"She is."

"Can we carry on t' the pub? I'll buy y' a beer."

"Y' losin' that magic touch, Sam?" Tim switched the indicator off and continued up the road.

"Never had it, Tim."

"That's not the story I just heard. Anyway, a cold one after that surf is just what the doctor ordered, and mixed with m' medication, it'll make a fine cocktail." He laughed and I joined in as if I had a compulsive disorder.

"When are y' folks' due home?"

"Don't remind me, it's somethin' I'd rather not think about." Tim swung into the car park beside the pub, coming to an abrupt halt a few centimetres from the fence.

"Y' don't want t' be drawin' that kind 'f attention t' y'self, Tim."

"A man's got t' have some fun in his dreary life."

I'd never seen 'm so cocky. Was it a high before another low, or was he genuinely getting better?

30

Band Night

We cruised through the double doors into the pub, where locals were playing pool, and they nodded their 'Giddays' as we entered, the old boys who were sitting at the bar watching the telly and sipping on their beers barely noticing us — the league was on.

"Two schooners 'f Tooheys, thanks Trev." Trev was the son of the publican. He was a good guy and organised all the live music in the pub. "Cheers!" I said to Tim, raising my glass.

"Cheers. Here's t' Casanova 'n a good day on the water," Tim said, raising his glass and taking a sip.

"Fancy a game 'f pool?" I asked. There were already a few names on the board. I walked over and added each of our initials to the collection.

"Tim, how are y'?" asked Jake, the top local surfer and boardmaker in the shire. He stood with pool cue in hand, watching his mate take a shot into the corner pocket.

"Good," Tim said.

"Been gettin' any waves lately?"

"A few." It was obvious Tim wasn't comfortable around other people, instantly reverting back to his monosyllabic speech. Shy people are often that way, and I couldn't help thinking that perhaps Tim was naturally shy, even before the medication.

"Been out t'day?" Jake asked, persevering.

"Yeah," Tim said, resting his glass on a bar leaner that ran just below chest height along the wall.

"Whereabouts?" asked the other pool player who hadn't said anything until now, but who had obviously been listening to the conversation. I'd seen him around but didn't know him.

"Nelson Beach," Tim replied.

"Oh yeah. Thought that might've been workin' t'day." Jake sank two balls in quick succession and was lining up the black. With one smooth stroke he potted it and stood watching the white ball roam around the table before coming to rest against the cushion.

"Nice shootin', Jake," said the guy who'd been playing him. They shook hands.

"Y're up, Tim. Those other names are dead," said Jake, pointing to the blackboard.

Tim slotted his money in the side of the table and the balls rolled out into the catchment area. He picked up the wooden triangle and proceeded to set up the balls. He walked to the cue rack, looked at a couple of cues, picked one and chalked his cue. Tim picked up the white ball and placed it on the line that divided the circle, favouring the right-hand side. He casually lined up the white ball and gave it a good nudge with his cue, sending the ball down the table where it collided with the triangle of balls, scattering them in every direction.

It was a good break, made better by the fact that he sunk two stripes. Tim picked out the best shot on the table and stroked another ball neatly into the bottom right pocket, leaving himself set up to put away another ball in the bottom left pocket. The rest of his balls were up the other end of the table and not easy shots. He got his head down low over the cue and lined up the ball he could see best, gently hitting the white, favouring the left side so the ball would trickle into the top right pocket. His shot was accurate, but the lack of power caused the ball to pull up short of going in the hole.

Jake came to the table with most of his balls in the middle and up the top end of the table. He liked to win and wouldn't take well to being beaten by Tim. He had three easy shots, while his fourth was difficult with the white ball being down the bottom end of the table, not an easy angle. He smacked the white ball hard and it raced down the table hitting his coloured ball on the wrong angle, causing it to ricochet around the pocket, scattering some of the balls at that end of the table, and one nudged Tim's ball into a pocket.

"Fuck'd that up," said Jake, as much to himself as anyone else, walking back to his position at the bar leaner.

Tim had a good shot straight on from a short distance and sunk the ball in the middle right pocket. To sink his last ball before the black, he had his most difficult shot: a double off the cushion rebounding on the right angle into the middle left pocket. He performed it beautifully for a fifty-fifty shot. The black sat nicely for him to drill into the top right pocket, and he didn't disappoint.

Jake came straight over and shook his hand. "Nice t' see y' haven't lost y' touch, Tim."

It was my turn on the table playing Tim, and I wondered how good my game would be, having just witnessed him dismantle Jake. As the game progressed, it was not looking good for me, and I thought I was facing a 'down trou' of massive proportions. Next thing, Tim had a clear shot at his last ball, sinking it neatly in the bottom right pocket. Then he was onto the black and looking like a winner when he sank it in the middle left pocket.

"Nice one, Tim," I called out prematurely as the white rolled into the top left pocket, giving the victory to me. Tim shook my hand.

"Nice come back," he said, showing a hint of a grin from behind his beard, with that mad twinkle in his eye.

I survived a couple of games on the table before being pipped by some local I'd seen around but never had anything to do with. I noticed Brigitte was now at the bar. She must've finished doing the cellar work and taken over from Trev who was probably taking a tea break before the band played tonight. She caught sight of me, so I popped over, feeling more relaxed now.

"Y' comin' back t' see the band tonight?" she asked.

"Maybe. Maybe not. I'm tryin' t' talk Tim int' comin'."

"What for?"

"What d' y' mean what for?"

She leaned over the counter and whispered, "Everyone says he's crazy."

"Well, that depends on who y' listen to! Who do y' want t' believe?"

"Oh … I see," she said, looking a bit sheepish. "So he's alright then, is he?"

"You can be the judge 'f that," I replied, feeling slightly irked by her comments.

* * *

Back home, I cooked Tim and myself some steak with boiled new potatoes and salad. We sat in our usual chairs watching the news while we ate.

"I'm goin' t' see a band up at the pub t'night. They're s'posed t' be good, accordin' t' Amanda at the coffee shop in Wodyn. She's goin' with a friend."

"I'll come," he stated without a moment's pause. I was pleased, as I didn't really want to hang out with Amanda and Rose on my own. I watched Sale of the Century while Tim showered.

Tim drove us up the hill because he didn't have the energy to walk.

He said I could pick the car up in the morning on my way to Wodyn. We pulled into the pub car park, taking one of the last remaining spaces.

We walked into the pub pleased to find that the band, Midnight Oil, hadn't started yet. A local band was thrashing out seventies covers, and the place was rocking. I scanned the room to see if I could spot Amanda and Rose anywhere.

"Can't see the girls I'm suppose' t' be meetin'," I said to Tim in a raised voice. There was a small round table with two chairs tucked in the corner near the doors we'd entered through. "Sit there 'n I'll get the first round," I said, pointing to the table. He moved towards it and I made my way to the bar through the beer-swilling punters. After much jostling, I arrived at the bar where Brigitte and Trev were frantically pouring drinks. Brigitte caught sight of me and flashed me one of her beamers. I felt like the most special guy in the pub. She wore a body-hugging white top with a low-cut V-neckline, revealing her breasts held firmly in shape by her push-up bra. The heat of the night added a bonus: her dampened top stuck to her bra, revealing her nipples.

"What'll it be, Sam?" she asked, keeping it professional.

"Two schooners 'f Tooheys, thanks. Jeez, it's going off in here t'night, isn't it?"

"Y' tellin' me, I'm stuffed already." She had one beer almost poured, smoothly replacing the glass with an empty without missing a beat.

"That's the ticket," I said as she passed the glasses to me and I handed her a five-dollar note.

"There's y' change," she said, giving me back as much as I'd given her, in coins.

"Ta," I said, taking it and putting it in my pocket.

"See y' later."

My hands now full, I navigated my way through the punters back to where I'd left Tim. Rob was sitting at our table, talking earnestly to

Tim, probably asking after Tania. When I reached the table, Rob looked surprised to see me, and he grunted an acknowledgement. I put Tim's beer on the table and walked off with mine into the expectant crowd. As I nudged my way through, I caught a glimpse of Amanda and Rose sitting at a table to the right of the stage, sipping on large cocktails and laughing about something. I looked back over to where Tim was sitting. Rob had gone and Tim was alone, drinking his beer. I made my way back over to him.

"I've found the girls. They've got a primo spot up the front. We should join them." He nodded, picked up his beer and followed me through the crowd. Amanda had her back to us, but Rose spotted me, and she tapped Amanda on the arm and pointed at us. Amanda turned to see me and waved enthusiastically.

"Hi, Amanda. Hi, Rose. Okay if we join y'?" The pub was noisy with chatter and music, making it hard to hear and I felt like I had to shout.

"Of course, sit down," replied Rose, pulling out a chair for me.

"This is Tim, he's a friend 'f mine. Tim this is Rose … 'n 'f course, y' know Amanda," I said, gesturing towards them.

"Hi, Tim," they simultaneously chorused. Tim nodded to them then took a sip on his beer.

"Thought y' weren't comin'. We couldn't see y' anywhere when we first arrived. We got the best spot though."

"Sure have," I said and smiled.

Amanda wore a dress that portrayed her best assets well. It was turquoise with sequins, shimmering like a mirror ball in the soft, smokey light of the pub. She'd applied make-up to highlight her eyes and bright red lipstick coated her lips. She looked shaggable, and I noticed Tim giving her a not-so-subtle once-over.

"How's y' day been, Rose?" I asked.

"It was alright," she replied nonchalantly.

"So, what do y' do?" I asked, attempting to get the conversation flowing.

"Not much really. I run a gift shop just down from Amanda's coffee shop." I detected bitterness in her young voice.

"Okay," I nodded, searching my memory for a visual, recalling a tacky-looking shop a few doors down from Amanda's.

"What about you?" she asked. Her facial structure was refined, but her nose and chin had a sharpness to them, and she held herself very erect, almost stiff. She wore a tight-fitting, black satin dress cut low at the front to reveal enough cleavage to be noticed but still covered her sufficiently to leave something to the imagination.

"I'm on holiday, y' could say."

"What's the attraction to Yaringa?" She didn't mince her words. "I mean, it's not the most well-known destination on the holiday calendar."

"My ex-girlfriend is from round here," I replied.

"Oh yeah, who's she? We might know her, eh Mands?" she asked, pursuing the matter.

"Tania Smithell."

"No, doesn't ring a bell." She glanced at Amanda who shrugged her shoulders and shook her head.

"How old is she?" asked Amanda.

"Mid-twenties," I replied vaguely.

"Ahh, no wonder. She'd have been a few years ahead of us at school, maybe not even there when we started." Amanda was almost shouting now, the noise in the room increasing.

"She would've been a senior by the time we started," responded Rose. "So what's keeping you here if you're not with her anymore?" Rose continued probing.

"Well, I like it here 'n the beaches are great. It's summer, s' why not?"

She shrugged her shoulders and nodded. "Fair enough."

I was grateful for her acceptance of my explanation. *Jesus woman! Why don't y' apply f' the detective's job with the local Police?*

"Want 'nother?" Tim waved his empty glass at me.

"Cheers," I replied, then looked to the girls. "Y' right f' drinks?" Their glasses were still almost full, and they shook their heads in unison.

Tim extracted himself from his chair and shuffled his way through the heaving crowd. The lights dimmed and the background music was cut. The crowd let out a loud cheer and I could make out figures stepping onto the stage as soft light revealed four silhouettes. Suddenly it was all on — guitars, bass, drums and vocals exploded in a wall of sound. Within seconds there were people on the dance floor. Before long, Amanda and Rose were up dancing and signalling me to join them. I needed another beer, some Dutch courage, before I was going to be seen up there. Amanda and Rose were like chalk and cheese on the dance floor. They danced facing each other, Rose — tall and graceful compared to Amanda — comfortable with herself, moving easily, whereas Amanda was a big, self-conscious bowl of wobbly jelly.

Tim arrived back with two more schooners, the tide out a bit. It must've been a battle getting through a lively crowd. He passed me one across the table and shrugged his shoulders. As the band warmed up, so did the crowd, and in a short time the entire floor was a sea of people dancing.

The band played two lengthy sets with a thirty-minute break in the middle. During the break, Detective Rose grilled me some more about why I would want to hang out in Yaringa. Halfway through the last set, Amanda and Rose accosted me, and I found myself on the dance floor, waving my arms by my side, trying to get into the beat and doing a bit of hoof stomping and hip twisting. Amanda and Rose had the same approach to dancing, whether it was the two of them or the three of us, as we now were. We faced one another as if doing the do-si-do, smiling stupidly as we shuffled and twisted on the dance floor. I cringed inwardly and thanked Christ that most people were blind drunk, and I wished I were. Tim sat drinking his beer on the sideline, probably pissing himself quietly at the fool I was making of myself.

The band ended their playing as abruptly as they had started, and we sat back down at our table. I made my way to the bar.

"Who are the cocktails for?" Brigitte asked snidely.

"Just some girls I know from town, where I go for m' cup 'f tea."

"Y' mean that fat chick Amanda whose parents own the coffee shop?"

"Yeah, that's her."

"What're y' doin' with her? She's a dog."

"Like I said, I have a cup 'f tea there sometimes. They had a table goin', so we sat with them."

"Come on, mate, the bar's closin' soon, save it f' later, will y!" a man standing behind me remarked.

"Yeah, yeah, keep y' hair on," I said, turning to him. I didn't recognise him as a local, but he looked drunk and happy to rumble, and I wasn't looking for trouble. I paid Brigitte and picked up the tray of drinks.

"Are we meetin' up later?" she asked. I shrugged my shoulders.

"See y' before I go, eh?"

Back at the table, Amanda had muscled in closer to Tim. *Tim might get laid t'night. That wouldn't be a bad thing.*

The pub was back to its noisy self with loud background music and the punters milling and chatting. It had been a good night. A band of that calibre was seldom experienced here, and everyone was buzzing. Detective Rose moved in on me for another hundred-questions session. She wanted to know where I lived and who Tim was. She was boring me, so I excused myself, saying I needed the bathroom, but I slipped out a side door onto a balcony. I pulled my packet of Drum from my pocket and rolled a cigarette, lit it and inhaled deeply. The moon resembled a croissant suspended high in the night sky, reflecting a beam of shimmering light on the sea. I took another puff on my cigarette before blowing the smoke out into the night air. I flicked the rest of the cigarette on the ground and extinguished it with my foot. I couldn't be bothered going back inside to listen to Rose's questions. I stepped off the balcony onto the road, making the decision to head home. Tim could make his own way home and Brigitte would figure things out and probably swing by my caravan after she finished work.

31

Waiting

I woke to the sound of feminine voices and a shaft of sunlight across my face.

"So you shagged him all night long?"

"Not quite, but most 'f the night. We got a bit 'f sleep. What happened with you 'n Sam?" Amanda asked.

"Nothing. I don't want to talk about it," Rose replied.

"What do y' mean?"

I heard car doors opening and closing, followed by the sound of a car engine starting. The engine idled for a moment before Amanda reversed down the drive, gears crunching as she struggled to find first gear. The wheels spun on loose gravel, and then there was silence except for the kookaburras laughing in the trees.

Brigitte was well and truly wrapped around me, my right arm dead from her sleeping on it. I tried to free my arm, causing her to stir and roll over, putting her back to me. I liked her soft, warm skin and firm, rounded buttocks against me. I felt aroused but didn't want to wake her, as she seemed so peaceful in that moment. Working my arm free from under her body, I lay there waiting for the pins and needles to kick in, holding my breath and trying to distract myself from the discomfort.

I carefully got out of bed and made my way to the downstairs shower. Soaping myself from neck to foot, I stood under the spray, washing away the night before and enjoying the pressure of the shower. I thought of Erika and how we used to shower together, her beautiful face, her wonderful body, her delightful smile. She'd been a welcome friend and lover over the summer. I thought of Sarah, an unusual woman, with two very different sides to her, one so caring and smart, the other so obsessive. I thought of Brigitte, lying serenely in my bed, her unrelenting attempt to sleep with me on New Year's Eve, the crazy passion in the back of my car, and my unexpected fondness for her.

I opened the door of the caravan to find Brigitte lying awake, the sheet wrapped around her. "Do you like me or just fancy me?" she asked, searching for an answer in my eyes.

"Look, Brigitte, I dunno what t' say. I like y' but y' know I'm not lookin' f' anythin' serious. Y' don't own me, 'n I don't own you." I thought about telling her about my situation, but she must've heard something on the grapevine. After all, she worked in a pub in a small town. "What do y' know about me, Brigitte, besides the fact I come t' the pub from time t' time?"

"What do y' mean?" she asked, holding my stare.

"Well, just tell me what y' know about me."

"I hardly know y', Sam. I want t' get t' know y'," she exclaimed, wiping tears from her face with the back of her hand. "I like what I know of y'. Like y' say, y' come in the pub 'n y' hang out on the beach, those are the only two places I've seen y'. Oh, y' picked me up hitchin'. That was the highlight 'f our acquaintance till now," she said, smiling warmly.

"Anythin' else?" I asked casually.

"Oh, 'n apparently y're in some kind 'f trouble with the cops f' havin' dope on y'. Someone said y' dropped Bruce in it."

"What! What the fuck would any 'f them know? They weren't there, they didn't go through what I went through." *They don't know what a shithead Frank is, or the sarge for that matter. They don't know any 'f that! They all stick their heads in the sand, pretend not t' hear, 'n then they talk.* "They all fuckin' talk, don't they? Talk behind m' fuckin' back! At the pub havin' a pint, at the beach when I'm swimmin', 'n even in town when I go f' tea. They all know, 'n they all say nothin'. Really, they don't know jack shit!" I was ranting and Brigitte was looking at me in silence, nodding her head occasionally. There was empathy in her eyes.

"It's true I'm up f' a hearin' in the District Court in a few weeks or so. It's serious! As far as Bruce goes … well, he got himself in the shit! He caused the whole thing! I don't have a great deal 'f sympathy f' him. I tried t' help a few people out 'n ended up on the wrong side 'f the fence, so to speak!"

"Hey, I don't know anything except what's been said here and there. I believe y', Sam," interrupted Brigitte gently.

"I don't care if y' do or if y' don't. I'm just tellin' y' m' point 'f view. I've got t' face the music. The outcome's unknown. It's not favourable. Bruce wants us to stick t'gether. Well, I'm not sayin' anythin' t' anyone, so I dunno what will happen. Bruce'd like t' see me dead, I'm sure! Sometimes I wake up at night from this reoccurring dream 'f havin' bricks tied t' me 'n being dropped off a bridge, fallin', fallin' int' bottomless water. Bruce doesn't give a fuck about me, he's out t' save his own bacon!" I was getting myself increasingly wound up, feeling the pressure of it all looming so close — the wait, the frustration, the despair. Some days it felt like such an effort to maintain my sanity.

"Sam, I'm sorry. I'm sorry y're in all this trouble. Y' don't deserve it, y're a good guy. I can't imagine what it must be like t' be so far away from home 'n in this kind 'f trouble."

I couldn't stop the runaway train now. Brigitte took me in her arms and held me. I was surprised by my lack of resistance. She held me so tightly to her breasts I could hardly breathe, and I was crying into them like a baby.

"I want you inside me, Sam. I just want to feel the gentle side of you." She said it so sweetly, with such feeling that I couldn't refuse her that moment, a moment more intimate than carnal. Our loins met, and I found myself inside her, felt her warmth, her compassion that came from a physical place and which soothed me in a tender way. Our union was heartfelt and powerful, and then the moment was gone.

"I've got t' get up n' go int' town," I whispered, still lying entangled in her arms.

"Do y' mind if I stay awhile?" Brigitte was glowing.

"Please y'self, the caravan ain't goin' anywhere." I hauled my relaxed body out of bed and dredged my shorts and jockeys up off the floor.

"Ta," she said. "Y' look so handsome, Sam."

"I don't feel it," I said, pulling on my shorts.

"But y' sure look it."

"Thanks. Might see y' later if y' still here. I've got t' report t' the police. I do it every day."

"Y' kiddin' me."

"No," I said, juggling my feet in my shorts as I found one leg hole then the other.

"How long've y' been doin' that for, Sam?"

I shrugged my shoulders trying to think. "I suppose it must be comin' up f' six months."

"That's a long time."

"Yeah, I know. I've got t' go."

'Bye," she said, and I bent down and kissed her.

When I returned from Wodyn, I was disappointed to discover Brigitte had gone. I lay on the bed staring at the ceiling, allowing my mind to wander. *I wonder how Erika's gettin' on? She'll be back at school by now. Shit! Ted 'n Val will be home any day. What a challenge that's goin' t' be adjusting t' them being back. Life has certainly been blissful without them.*

The caravan door suddenly opened and there was Brigitte with a towel wrapped around her, looking as surprised to see me as I was her.

"That was quick," she exclaimed as she flopped on the bed next to me, letting her towel fall away. "So what's it like in New Zealand, Sam? It's s'posed t' be really beautiful."

"Yeah, it is. The postcards show it is, 'n they don't lie. But y' know, I think Australia's beautiful too, all its eucalyptus trees 'n interestin' animals. The beaches are just stunnin' with their golden sand 'n amazin' rock formations.

"It's all true, but inland it's just desert."

"Well, even that's got its own beauty, hasn't it? Think of Ayers Rock."

"I s'pose y're right. But I'd like t' go t' New Zealand one day."

"Maybe y' will." I pulled her in close, feeling the warmth of her skin against mine. Then she pulled away.

"I've got to get up to the pub, Sam, or I'll be late." She found her knickers and slipped them on. I watched her dress without saying anything. "Will I see you at the pub later?" she asked, bending down hurriedly to kiss me.

"Maybe," was all I could say. She was halfway out the door.

"Okay, I'll see y' if I see y'. Bye." She closed the door.

I remained lying there with my thoughts, wondering what I'd do with my day. I found the book I'd been reading laying randomly face down on the floor next to the bed. I picked it up and began to read.

I must've fallen asleep because I woke to the sound of someone banging on the side of the caravan, then the door opened and sunlight blasted in, causing me to squint.

"Oh, y' are in here!" It was Tim. "Y've slept f' a day 'n a night, do y' know that? I never saw you yesterday. Don't y' have t' report t' the cops?"

"No! How can that be?"

"Too much shaggin'!" he mused.

I groaned, rubbing the sleep from my eyes. "Now I've got t' go int' town again. Feels like I only just did that."

* * *

I reported to the police station, pleased to see Harry come through the door when I rang the buzzer.

"I need t' talk to y' sometime soon, but not here," he said. "Can I swing by your place after work?"

"Sure," I replied.

"Okay. I'll be 'round about six o'clock."

That done, I dropped in for my cup of tea at the coffee shop. Amanda was at the counter, her usual friendly self. She looked extremely radiant today.

"Hi, Sam. Did y' enjoy y'self the other night?"

"Hi, Amanda. Yeah, it was pretty good. A pot 'f tea thanks, and 'n asparagus roll."

"Sure. How's Tim?" she asked, her face blushing a deep crimson.

"Tim's good. T' be honest, Amanda, I haven't had a chance t' catch up with him since the other night."

"Oh, I see," she said, pouring hot water into the stainless-steel teapot. She put the lid on and placed it on the tray with the cup and saucer and the plate with the roll.

Finding a table by the window, I put the tray down and extracted the morning paper from the magazine rack. I buried my head in the newspaper and soon finished my belated breakfast.

"See y', Amanda," I said as I walked out.

"See y'," she said, somewhat awkwardly.

* * *

Back at home I found Tim in his usual relaxed position. The cricket was on, the final of the one-day games — The Decider. Australia were batting, no wickets down. It had been going for an hour and the Ozzies were looking good.

"Have fun the other night?" I asked.

"Can't complain," he grinned broadly. "How about y'self?"

"It was okay, nothin' worth talkin' about."

"By the way, the olds are home t'day. I had a call from Mum 'n hour or two ago. Can't say I'm excited 'bout havin' them back cos life's been sweet without them."

"Have t' say I feel the same," I responded.

"Y' might want t' do some vacuuming just t' keep Mum happy."

"Yeah, I s'pose." The thought of having to share the house with Tim's parents again didn't do much for me at all. "Don't y' have t' pick them up from the airport?"

"Yep, but not till later, and we'll probably get takeaways on the way home. Mum won't want t' cook."

"I could cook."

"Nah, not worth the hassle."

It was five o'clock and we were at Wodyn Airport waiting for Ted and Val's plane to land. It was small, but there was no other commercial airport around for kilometres, and only a few flights operated in and out each day. Crows and cockatoos squawked loudly in the surrounding eucalyptus trees, and the sun still packed some heat for the time of day as Tim and I walked from the car park to the terminal's arrival lounge.

An announcement informed us that the plane was delayed by fifteen minutes. We sat waiting in silence, and twenty minutes passed before another announcement confirmed the plane had landed. After another five minutes, Ted and Val appeared in the small arrival lounge, and I nudged Tim.

"Here they are."

Tim pulled himself slowly to his feet and shuffled towards them with me in tow. He seemed to slip back into his unhealthy way of being, as if he had a chemical reaction, a physiological response, to their arrival. A blank, distant expression appeared on his face, and there was a marked difference in the way he walked, more stooped, the way he was when I first met him. Perhaps his parents had more to answer for in terms of his condition than I realised, though it also seemed that this may have been a bit of an act, a way to deal with them or, perhaps, to not deal with them.

"Hello, Tim darling," oozed his mother, as she moved in to hug him, suffocating him in her smothering embrace.

My God, y're so overbearin' 'n all consumin'. If my mother were like you, I'd have run away a long time ago. I wonder if that's why Tania wanted t' go back t' New Zealand?

"Good trip, Ted?" I asked, shaking his outstretched hand.

"Very good trip, Sam. We weren't ready to come home yet, but that's the way it goes sometimes." Ted looked as unhealthy as ever, his face a blush of bright red with the broken blood vessels on his nose and cheeks more pronounced than before they went on holiday. His eyelids were heavy, the lower lids sunken, making his eyeballs prominent, as if they might pop out at any moment.

"Oh well, y'll just have t' go again sometime," I suggested.

"Indeed."

"Sam! How are you? Come here and give me a hug," Val drawled, coming toward me with outstretched arms as if I were her favourite son.

I hugged her briefly and pecked her on the cheek. "Welcome home, Val."

"Thank you, Sam. We had such a good time." Val appeared far more rejuvenated from the holiday than did Ted. He'd probably been henpecked close to death, having nowhere to escape to, being stuck in motels night after night with Val. Most likely he drank and smoked more than his normal quota, which was already in the upper end of the range, just to endure Val. *The poor bugger.*

"We've got so many photos to show you. New Zealand is so beautiful," she drawled. "A very special country."

I was amazed she liked it. I thought the weather would be too cold for them, and that she would somehow find fault with everything. We walked out of the arrival lounge to collect the baggage off flat-deck trailers towed by a green John Deere mini tractor. Val continued her praise of their trip while Ted and I removed their luggage and Tim assumed his zombie pose.

The drive home was a challenge, reacquainting myself with Val's high-pitched, penetrating voice and Ted's chain-smoking. Val never came up for air as she extolled New Zealand in a blow-by-blow account of their trip. I had to give her credit for her enthusiasm, and it was nice to hear about my homeland. Tim turned off the main road and into the golf club's grounds. The club's restaurant did Chinese food and Tim had pre-ordered our meal.

"Just got t' pick up the takeaways I ordered," he said.

"Oh, that was thoughtful of you, dear," said Val.

Tim parked up, opened his door and made his way slowly into the club.

"Your mum and dad send their love, Sam. They dropped us off at the airport this morning," Val said as she fixed her hair in the visor mirror. "Your parents were very good to us," she continued. "But I suppose they had to be."

Tim reappeared with a brown paper bag in each hand and passed them to me in the back seat where I placed them on the floor between my feet.

* * *

Tim soon pulled up into the drive at their house, and he and I collected a suitcase each from the boot. We left his parents to handle the small stuff as we made our way up the stairs onto the balcony. Tim put the suitcase down to unlock the front door.

"Can y' handle another month or so 'f them?" he asked, his wide eyes smiling at me. We left their suitcases in the hallway, and I popped back downstairs to make sure they could manage everything else.

"We've pretty much got it, Sam, although the Chinese food needs taking up," said Ted.

I walked into the lounge with the bags of Chinese takeaway to find Tim already slouched in his armchair watching cricket, the second to last over just completed.

"Y' need fifteen from the final over, 'n I guess y've got enough wickets, but I don't know if y' can do it," teased Tim.

It was looking close, too close to call, and I wasn't going to miss it. I took the takeaways into the kitchen, dumped them on the bench and rushed back into the lounge, diving into my armchair. The match was at the SCG in Sydney. Richard Hadlee was on strike and Trevor Chappell was bowling. Chappell ran in, and the crowd made a thunderous roar as he released the ball. Hadlee smacked it to the boundary for four.

"Ha! Take that!" I shouted, raising my arms in the air to celebrate. Ted entered the room. He never showed a great deal of interest in the game but was curious to see what the excitement was about. When I told him how close it was, he sat himself down on the couch.

"You seem to have a good team at the moment. That Hadlee is quite brilliant, isn't he?" Ted observed.

"Yeah," I said. Hadlee composed himself for the second delivery. Chappell struck Hadlee on the pads as he came forward to defend the ball. Chappell leapt in the air and spun round to appeal to the umpire. The umpire's finger went up and Hadlee shook his head in disbelief as he walked from the pitch back to the pavilion.

"A harsh decision," Ted said.

"I reckon." I replied in disbelief.

"Plum, absolute plum." Tim was poker-faced, looking at me. I grinned and shook my head.

Smith, the wicketkeeper, entered the pitch. He was reasonably handy at the end of a game, known for being able to hit big, but just as likely to swing and miss. Chappell bowled to him. Smith stroked it away, ran one, saw two was on offer, so ran another. Smith offered a similar shot for the fourth delivery, running another two.

"We're goin' t' do it, I'm tellin' y'."

"No y' not," retorted Tim.

"It's fifty-fifty," chimed in Ted.

"We should eat, the Chinese is going cold on the bench in here," Val said, entering the lounge.

"We'll be there in a minute, Val. The boys just want to watch the last over of the cricket."

"Don't make it too long." Val stood right in front of my view of the telly, oblivious of me trying to look around her. I could hear Richie Benaud, the commentator, saying, *He's got him. He's gone.* Val finally moved, allowing me to see Smith walking away from the crease, swinging his bat in disgust. The replay revealed Chappell had clean bowled him, he'd swung and missed, and the ball had dislodged the middle stump.

Brian McKechnie came to the crease to face the last ball.

"Y' can't win now, can y'?" Tim said, looking like a smiling assassin, and I wanted to thump him. Tim didn't care much for the result of the cricket. He got his pleasure from winding me up.

"Well, it's still possible t' win," I said. "If Chappell 'no balls', that'd be one run, 'n he'd have t' bowl an extra ball, which McKechnie would have t' hit f' a six. Unlikely, I admit, but possible."

"Clutchin' at straws now, are we?"

Chappell was in conversation with his brother and captain, Greg Chappell, who'd been in conversation with the umpire; they were obviously hatching a scheme. Chappell didn't take his usual run up for the final ball. He hardly took a run up at all — only two paces — and not taking the arm back over the shoulder either. Instead, he under-armed the ball, sending it rolling down the pitch like one of the old boys would at the bowling green. McKechnie threw his bat away in disgust and walked off the pitch, glaring at the umpire.

The commentators were in disbelief. Richie Benaud said, "I cannot believe it, I cannot believe it! In all my years of commentating I have never seen such a sight!"

"How ridiculous, how bloody pathetic is that?" I was outraged by the bad sportsmanship demonstrated on the pitch.

"Yeah, that's pretty bad," Tim conceded.

"Bad!" Ted exclaimed. "It's an embarrassment. It couldn't be more appropriate than to say, 'It's just not bloody cricket!'"

"Is the cricket over?" Val whined as she entered the lounge again. "Come on, boys, dinner's going cold. I've served it onto plates so come and sit up."

Our days of doing as we pleased were over. Val was back ruling the roost already. I was still in disbelief at the cricket's outcome as I headed into the dining room. Val poured drinks for herself and Ted.

"Would you like a glass of wine, Sam? We brought some New Zealand wines back with us."

I bet y' did y' ol' lush. "Yes, please," I said, thinking it would be nice to try a New Zealand red.

All through dinner Val and Ted rambled on about their trip again as we quaffed a couple of bottles of red wine. There was little mention of Tania, how she was doing or where she was living. It was all about Val and how wonderful everything they did was. She occasionally looked to Ted for back up on something they'd done, or something she couldn't quite remember the details of. I wasn't really taking too much notice of anything she said, since I was still smarting at the ungracious deeds of the Australian cricket team under the auspicious guidance of their win-at-all-cost captain, Greg Chappell.

After dinner I helped with the dishes, then made my excuses and escaped to the caravan to read *The Day of the Jackal* again. Lying there I remembered that Harry was supposed to drop by. I impulsively decided to walk down to his place and pay him a visit instead. Even though I didn't want to see Sarah, I felt I had to see Harry to keep things on the level with him, to demonstrate that I did appreciate his efforts to help me.

* * *

The evening was incredibly humid as I left the caravan. The sun was about to set behind the hills, and the cockatoos were out in force, singing their final song as the sun disappeared. In truth, it was more of an orchestral racket than a song, but I liked their boisterous cacophony.

There was something soothing about their presence as I made my way, silhouetted by the fading light, along the street to Harry's place.

I walked up the drive past Harry's car to the wooden front door, raised the ornate brass knocker, and banged it several times. The door opened to reveal Sarah with Sophie and Daniel in tow.

"Sam, what brings you here?"

"Hi, Sam," said Sophie.

"Hi, Sophie," I responded.

"Hi, Sam," Daniel mumbled shyly.

"Hey, little man," I said, bending down and tickling his stomach.

"I came t' see Harry. Is he in?" I asked Sarah as I stood up.

"Yes, he is. Come in."

"Thanks, but I don't really have the time t' come in. Just tell him I'm here."

"Don't be silly, Sam. Come in, it's hot out there."

"Yeah, Sam. Don't be silly, it's hot out there," Sophie repeated like a parrot.

"Okay, I think I get the message," I said, grinning at her.

"Look who's here, Harry."

He was in one of the easy chairs, looking very relaxed in front of the telly.

"Hi, Harry. Thought I must've missed y'. Ted 'n Val got back today, but I didn't realise they were comin' back till after I'd seen y'. Then I completely forgot about y' comin' over till I was in m' caravan readin' a book, so I thought I'd better pop down 'n see y'."

"Y' didn't have t' do that. Come in 'n sit y'self down."

"You two fancy a beer?" asked Sarah, already at the fridge.

"Yes, please," said Harry.

"Sam?"

"Yes, thanks."

Sarah returned with two cans of Fosters and passed me one, my fingers touching hers as I took the can from her hand. Then she passed Harry his. Simultaneously we opened our beers and put them to our mouths. I greedily gulped at mine. The taste and coolness refreshed my mouth and helped me relax.

"How've things been, Sam?" Harry asked between sips.

"Okay."

"What does 'okay' mean?" He was inspecting his can as if he might find something of interest on it.

I shrugged my shoulders. I didn't really know what to say. "I guess it's just that it's such a long wait. I'm sick 'f waitin', 'n now that Ted 'n Val are back, it's not the same at their home. I'm tired of being here, I want t' go home."

"That's understandable," Sarah said sympathetically.

"It's not long t' go now. The next few weeks will fly by," Harry said, attempting to console me.

"I miss m' family."

"Of course you do, Sam," said Sarah, giving me her compassionate look.

"Listen, Sam. We were wonderin' if y'd like t' babysit the kids f' us next week. We're havin' trouble gettin' a babysitter," Harry said.

"Y' want me t' babysit y' children? Aren't y' takin' enough risk just havin' me over here? I mean, it wouldn't be viewed well in the eyes of the world. Listen … I don't think it's such a good idea. T' be honest, it makes me feel uncomfortable."

"Oh, come on, Sam. Your mind ticks over too much," responded Sarah.

"Look … Okay, I'll do it." I felt like I was buying my way out of the situation, that I was purging Harry of his guilt in the hope that he might have the ability to plea bargain my case with the judge.

"Thank you," said Sarah. "It's important for us to be able to go to the evening's event knowing that the kids will be well looked-after. It shouldn't be too challenging as I'll put the kids to bed before we leave. Why don't you come around for dinner first?"

"What night is it?" I asked.

"Wednesday," replied Harry.

"I'll see y' Wednesday night then," I said, getting up, having drained my can of beer.

"You know, you don't have to go just yet," said Sarah.

"Thanks, but I'm engrossed in a really good book and want t' get back t' it. See y' soon, Harry."

Harry put his beer down on the side table beside the couch. "I'll see y' out," he said.

"Bye, Sarah. See y' Wednesday evenin'."

"Bye, Sam." She kissed me on the cheek.

I followed Harry to the front door, and he closed it behind us. We walked onto the driveway together.

"Sarah worries about y', Sam."

"What for?"

"I s'pose because she's a woman and a mother. It's an intuitive thing, isn't it?"

Why the fuck's he askin' me? "I dunno, Harry. I s'pose y' right."

Suddenly I wanted to go. I didn't want to babysit their children. I didn't want to have anything more to do with Harry or Sarah. I felt like I was between a rock and a hard place, anxiety building up inside me.

"My life already feels better f' me handin' in m' resignation," Harry said. I didn't want to know about how good his life was.

"M' life feels like shit, Harry. Sometimes I wake up havin' nightmares about being lifted over the rails 'f a bridge. Bruce is there laughin' his fuckin' head off 'n sayin', *That's what y' get f' narkin', y' fuck'r.* He laughs some more then he pushes me off. I've got bricks strapped t' me 'n I'm fallin'. I hit the water, Harry, 'n I'm sinkin' … it's bottomless. I'm still sinkin', Harry, and when I wake up, I'm chokin' as if m' mouth is full 'f water. I manage t' catch m' breath 'n I just lie there, Harry, not sure whether I'm relieved it was only a dream. And the next night I'm dreamin' it again. I dread goin' t' sleep and I read every night till I fall asleep. I wake up the next mornin' with the readin' light still on, 'n my book's fallen off the bed, or made its way under the covers 'n I'm sleepin' on it. The whole thing 'f goin' t' sleep is as reoccurring as the dream itself."

Harry looked uncomfortable. But I wanted Harry to feel my pain, my anxiety. I wanted him to know that he put me in the situation I was in. I didn't want to take responsibility for my part, right now it was all Harry's fault. Harry squirmed as he struggled to say something, and I couldn't quite hear him because he wouldn't look at me.

He was mumbling, "Canberra Police … phone call … informin' us that there was somebody in a Holden station wagon goin' t' pass through Wodyn. The person in the car would be in possession 'f hash oil capsules …"

Cosmo had dobbed me in! There it was, straight from the horse's mouth. Mr Fuckin' Smooth had done some kind 'f deal with the cops! Told them if they sat on me heavily enough, they'd get the bigger fish!

I wasn't going to allow his uncomfortable moment to subside easily.

"Why did y' let Frank 'n the sarge beat me up that night, Harry?"

He kicked at the ground, not looking me in the eye. "Because that's the way cops operate when they want somethin', Sam. Cos that's the way it's always been. Different strategies f' different situations. It was obvious we weren't goin' t' get anythin' from y' through orthodox means. And Frank loves the confrontational stuff. He was born t' be a cop. I'm ashamed 'f m'self f' not standin' up t' him that night, but it's pointless t' make excuses. It's more or less impossible t' fight the status quo, it's so firmly ingrained in all cops. There's as much corruption inside the police force as there is outside. We're often not much better than the criminals we bring t' justice."

"I've got t' go, Harry. I dunno what t' say." I wanted his night to be as sleepless as mine would be.

"I understand, Sam. Will we see y' Wednesday night?"

"Maybe," I said, already walking away.

As I walked down the road, I wondered what sort of plea bargain Cosmo had negotiated and whether it was going to make a difference to the power of shit he was in.

***

On Wednesday night I reluctantly babysat. Sarah hired videos for me to watch, left a biscuit tin full of baked goodies, and told me to help myself to beer in the fridge. I never heard a squeak from the kids, and Harry and Sarah arrived home to find me asleep on the couch. They insisted I stay the night, but I said I'd rather wake up in my own bed, so Sarah drove me home.

When we arrived at my place, she wanted to talk in the car, but I didn't, and I made my exit for the caravan. I was only in there a few minutes when there was a quiet knock on my door.

"Who's there?" No answer. A few seconds passed, and there was another soft knock on the door. This time I opened it to find Sarah standing there. The dim light from my reading lamp spilled across her face to reveal she'd been crying. "What's the matter, Sarah?"

"Can I come in?"

"Of course," I said against my better judgement.

"Harry told me about your reoccurring dream," she began. "He also said that he told you about the phone call they got from Canberra, the tip-off about you. Harry had no choice but to check you out and make the ensuing arrest. We all know what an arsehole Frank can be, so there's no surprise that he beat you to get what he needed. Harry's very upset about the whole thing. I can't tell you enough how sorry he is, and I know it doesn't change what happened to you or necessarily make it alright."

"Tell Harry I understand and that I don't blame him f' what happened to me."

"Thank you, Sam."

She reached out to hug me, pulling me into her, embracing me as a mother might a child. I returned the embrace, becoming intoxicated by her scent, the softness of her skin against my face. I didn't want to let her go. She must've sensed it, as she continued to hold me. I felt desperate for her now, and I didn't care any more. I had nothing to lose. I could feel a swelling in my loins and a quickening beat to my heart. I turned my face inwards, my lips found hers and for a moment I thought she was responding. Instead she was pulling away.

"Sam, what are you doing?"

"Kissing you."

"You're so sweet, Sam, so very sweet, so young and innocent."

She was in her other, alternative state of being, the caring compassionate woman, not the wild femme fatale I had also been exposed to. *Strange the many different shades of light in which a person can be seen, or how someone perceives y' in contrast t' how y' perceive y'self.*

Sarah placed a hand on either side of my face like Oma would, holding it, looking at me as if she expected to extract something from me by studying my face long enough. Then she kissed me. Her tongue was in my mouth, hungry, exploring. I placed my right hand on the exposed flesh of her left breast. She gasped lightly and I took it as a signal to probe further, managing to get my hand inside her bra where

I could feel the erectness of her nipple. Dick was aching in my pants and, as if on cue, her hand found him. Sensing the urgency in me, she deftly undid the press studs of my pants and whipped the zip down, all in one move. Magically, Dick was out like a jack-in-the-box.

She pulled away from my lips. "My, Sam, you're bursting," she said in a matter-of-fact tone, a smile on her face.

"Couldn't y' do somethin' about it?" I pleaded.

Sarah took Dick in her mouth and expertly brought me to the brink of orgasm. Sensing my closeness, she pulled away, pushing me down onto the bed. She pulled up her skirt and drew her knickers to one side and straddled me. She rode me into the west bareback, and I broncked and bucked until the fire in me was completely extinguished. Sarah cried out in whoops of excitement as her own pleasure arrived.

It finished as abruptly as it had started. Sarah stood and straightened herself out.

"I'd best be going, Sam," she said.

I felt cold and distant now. I didn't care if she flew to the moon and exploded. I also felt a great sense of satisfaction knowing that Sarah was going home to bed to sleep next to Harry with a part of me inside her. She could shower, she could do what she wanted, but she wouldn't be completely rid of my essence.

* * *

Sleep came quickly and lasted well into the following morning. I reluctantly dragged myself out of bed and down to the beach for a swim. The waves were small and insignificant, the sea a deep turquoise and dead calm. As usual, the sun was shining and there wasn't a cloud to be seen in the sky. Rain would be a godsend, but it wasn't going to happen today, nor tomorrow probably, nor even the next day. I dived into the sea and swam out a little, then across the bay a few hundred metres and back again.

By the time I returned to the house, the only reminder that I'd been swimming was my wet shorts, the rest of me was bone dry, apart from the sweat beading on my forehead. I decided to hitch into town and get that part of the day out of the way. Standing on the side of the road waiting for a ride, I felt a demented pleasure in the knowledge that I had taken something precious from Harry — his wife — just as he had taken something precious from me — my freedom.

With Ted and Val back home, I spent more time on the beach and in my caravan. Tim and I hung out during the week while they were at work. I usually made sandwiches for lunch, and we watched cricket if there was a game on, and soaps and infomercials. Tim remained introverted since his parents' return, and I read a lot in the caravan. I finished *The Day of the Jackal* and found *The Odyssey*, another Frederick Forsyth novel, at the second-hand bookshop in Wodyn, and devoured that too. Brigitte would come by a few times a week and stay over after she'd done a night shift. I liked her quirky sense of humour and having someone to talk to. She provided the close contact I so craved but didn't understand.

32

The Old Man

My father arrived in February, a week before the court case, as he had promised. Tim and I collected him from the airport. He arrived on a late morning flight from Sydney where he'd spent a few nights. I picked him out as he walked across the tarmac away from the plane. My father had a distinctive walk, his feet turning broadly outwards, and he held himself upright, making him appear taller than he was. He had a small faded-blue canvas backpack hanging off one shoulder. My father had a good head of hair, fine and silvery grey, almost white, as it had been ever since I could remember, but now somewhat thinner than it once was. He grinned broadly as he approached. We embraced warmly in the arrival lounge. It had been almost a year since I'd left home. Tears welled up in my eyes and I was afraid I wouldn't be able to control my emotions, so I pulled away.

"Tim, meet m' dad. Dad meet Tim." Tim shook his hand silently.

"Hi, Tim, nice to meet you," the old man said.

"Do y' have any luggage, Dad?"

"Yes, a suitcase."

"Okay. They bring it out the front," I said, leading the way. "How was the flight from Sydney?"

"Good."

"Y' stayed in Sydney a couple 'f nights, didn't y'?"

"Yes, just to meet up with some people there."

"What people might they be?"

"Oh, no one you know."

He was keeping something from me. The mini tractor with the two flat-deck trailers came through with the luggage. The old man went up to the first trailer and plucked a well-travelled, brown leather suitcase from it.

In the car on the trip back to Yaringa, my father and I talked like old friends who hadn't seen each other in ages, as there was a lot to catch up on. I'd always been a challenge for my father. It wasn't that we didn't get on, more that we didn't often see life in the same light. He struggled to accept that I was different to most people in my ways of thinking and doing. I suppose I disappointed him — I hadn't pursued an academic path or a professional career, I pushed boundaries, and now I'd broken the law.

As we approached Yaringa, the view looking up the coast impressed and delighted my father.

"You couldn't find a better place to live, could you, huh?" The old man was keen on the outdoors; he loved the mountains, the bush and the sea. This was the common thread we shared.

"It's pretty good, isn't it," I said, pleased he liked it. "Tim, can we drive up the road a bit t' show Dad more 'f the coastline?"

"Sure."

We drove to the northern end of the beach that overlooked the inlet where I had lived with Tania, Bruce and Sally. I pointed the house out to the old man.

"It's a bit rustic, but it was a great place to live."

"I can see why you like it," he responded.

We drove back towards the village, to the house. I collected the old man's suitcase from the boot, took him up to the house and showed him the room he'd have for the duration of his stay.

"Do y' want a shower or anythin', Dad?"

"No, I had one this morning. I'll be fine. Could go a cup of coffee though."

"Right then. I'll put the kettle on."

* * *

The old man's arrival marked the end of my era in Yaringa as I had known it. *Once he heads back t' New Zealand next week, things will be diff'rent one way or the other.* A massive knot was forming in my stomach as D-Day loomed. I imagined getting on that plane back to New Zealand. I imagined each step down the gangway — being greeted by the air hostess, being ushered to my seat, putting my seat belt on, the plane taxiing down the runway, and the final sensation of being airborne. I imagined it every morning when I woke, and I fought off other thoughts, even though the fear was eating away at me.

As I waited for the kettle to boil, I saw the plane land on New Zealand soil, the doors opening, and me stepping out onto the tarmac, into freedom, the mountains at my back. I was home. *I'm Billy in the movie* Midnight Express, *after he escaped from the Turkish prison dressed in a guard's uniform, skipping down the street, tossing his cap in the air. I toss my bag in the air, my salute to Billy.*

Once the kettle boiled, I made coffee in the plunger and poured three cups, topping them up with milk. Tim seldom turned down a cup of coffee or tea, so I hadn't bothered asking if he wanted one. I offered my father the armchair I usually occupied, and he accepted. Tim had the telly on and didn't have the awareness to turn the volume down while we tried to talk.

"Would y' like t' go f' a walk, Dad?" I asked, hoping he would.

"Yes, that'd be good. I could do with the exercise after being on that plane all morning."

We finished our coffees and the old man sorted out his footwear. We walked through the park and over the track through the sand dunes.

"The temperatures at home are nothing like this," the old man said, wiping his brow. "I could do with a swim. The water looks nice."

"Well, we could go in our undies further up the beach if y' want," I said grinning.

"That's probably not a bad idea," he said, smiling back at me. "So, how've things been going with you?" He looked earnestly at me, the way he always looked when he felt genuine concern. I'd been around him enough to recognise when he was being sincere and when he was just going through the motions.

"Pretty good overall, I guess. It was good with Oma and Opa here. Oh, 'n I had friends visiting over the Christmas holidays."

"Really? From New Zealand?" he asked.

"No. Some guys I met here while hitchin' back from Wodyn one day."

"Oh yeah," he said, in an 'I see' sort of way.

"But they are Kiwis, funnily enough, living in Woolongong."

"And Oma said you'd met a girl."

"Yeah, but she's gone back home now. Erika. She's still at school, Dad. She and her family went home a few weeks or so ago."

"Aha," he said, which suggested a dulling down, a switching off, a more automated response.

"But I'm kind 'f seein' someone else now," I said, more to get his attention again than for any other reason.

"Really? That's very soon after the other girl. What's her name again?"

"Erika. She was just a bit 'f a holiday fling."

"You shouldn't talk about your girlfriend that way," he said all righteously.

I wasn't looking for an argument with him, as he'd just arrived, and I needed him on my side. I'd seen his wandering eye before, when we were out driving or at the beach. It was nothing to be ashamed of.

"Sorry, Dad, I didn't mean t' sound derogatory towards her."

He's got the same jewels 'n plumbin' as me. Even his old man, Opa, still has a bit 'f an eye f' appreciation. Good on him! A feelin' 'f youthfulness 'n lust in an ageing body has got t' be a good thing. I've sprung Opa on a few occasions flickin' through nude mags on the smoko table at the old man's work. Lingerin' too long on the centre-page spread t' be able t' get away with it. He wasn't tryin' t' hide it anyway. "Beautiful," he'd say in his heavily accented voice. "Absolutely beautiful." I respected his honesty. "If only I was young again," he'd said. Then he got a faraway look in his eyes as if he remember'd long ago days. Y' weren't too happy when y' were told at seventy or somethin', that y' couldn't sleep with y' wife any more, that she didn't want it. That's a cruel blow f' a man. Sucked a bit 'f life out 'f y' there 'n then, didn't it?

Erika might have been a holiday fling, but in truth she was far classier than that. She had ambition, a head on her shoulders; she'd go places. We arrived at the end of the beach having walked in silence for a while. It was going to be good to have a few days with the old man and for him to acquaint himself with Yaringa, get the lay of the land before the shit started to hit the fan.

"How's Mum?" I asked.

"She worries about you too much. Her worst fear is that you end up in an Australian prison."

"Mine too," I said laughing, trying to make light of it.

"You do know there is always that possibility? You have to be prepared to consider it."

"I'm all too aware 'f that possibility, Dad. I wake at nights from bad dreams that y' don't wanna hear about." I didn't mention handbasins or showers to him. I was sure my father knew what really went on in prison.

We reached what I judged was halfway down the beach and we stopped for a swim. The sun was beating down on us, frying me to a cinder and forcing my hand — I was going to swim in my underwear. The old man was unfazed by the scenario and followed suit. The waves were relatively benign, nothing worth bodysurfing. We swam out beyond where the waves were innocuously breaking, and treaded water.

"So the barrister arrives on Monday," the old man stated. "But in the meantime, I'd like to meet your solicitor."

"I haven't seen Dennis since Mum and Oma were here and I had that miserable experience in the Magistrates' Court, which they still call the Court of Petty Sessions 'round here, even though the name was changed in the early seventies. I can ring t' make 'n appointment with him if y' like," I responded.

"That'd be good."

"I think I need t' get out before the sun gets the better 'f me." I began swimming back to shore.

"Yes, I agree," he said, taking up his stroke next to me.

"Australia's predominantly a desert, Dad," I reminded him as we swam. "And that much closer t' the equator. They reckon Australia was part 'f the African continent before it broke away many millions 'f years ago."

"That's right, they do. I recall seeing a documentary on it," the old man said as we casually breaststroked our way towards shore. "The water's so much warmer here too."

"I s'pose it's part 'n parcel 'f the whole desert thing, Dad."

"Mmm," he said, his thoughts drifting off elsewhere.

* * *

By the time we returned to the house, we were both hotter than a buzzard's crotch. It was cooler inside, but we had to put up with Tim watching all the afternoon soaps.

"Y' hungry, Dad?" I asked, knowing he was never one to turn down an opportunity to put a bit of food in his belly.

"Something to eat would be nice, son," he replied warmly, smacking his lips together at the prospect of a feed.

Fuck knows why he never puts weight on, he eats like a horse. He must have a lot 'f nervous energy, or somethin' that helps burn it off. I opened the fridge. It was overflowing with vegetables, cold meats, cheeses, soft drinks and wine. I hauled out everything that looked good for lunch and placed it on the table so we could make our own sandwich concoctions. The old man was in there like a pig in shit, buttering up two slices of bread and peeling off leaves of lettuce, while I sliced up tomatoes, gherkins and cheese. He piled everything onto the one sandwich, topping it with the smoked chicken I'd broken up into pieces. He cut the sandwich into halves and halves again, so it was manageable to get into his mouth.

"Tim, all the food's out if y' want t' make a sammy," I called out. No response. I started making up my sandwich and as I was about to bite into it, Tim appeared at the table and sat down opposite the old man, grabbing a plate and bread without saying a word.

"So, what do you do with yourself, Tim?" The old man asked, trying to make conversation.

"Nothing really." He sure knew how to put an end to a conversation.

"Nothing at all?" The old man asked in a second attempt to get the ball rolling as he lined up another quarter of his sandwich.

"I watch telly if that counts," Tim stated in his characteristic monotone.

The old man's mouth was full now as he masticated his sandwich to a pulp, his cheeks bursting with the contents, his conversation with Tim bordering on being over.

"Tim surfs, Dad, but lately his health hasn't been as good as it was, so he's more limited with what he can do. Taking it easy is good f' him."

"Oh, I see," Dad said, but he didn't really. "What's wrong with your health, Tim?" He might have been better off letting sleeping dogs lie.

"I've just come out 'f the loony bin. Apparently I was spyin' on local women, 'n I've been accused 'f removin' underwear from clotheslines." The old man looked to me, searching my face for confirmation. "They decided I was a menace t' society, so they medicate me. It slows me down, takes my energy away, renders me useless."

The old man looked uncomfortable as he digested the information along with the last mouthful of his sandwich. I kept my face blank, wanting him to make up his own mind.

Tim put the finishing touches on his own sandwich, spreading mayonnaise all over the tomatoes he'd just laid on top of everything else, arranging the top slice of bread, then compressing it down. Taking the whole thing in his hands, he lifted it to his mouth which was wide open, ready to receive it. We sat there with our mouths full. All that could be heard was the odd clicking or grinding of someone's jaw as we consumed our sandwiches in comfortable silence.

Afterwards, the old man and I cleaned up, and Tim went back to his armchair and soaps.

"So what's the story with Tim then?" my father half whispered as he dried cutlery with a tea towel.

"Just that, Dad."

"What do you mean?" He was looking at me all earnestly, expecting an explanation but none was forthcoming.

"What Tim told y' is the same as what I know. And yes, he is on medication, although they've cut it back a bit, I believe."

"And the stuff with the women?" he asked with genuine concern.

"Dad, I don't know! Apparently, it's the word 'f the two women versus Tim's. There are no other witnesses. The cops picked him up, then locked him up, and he went nuts 'n attacked one 'f the cops. They brought in a shrink who signed an affidavit committing him t' the loony bin. He's on medication now, no longer a menace t' anyone. He hasn't even had a proper trial. It's insane!"

"The whole thing sounds very messy."

"That's what I reckon too, but what can y' do?"

"What about his parents?"

"I guess they feel like their hands are tied." I put the last of the perishables in the fridge while the old man washed the plates.

"I feel a bit shagged," I said. "Think I'm goin' t' have a bit of a nap, Dad. It's too damn hot t' be doin' anythin' else."

"That sounds like a fine idea to me," the old man responded. On the weekends at home, he always had an afternoon nap, and when we were kids, driving somewhere long distance, he'd get Mum to drive while he had a power nap in the car.

"I'll see y' later then," I said. "Oh, anythin' y' need?"

"No, you go, I'm fine. See you in a bit," he said as he reached out to embrace me.

"It's great to have y' here, Dad," I said, releasing him from our embrace.

* * *

I'm on the rail of a bridge and Bruce is there. He's tightening the last strap that's looped through the steel weights strapped to my chest. There's a couple of bogans with him, tying my feet together so that I've no chance of getting free.

"I told y', Sammy, y' can't go openin' y' mouth t' the wrong people. Y're too much 'f a liability f' everyone involved." He shakes his head adamantly. "Y' fuck'd up, Sammy. Do y' understand?" He looks at me as if he expects an answer but how can he possibly? I can't reply because there's a rag shoved in my mouth. My lips are parched, and my tongue feels like dried out cardboard after rain and a day of sun. I can't see anything except the blueness of the sky.

My hands! I can't feel them, it's as if they've been removed. But still, they must be there, or I'd be dead from the loss of blood. My circulation's been cut off, my arms are behind me, my hands are bound. It's hot and sticky and I'm sweating, and my pants are wet. I've pissed myself. Fear overwhelms me.

My head aches as though I've been whacked with a mallet after drinking all the top-shelf whisky in some sleazy side-street bar. Flies are buzzing all over my face and up my nose, sensing death the way a buzzard does when circling its prey, waiting until it's too weak to move. Then it's in there without mercy, feasting, before its prey has even gasped its last breath. The drying piss on my pants smacks me in my nostrils, the odour of a men's toilet in a suburban park, one that hasn't been hosed out for more than a week. I feel I'm going to pass out. Bruce is talking to me again, but it's only his lips moving, there's no sound coming out. He looks all twisted and contorted like the reflection in a trick mirror that elongates and warps one's features.

I hate y' Bruce, y're a fuckin' cunt. Y' think y're so fuckin' cool 'n have got it, got the way about y'. But y' just a twisted, fuck'd up, bitter cunt who thinks life owes y' somethin', but it owes y' nothin'. I wish he could hear me, hear my thoughts.

And then I'm falling, falling, falling. The sky isn't blue any more, and I realise it's not the sky, it's water, the sky's reflected in the water. I'm still falling but I'm close to impact. I hit the water and I'm still falling. No! I'm sinking, there are fish and weeds passing by, and still I'm sinking. There seems to be no bottom. The rag in my mouth comes free, but it's no consolation, as I can't breathe, I've run out of air and I'm still sinking … down … down … down. The light has gone. I've blacked out and somewhere I can hear distant sounds; they're a long, long way off. But now the sounds are getting closer … But the air … there's none left. Then the sound is right there in my ear like a loud banging, and I'm in a cold sweat.

I was awake, bolt upright, and a huge sense of relief washed over me, while another part of me wished it was all over.

"Are y' in there, Sammy?" I recognised the voice. It was Bruce. I was a wreck, I was exhausted, and I was saturated in my own sweat. I must've nodded off while reading Frederick Forsyth. I got up very slowly. My mouth was too dry, it felt like sandpaper. I opened the door and there he was, looking at me in much the same way he did on the bridge in my dream.

"Jeez, y' look terrible, Sammy. Are y' crook or somethin'?"

"No, I don't think so. I've just woken up. I was readin' 'n I must've fallen asleep, like a very deep sleep 'n it's like a cooker in here. I'll be alright, I just need a swim or a shower."

But in truth I was still in shock — the nightmare, the distant banging noise, waking to the sound of Bruce's voice, opening the door to face him — it was too much to comprehend. He had never been here to see me before, but it was getting close to D-Day, and he'd be wanting to put the squeeze on, make sure I was not going to drop him any further in it. Really, it wasn't possible for me to do so. He was in the shit as a result of his own actions, and it was up to him to find a way of weaselling out of it.

"I haven't seen y' about," he said. "Thought y' were goin' t' drop 'round?"

"Yeah, I've been meanin' t', but Tania's parents have just got back, 'n now m' dad's over too, so things are busy f' me at the moment."

"Y' dad, eh? How's Val? She still got that voice worse than a crow's? Drives y' up the wall, doesn't it?"

"You too, huh?" I wished he'd just go. He was giving me the creeps. My nightmares were becoming more and more intense. "Look, I'm goin' t' have a swim 'n get rid of m' sleepy, sticky feelin'," I said.

"Can I come in f' a minute?" he asked.

Fuck off! "Sure," I said.

I moved backwards to let him in, and he pulled the door shut behind him.

"Christ, it's hot in here!" He reopened the door, but it didn't help much. There was not enough of a breeze to make a difference. Bruce's hair looked like it had been cut, and he appeared tidier than I'd ever seen him. Perhaps he was working on his image for his own day in court. "Look, Sam, don't fuck things up f' me. I don't want t' end up in the slammer courtesy 'f you. So, stick t' y' story 'n don't sway from it! Right?"

"Right," I said.

"We'll see y', eh?" he said, giving me his most intimidating stare.

"Y' will," I said. He patted me on the back as if we were buddies.

I watched him drive off in his van, then removed a towel hanging on the back of the door and ran to the beach. I left my towel a few metres up the beach and waded out up to my waist. I dived in and held my breath, staying under as long as I could, making breaststroke moves underwater and moving forward simultaneously. I surfaced behind the breaking waves, treading water, and looked back at Yaringa and at all the houses that dotted the horizon. In each house there was a person or persons, unseen, going about their daily existence. I wondered, as I continued to tread water, what was on their minds, what was important to those people right now. A good wave came along, and I caught it, riding it all the way back to the beach. I felt cleansed by the ocean, cleansed of all the filth I had attracted in my life here.

* * *

That night we all sat down to a dinner Val had cooked.

"It's pan-fried fish with baked potatoes and salad. The perfect summertime meal," she announced, looking pleased with herself.

Tim and I hoed into ours as if we hadn't eaten for a month while Val rabbited on to my father about their fantastic holiday. Ted made himself busy filling everyone's glasses with white wine so he wasn't drinking alone. He'd already slipped back a couple of quiet whiskies while hanging out on his bar stool doing the crossword, waiting for Val to get dinner ready. The old man wasn't much of a drinker, so it was interesting for me to see how he'd cope with Ted constantly topping up his glass.

"I've arranged for you to see Dennis Greenwood tomorrow," Ted said as he quaffed his wine.

"Who?" the old man asked.

"Dennis Greenwood. He's Sam's lawyer, and he helped jack up the barrister who will represent Sam in court on the day."

"Oh yes, of course. I'm with you now," the old man said.

"Den's a lovely man," Val chimed in, wanting to be in on the conversation. "He's been a friend of the family ever since I can remember. He looks after all our affairs. I think you'll like him."

"I look forward to meeting him," said the old man convivially.

* * *

The following morning, I borrowed the Valiant and drove into Wodyn with my father to make the ten o'clock appointment with Dennis. It

394

seemed like a waste of time as Dennis wasn't representing me for my big day in court. We sat for fifteen minutes in the waiting room, and I wished the pretty receptionist were there to distract me from my dark thoughts. Instead, a very plain-looking older woman was on duty that day.

Strange how dentists, doctors 'n solicitors all seem t' think they've got the right t' fuck with y' time. How very unprofessional 'f the professionals. Finally, the door opened, and Dennis ushered a frumpy, middle-aged couple out, talking non-stop until they escaped through the front door.

"Ah Sam, this must be your father," he said, turning to us with his wide smile. "Dennis Greenwood, pleased to meet you," he said, putting his hand out. The old man stood and shook his hand firmly.

"Henry Gorzman. Pleased to meet you."

"Come in. Please, come in." He ushered us through the door to his office.

"Thank you," said the old man, following him obediently.

Dennis sat down behind his desk and we sat facing him in the two chairs opposite. He looked terrible, his face blemished with broken blood vessels. His cheeks hung off the bone like jowls, and his pale blue eyes were bloodshot. Excess weight oozed from his frame. The state of the room reflected his poor health: there was a messy stack of files on his desk, the ashtray was full of cigarette butts, and the rubbish bin overflowed with discarded paper. His badly-stacked bookshelf was spilling over, but his drinks cabinet was tidy and as well-stocked as ever.

"So," said Dennis, picking up his cigarettes. He removed one from the packet and with the other hand he picked up his lighter. "As you know, the hearing for this case is up next Tuesday." He blew a large plume of smoke straight out in front of the old man. "I've arranged for Simon Cottrell to present the case. I think it's better that way since he has a wealth of experience in drug cases."

I half expected my dad to say something about Dennis smoking, but he remained silent. "What time is Sam's case up that day?" asked the old man.

"At ten, if I'm correct, but we won't know for sure until the day," replied Dennis, tapping some ash into his overfull ashtray.

"Right, and when are we meeting Simon?" my father asked, agitated by the smoke.

"You can meet with him the day before the case, here in my office. He arrives early afternoon, I believe, but I'll get back to you on that." He sucked hard on his cigarette, the end glowing red with intensity. Particles of ash hung in the air like dust.

"What else do we need to do at this point?" The old man continued with his line of questioning, shifting around in his chair, trying to get comfortable.

"There isn't a lot that can be done. A plea of guilty will be made, has to be made as Sam's already pleaded guilty in a lower court. There would be no point in making any other plea as the evidence is there, as solid as concrete. It's Sam's word against the two arresting police officers." The old man nodded.

"What is the most likely outcome?"

"Who knows for certain?" replied Dennis, shrugging his shoulders, and stubbing his cigarette out on the edge of the ashtray. Smoke billowed in all directions as he pushed the cigarette hard into the vessel. "A glass ball is required for that prediction. As you know, there is a maximum ten-year sentence, and counting down from that, there are varying levels of sentencing that could be imposed. That's about all I can tell you. It is most unlikely that they would go for the maximum. Depending on the presiding judge and the events that unfold on the day, Sam may well end up doing prison time." He clasped his hands together then flexed them forward as if relieving his tension. I shuddered as a shiver slithered up my spine.

My father was silent, and Dennis looked directly at me for the first time since we had been in his office. "The purpose of having Simon represent you, Sam, is to present a compelling case, highlighting mitigating factors, to prove that you were a minor player in something a lot bigger and that your naivety got you into trouble, not your intentions. That will be his case to the judge."

"So … there's a real risk he'll go to prison?" the old man asked, looking grim-faced as the reality of my situation sank in. I suddenly felt sorry for him. He'd just arrived and was immediately forced to deal with the final days of my ordeal.

"Of course there is. We wouldn't be bothering with a Sydney barrister if there wasn't. Look, Henry, how can I promise you a result when there are so many unknown variables? It also depends on how the police present their case. They can influence a judge by how they perceive a defendant."

The old man looked from Dennis to me and back to Dennis, somewhat bewildered, then he shrugged his shoulders.

"Sam … Henry … We'll finish here for now until we meet with Simon," said Dennis going for his cigarette packet again.

"Sure," I said, gazing at his drinks cabinet, wondering if he'd have a tipple once we departed. The old man looked like he could sure do with one right now. I nodded, feeling detached, wondering how much influence Harry might have with the police prosecutor, if any. "I guess it's all about Simon now," I said.

"Simon and you, Sam. Sometimes it's best to expect the worst and hope for the best." If he thought his words were comforting, he was mistaken.

* * *

We drove back to Yaringa, the old man thoughtful and silent, me lost in my own head. Reality loomed, approaching at a rapid rate of knots, my fate all but decided. There were a few scenarios for me to consider. One, the judge finds my crime serious enough to send me away for a few years, all my 'bent over a handbasin' fears realised. The end. Two, I get off with a serious warning and if I reoffend, I'll be inside 'bent over a handbasin', done like a dog's dinner. The end. Both of these scenarios had a common, predominant action and a prop: 'bent over a handbasin'! Three, I get off scot-free with nothing more than a slap over the wrists, and I'm a free man. No handbasins involved! End of story. I wondered if Harry could really swing something like that.

"I wouldn't have a clue how things are going to pan out, Sam," the old man said, interrupting my thoughts.

"Nor me, Dad," I replied, glancing at him only to see his face still carried a significant worry frown. "There's nothin' much y' can do about it, Dad, 'cept meet with the barrister 'n discuss our options." The old man always worried excessively about things he had no control over, so this was a real test for him. Sure, I was worried as hell about going inside, but if I spent every day in that state, I'd be a mess.

"I suppose you're right, Sam. I can't believe how calm you are about all of this. Why didn't you just come home?"

"Oh, come on, Dad! We both know that wasn't a real option. I can see the news headlines: *Young Kiwi in Drug Scandal Disappears Off Radar!* They'd keep the case open 'n Interpol 'd come in t' play, they could extradite me if they felt my case warrant'd it. I've read heaps, too many books 'n newspaper articles, about Interpol becomin' involved when countries are harbouring wanted suspects and criminals."

"You're not a criminal, Sam," the old man interrupted.

"Not in your eyes, but in the eyes of the law I am."

"It's all fiction and movies! You're living in a fantasy world. This is reality here, right here!" He banged his hand on the dashboard to emphasise his point.

"Well, occasionally there are articles in the paper about someone being extradited due t' a crime in another country. Are y' goin' t' tell me that's fiction too?"

"Okay, maybe you're right," he conceded.

"The thing is, Dad, this town has viewed my action as a serious crime. They're treatin' it as a big deal. That's why it wasn't resolved in the Magistrates' Court."

"I see your point." The old man hated arguing with me.

We arrived back at the house and decided it was too hot and sticky to do much more than swim. After cooling off in the sea, I lay down on my towel. The old man had picked his up and was drying himself, which seemed pointless as he'd be cooking again in seconds. He spread his towel out in the same way I had spread mine and proceeded to lie on it.

"Just a few minutes for me, I can't afford to burn," he said. Mum had rammed that home to him like a teacher to a schoolboy. Now he obediently followed that rule of thumb. It was said that Australia and New Zealand had the most intense exposure to ultraviolet rays in the world, something to do with the ozone being thinner in the southern hemisphere. I couldn't handle the sun's heat for more than twenty minutes at a time anyway, after that I'd rather be in the shade reading a book, so it wasn't really a problem for me.

I must've nodded off for a few minutes, and I awoke all sweaty. My face stuck to the towel as I lifted it off. I had to peel the fabric away from my skin. The old man lay there sound asleep, a light snore resonating from his nostrils.

"Hello, Sam." Sarah's familiar voice filled my ears as footsteps squelched in the sand behind me. I rolled over onto my back to face her. She was topless as usual, wearing the most revealing bikini bottom.

"Hi, Sarah. How are y'?"

The old man stirred.

"I'm good and you? Is this your father? Do I get introduced?"

The old man stirred again and turned over onto his back, making a few grunting noises as he slowly woke from his slumber.

"I must've dozed off," he said as he looked around with sleepy, unfocused eyes.

"We both did," I said.

He noticed Sarah and his attention was suddenly there. "Are you going to introduce me, Sam?" he asked, all alert now.

"This is Sarah. Sarah, meet m' dad."

The old man was giving her the up and down treatment, failing to give her eye contact as his eyes were fixed upon her breasts.

"Pleased to meet you, Mr Gorzman."

"Call me Henry." He stood up rather ungraciously and shook her hand, trying desperately to keep his gaze above her breasts.

"You have a wonderful son." I wished she would just go. I didn't want the old man to know anything about her or Harry.

"How do you know Sam?" asked the old man.

"We live in this village and it's not very big, as you will have noticed."

"Yes, it is a small town … and I suppose it wouldn't take long to get to know people."

"Sarah is the local police officer's wife, Dad," I decided to say.

"Oh really?" His bushy eyebrows involuntarily raised and lowered. "I think I should be getting out of this sun," he said, adjusting himself on his towel.

"It's been hot today, hasn't it? Hotter than usual, I think," said Sarah, standing there like a sun goddess, my father transfixed. "I'd better be going too, not long until the kids will need picking up from school."

"Nice meeting you, Sarah," he responded, snapping out of his trance.

"Bye, Sarah," I said, standing to shake the sand off my towel.

"Bye, Sam. Nice meeting you, Mr Gorzman."

"Henry, please," the old man reminded her.

"Of course, Henry."

As we walked back to the house the old man started his quiz session. "So how do you come to know the local police officer's wife, Sam?"

"If y' really want t' know, her husband, Harry, is the officer who arrested me."

"But I don't see how that would mean you're acquainted with her." We crossed the main road, passing the shops near the bowling green.

"Look, do y' fancy a coffee or a cold drink?"

"I haven't got any money on me."

"Don't worry." I led him across the road to the burger bar. There were tables outside with bright yellow, Lipton Tea-branded umbrellas offering some shade. "Coffee or a cold drink?" I reiterated.

"Maybe a tea."

"Sure. Grab a table 'n I'll order it."

Costa, the man who owned the joint, was an unhealthy-looking, overweight Greek with classic dark rings under his eyes. His face was jowly, and he wore white singlets that were always covered in grease and filth, invariably drenched in his own sweat.

"Sammy, my boy. How are you? What can I do for you today?" he asked, greeting me with his usual enthusiasm.

"Hi, Costa. I don't have any cash on me, can I drop it by later?"

"No problem. Who's the gentleman with you?" He gestured to my dad.

"That's the old man," I told him.

"Your old man!" He laughed, big and hearty. "He doesn't look old to me, Sammy. You shouldn't be calling him that."

"Well, y' know, it's just a term 'f endearment."

"Not where I come from, my friend." I liked Costa. He was a

passionate man despite his bad health, always welcoming, always enthusiastic with his customers.

"For m' father then, can I have a pot 'f tea, 'n f' m'self, I think I'm gonna have one 'f those smoothies with banana that y' make so well."

"Consider it done! Have a seat, I'll bring it out to you."

"Champion."

I left him to make our drinks and joined the old man at the table he'd chosen, which was shaded by an umbrella secured in a hole in the middle of the table.

"So … you were saying," the old man said, anticipation in his voice.

"Well, it's a really weird thing, Dad." I shifted, feeling uneasy as I considered what I was about to tell him. In some detail, I explained to my father the situation with Harry and his personal interest in me.

"Why would a cop, who has arrested and charged you, then turn around and invite you round for a drink, and for dinner, and to look after his children?" my father asked. "It doesn't add up." The old man scratched his head as if expecting some revelation. "I don't understand his motivation."

Costa arrived puffing and panting with the tea and smoothie on a tray. "There you go, Sammy." He placed the tray on the table and turned to my old man. "So, you're Sam's father?"

"I am."

"I'm Costa," he said, reaching out his large hand. "And I'm very pleased to meet you."

"Henry. Pleased to meet you too," said the old man as he shook Costa's hand.

"You have a great son," he said, nodding his oversized head in my direction. "You should be proud of him." Costa might think differently if he knew about my brush with the law. "Enjoy your tea." He shuffled his large frame back towards the kitchen with the empty tray.

"Cheers, Costa. See y' later," I called out.

"No doubt." He waved his hand dismissively in the air.

The old man poured the tea then added some milk. I took a long sip of my banana smoothie. It was cold and sweet, just what the doctor ordered. The old man had gone silent.

"Ahh, good tea," he eventually said. "A very odd story, Sam. I can see why you would have gone to Harry's place, you had nothing to lose. Nothing ventured, nothing gained."

"I'm glad y' see it that way," I said, sucking loudly at the last bit of my smoothie.

"I wonder if we should tell the barrister about this situation with Harry?"

"Ah, no! I'm not makin' this any kookier than it already is." I shook my head adamantly.

"But he may be able to use it to your advantage, Sam."

I leaned forward and eyeballed the old man. "Dad, I'm not involving Harry in this. There's too much at risk doing that. Let Harry do what he can in his way." As much as I feared going inside, I wasn't interested in entangling Harry in the web of my defence. I didn't want to be seen aligning myself with the cops to get off. It could just as easily backfire on me. The old man looked at me with a frown as he tipped his teacup back, draining it into his mouth, then gazed at the inside of his cup the way a reader of tea leaves would.

We finished our drinks and headed back to the house. Once inside, we made ham sandwiches. The old man always needed to eat at certain times of the day, or he became grumpy. He told me it had something to do with his blood sugar levels. Opa was the same, so it ran in the family.

The drone of an infomercial carried from the lounge where Tim was firmly seated, filling his mind with stimulating images of scantily dressed blondes promoting a 'Build your Abs' product. He probably snuck off to his bedroom afterwards to fantasise about them.

The rest of the week with the old man went by in similar fashion. Sometimes he'd travel into town with me in the Valiant, other times I'd hitch and be back by mid-morning. Sometimes Harry was at the cop shop but most of the time it was the new cop. I hadn't seen Frank in a long time. The old sarge was always loitering somewhere in the background, waiting for a quiet moment, no doubt, to whip one of his well-stained mags from its hiding place so he could salivate over the Playgirl of the Month.

33

Falling

The days continued to be unreasonably hot and there was no sign of a let up in temperature or any prospect of rain. The countryside had become a dust bowl, void of greenery, everything scorched and dead, even the hardy eucalyptus trees looked browner than usual. Ponds were drying up with scant amounts of water forming murky puddles on the cracked earth. Farmers were selling or relocating their stock, and those who could afford it were buying in feed to prolong the inevitable. On most days that I hitched to town, I would see a brown snake or two lying coiled up beside the road, baking quietly in the sun, uninterested in me as I warily walked by. I was curious about them coming out onto the road. It appeared they enjoyed the heat of the tar-sealed surface.

I was hitching back to Yaringa again, two days before I was expected in court. As I stood by the roadside, several cars passed, followed by a police car, which pulled up in front of me. For a moment I thought it was Frank, then the window unwound and there was Harry looking back at me.

"Jump in. I'm goin' t' Yaringa." I hesitated for a moment, as I didn't like to be seen conversing with cops in public, and with Harry in particular. People talked and I didn't want Bruce to have a reason to do something irrational. It was bad enough seeing him in my dreams most nights. I climbed in reluctantly and Harry pulled swiftly away from the kerb as if he sensed my discomfort.

"How y' been keepin', Sam?"

"Alright," I replied.

"So y' dad's here now," he stated more than asked. "Sarah said she bumped int' you 'n y' dad on the beach."

"Yeah."

"Nervous about Tuesday?"

"I'd be lyin' if I said I wasn't." I tried to make myself comfortable by fidgeting in the seat, and I wriggled my arse around as if that might make a difference. I pulled the sun visor down, pretending the sun was in my eyes, but in truth I was worried someone coming the other way might see me.

"It's only natural that you would be."

What the fuck would you know? It's not you who's on trial, Harry.

"Would y' come f' dinner t'night, Sam?" Harry asked nonchalantly.

"T'night? I can't Harry! It's too close t' Tuesday, 'n besides, the old man's here. I can't leave him t' put up with Ted 'n Val on his own f' a night," I lied, desperately trying to find an excuse.

"I understand, but if y' could, it would be good, as this may be our last opportunity t' have y' over."

"What's that s'pose' t' mean?"

"What I mean is … Look, whatever I say it's goin' t' sound wrong." He was right about that.

"Any more word on who the judge is, or what he's like?" I asked, scanning the road for Kombis.

"He's new t' this area 'n unknown, hails from Sydney," replied Harry, scratching his head.

"I guess none 'f that means anythin' at the moment. I'll try 'n keep an open mind."

"That's right," said Harry as he drove through the main street of Yaringa, stopping to drop me off on the corner of the street behind the bowling club. "It'd be good if y' could make it, Sam," he said, looking at me earnestly.

I shrugged my shoulders and opened the door. "I'll try." I let out a long sigh.

"Otherwise, I'll see y' in court on Tuesday, 'n good luck for the day." He reached out to shake my hand.

"See y' Tuesday," I said, and extracted myself from the car, ignoring his gesture and closing the door. I stood there and watched Harry drive off, realising that my feelings for Harry were more complex than I cared to acknowledge.

***

The next morning I had breakfast with the old man. Ted and Val had already left for work, and we sat down to cereal and milk, neither of us with much to say. The night before had been an ordeal — having dinner with Val and Ted and listening to life according to Val. Ted had become bored and somehow managed to slip away to the bowling club. Tim had escaped to the telly, leaving me to sit with the old man as we politely listened to Val's distorted take on life. I finally waved the white flag and retreated to the caravan where I stupidly allowed myself to feel guilty that I didn't make the effort to get to Harry's for dinner. The *Harry and Sarah Show*, though, was way too complex for me to continue dealing with.

The old man always liked an egg for breakfast. He reckoned it set him up for the day. So I put a couple of eggs on to soft boil. I was aware he was feeling anxious this morning, as he wasn't saying much, a sure sign he had things on his mind. We were meeting the barrister at ten o'clock. There was a twisted knot in my stomach, and I couldn't eat my cereal. I tipped the remains in the scrap bucket and rinsed my plate in the sink.

We had time for a walk on the beach before we needed to leave for town. I hoped the walk might get the old man talking or at least relax him a little before we met the barrister. He stopped suddenly, looking exasperated and removed his hat to wipe his brow with his forearm.

"I really don't know how these Ozzies do it!"

"Do what, Dad?"

"This heat is unrelenting," he said, placing his hat back on his head.

"They're acclimatised to it. It's normal f' them."

"I suppose you're right." He cleared his throat as if making space for what was to follow. "Sam, I've been talking with people in Sydney, looking at an option for the worst-case scenario. There's a centre up there for young offenders, for those involved in what's considered more serious crimes," he said, then paused.

"So y' think m' offence is considered a more serious crime?" I asked, filling the space.

"It's not what I think, Sam, it's what the law dictates that counts. So hear me out."

"Sorry," I apologised. I kicked at the sand and poked it with my toes, watching it change colour as I burrowed deeper with my foot and the sand cascaded over it.

"The periodic detention centre I found out about, runs for thirty-six hours on the weekends. Offenders go in late Friday afternoon and are released again on the Sunday morning. Their time is spent doing rehabilitation workshops," he explained as we resumed walking down the beach.

"Whatever that means!" I snarled, feeling totally unwilling to consider this place as an option.

"They also do creative projects such as art and writing. I visited the people who run it. They seem like really good folk, and it has a very high success rate. Something like over ninety per cent of the young people never reoffend."

"So what are y' tellin' me, Dad?" I stopped in my tracks and stood facing him with my arms outstretched, the palms of my hands facing upwards.

"Sam, I'm not telling you, I'm just saying there's another option if you would just listen."

"I am listenin'," I snapped.

"If things look bad there is a better option than going to prison."

"I don't want t' consider 'if' right now, Dad." Tears came as I stood in the middle of the beach. The old man stepped forward and held me as tears spilled down my face onto his shoulder. The isolation, the loneliness and emptiness I had felt for so long overwhelmed me now. The tough 'she'll be right' façade had crumbled badly in the past twelve hours, leaving me exposed and raw. I realised the old man was crying too, and I pulled away to look at him. Our tear-stained faces broke into smiles and we both burst into infectious laughter.

"What a couple of silly billies!" exclaimed the old man. We continued up the beach, wiping tears from our eyes, the heated discussion abandoned now and replaced by the spontaneity of this lighter moment.

* * *

I borrowed the Hemi Valiant to drive to town as I didn't fancy hitching with the old man, nor did I want to risk being picked up by Bruce. Our first stop was the cop shop. It felt strange to think that after six months this was it, my last day of reporting. The sarge was at the counter, dealing with some elderly lady's complaint about noise in her neighbourhood the previous night. He appeared more interested in what was under his fingernails as the old biddy rabbited on about how loud and awful it had been.

The sarge caught sight of me and shot a menacing look. "There's someone else waitin', love. Like I said, next time ring us at the time of the disturbance 'n we'll send someone over."

"Alright then, but you jolly well better." She turned with walking stick in hand and hobbled out, scoffing at me as she passed.

"What d' you want?" the sarge snarled as I approached the counter.

"Just come t' report f' the last time," I announced, grinning at him.

"That's right, t'morrow's the big day for y'," he said, opening the book for me to sign. "Y'll be goin' down." He grinned to reveal his stained, yellow teeth. "Which I might add is nothin' less than y' deserve."

"Y're the one who should be goin' away," I said as I initialed the book. "Y're a sicko!"

"Why y' cheeky bloody prick. I'm goin' t' have y' f' that." He lifted the hinged wooden bench on the right side of the counter.

"See y'," I said, starting to walk out.

"Y' come back here, y' cheeky prick! I haven't ticked y' off yet f' reportin'!"

I backed into something solid and realised the something was someone as their arms wrapped around me, then there was a voice. "What's goin' on here?"

Harry! His arms remained around my shoulders as the sarge came at me.

"This little prick was givin' me an earful 'f abuse b'fore y' arrived."

"And what might've provoked such an outburst?" probed Harry.

"Nothin' really. I was just checkin' him off 'n he ..."

"Y' lyin'! Y' said that I'd be goin' away tomorrow 'n it was nothin' less than I deserved."

"I get the picture," said Harry, releasing me from his hold. "That wasn't very thoughtful of y' was it, Sarge? This young man has his day in court t'morrow, 'n that's where his fate will be decided. Not here and not by us." Harry winked at me. "Now on y' way, Sam."

"I just want t' say…"

"On y' way, Sam," he repeated in a firmer voice.

I took heed and left. I found the old man standing on the pavement next to the car.

"I can't decide if it's hotter in or out of the car. What took you so long?"

"An old lady was layin' a complaint."

"I think we've got time for a cup of tea before we meet the barrister. I'm parched," he said, looking at me longingly.

"If y' like, I have a place I go."

I took the old man to my regular. Amanda was, as usual, behind the counter, pouring a pot of tea for a customer and looking as plump and pretty as ever. She took a lot of pride in how she presented herself. Her face lit up when she saw me.

"Hi, Sam. Where've y' been?"

"Been busy lately."

"Oh, so y' haven't been away?"

"No. Can I get a pot 'f tea f' two, thanks?"

"Want anythin' t' eat?" I asked, turning to the old man.

"Maybe a muffin or something," he said, pointing to a plate of savoury muffins on the counter.

"Oh, and a muffin, too. Grab a seat if y' like, Dad." The old man wandered off to the far side of the room to claim a table.

"Y' know, I don't know what happened between you 'n Rose, but there isn't a problem with me, is there?" Amanda asked, taking my money.

"No, there isn't, Amanda. It just didn't seem like a good idea t' come here, as I didn't want t' bump int' Rose after the hundred-questions interrogation I endured last time."

"How's Tim?" she asked, blushing.

"Tim's Tim."

I sat down with the old man. He'd grown increasingly anxious about tomorrow and the appointment with the barrister. There wasn't a lot we could do other than hope the barrister was good at his job. Amanda arrived carrying a tray with the tea and muffin.

"There y' go," she said, putting the tray on the table. "I don't mean t' impose, but y're Sam's father aren't y'?"

"Yes, I am," replied the old man.

"Pleased t' meet y'. Sam's become one 'f our regulars here. We often get talkin'. Y' have a very nice son. Sorry, I won't bother y' further." She blushed, bowed slightly and scurried away.

"I think she might like you, Sam," said the old man.

"Really, do y' think so?" I laughed. "Yeah, I guess she might. Not really my type, Dad."

"She makes a great cup of tea."

"Well, that's a bonus." We broke into laughter. The old man tucked into his muffin while I sipped my tea in contemplation.

We finished our tea and left, but not before I made a point of saying goodbye to Amanda, even though she was busy serving a customer.

"Thanks, Sam. Drop by again soon."

"I will," I replied. I hoped I wouldn't need to.

* * *

We arrived at Dennis's office and were greeted by the same pretty receptionist from the earlier visit. She gave me an exceptionally wonderful smile, but I wasn't in the mood for flirting.

"Dennis will be with you shortly. Please have a seat," she said warmly. We sat down in the seventies-style chairs that had been cheaply reupholstered. A fan was on high speed in the corner, turning from left to right and back again in an even movement, offering some relief.

The old man gruffly whispered to me, "I thought we were meeting the barrister from Sydney."

"We are. Dennis prob'bly wants t' introduce us."

The old man was all fidgety. He kept on crossing and uncrossing his legs. He clasped his hands in awkward positions, then flexed his arms out in front of him, his fingers interwoven and his palms facing outwards as if he were warming up for a physical event of some kind. I picked up a magazine from the coffee table and thumbed through it. The *Woman's Weekly* was a trashy magazine, full of silly photos and brainless stories about some celebrity or other, or about someone turning tragedy into triumph. It was all pretty superficial stuff, but I guess it sold or they wouldn't be publishing it.

Just as I flicked to the end of the magazine, the door to Dennis's office opened. I felt a dryness in the back of my throat and a sudden cramping in my stomach, as if someone were squeezing my insides.

"Sam ... Mr Gorzman, please come in," Dennis said, standing to one side and gesturing with a wave of his arm for us to step into his office. I left the magazine on the chair and the old man and I stood up simultaneously.

"You first," he said, trepidation in his voice. I walked past Dennis and into the office, coming face to face with a man sitting beside Dennis's desk.

The man stood and reached out his hand. "You must be Sam," he said.

"Yes, I am. You must be Simon, pleased t' meet y'."

"Pleased to meet you too, Sam. Simon Cottrell, your barrister." He looked at me with an intense stare, never once breaking eye contact. I always thought the measure of a person was in their ability to engage in eye contact, and he passed the test, instantly putting me at ease.

"And you must be Henry," he said, turning his attention to the old man.

"Yes, that's right. Henry Gorzman, pleased to meet you."

"Very pleased to meet you too," he said, shaking the old man's hand and giving him the same intensive stare.

"Have a seat, gentlemen," said Dennis.

Simon was a well-dressed man, far more dapper than Dennis. He wore a handsome, dark-blue suit clearly bespoke and hot off the dry-cleaners' press. His off-white shirt and broad paisley tie, in deep reds and blues — not so loud that it leapt out at you — was just enough to offset the rest of his attire. He had a youthful face devoid of lines or frown marks, and I picked him for being in his mid-forties, similar in age to the old man. A good head of mousey blond hair, carefully styled, indicated he was a regular at the hairdressers. His eyes were bluish green in colour and commanded respect, yet there was a cheeky twinkle dancing within his serious gaze. I liked him.

"Okay, we may as well launch in at the deep end," began Simon. "Sam, you've already pleaded guilty to the charge." It wasn't a question, but I answered that I had. He looked thoughtful for a moment.

"I have to point out that drugs are not viewed in a good light in this country and drug-related offences incur harsh penalties. To recap, your offence, originally of 'Possession', has had the offence 'Intention to Supply' added because a large enough quantity was found in your possession."

"Of course," interrupted Dennis, "Simon is going to give you the worst-case scenario."

"That's true," Simon said, smiling. "I don't intend to alarm you both, but we do have to bear it in mind."

"What is a likely outcome?" the old man asked, looking rather pale.

"Since we're not defending this case, we are working on presenting Sam in the best light and on emphasising the extenuating circumstances that need to be considered," articulated Simon, rolling his fancy ink pen around in his hands while looking directly at me.

"You have all the character reference letters I sent you?" questioned the old man.

"Yes, I have," Simon replied. "I'm not sure what else I can say at present, but I'm pleased to have had the opportunity to meet you both. Do you have a good suit to wear tomorrow, Sam?"

"Yep! Special delivery from New Zealand," I replied, smiling and feeling strangely lighthearted.

"Okay. That's great. It was nice to meet you both. We'll meet again on the steps of the courthouse tomorrow at ten o'clock sharp. I'm not sure of the schedule for the day, as it's not finalised until the actual morning, so it can be a long day of waiting around for our case to be called. So be patient tomorrow and bring something to read." With that he stood up and Dennis, like a jack-in-the-box, responded as if the lid had been lifted.

Then it was our turn to stand. It was like a mini Mexican wave, and I almost expected Simon and Dennis to sit down again. Instead, Simon stepped forward and reached across the desk to shake the old man's hand.

"Good to meet you," he said reassuringly. He then turned to shake my hand. "Sam, get a good night's sleep and I'll see you tomorrow." And, as if not wanting to miss out on the handshaking session, Dennis stepped forward to have his turn.

"I won't be in court tomorrow," he told us. "There's no real need for me to be down there. You're in very good hands with Simon. I wish you all the best for tomorrow. God willing, we'll get the result we all want."

Walking out of Dennis's office onto the street, we were hit by a wall of heat so intense it dried the back of my mouth as I breathed in.

"I need a swim badly," gasped the old man, loosening the tie on his shirt. We made our way down the street to where we'd parked the car. Inside it was like an oven, the sun beating down on the dark upholstery had heated it up so much that it was too hot to touch. Lowering the windows offered no reprieve because the oppressive heat filled the car. It wasn't until we were out on the road that the air began to circulate inside, forced in through the open windows.

"That's starting to feel a bit cooler," said the old man. "What did you think of the barrister?"

"He seems pretty slick, like he knows his stuff," I replied.

"I thought he seemed pretty good too. I've only spoken to him on the phone before."

"I'd rather him than Dennis."

"I can see why you'd say that," he said, having a chuckle to himself as if he'd said something funny.

* * *

I parked the car in the driveway, and we quickly changed into swimming shorts. We grabbed our towels and headed for the beach. There was a light onshore breeze blowing, making it slightly more bearable to be in the sun. The sets of breaking waves were holding up nicely, and there were a few more people on the beach than there had been recently, perhaps a late wave of childless holidaymakers. We dropped our towels halfway down the beach and continued to the sea, where we waded in up to our thighs. The old man dived into the first wave that threatened to take him out. I was slower on the uptake and got caught in white turbulence as it broke around me. The waves were bigger than they had first appeared. I became immersed in bodysurfing, happy to forget about the world for a while.

"There must be a good storm somewhere out at sea," I remarked to my father, who nodded in agreement.

After our swim we headed back to the house for a light lunch before the old man took his nap and I disappeared to the caravan. As I lay on the bed, my thoughts wandered, and I found myself thinking about Erika. She seemed a distant memory now. I suddenly missed her deeply. I wished I could feel her soft skin next to mine, hold her, smell her, kiss her.

The next thing I was aware of was a loud banging on the caravan door that woke me from my dream.

"Hang on … Hang on!" I called out in a hoarse mumble. Before I could reach the handle, the door opened and there was Brigitte, climbing into the caravan dressed in a green bikini top with a towel wrapped around her.

"I came to see y' cos I know it's y' big day in court tomorrow, 'n y' haven't been at the pub lately. I've just been t' the beach f' a swim before work. Thought I might catch y'."

"Hey, come in. It's great t' see y'," I said, meaning it. My eyes gravitated effortlessly to her bountiful breasts as she sat herself on the end of my bed.

"How've y' been?"

"Not bad," I replied, propping myself up on an elbow.

"Are y' nervous?" she asked as she shuffled further up the bed.

"No. Strangely, I feel calm about it now."

"The calm b'fore the storm, huh," she quipped, smiling and looking into my eyes. She leaned forward and kissed my cheek, then my lips. I responded too urgently, biting at her lips and pushing my mouth up hard against hers, but she met me with equal passion. Her hands were on my buttocks and down the back of my thighs. My urge was to let go, take her breasts and feast. Then I stopped.

"Brigitte, I can't do this right now. My father's here 'n he's upstairs, he could be down here any minute. I'm sorry."

"Hey, it's okay," she said, looking sincere.

"Would y' come back t'night after work?"

"Sure," she replied. "It won't be a late one t'night." We kissed lingeringly before she pulled away. "I'll see y' after work then." And she was gone.

* * *

Val cooked the evening meal. "Everyone eat up and enjoy," she commanded. "Sam, we hope it all goes well for you tomorrow. I also hope you appreciate everything that has been done for you." It was typical of Val to need to be acknowledged.

"Thank you, Val. I do appreciate everyone's support. It's very generous of y' t' take me int' y' home the way y' have," I said in almost a mocking tone as I raised my half-full glass of cheap Ozzie Chateau Cardboard in a show of appreciation.

Ted followed suit. "I'd just like to say that I hope tomorrow goes well and may you be able to return home at the end of it."

"Hear! Hear!" chimed the old man. "And if I may add, I would like to say thank you for being able and willing to offer your support and a place for Sam to stay during this ordeal. I'm sure he has learnt a lot about the human spirit and kindness. I thank you both with all my heart."

Val beamed from ear to ear, soaking up the acclaim as if she had single-handedly rescued me from the brink. "Thank you, Henry, for that." I wanted to vomit on my plate.

418

As dinner progressed, the conversation around the table became stilted and awkward. Tim remained silent and I was uninterested, distracted by my own thoughts. The old man wolfed his meal, seeking comfort in the food. Val and Ted maintained their babble. There were all these people around the table, but no one was taking any notice of anyone else, like a film montage, the images all integrated and layered over one another, each person in their own private bubble.

Tim finished eating and left the table, putting his empty plate on the kitchen bench. I excused myself and did the same. Tim made his way back to the comfort of his armchair and the telly. I flopped into the other armchair to blob out, abandoning the old man to contend with Val and Ted alone.

"Tomorrow's the day," Tim said, out of the blue.

"Yep," I said, looking at him, his eyes fixed on the telly, his face void of expression, still hidden behind his overgrown beard.

"Judgement day."

"Yep."

"To prison or not."

"Yep." I left the room. I didn't need the wind up. "Think I'm off t' bed," I said, walking into the dining room.

"It's so early still," said Val.

"Might go f' a small walk on the beach first."

"Would you mind if I join you?" the old man asked.

"Nah, come along if y' like."

He pushed himself up out of his chair and it scraped noisily on the floor like fingernails on a blackboard. "Excuse me," he said. "Thank you for a lovely meal, Val. Perhaps I could dry the dishes when I get back."

"Don't be silly, go and enjoy your walk, Henry."

* * *

The sun hadn't dropped behind the hills yet, and the sea was a smooth deep blue with sets of waves rolling in constantly, breaking in white tumultuous foam just short of the shore.

"So how are you feeling?" the old man enquired cautiously.

"As good as can be expected, I s'pose. I dunno really. One moment I feel hope, the next despair. How should I feel? Don't y' think they just wanted t' put the frighteners on me f' a while? I mean Harry seems t' think that things will work out. I'm the little fish. Bruce is the one they want. He should never have sent me off with that stuff in the first place, 'specially with Cosmo, knowing what I know about him now."

"You've lost me. What do you mean?"

"Don't worry, Dad. It's all irrelevant now. We talked and walked our way down the length of the beach. The sun had dropped behind the hills at the back of the lagoon, casting everything in silhouette. Dark shadows and shapes created eerie images on the dunes, the lagoon shining black like a polished stone. The water was calm except for the odd fish breaking the surface, creating small circular ripples that faded to nothing. The heat of the day was still noticeable, but bearable now in the early evening. We turned and strolled back along the tracks we'd made coming up the beach.

By the time we reached the house it was completely dark except for the lights coming from the windows of houses on the hills.

"I'm not comin' inside, Dad. Think I'm just gonna hit the pillow, maybe read f' a bit."

"I understand," he said. "I hope you manage to sleep."

"Yeah I hope so too, Dad."

"Don't imagine I'll sleep too well either. Goodnight, son," he whispered, wrapping his arms around me in a brief embrace. "See you in the morning."

"Y' will." I stood outside the caravan and watched him walk up the stairs, open the door and disappear into the house. I stayed there for a moment, looking up at the night sky. The stars were out in force and the night was clear, so incredibly clear, just a mass of magical, shimmering lights, a carpet of jewels twinkling in the night. I wondered if my fate was already written somewhere out there in the stars. I put my fingers on the handle of the caravan door and opened it. Stepping in, my hand floundered for the light switch.

"Jesus, Brigitte, I wasn't expecting y' t' be here yet! Fuck, y' gave me a fright!"

"Sorry. I finished work early. There wasn't much happenin' so I asked if I could go. You weren't here so I made myself at home. I figured y'd be here soon." She propped herself up in bed with the sheet loosely wrapped around her, gave me one of her big smiles, and patted the bed like I was her pet dog.

"Look, I've got t' get ready f' tomorrow. It's such a big day. I wasn't expectin' y' t' be here yet."

"Hey, y' just do whatever it is y' need t', baby. I'll be here when y' done."

"Look, I'm not y' baby, right."

Her eyes went to the floor. "Sorry, babe," she said, looking mildly offended.

"It's okay," I said, feeling bad for a moment. "Just don't talk t' me like I'm a baby, I don't like it," I said, opening the wardrobe door. I reached in and lifted out the suit Mum and Oma had bought for me.

"Y' don't need t' get shitty with me, Sam."

"Maybe not. It's just that I've got a lot goin' on in m' head. I've no idea what's gonna happ'n t'morrow, so it's quite a big deal. They might decide t' lock me up."

I laid the suit down on the spare bed, feeling a tinge of despair and a familiar tightening in my stomach. I went back to the wardrobe to find the black shoes that went with it.

"They wouldn't lock y' up f' havin' a few drugs on y', would they?"

I found the shoes and removed them from the wardrobe, checking that they still looked polished. "You bet they would!"

"Gee, Sam, I didn't realise it was so serious."

"Well, 'f course y' didn't cos I've never really told y' about it!" I looked at the shoes and decided they were still shiny enough. I wouldn't have to polish them.

"Sam, do y' want me t' come t' court with y' t'morrow?" she asked, all sprawled out on the bed, breasts revealed above the sheet as if she expected me to drop everything and join her.

"No, m' father's here t' do that. I just want t' keep things simple, uncomplicated, y' know." I sat down on the bed beside her and looked her in the eyes. As she sat up to meet me the sheet fell away.

"Come t' bed, Sam," Brigitte whispered ever so softly in my ear, and there was a sweetness in her voice that softened me. She pulled me into her and lay back, taking me down with her. I lifted the sheet and slipped in beside her.

34

D-Day

I woke to loud knocking on the caravan door. "It's time to get ready, Sam." It was the old man's voice. I sat bolt upright. Brigitte stirred and rolled over next to me.

"Okay," I called out as I checked my clock which read seven fifty-five. "I'll be up shortly," I added sleepily.

"Don't be long," he sounded anxious. I listened to his footsteps fade away while stretching my arms out in an effort to wake up, feeling surprised that I had fallen asleep so easily in Brigitte's arms.

"Must've fallen asleep, I've still got m' clothes on."

"Yeah, y' did," Brigitte replied with her sleepy-looking eyes and her bird's nest hairdo.

"I've got t' get ready." I leaned over and kissed her, and she pulled me in close. I withdrew from her, knowing I had to go. I wrapped a towel around myself, needing to wash and freshen up, and exited the caravan, heading for the shower.

Black crows perched high in the eucalyptus trees greeted me with harsh squawks, and a kookaburra responded with its own rendition. The sky was a hazy blue, the sun was well and truly up. It would be yet another hot, sweltering day. I turned the shower on and stepped under the spray, unbothered by the initial cold water, and relaxed as the water warmed up and pelted down on my face, washing away any remaining sleep as I breathed in and out slowly. I was convincing myself to remain calm for the day.

Back in the caravan, I dressed quickly, slipping on fresh underwear and pulling my dress trousers on. The belt was still in place from my Magistrates' Court appearance, and the crease down the front of the trousers was still perfect. I lifted the inoffensive, cream-coloured cotton shirt off the bed and slipped my arms into the sleeves, tucking the shirt into my trousers. I stood there for a moment feeling strange, all dressed up as if I were about to head off to church. I sat on the bed and pulled on black cotton socks.

"Are y' scared, Sam?" asked Brigitte, sitting up in bed.

"I dunno. I'm tryin' to feel relaxed. Guess I've been waitin' f' today f' so fuckin' long it doesn't feel real, but I imagine I'll be worried once I'm in court." I slipped my left foot into one of the black shoes.

"Sorry. Didn't mean t' get y' worried about it," she responded as she wrapped the sheet awkwardly around herself.

"Hey, y' didn't," I said, lacing up a shoe.

"D' y' think y'll be back tonight?" I saw the concern in her eyes.

"No idea, but I hope so." I laced up the other shoe and stood up. "How do I look?"

"Y' look like y're off t' some posh office job, all swanked up like that, or like one 'f those Bible bash'rs who go door t' door," she said, trying to force a laugh.

"Well, that's a pass then." I grinned, and throwing myself at her on the bed, I kissed her smack on the lips. "See y' soon, eh? Oh, 'n maybe it's better t' wait till y' hear both cars drive off before you exit the caravan. Ted 'n Val will probably leave before us, then the old man 'n I will take the Valiant."

"Okay, I'll wait. Good luck." She looked serene with the sun shining across her face through a crack in the curtains. I opened the door and stepped out into the morning sunlight.

As I climbed the stairs to the house, I could hear Val's voice in full flight. It was enough to make me want to turn around and walk back down, except that the old man would be fretting.

Val was yelling at Ted. "It's time to go! I've got an appointment this morning, so get a hurry on, will you." Ted never hurried, even less so when it was demanded of him.

"If you stopped your bleating, I might be able to concentrate on what I need to do to get out of here," he responded gruffly, without raising his voice.

She caught sight of me. "Sam, how can you be so casual when you're due in court at ten? Your father's worried sick." She was like a screaming skull, her skin taut across her face, nostrils flaring, her intense blue eyes glaring.

"There's ample time," I said. "I'm not goin' t' put extra pressure on m'self this mornin', thank you." I felt pleased, almost smug.

"What's happened to the youth of today?" she uttered, giving me her look of disapproval, rolling her eyes around in her head. "Good luck today anyway." She hugged me. I remained as rigid as an ironing board.

"Thanks."

Ted appeared in the hallway, briefcase in hand, ready to face the day. "Sam, I hope the day is favourable." He looked me directly in the eye and I knew he really cared.

"Thanks, Ted." We shook hands. "Thanks for everything."

"You're welcome." He opened the door onto the balcony and headed down the stairs. I wondered if he had a bottle of whisky stashed in his office desk for medicinal purposes, required after his morning drive with Val.

I found the old man sitting at the dining table, eating breakfast cereal. "Mornin', Dad."

"Morning, Sam," he mumbled through a mouthful of food. "You'd better get some breakfast in you. It could be a long day."

I walked into the kitchen and checked the water level in the jug. It was half full, and I flicked the switch on. "Don't think I'm really up t' eatin', think I'll just have a cup 'f tea," I said.

"You're crazy, Sam! You won't last the day in court if you don't eat," he said, getting all animated, as if breakfast would make a difference.

"I'll be fine, I'll take an apple 'n buy somethin' if I have t'."

"I'm going to make some sandwiches, so I guess I can make a couple for you. Okay?"

"Sure," I said, not wanting to continue the conversation. The truth was my stomach was so knotted with anxiety I couldn't have eaten even if I wanted to. There was no way I was going to get food down and keep it down. I made myself a cup of tea instead and sat at the table opposite the old man who was sawing into the top of a boiled egg with great urgency.

"How are you feeling this morning?" he asked, eyeballing me after he succeeded in removing the top off his egg.

"Okay. A little anxious, I guess."

"Not surprising," he responded, dipping a teaspoon into the egg. I liked my yolk soft and runny. His appeared hard and had that sickly, mustardy look about it. He put the egg into his mouth, his jaw muscles flexing each time he chewed.

"What about you?" I enquired. He took a bite of his buttered toast and I found myself focusing on his jaw muscles as he masticated the mouthful slowly.

"Anxious, I admit. I've never experienced something like this before." He spooned more egg into his mouth and stared at me, his eyes slightly glazed, unfocused, staring ahead.

"Neither have I, 'n I don't want t' ever experience something like this again," I responded in a matter-of-fact way.

"No, I shouldn't imagine you would." His eyes refocused back on me. "We've just got to deal with it now and hope for the best outcome." He shovelled the last of the egg into his mouth.

"Well, I guess it's time t' hit the road." I gulped down the remaining tea and went to the kitchen sink to rinse the cup, leaving it upside down on the bench to drain.

"You seem surprisingly calm, Sam."

"Yeah well, what else can I do?" I wasn't about to tell him the knot in my stomach was so tight I might be sick any minute, that my throat was so dry no amount of liquid would hydrate it.

"I'll just get my jacket," he said, brushing past me, heading for the bedroom. He had donned a suit and tie for the occasion. Dad returned from the bedroom sporting a navy-blue, mid-weave jacket that matched his trousers and brightly coloured paisley tie.

"Ain't we the right duo?" I said, admiring my father's attire. 'It's goin' t' be a pig 'f a day in the courthouse. It's already hot outside 'n it's not even nine o'clock."

"Were you talking to me?" he asked, struggling with his collar.

"Yeah, I was just sayin' it's goin' t' be hot in the courthouse. Here I'll sort that," I said, coming up behind him and turning the collar down to sit evenly on the contour of his neck.

"Every day's hot here."

"Yeah, I guess. Are y' ready?"

"I am now," he said, patting his pockets to check he had everything he needed. "I was going to make sandwiches, but I guess it's too late."

"Yup. Let's go. We can buy something in town. You can slip down the road even if I can't." I gestured toward the front door, noticing Tim was nowhere to be seen. There was nothing unusual about that as he seldom rose before ten o'clock.

Tim had given us free range with the car since the old man had been over, for which I was grateful. *Sure y' can borrow the car, but y' old man'll have t' drive it home afterwards. Y'll be goin' inside*, he'd said, grinning mischievously.

I backed the car down the drive and out onto the road, fully aware that Brigitte was still in the caravan. I wondered if I'd ever see her again. I noticed a curtain lift slightly and thought I saw her eyes peering out. The old man was staring into space again, so he hadn't noticed. I tooted the horn.

"What was that for?" he asked, snapping back to reality.

"Just t' see if y'd notice, y' look so far away."

"Do I?"

"I was givin' Tim a wake up 'n a farewell at the same time."

"Oh, I see." He continued to gaze trance-like out the window.

"Y' know, if things go badly, you'll have to drive this beast home tonight, Dad," I said. He looked at me with his soft, blue-grey eyes, full of deep concern.

"Really?" he said. I shrugged as I put the gear shift into drive and accelerated hard, the spinning wheels spitting gravel as I steered the car fully onto the main road. Then I headed up the hill.

* * *

The drive to Wodyn was mostly in silence. Neither of us had much to say, our minds preoccupied with what the day might bring. I parked the car down a side street, so we didn't have to pay the parking meter fee every few hours. From there it was a short walk to the courthouse.

"I might buy a paper," the old man said as we passed a newsagent. "Want anything?"

"Yeah, a magazine could be good. I'll come with y'."

He was fidgety, his hands in and out of his pockets as we walked the short distance to the store. Once inside, I made my way to the magazine

428

stand, eyes searching for something appealing. Nothing leapt out at me, and I picked up a sailing magazine. I liked yachts, having sailed them as a teenager, and it seemed like the best choice. I went to the counter where the old man was and gave him the magazine, which he paid for along with his newspaper.

Approaching the courthouse, I felt the knotting in my stomach intensify and I needed a bathroom. It was as though someone were reaching inside me and twisting my guts. I was sure I would be sick any minute. As we climbed the steps leading to the entrance of the courthouse, I saw a man waving at us. It was Simon.

"Dad, y'll have t' cover f' me, I need t' go t' the bathroom."

"Right, off you go. I'll explain."

I bounded up the stairs two steps at a time. I made it into a cubicle and leaned over the bowl, holding back my tie so I wouldn't throw up on it. It was more of a dry retch than a proper chunder. I washed my face thoroughly and checked myself in the mirror to make sure I was looking fairly decent. My face looked pale and full of worry. *Come on, Sam, pull y'self together! Y've got the whole day t' get through.* I slapped my cheeks to invigorate myself.

On the verandah of the courthouse, I saw the old man with Simon and made my way over.

"Sam, are you alright?" Simon asked, seeming genuinely concerned.

"I guess so, just a bit 'f anxiety."

"Understandable," he said reassuringly. "We can either wait outside until we are called or sit inside and observe proceedings. My guess is we won't be up until later in the day."

"Think I'll sit out here if that's okay. Don't really fancy watchin'."

"Of course." Simon gestured for us to sit down on one of the wooden benches placed against the exterior wall of the covered courthouse verandah.

"I'll sit out here too," said the old man, sitting down on the bench next to me.

"That's fine. I've got a few things to do, so I'll be inside if you need me," replied Simon.

The old man passed me my magazine. "Are you alright?" he asked.

"As good as I'm goin' t' be. It's all a bit nerve-rackin'. I've had t' wait f' this day f' so long, 'n now it's finally here I feel overwhelmed. I mean, this afternoon they might send me off t' prison."

"You're not going to prison, Sam!" said the old man, unfolding his newspaper, his voice full of emotion.

"Y' don't know that, Dad."

"Okay, maybe I shouldn't have said that, but we've got to hold onto some hope here."

"Yeah, how does that saying go … Dennis says, *Expect the worst 'n hope for the best.* Hopin' is fine, but t' say outright that I'm not going t' prison is presumptuous, cos what if I do end up goin' inside? Then how'd y' feel?"

"Point taken." The old man raised his newspaper and glanced over the front page, looking for an article to read, hoping to distract his thoughts. I opened my magazine.

* * *

Time dragged on, and by late morning I'd read my magazine three times over and I'd paced the verandah more times than I cared to count. Then Simon appeared around the corner.

"Hi, guys." The old man folded his newspaper, sitting to attention. "It looks like we won't be on until mid-afternoon. There's quite a big case where the defendant's pleaded not guilty and it's taking forever. Word has it we'll be up after that. I'm predicting" — he glanced at his watch — "our case being up at three o'clock, all going well."

"Okay if we disappear for a bit? I need to stretch my legs and get something to eat," the old man said as he stood up. I knew he wouldn't last the afternoon if he didn't eat.

"Fine. Go ahead. Court will be adjourning for lunch soon anyway. I'm sorry about all the waiting, but that's the way it goes sometimes."

"No big deal," I said, shrugging my shoulders. "Shall we go then?" I looked at the old man. He nodded and placed his folded newspaper under his arm.

Once out from under the courthouse verandah, the heat was instantly intense, creating beads of perspiration on my forehead as we walked down the street to the coffee shop.

"I couldn't live here, it's way too hot for me," said the old man.

"I know! Y've already told me!"

"I'm telling you again." He wiped the back of his hand across his forehead then looked at his hand. "And the flies! They're something else, aren't they," he stated, swatting the air in front of him. "Jesus, Sam! I don't know why you didn't just hop on a bus to Melbourne and a plane back home. You could've done that all in the space of twenty-four hours and no one would have batted an eyelid."

"Look, Dad! I realise this is hard f' y', but I told y' why I didn't. I don't need y' sayin' this kind 'f shit t' me now. If y' knew how many times I weighed that up as an option, then y' might appreciate why I chose not t'."

We ended up outside the coffee shop and the old man opened the door for me. I was about to finish my diatribe when I noticed Amanda looking at me strangely. I wanted to walk out, but the old man was behind me and feeling the heat of the day in more ways than one.

"Hi, Amanda," I said.

"Hi," she said, staring at me as if I were part of a freak show. "What's with the suit? I've never seen y' dressed that way before."

"Oh, we've got a bit 'f business we're doing together that requires me t' look more presentable. Y' know first impressions are lastin' impressions."

"Yes, I guess they are," she said, looking at me oddly.

"Anyway, can we have a pot 'f tea f' two, 'n I'll have a BLT. What y' goin' t' have, Dad?"

"I suppose the same."

"Right. So a pot 'f tea f' two 'n two BLTs," said Amanda, ringing it up on the till. "Ten dollars even. Thanks, Sam."

"I'll get this, Sam," said the old man, opening his wallet and passing Amanda a note.

"Have I given you the right note? I haven't gotten used to the different colours of your money yet."

"Yes, y' have, thanks," said Amanda, smiling at him.

"Great. Thank you," said the old man, putting his wallet back in his pocket.

We found a table on the other side of the room, close to the window.

"Can we move on, Dad?"

"Yes, sorry," he replied.

Amanda appeared with our pot of tea on a tray and placed it on the table.

"There y' go, boys, 'n the BLTs aren't far away." She smiled and made her way back to the counter.

I waited until she was out of earshot. "Where was I? Oh, yeah. So this whole time I've had a voice inside tellin' me t' stay 'n face the music. Of course I've wanted t' run, but I've run from stuff before, Dad, 'n it solves nothin'. I can't help thinkin' that if I see this out then I'll be better f' it."

The old man's brow furrowed as he listened, maintaining eye contact and trying his best not to interrupt.

"I know that sounds strange, perhaps it is, but it's somethin' I've got t' do 'n I'm shit-scared. But I've got t' do it."

I reached for the upside-down teacups, sat them on the saucers and poured the milk into them. The old man picked up the tea pot and poured the tea. As he finished pouring, he sighed heavily.

"I'm sure you've done the right thing, Sam. Besides, it's neither here nor there now. Sorry for mentioning it again."

Amanda returned to the table with our BLTs, placing them carefully in front of us.

"Thanks," I said, making brief eye contact with her.

"Y' know, Sam," she said bemused, I can't believe how different y' look all dressed up like that. I never picked y' f' a businessman."

"Well, I'm not really a businessman. All I said was I had some business t' do with my father."

"Oh, but … I don't get it. Doesn't that make y' a businessman?"

I just wanted her to leave. "If y' like, then yes, I s'pose it does." I forced a smile, hoping she'd get the message.

"I'm confused, but whatever. I think y' look very smart all dressed up like that."

"Thanks."

"He does, doesn't he," the old man said. "And he's an excellent businessman."

"There y' go, I knew it! Y're so modest, Sam. Y're a funny one." The bell on the door chimed as someone entered and she was gone, her attention required elsewhere at last.

"She really does make a good cuppa," the old man said, "and she's very pretty. You sure you don't want to ask her out on a date?" He grinned cheekily.

I just about choked on my BLT, swallowing too quickly in my eagerness to reply. "Are you kiddin' me? Y' really think she'd be my kind 'f girl?"

"You are in a small town. It might be hard to meet a girl round here."

The old man was getting into his BLT, jamming a huge piece into his wide-open mouth, bits of bread and tomato falling out onto his plate. His mouth was bursting as he pulled the BLT away and began chewing noisily, all the time looking at me as if he were about to say something but couldn't because his mouth was too full. His eating manners annoyed me. He seemed oblivious of how inelegant he looked.

"I'm sure" — he stopped as he swallowed, then chewed what was left in his mouth — "she's attracted to you."

"Jesus, Dad. Not now!"

He swallowed what remained and laughed out loud as if he'd just come up with something profoundly amusing. I found his infectious grin spreading across my face, and I couldn't suppress my own laughter, and we laughed for what seemed like an age. Each feeding off the other, we laughed so hard our stomachs hurt, our eyes watered, and it was painful to take a breath.

The old man glanced at his watch. "Perhaps we'd better get back."

"Yeah, I guess we should. I've got a date with destiny."

We walked the short distance to the courthouse. The heat engulfed us and the flies were there on cue to annoy the old man. He resumed his swatting with great vigour, making use of his newspaper until we were back beneath the shade of the courthouse verandah. There were less people around and the court warden, who'd been outside the front doors most of the morning, was nowhere to be seen.

"They must be still at lunch. There's hardly anyone here," I said.

"Huh, I'm going to sit back where we were. It's too damn hot to do anything else," the old man responded. He walked to where we'd been sitting before and sat down, leaning his head back against the wall of the building, and he closed his eyes. He was good at being able to catch small amounts of sleep in unusual places.

The old man must've slept for a good twenty minutes before Simon appeared around the corner.

"Ah good, you're back." The old man sat upright, instantly awake and present to Simon's voice. "Court recommences in five minutes," he said, glancing at his watch. "Sam, I predict you'll be up within the hour."

I gulped and felt the back of my throat go dry. Time was counting down. The moment I had waited six long months for was finally about to arrive, and my body was brimming with anxiety.

"Sam, when they call you in, I want you to come and join me up the front. On the right-hand side there will be a seat next to mine for you. Henry, you can come up to the front row of pews. There will be an empty space for you to sit. If you prefer to come in now, that's alright too."

The old man shook his head. "No, thanks, I'll sit out here with Sam until he's called."

"That's fine. Okay, I'll see you when you're called," he said, affirming me with a hint of a smile before he turned and headed back along the verandah. I stood up and watched him leave, all elegantly dressed, with his purposeful walk. He disappeared through the front doors of the courthouse.

Beyond the doors, further along the verandah, there were several police officers standing in a group. They looked as though they were laughing as they stood around in a circle, inhaling on cigarettes. As I stood there, acutely aware of my heart banging loudly against my chest, I realised Harry and Frank were amongst them. Seeing them standing together just added to my anxiety.

"Sit down, boy, you'll give yourself an ulcer standing there worrying like that. You need to take some deep breaths. It'll help you relax," commanded the old man.

"I'm not in the mood, Dad," I snapped. I hadn't taken my eyes off the group of officers and my mind was full of paranoid thoughts as I started to walk the distance between them and me.

Y' pack 'f fuckin' scum! Y' no better than the so-called low life that y' pick up 'n lock away. How can y' tuck y' kids int' bed at night 'n sleep with y' wives 'n look them in the eyes 'n believe that what y' do is a good, honest day's work? Y're as scummy as the ones y' see as scum. God fuckin' help you. My thoughts ran riot, and as I passed the policemen, they all stared at me in silence. I'd been in contact with each of them at some stage in the last six months, reporting to the station every day.

"Afternoon," I said as casually as I could muster. There were a few grunts but nothing resembling a word. I rounded the corner and opened the door to the men's toilets. As I stood there peeing, feeling great relief as the steam rose off the stainless steel, the door opened and closed. There were footsteps behind me as someone shuffled up to the urinal. For one brief second, I expected to turn and see Bruce standing there. Instead, I was face to face with Harry.

"Alright, Sam?"

"Yeah."

"Y'll be up soon, won't y'?"

"I know." I stopped pissing. Harry's entrance had put me off. I shook myself carefully so as not to get any drips on my flash trousers, and quickly zipped up.

"Y' must be feelin' nervous," said Harry as he unzipped.

"Yeah. Guess I am." A wild tremble raced through my body.

"Hey, there's nothin' t' worry about, y'll be walkin' away from all 'f this by the end 'f the day."

"How d' y' know that, Harry?"

"Just a hunch," he said, looking pleased as he relieved himself. I felt uncomfortable and stepped back away from the urinal. I walked over to the handbasin to wash my hands.

I didn't need Harry lifting my hopes with hunches that could just as easily be false promises. I needed to keep my head above all that and believe that the judge would see things beyond the black and white world of right and wrong.

"Well, I guess time'll tell. But y' shouldn't be comin' in here raisin' false hopes. What's gonna be is gonna be, Harry."

"Y' think too deeply, Sam."

"Do I? My old man says so too. It must be all the time I've had stuck in this place, stuck in m' head all day long. Most people get up in the mornin' 'n have a job t' go t'. I get up 'n hitch t' town every mornin' t' see you or one of y' mates so that y' know I haven't done a runner. I'm such a threat t' the community, aren't I, Harry? A big catch in a little pond that's what I am! Somethin' t' make a scapegoat of," I snarled, and moved to walk out.

"Oh, come on, Sam. That's not true," exclaimed Harry.

"Y' know, I should've listened t' m' old man. He told me t' come home, that I wouldn't be missed, that it wouldn't be worth y' resources t' track me down 'n bring me back. But I didn't, did I? I've read too many crime stories, seen too many movies. My over-imaginative mind told me if I did a runner, like the old man suggested, I'd be tracked down and sent back. Then I'd be in one 'f y' scummy jails f' sure, with an added sentence f' abscondin'!" I glared at him and stormed out of the toilets, back past his colleagues and down towards where the old man was sitting.

I walked past the main courthouse doors and they suddenly opened. A voice called out, "*Samuel Gorzman.*" I stopped in my tracks and turned to reply. All I could see were the policemen beyond the court warden, all staring at me.

"That's me," I mumbled to the court warden. My dry mouth caused my tongue to stick to the roof of my mouth. All my blood seemed to drain to my toes.

"Your presence is summoned in the court. Please enter," trumpeted the court warden.

"I'll be there in a minute. I need t' get m' father."

On cue the old man appeared from around the corner. "I'm here," he announced. "In you go, I'm right behind you."

As I took each step towards the doors, my legs became like lead, each step an effort as though they might give out.

* * *

Inside the courtroom the judge sat behind the elevated bench at the front of the court, peering over his spectacles. The stenographer, who recorded all the court's proceedings on a shorthand machine, was at a desk in front and slightly to the left of the judge's bench, but lower, at floor level. The pews on either side were scattered with people. Some of the men were dressed in suits like me, and the women were mostly well-dressed too. There were others casual attired, in beach shorts, T-shirts and thongs.

The courtroom felt morbid, like a church congregation attending a funeral, and I suddenly felt as though I was falling. As I approached the front, where Simon was seated, something caught my eye. A second look made me jump. It was Bruce sitting there, a few rows behind Simon. *What the fuck's he doin' here?* He gave me a wink and a thumbs-up sign. I kept walking, pretending I hadn't seen him. I approached Simon, who smiled and gestured for me to sit in the empty seat next to him. I sat, and the judge, who looked down at me through heavy-framed spectacles, began to speak.

"Samuel Gorzman, you have been charged with being in the Possession of a Class B drug with the Intention to Supply. How do you plead?"

My heart banged loudly against the inside of my chest, my throat constricted, and I wondered how on earth I was going to be able to speak.

"Stand up, Sam," whispered Simon. I look at him blankly. He gestured with his hand, encouraging me to my feet. I attempted to stand, wondering if my legs would support me. My knees trembled, my lips were cemented together, but I was standing now, my hands firmly clasped behind my back.

The judge looked at me with anticipation, the room dead quiet. I stared back at the judge and wondered why he wasn't wearing a big white wig.

He spoke again, repeating his question. "Samuel Gorzman, how do you plead?"

I hesitated, then the words that came out of my mouth sliced through the air like a guillotine. "Guilty, Your Honour."

"Mr Cottrell, I believe you have something to say in defence of this guilty plea?"

"Yes, Your Honour, I do," said Simon, pushing back his chair to stand. He made a guttural noise as he cleared his throat to speak, gesturing for me to sit down. "It is my intention to convey to you that although Samuel has pleaded guilty to the crime he's accused of, he was led along by men far older and more sophisticated than himself. On the one hand yes, Samuel is guilty of being in Possession of a Class B drug, and on the other hand there was no Intention to Supply. He had the misfortune of falling into devious company for which he has paid the price."

"Get to the point, Mr Cottrell," said the judge, looking at Simon with an air of impatience.

"That is what I am doing, Your Honour," replied Simon, seeming unperturbed by the judge's interruption. "Sam is a young man, only eighteen years old. He arrived in Australia from New Zealand in May 1980, just under a year ago. He came here with an Australian woman he met back in New Zealand where he fell in love with her. Through his relationship with her, he was introduced to her previous partner, Bruce Langer, who is also up on charges of Possession to Supply and who the police believe was the supplier of the Class B drug Samuel had on his person when he was arrested." I cringed as I imagined Bruce's fury as he sat listening several rows back.

"That's another matter altogether," intervened the judge.

"Samuel was arrested," continued Simon, "in the early hours of the morning, having travelled to Canberra from Yaringa to drop off a friend of Bruce's whom he had met on one other occasion. Bruce asked Samuel if he could take the friend to Canberra because he wanted him out of the way. Samuel, unsuspecting of the true motive, happily obliged Bruce's request and looked forward to the prospect of a road trip. I suggest that Samuel was caught in the middle of this situation. On the way back from Canberra, Samuel was pulled over by Wodyn Police for a routine check. It was then that he was found to be in Possession of a Class B drug. This brings me to call upon my one and only witness, Senior Sergeant Harry Raffles."

I took a deep breath and another. I was hyperventilating. Simon had not informed me that he intended to summon Harry.

The court warden called out, "Harry Raffles, please take the witness stand." Harry appeared through a side door, dressed in full uniform, his cap tucked under his right arm. He stepped up to the witness stand. The court warden approached the witness stand and held out a Bible in the palm of his hand. "Please place your hand on the Bible and repeat after me. "I, Harry Raffles, do solemnly swear to tell the truth, the whole truth, and nothing but the truth, so help me God."

Harry placed his hand on the Bible, repeating the oath word for word, and the court warden assumed his previous position.

"Senior Sergeant Raffles," said Simon, approaching the witness stand.

Harry raised his eyebrows in response. "As the arresting officer, what were your first impressions of Samuel that night?"

"Well, my first impressions were that he was nervous and possibly hiding somethin'."

"Wouldn't most people feel nervous being pulled up in the middle of the night on a quiet stretch of road?"

"Yes, that's true, I s'pose." Harry shifted his weight from one leg to another. "However, my hunch proved right. We did find Sam to be in possession of a Class B drug."

"We?" Simon was sharp and on to Harry.

"Well, yes. By this time my colleague, Frank Capella, had shown up and was assisting me with my search." Harry breathed deep into his chest.

"So you arrested him, then took him back to the station to get a statement?"

"Yes. We questioned him as to who he had acquired the capsules from."

"Because?" The air hung heavy in the courtroom and the slightest noise amplified in the stillness of the high-ceilinged space.

"Standard procedure, of course! But he seemed very naive, so we suspected he was the mule or, if you like, the carrier."

"How did he respond to your questioning?"

Harry shifted awkwardly as his eyes met mine. "He seemed scared and vulnerable. We told him in no uncertain terms he was in deep trouble and that he could go away for a long time."

"So would it be fair to say that in your eyes, Samuel was the innocent young man, who became acquainted with older, more influential men who took advantage of his naivety?"

"I believe that t' be the case."

"Thank you, Harry Raffles. That is all, Your Honour."

"You may stand down, Senior Sergeant Raffles," said the judge.

Harry nodded, glanced at me with a faint smile, and stepped down from the witness box. The judge looked intensely at Simon over the top of his glasses, and said, "Mr Cottrell, have you anything else to add in summing up?"

"I have, Your Honour."

"Very well. Continue please," said the judge, leaning back in his oversized wooden throne.

"It is my belief that Samuel was taken advantage of by Bruce Langer and Cosmo Rogers. He was asked to take Bruce's friend, Cosmo, to Canberra. I suggest that it was this friend Cosmo, already in trouble with the law, who was planning to distribute the Class B drugs Samuel had in his possession, in Canberra. But Cosmo didn't. Instead, he sent them back with Samuel to return to Bruce. Although Samuel was found in Possession of a Class B drug and pleaded guilty to the charge, sending Samuel to prison as a result of this comedy of misfortune will not benefit anyone, least of all Samuel. It is a proven fact that most young men sent to prison reoffend within six months of being released. Samuel comes from a stable home environment in New Zealand, and his parents have stood by him throughout his entire ordeal."

Simon was in full flight. It was a concerto, impressive and embarrassing simultaneously. God knows what Bruce was thinking three rows back. Simon articulately built his case, rising to the final crescendo, and I began to feel compelled by his description of the situation.

"His father is here in court today and has been Samuel's support these past few days. He brought with him many character references from employers, teachers and grandparents." Simon picked up a bundle of papers and walked to the judge's bench. He handed the papers to the judge who browsed briefly through them as Simon continued talking. "His mother and grandmother were here for the original hearing in the Magistrates' Court six months ago. This demonstrates the care and concern his family have for him. He has reported to the police station *every day* since the day he was arrested six months ago, which has often meant hitchhiking into Wodyn from Yaringa as he has no vehicle of his own. It hasn't been easy for him to find full-time employment in a small farming community affected by drought and high unemployment, but to his credit he has gotten by. I cannot emphasise enough the importance of giving Samuel another chance. These past six months have been punishment enough for him, a time to take stock and reflect on his mistake and make good for the future. I firmly believe Samuel deserves this opportunity." Simon went silent for a moment. You could hear a pin drop. "That is all. Thank you, Your Honour." Simon made his way back to his seat beside mine and casually winked at me as he sat down.

The judge was silent. He peered sternly over the top of his glasses then looked down at the character references, frowning as he shuffled through them for several moments while the court sat in silence. I heard people behind me shuffle their feet; someone crossed, then uncrossed, their legs; someone blew their nose into a hanky in the row across the aisle. It didn't look as though the judge was reading the references, or perhaps he was a speed-reader like my mother. Then he looked up and straight at me, his stare intense, as if he were burning a hole through my head.

"Samuel Gorzman, please rise," he said. I gulped and attempted to stand without pushing my chair back, and as I stood, I clasped my hands behind my back again. "Do you have anything to say, Samuel?" he asked, looking earnestly at me.

I felt myself clear my throat, but I didn't want to say anything because I was terrified to speak in this public forum, but I had to. I had to say something even if it wasn't much. My throat was still dry. It felt as if something was stuck in it, like chunks of carrot swallowed too quickly.

I opened my mouth in the hope that something decipherable would come out.

"Your Honour … I do … I … realise that what I did was very foolish. And I'd like t' say it's been a hard lesson so far. This is a lesson in life. I've learnt a lot about m'self 'n about other people. I'm very sorry for what I've done, and," I finished, "I can promise you it won't happen again."

I didn't know whether I should remain standing or sit back down. I decided to remain standing, hoping Simon would tell me when I could sit. The courtroom remained eerily quiet as the judge exploited the moment of silence to great effect, shuffling papers and looking grim as he peered at me again through the distorted lenses of his glasses.

"Samuel, this is a very serious offence. I feel it requires more thought before I can make a decision." My knees went weak and I began to tremble. For a moment the room became blurred, and I felt dizzy, as though I were falling. "I hereby remand you in custody overnight. My final decision for sentencing will be tomorrow morning at ten o'clock." My eyes refocused and I was still standing.

"This court is adjourned for the day and will resume tomorrow morning at ten o'clock," the judge said and banged his wooden gravel on the bench to conclude matters.

The court warden stood in front of the judge's bench and in a loud booming voice said, "Would the court please rise." Everybody stood.

I looked to my left where Simon was standing. He gave me a quick wink and a smile. Nothing seemed to faze the man and he stood proud, as though he commanded the world's attention. The judge was the last to stand, and he took one very definite final look at me, then departed from his bench through a door at the rear of the courtroom.

Being in court had been so intense that I'd forgotten about the old man. I quickly glanced around to see where he was. Instead, I caught sight of Bruce who sneered and gave me the fingers. Fortunately, he was not able to get close to me. I couldn't blame him for his feelings, but strangely, I didn't feel bad or that I owed him anything or that I'd let him down. If he hadn't asked me to take Cosmo to Canberra, I wouldn't be standing where I was now. I watched him storm down the aisle and out through the large front doors.

"So, Sam." The old man appeared beside me. "Things aren't looking so good, are they?"

"I guess not," I said.

A police officer arrived to escort me to the station. I didn't know him, but he was the young bloke who occasionally checked me off when I came in to report each morning.

"You need to come with me," he said, all matter-of-fact in his tone.

"Could we just have a few minutes together, please? I'm Sam's barrister and this is Sam's father," said Simon.

The police officer nodded. "Make it quick, sir."

"Thank you," said the old man, looking concerned.

"We need to talk a couple of things over," explained Simon.

"What's there t' talk about? I'm goin' inside for the night 'n tomorrow the judge is goin' t' reveal m' fate. I'm still in limbo," I stated with sarcasm.

"I'm sorry it's panned out this way," said Simon, "but there isn't anything particularly unusual about a decision pending."

"Sorry, folks, but I'm going to have to take Sam now. You can visit him later if you need to," interrupted the young officer.

"I guess that's the way it's got to be then," said Simon, shrugging his shoulders.

"Sam, you'll be fine, huh? Hopefully, I'll see you later today, before I go back to Yaringa."

"Whatever y' think, Dad." The police officer took me by an arm and guided me away.

35

Returning

I was going back to where it all started. The door through which I had been taken at the courthouse led into a corridor that the young police officer at my side marched me down.

"So the judge couldn't decide, eh? Maybe he's a bit soft. If he wanted to lock y' up, he would've done it today, I reckon. He's just winding you up, trying to freak you out."

"Well, I ain't holdin' m' breath," I said.

We had come to the end of the corridor, and he put a large, old-fashioned key into the keyhole of the vault-like steel door and opened it. Bright light streamed through as the gap opened to reveal daylight and a parked paddy wagon. He opened the back door to the vehicle and bundled me in, closing the door behind me. I had a flashback to where it began all those months ago, late one September night on the side of the road, just shy of Wodyn. The vehicle lurched forward, throwing me off balance as it pulled away from the courthouse.

Moments later the vehicle stopped, the door opened, and the young officer assisted me out the back. "Back to where it all started for you, eh?"

"Mmm, I guess so." I felt numb as I stepped out of the paddy wagon. He led me up the path to the police station entrance and through the doors out the back, past another officer sitting at a desk. When we

446

came to the far end of the room, he reached for a set of keys on a hook and nudged me into the corridor that led to the cells. These were all empty except for a solitary bed in each, with the standard grey blanket folded up at the foot of the bed. It was a déjà vu experience, and not an attractive or welcoming sight. From his jingling set of keys, the young police officer selected the one that would open the cell door before me. Steel clanged noisily, hollow and empty like the cells, and a cold shiver rose up my spine and hovered between my shoulder blades.

"Welcome to your hotel for the evening," the officer said, a malicious grin spreading across his face. His baby face hinted that he wasn't much older than twenty, yet he already showed signs of being another Frank.

"Why, thank you," I said sarcastically, playing along with his warped sense of humour as I stepped into the cell. The door closed, reverberating with the stark sound of steel against steel and then the jingle of keys as he locked it shut.

"Have a pleasant stay," he said and left.

I sat down on the bed and put my head in my hands. It had been a long day, too long, and I couldn't think straight. I couldn't see the future one way or the other. I didn't know what was happening to me, I couldn't process anything, and it was all too much to comprehend.

I must've nodded off until a slight noise disturbed me. I looked up as keys jangled in the lock, and a silhouetted figure opened the door. Harry's frame appeared, casting a shadow along the length of the corridor.

"Hey," he said, looking at me sheepishly.

"Hey," I said back, not bothering to get up off the bed and placing my hands behind my head.

"Not what y' expected in there today, eh?" Harry asked, taking the liberty to sit on the end of the bed.

"I don't know what I expected, Harry. Either way, I just want it over 'n done with so I can move forward."

"I imagine it's quite challenging, but it ain't over till the fat lady sings, 'n t'morrow mornin' she will."

"Y' seem to have y' doubts, Harry," I said, swinging my legs over the bed so I could sit up and look him in the eye.

"I don't have doubts, I have hope, Sam, or maybe it's faith."

Sarah entered my mind — the smell of her hair, the softness of her skin and her gentle, soothing voice. "Would y' have invited me f' dinner if y' weren't with Sarah?"

He looked at me, his eyes wide with surprise.

"I hope I would've … But how can I assume that? My life would be completely different if I wasn't with Sarah. We've made a family t'gether. It's through being with her that I've been able t' see things more clearly, t' understand that life isn't just black 'n white like so many of us make it out to be."

"Yep," I nodded.

"It'd be hard t' think 'f life without Sarah. Look Sam," he said, suddenly getting up. "I've got t' go but I'll see y' tomorrow. Get some rest, eh?" He straightened his clothing like a man who'd just been with his lover. He stood there for a moment, looking at me as if he wanted to say more before he walked to the door. It clunked closed behind him and his keys clattered against metal as he locked it shut. "I hope y' sleep well."

"I guess," I replied. "Y' know, it's a funny thing, but that night y' arrested me 'n left me here in the cell so y' could go after Bruce, I slept like a baby.

"Y' kiddin' me," his face looked surprised.

"All I'm tryin' t' tell y' is that I seem t' be able t' sleep regardless 'f how bad things are. It's like escapin' t' another world where, if I come across danger 'n demons, they're only in m' dreams. The real danger lives outside 'f m' dreams, in the real world," I said with calm clarity.

"Life's a funny thing," he said, relaxing his grip on the bars.

"If y' think it is then I guess it is." I stood up as I needed my blood to circulate.

"No, I just mean the whole thing 'f comin' across you that night, 'n everythin' that's unfolded as a result 'f it. I've never involved m'self with a defendant b'fore, beyond the duty 'f giving evidence. I've never even contemplated it b'fore." Harry searched my face for acknowledgement.

"I guess that's the beauty 'f life, that we can change our minds about how we feel about things 'n we can make a diff'rence," I responded. "A small but significant diff'rence if we want to … by doin' somethin' even if it doesn't seem like very much."

"Y're a wise young man, Sam."

"Not really. If I was, y'd like t' think I wouldn't be here now."

"Circumstances, Sam. Circumstances. Got t' go. Goodnight." He tapped his hand on one of the bars for emphasis.

"Night, Harry," I said and lay back down on the bed.

* * *

I awoke to the clanging of keys in the cell door and the old sarge's voice. "Come on, sonny, wake up! Y've got a visitor."

"Hello, Sam." It was the old man. Looking the worse for wear, he followed the sarge into my cell. The day seemed to have impacted him more than it had me.

The sarge stepped back out, closed the cell door and locked it. "I'll be back in twenty minutes, so make the most 'f it," he sneered as he walked off.

"Nice bloke," said the old man sarcastically as he sat down at the foot of the bed.

"Y' could say that," I said, grinning weakly and rubbing the sleep from my eyes.

"You managed to get some sleep. That's surprising in a place like this," he said, looking around with distaste.

"Yeah, I lay down with all sorts 'f thoughts goin' through m' head, 'n the next minute there's the sound 'f keys 'n the doors openin', 'n here y' are."

"I suppose that's a good sign, huh." He shifted uncomfortably. "I asked Simon if we should push for you to do weekend detention in Sydney, as things aren't looking that great, are they?" The old man leaned forward, buried his head in his hands and began to sob.

I propped myself up on my elbows, swung my feet onto the floor and sat up. I shuffled close and put my arm around him.

"Anyway," he managed to say, wiping his eyes, "he reckons we should leave things be and see what unfolds. He doesn't want to confuse the judge with options at this stage. I'm more of a mind to propose it now, but Simon's the barrister and he seems to know what he's doing, so I thought I'd run it by you first. What do you think?"

"I don't have answers, Dad, but he's probably right. Let's just leave it, eh. If the judge sends me t' prison, then perhaps that can be offered up as an option, don't y' think?"

"The only thing is that once you've been sentenced, it's much harder to propose something like that," continued the old man.

"Well, that's the risk we'll have t' take!" I surprised myself with the strength and clarity in my voice. "There must be a way 'f proposing the periodic detention option after the fact, the police must be able t' get involved in the nature 'f the sentencin'. Don't they make sentencin' recommendations?"

The old man shrugged his shoulders and looked at me blankly through his tear-stained eyes. "Maybe, but why would they want that?"

"There's a possibility that they'd rather see someone like me in rehabilitation."

The door opened and the sarge appeared in the corridor. "Y' twenty minutes is up," he announced.

"Anyway," I said, suddenly feeling exhausted, "I don't know 'n I don't care at this stage. I just want t' get some sleep 'n see what t'morrow brings."

The sarge fumbled noisily with the keys as he unlocked the door.

"Sure," said the old man, putting an arm around me.

"Sleep well. I'll see you in the morning."

"Here's y' evening meal," interrupted the sarge, placing a tray with covered dishes on the floor. "It's hard t' sleep well in here," the sarge sniggered to himself as the old man stepped out of my cell into the corridor. The sarge locked the door behind him.

"Goodnight, Sam," the old man called out, louder than necessary.

"Night, Dad."

* * *

I was awoken by the young officer in the morning. "Breakfast before court," he said, juggling the tray and keys. I sat up on the bed and reached for my trousers and shirt. "Your father said he'd bring you fresh clothes when he comes in," said the officer as he placed the tray on the floor beside me and picked up the dinner tray, which I hadn't touched.

"Tell him not t' bother. Tell him I didn't sleep in m' clothes so these ones are fine," I said, standing up and pulling on my trousers.

"I'll pass it on," he said, not lingering and locking the door as he left.

"What time is it?" I called out, finishing off the buttons on my shirt.

"Eight-thirty! You're required in court at nine-thirty."

"Okay." There was no mirror in front of which to do my tie, so I struggled as best I could. It didn't feel like it was sitting right, but there wasn't much I could do about it. I picked up the tray on which there was a cup of tea with the tea bag still drawing, a small jug of milk, overcooked fried eggs on white toast, and bacon cooked to a crispy dark brown. It wasn't the greatest breakfast but, despite my anxiety, I was hungry.

The young officer led me into court via the same route we exited the night before. I entered the courtroom knowing that now was my moment of truth. I was amazed to find the room full of people again, considering the size of Wodyn. It seemed that attending a District Court session held a strange fascination for the locals. As I walked across the courtroom to where Simon was sitting, I noticed that the judge was already seated at his bench, suggesting court had commenced and they were waiting on me. My father was seated behind Simon in the front row of benches. He nodded and attempted a smile. I sat down next to Simon, who leant across and whispered, "Good morning."

"Mornin'," I replied.

The young officer made himself scarce, moving over to the door. No sooner had I sat down than the court warden called out in full voice, "Samuel Gorzman, please stand!"

A familiar, violent shiver raced up my spine, and my legs trembled as I rose. I prayed it was not too obvious. My head was slightly bowed, and my hands were firmly clasped behind my back in an attempt not to reveal the tremble that possessed my body.

"Samuel Gorzman," said the judge, lingering on the pronunciation of my surname, drawing the word out. I looked up, as if summoned to do so. My eyes met his and for a few moments the room was deathly quiet as we held the other's gaze. "The crime you have committed, that of being in possession of a Class B drug with Intention to Supply is viewed as very serious. In point of law it holds a maximum sentence of nine years in prison. Drugs are viewed as a serious problem in Australian society, hence the laws to fight it, not dissimilar to your own laws in New Zealand. These sentences are upheld to deter potential offenders. I cannot stress enough how serious your situation is." I was trembling so badly by then that I was sure everyone could see my knees knocking.

"However..." he said, holding my gaze, looking like the Grim Reaper with his beady eyes and his wrinkled face framed by fine, black, receding hair with wisps of grey streaked through. "Under the circumstances it is my belief that you have been led astray through associating with older people who influenced you in unfortunate ways. I hereby sentence you to three years —"

My heart leaped into my mouth. I became light-headed. My legs were barely holding me vertical. *My God! I'm goin' t' prison. No hang on ... What did he just say?*

"— suspended sentence —"

Suspended sentence! What does that mean? Oh, help me God!

"— and a fine of three thousand dollars."

I turned to Simon, but he was too busy looking at the judge.

"As part of your sentence, you are required to appear as a witness in the trial of Bruce Langer, due to be held in this court one week from today." The judge banged the gavel down on the bench.

Simon was on his feet, holding out his hand to me. "Sam, well done, you're free! You're a free man, Sam." He shook my hand with great enthusiasm.

"What? It can't be..." The old man was there with tears in his eyes, and we embraced, holding each other tightly. It was only just sinking in that I was not going to prison. "We did it, Dad," I whisper in his ear.

"You sure did."

The young police officer arrived to usher us out through another door, one leading to the bailiff's office.

"You need to wait here until documents have been drawn up for you to sign, stipulating the conditions of your suspended sentence and release," he informed me.

Through the throng of people congregated in reception, I saw Harry beaming as he made his way to me. He was dressed in full uniform but that didn't stop him giving me a huge bear hug. I was so happy I didn't care what anyone would think, and I hugged him right back.

"Harry," I said as he released me. "Can y' explain a suspended sentence t' me?"

"Sure," he said. "A suspended sentence means that y' free t' go. However, if y' should break the law again within the time frame 'f y' sentence, then the court, at its discretion, can put y' in prison for those three years. I believe you also have a condition attached to your sentence?"

"Yeah. Not one that sits well with me, but hey, I'll do what I have t' do."

"Good on y', Sam," he said, patting me on the back. "Bruce hasn't done y' any favours and wouldn't do y' any, either. Testifying at his trial is the right thing to do. I'd like y' to come 'round f' dinner before y' leave."

"Course I will, Harry."

"Your papers are ready to sign, Sam," the old man said, appearing beside me.

"I don't believe we've had the pleasure of meeting. I'm Henry, Sam's father," he said.

"Harry. Senior Sergeant Harry Raffles."

"I appreciate what you said in court yesterday," said the old man warmly. "Thank you."

"Well, it's the truth."

"Yes, you're right there. Thank you again."

"Bye, Harry," I said.

"See y', Sam." Harry sauntered off as if he'd single-handedly gotten me out of this situation. He went out through the bailiff's door that led to the back of the courthouse.

Whatever, Harry. It's been my journey.

In the presence of the young officer, Simon talked me through the three-year suspended sentence document and what it meant, before he asked me to sign the papers.

"What now?" I asked, turning to Simon, having signed the papers.

"That's it, Sam. You're free to go." He put out his hand which I took and shook firmly.

"Thank you so much for coming down here to help me," I said as I struggled to believe it was over.

"My pleasure," he said and laughed. "That's what makes my job worthwhile. Take care, Sam. I have a plane to catch."

I'm goin' home! I'm goin' home!

* * *

The old man drove us back to Yaringa. I felt like I was floating on a cloud. All the months of waiting were over, and I hadn't gone to prison. I wondered whether Bruce had been in court this morning. If so, I hadn't noticed him. I'd been so preoccupied I hadn't even looked for him, not even after the verdict, what with all the excitement. *When he finds out he'll kill me. He'll know he's fuck'd f' sure!* Bruce most likely wasn't so irrational that he'd come around to waste me, but those who supplied him might think it was a good idea. I wasn't in a position to implicate anyone else, so in fact I wasn't a threat to them. The types of characters with whom Bruce was involved probably didn't rationalise this sort of situation, so I couldn't be certain about my safety.

Fuck, what a fool I am! I should've requested police protection. Why didn't the police offer me that the moment I was called upon t' be a witness? They should know the score. They should know that I could become a target. Maybe they factored this int' the equation — Bruce would terminate me 'n then they'd get him f' life. That's how cops think, isn't it? They'll be thinkin' 'f me as the sacrificial lamb. Sweet Jesus, I wish I didn't read so many cop stories. It's all about deceit 'n manipulation. I can't trust anyone!

Now I wondered whether I could even trust Harry. Was he playing a game of charades to lure me into a false sense of security? *Harry wants me over for one last supper. What's that all about?* My mind was running wild like a horse that bolted.

The old man's voice dropped gently into my polluted world. "Are you alright, Sam? You seem awfully quiet for someone who's just been let off the hook."

"Yeah. Just thinkin' too much. I don't really like the idea 'f being a witness f' the prosecution at Bruce's trial," I said, gazing out the window at sun-scorched paddocks of farmland, wondering if the rain would ever come.

"He got you into this mess, so he can pay the price for that."

"You may see it like that, but I got m'self int' this mess agreein' t' things I shouldn't've in the first place."

"That's what I'm saying, Sam! You were taken advantage of," he replied as the car wound its way uphill through the eucalyptus trees to Yaringa.

"Well, no. Actually, I just thought I could help out, 'n I've been smokin' dope since high school, so it's not like I ended up with these guys 'n started smokin'."

"Yeah. Well, half the teenage population experiments with smoking drugs these days," the old man said, sighing heavily as we entered the township.

"I guess there was a bit 'f pressure from them f' me to drive him t' Canberra, 'n f' him t' get rid 'f some merchandise. I wasn't real happy about that, but I just thought it would be fine. Once we got t' Canberra things weren't as they seemed, 'n I began t' feel freaked out by it all. Turn left here, Dad, unless y' want a drink at the pub t' celebrate."

"Sure," the old man said, continuing straight ahead. It had just gone midday. "You see, if you look at it like that, you were naive enough to go along with it, even though you didn't feel comfortable about it."

"I guess. I take y' point, but ultimately, I made the bad decision, so I'm responsible. That's the pub," I said, pointing. "Pull up anywhere in front or in the car park." He pulled up right outside and wrenched the handbrake on. We clambered out of the car and closed the doors behind us.

"But you did take responsibility!" The old man was like a dog with a bone as we made our way inside to the bar. "You stayed here and faced the music."

"Yeah, but I snitch'd on someone."

The old man threw his hands up in the air. "You were under extreme pressure! Your life was in danger!" he proclaimed, raising his voice.

"Oh my God, Sam, I thought something terrible had happened!" cried Brigitte, lifting the hinged bench bar she was standing behind, and rushing towards me. "I can't believe I'm seein' you. I thought the worst when y' didn't come home last night." She threw her arms around me.

"I thought m' goose was cook'd last night. They lock'd me up cos the judge couldn't make up his mind."

"They just wanted to scare him," chimed in the old man.

"I'm so happy to see y', Sam. Is this y' dad?" she asked, releasing me from her hold.

"Yeah. Brigitte meet m' dad, Henry. Dad, this is Brigitte." They shook hands.

"Pleased to meet y', Henry."

"Nice to meet you too, Brigitte," he said, eyeing her up.

"Can we have a couple 'f schooners 'f y' finest?" I requested.

"Most definitely," she replied, smiling broadly.

We sat outside on the balcony under a sun umbrella and admired the view across the bay.

"You know, most people in your situation would have done exactly the same. In fact, they may not have held out the way you did," stated the old man, picking up where he had left off. "It was perfectly normal what you did. You're not part of the Mafia. If the roles had been reversed, you can bet your bottom dollar Bruce would have talked, too."

"Maybe. It's okay, Dad. I get y' point, and y' prob'bly right."

Brigitte arrived with a tray carrying two schooners of cold beer. "Here y' go," she said, placing them on the table. "I'll leave y' to it."

"Thanks, Brigitte." I picked up my schooner of beer.

"Cheers!" said the old man as we clinked glasses.

"Skol!" We greedily gulped down mouthfuls of refreshing golden liquid.

"I know I'm right! You have to let go of that feeling of having done something bad. It'll consume you, Sam."

"I will. It just might take a bit 'f time. I'm also a little worried that Bruce might come 'round one night 'n machete me t' death in m' caravan," I said, not wanting to be dramatic but feeling quite certain it was a possibility.

"Hardly likely, Sam," said the old man, chortling at the idea. "He's in enough trouble without complicating his situation. He might only get three years for what he did. It's not like he had truckloads of drugs in his possession. He's just the next pawn up from you, making an illegal living on the side. He's been found out and might do a year of that sentence in prison, then get parole." The old man was on a roll, as if he'd suddenly become an expert in drug cases.

Christ, Dad! Y'll be seekin' admittance t' the bar next.

"How do y' figure that?"

"Simon told me. I asked him what he knew about Bruce. He also said that the sentence could be even lighter if he had the sense to plead guilty." He took another gulp of his beer then looked into his glass as if he had realised something for the first time.

"He won't, Dad."

"He won't what, Sam?"

"Plead guilty," I replied, attacking the last of my beer.

"You'll be surprised."

"Whatever," I drained the last of my glass.

"So … I'll be going home tomorrow afternoon if I can get a flight, Sam. I've got to get back to work," he said as he swivelled his glass on the table.

"Can't y' stay here till Bruce's trial's over?"

"No, I can't. Sorry. The business needs me," he said, shaking his head emphatically.

"That's a bummer. I'm sick 'f bein' here."

"Another week. It'll go by quickly," he enthused. Finally finishing his beer, he pushed the glass to one side.

"No! It'll drag, it'll feel like a month, I know. Just waitin' f this moment t' arrive has felt like 'n eternity in slow motion."

"Get out the violin, Sam," he laughed. We both laughed, and I laughed so hard I didn't even know what I was laughing about as the tears streamed down my face.

"Thanks, Dad," I managed to say once the laughter had subsided.

"No problem, huh. Come on," he said, pushing back on his chair. "I could do with a swim."

I stuck my head inside and called out to Brigitte. "See y' later. We're off for a swim."

"I'll come 'round aft'r work," she shouted from behind the bar.

"Cool."

* * *

Dinner that night was accompanied by champagne that Ted provided to celebrate my freedom. It was a rare occasion to see Ted and Val so upbeat. They were probably secretly thrilled to bits to know they were about to see the last of me. But my being here had more advantages than disadvantages for them. I was a companion for Tim, and I was able to get him out and about, which they were never able to do. I could talk with him, laugh with him; we were mates. Dinner and champagne were followed by whisky in the lounge. Ted insisted. We drank and talked and drank some more. Ted invited the old man over to the bowling club for a drink, and he graciously accepted. I took the opportunity to retire to the caravan.

While the household slept, I lay awake in bed, unable to sleep. There was a knock on the caravan door and I recoiled in fright. My heart raced furiously, and I lay there white-knuckled, gripping the duvet cover, feeling the blood drain from my face. Another knock. This time the handle turned.

"Are y' in there, Sam?" It was the rasping whisper of a woman.

"What do y' want?" I whispered back.

"It's me."

"Who's me?"

"Brigitte, silly."

"Are y' on y' own?"

"'f course I am."

I opened the door and let her in, looking over her shoulder, half expecting Bruce to appear out of the shadows of the night. I closed the door, locking it behind her.

"Sam, I thought y' were locked up! That was the word at the pub last night."

"Like I told y', I was, but only f' the night."

"So y're free now?"

"I guess y' could say I'm free. Come on! Get int' bed," I said, diving back under the duvet. She pulled her top off, then effortlessly removed her bra and undid her jeans. She let them drop to the floor and then flopped onto the bed next to me. I pulled her close, felt her warmth, her firm breasts pushing into my chest and the softness of her skin. I just wanted to hold her and breathe her in.

* * *

The next afternoon I took the old man to the airport in the Valiant.

"I'll see you soon," he said, looking at me, emotion welling in his eyes, his backpack slung off his right shoulder.

"I'll be on the first plane home once I'm not needed here any more," I responded, trying to maintain conversation, tears forming in my eyes.

"I bet you will. Take care, son, and don't worry. You'll be home soon, huh."

I watched him walk to the small pencil-shaped plane and stayed until it had taken off down the runway. I waved with big sweeping arms above my head as if I wasn't going to see him again, then trudged back to the car, filled with dread for the week ahead of me.

I felt as if I were still trapped. I filled the days by dragging Tim out of the house to come surfing with me, but most of the time it was me on the beach watching him surf because the waves were too big for me.

461

I didn't fancy a repeat of my near drowning. I swam, I bodysurfed, and I walked up and down the beach a lot that week. Every night Brigitte would come down after work and we'd rattle and shake the caravan to the point I was convinced it would fall apart. We'd lie there afterwards and giggle at our antics, like a couple of naughty kids. I'd grown to like Brigitte, as I could really let go and be myself with her. She was playful and light-hearted sexually, quite unlike anyone I'd been with before. Our last week together was a whole lot of fun.

* * *

Towards the end of the week, I went to Harry's for dinner. I knocked on the door and was greeted by Sarah.

"Hi, Sam, I'm so happy you're free. Congratulations!" She embraced me warmly. "You know, Sam," she said looking at me earnestly, "I've never heard Harry speak of a particular incident with such obvious remorse before. He'd spoken about his dislike of the New South Wales Police Force in general, but he'd never before come home and spoken about someone with the degree of concern he showed for you. So I encouraged him to do something about it, and yes, I was curious to meet you."

It was heartfelt and I could see how much she cared. "I'm glad you did, Sarah. Thank you," I said, feeling like my emotions might overflow.

"Come in." She grasped my hand and led me down the hallway into the living room. Harry was sitting in an armchair, reading a book. He placed the book on the coffee table when he caught sight of me and stood up.

"Hello, Sam." There was a bottle of champagne in a wine bucket on the coffee table and three champagne glasses next to it. He picked up the champagne bottle, popped the cork, and deftly filled the glasses.

He handed one to me and one to Sarah before picking up a glass for himself.

"Here's t' you, Sam," he said, raising his glass.

"To Sam," joined in Sarah.

"Thanks," I said as our glasses chimed. I took a large mouthful of champagne and let it sit in my mouth before I swallowed. "Well, it's not quite over yet," I said. There was silence for a moment.

"Y' won't need t' appear at Bruce's trial," Harry announced casually.

"Who won't what?" asked Sarah.

"Sam won't," replied Harry, nodding his head at me. "You're free t' go, Sam. Bruce's lawyer informed us that he's changed his plea t' guilty, which means you're no longer needed. And that's official," he said, raising his glass to salute me.

"Y're kiddin' me," I said, barely able to contain my excitement.

"I'm not the kiddin' type, kiddo," he said, beaming.

"Y' mean I can go home?" I asked, feeling the blood rush to my head.

"Yep."

"That's fantastic, Sam," Sarah said, reaching across and hugging me. "You can go home."

"I can't believe it," I said, returning her embrace and trying to contain my emotions.

"You'd better believe it," said Harry. He took another large sip of his champagne.

"It's hard t' believe! I was worried about havin' t' show up at Bruce's trial, and t' stand up under oath with him glarin' down at me."

"Y' don't have t' worry now, do y'," said Harry.

"So I can book a ticket home now?"

"Y' can ring the travel agent in the mornin', 'n if they can put y' on a plane in the afternoon, I'd say go for it."

Sarah wore a smile, though the lines on her forehead were

pronounced with thought. I couldn't tell if she was happy or sad. I gulped down the rest of my champagne and announced that I needed to leave.

"By all means," responded Harry. "Go pack those bags."

I was grateful to Harry as we embraced. He'd been consistent in his support of me from the moment he invited me around to his house. Sarah looked less enthused as she maintained her smile and hugged me.

"Take good care of yourself, Sam." She didn't seem to want to let me go.

* * *

Outside, I skipped down the road, feeling a true sense of joy wash over me. I arrived back at the house sweating and out of breath. Val and Ted were still up watching telly with Tim.

"I can go home!" I announced, sitting down on the couch to catch my breath, having run the distance from Harry's.

"What do you mean you can go home, Sam? I thought you had to appear in court for Bruce's trial," questioned Ted.

"Yeah, I did, but now I don't."

"I don't understand. You're not making sense," Ted said, leaning forward and taking an interest.

"I did have t' appear, but Harry has just informed me I don't need t' now. Bruce has changed his plea t' guilty."

"Really?" said Val, sounding surprised.

"Yes really! I'm goin' t' ring the travel agent in the mornin' 'n see if I can get a seat."

"When, Sam?" Val asked, her whining voice washing right over me.

"As soon as they can. Tomorrow if possible," I wheezed, still catching my breath.

"Isn't that a bit soon?" Val asked.

"Not really, and m' bag's almost packed. I don't have much stuff, only a few clothes, a few books, 'n that's it."

"Hey, if you can manage it, why not," said Ted. "I can understand your desire to go straight away." At least Ted was on my wavelength.

"If I can get a ticket tomorrow, would y' be able t' drive me t' the airport, Tim?"

"Mmm," he grunted.

"Thanks, mate. You folk have been fantastic t' me, 'n if this'd happened t' me somewhere else, I'd have really struggled t' get through."

"You've become like family, Sam," said Val, sounding sincere.

"We'll certainly miss you," responded Ted, getting up to top up his whisky. "Want one?" he asked, waving his glass at me.

"Sure, why not," I responded, thinking it would be good to have a toast.

"I don't know what Tim will do without you," Val said, dabbing the corners of her eyes delicately with a white handkerchief she'd pulled from the sleeve of her cardigan.

"It's goin' t' be strange t' leave. I'm so use' t' this being home, 'n I love the beach so much. I'm gonna miss it, but I need t' put this all behind me 'n get m' life back on track."

Ted handed me a small glass of golden liquid. "Get that down you, son."

I took the glass to my mouth and felt the whisky warm the interior of my mouth. I didn't really care for the taste, so I swallowed it quickly, and it burned all the way to my stomach.

"That'll warm the cockles of your heart," said Ted knowingly. It had indeed.

***

I awoke the next morning and ran up the stairs to the house. I rang home and got my mother on the other end. She sounded surprised to hear my voice, and it felt strange to be talking to her since I hadn't heard her voice for so long.

"That's fantastic!" she said, sounding like she was in the next room. "I'll ring your dad and tell him now."

"I'm goin' t' ring the travel agent 'n see if they can get me a flight today. I'll call y' once I know what I'm doin', okay?"

"Alright, Sam. Good luck."

It took me a while to organise everything. After I'd spoken to the travel agent, I had to wait a long time before she rang me back.

"I've managed to get you on a flight tomorrow morning from Sydney. That means you need a flight from Wodyn to Sydney this afternoon. Can you get to the airport this afternoon?"

"Yeah, I think so." My heart was pumping hard. I could feel a surge of adrenalin in my veins. I'd do anything to make the flight.

"Okay," she said. "Then I'll book the late afternoon from Wodyn to Sydney. It departs at four-thirty. You can pick up and pay for the ticket at the airport. The second ticket is just a change of flight, so you will need to quote a number to them when you check in at Sydney Airport."

"Great. Thank you," I said and hung up the phone.

I frantically packed and as I did so I realised I hadn't said goodbye to Brigitte. I felt a pang of anxiety for a moment as I tried to decide what to do. I didn't even know where she lived, so unless she was doing days at the pub, there was little chance that I'd see her. I decided I would ask Tim to drop by the pub on our way out of town. Besides Brigitte, there was no one else I really wanted to say goodbye to.

I packed my bag quickly, deciding to leave behind most of the books I'd accumulated. I cleaned all the rubbish out of the caravan, then grabbed the vacuum cleaner from the house and gave it a quick going over. I threw all the linen in the washing machine downstairs next to the shower, poured in too much laundry powder, and hit the start button. I folded up all the blankets and left them on the end of the bed. The caravan looked better than the day I first entered it. My bag sitting on the bed, all strapped up, was the only sign I'd been here. I thought of Brigitte and felt sad for a moment. I wondered how Tim would get on once I'd left, and I hoped he would still get out and go surfing and take walks on the beach.

* * *

I walked down to the beach with a towel in hand for one last swim. I stood there watching the waves break as they rolled into the bay, the moving mounds of brilliant blue, coming in one after the other, building a crest that turned into a wave with nice, high ridges and perfect curves. As the sun shone through the clouds, the waves glistened before breaking, becoming a white, turbulent mass, then smoothing out to nothing. It was as if they'd never been there. One after the other I watched each wave repeat the same performance.

I removed my T-shirt and dropped it on the sand along with my towel, then walked into the surf, dived and swam out to meet the waves. I waited for the perfect wave to take me in and when it came, I was one with the wave. It was magical the way I raced down its face only to be tumbled unceremoniously in its white mass of breaking water. Like the waves that came into the bay to break on the beach, I, too, was finished on these shores.

The End

Acknowledgements

This book wouldn't exist without the encouragement and faith of my true love, Mariana Kolff. She has been the one to encourage me when I shelved this book for several years to concentrate on film work. Mariana was the one who sat with me and edited the first, rather rough, draft. She also encouraged me to find a good editor to finish the book with me, and she has maintained an unwavering belief in me throughout this journey.

I would also like to thank Renell Judais, my copy editor, whom I discovered when looking at publishing options. Renell has been a breath of fresh air and wonderful to work with. She is such a great communicator and very honest with me. It has allowed me to maintain a positive approach when in the past I have doubted the process. Thank you, Renell, for making it possible for me to complete this book.

And finally thanks to Rose Michel von Dreger, my proofreader for taking up the role at short notice, also for offering her opinion about certain punctuation which we agreed upon. No book is complete without a proofreader.

About the Author

David has written a variety of short stories and poems, some of which he has performed live. *Mad if Y' Do* is his first novel. He has a successful and creative career in film and a passion for the telling of a story, both in the written word and in moving image. He is an adventurous soul, always enquiring and seeking out the quirky side of life with an open mind and embracing heart. David sometimes lives in New Zealand and sometimes in the South of France, with his wife.

www.ingramcontent.com/pod-product-compliance
Lightning Source LLC
Chambersburg PA
CBHW010657100726
47900CB00010B/2695